DOOMSDAY CI

GRAVE

Tales of Mankind's Post-Apocalyptic, Dystopian and Disastrous Destiny

PREDICTIONS

Edited by Drew Ford

Introduction by Harlan Ellison®

DOVER PUBLICATIONS, INC.
Mineola, New York

ACKNOWLEDGMENTS: See page vi.

For mature readers only.
This work includes some violent and sexual content that may be
objectionable to some readers.

Bibliographical Note

Grave Predictions: Tales of Mankind's Post-Apocalyptic, Dystopian and Disastrous Destiny,
first published by Dover Publications, Inc., in 2016, is a new compilation of short stories
reprinted from standard editions. Illustrations that originally appeared in a story have not
been reproduced for this edition.

Library of Congress Cataloging-in-Publication Data

Names: Ford, Drew (Andrew), editor. | Ellison, Harlan, writer of introduction.
Title: Grave predictions : tales of mankind's post-apocalyptic, dystopian and disastrous
  destiny / edited by Drew Ford ; introduction by Harlan Ellison.
Description: Mineola, New York : Dover Publications, 2016. | Series: Dover doomsday
  classics | Includes bibliographical references.
Identifiers: LCCN 2016014993| ISBN 9780486802312 (paperback) | ISBN 0486802310
Subjects: LCSH: Science fiction, American. | American fiction—21st century. | Dystopias—
  Fiction. | BISAC: FICTION / Science Fiction / Short Stories. | FICTION / Science Fiction /
  Adventure. | FICTION / Science Fiction / Military. | FICTION / Science Fiction / General.
  | GSAFD: Apocalyptic fiction. | Dystopian fiction.
Classification: LCC PS648.S3 G693 2016 | DDC 813/.0876208—dc23 LC record available at
https://lccn.loc.gov/2016014993

Manufactured in the United States by RR Donnelley
80231001   2016
www.doverpublications.com

FINAL BLACKOUTS

Introduction by
HARLAN ELLISON

THAT ominous cloud descending on you is not the sun scurrying over the hill. It is the clawed hand of destruction. And this is a book of stories intended to describe that hand of mortal destruction in sixteen utterly different, yet all apocalyptically stunning ways!

Stop staring around like that . . . like a deer caught in the headlights. No cavalry is gonna be charging in to save you at the last moment. No fantasy troll or dungeonmaster will appear in a nanosecond and remove the threat. You're on your own; captain of your ship, master of your Fate. Warnings of impending doom are not new: the Mayan calendar posited the End of Times centuries ago—and yet that date has come, gone, and we're still sucking air; Those Who Believe made book on the prediction of the Reverend Bishop James Ussher that "God created the world on October 27, 4004 BC, at 6:00 PM"—and we would be gone by now. Happy 6029th birthday, suckers.

The Y2K "bug" was supposed to finish us off—and that was 15+ years ago. The Black Plague decimated humanity, World Wars 1, 2, 2.3 and yet we go on. Like rats and crocodiles, we are a stick-to-it species of cognitive lice on this green&blue body we call the Earth. Until we pave it over for parking lots and mini-malls. We are our own worst enemies . . . and even the most dire of the stories here isn't one-millionth as morbid as what Man or Woman has done to others.

These are stories of "what-if?" . . . stories of pulse and perspi-ration . . . the name for it is extrapolation. Alien invaders from space—time-travelling winged blue monkeys from the center of

the Earth—Global Warming, Nuclear Holocaust, attacks by were-
wolves—yeah, fantasists since before Jules Verne have had all these
frights for you. And written them intriguingly. Whimsies and wor-
risome wishes, perhaps—yet they all hear at their core the constant
yearning of the Kind Heart, the Calm Intelligence, that commends
to us always: Tomorrow Will Come.

You, I, all of us stand atop a towering hillside of History, the Past
replete with warnings as clear as those in this book. The remnants of
human overreach, greed, churlishnous, hatred, prejudice. How many
moments are left to us, to get our heads straight? These tales predict
the clock is ticking down to total blackout: time runs thin. You are not
alone. You have power in you; use it.

Feigned helplessness and adolescent distraction are the twin kill-
ers of Attempt; they cloud the mind, paralyze the limbs, drain your
courage, and put you in the pen with the sheep awaiting the shear-
ing. It takes balls and/or eggs to face the oncoming night, no matter
what shape the specter takes. The end may well be nigh, but you can
face it with your whimpering face in the bloody mud—or with your
fangs bared and a cleverly worded challenge on your forked tongue.
Your choice: lying down, or standing straight. The Lone Ranger or
Sojourner Truth—or the kid who gets bullied in third grade.

Writing an introduction to a book of stories as well-edited as
Drew Ford selected these, is so much a silliness, it's as if one had a
hysterical puppy-dog running a shadow's length ahead of you, yap-
ping, "The moon and your shadow are following you!"

Yeah; that, and an extra set of elbows will make you a star on
America's Got Tweekers! But having made my insincere apologies
for having staved-in between you and what follows, allow me to
attempt a few cleverisms to soften the beachhead:

I have gone before you; with the exception of only one of the forth-
coming sixteen, I have read every and each of them—some of them
I've edited or anthologized myself (as Dorothy Parker used to say,
"You could look it up." You could even look *her* up, if you don't want
to be standing there looking stupid when the curtain falls). They are
all quite good and encapturing yarns. I knew or know all but three of

the authors and personally vouch for the quality of the product being offered here. The three I didn't know were sent to me by your good editor, Mr. Drew Ford . . . and I smiled lovingly at two of them; one of them I thought was silly.

Fifty-three million cold cash dollars to the first one of you who buys this book, tracks me down, and correctly names the one story herein that was to my taste "silly." Now, *that* ought to be worth the price of admission! (Did I ever tell you that when I was a runaway kid, pre-teen, I worked on the road in the carny?) (Look it up. The end is nigh.)

HARLAN ELLISON

ACKNOWLEDGMENTS

Bear, Greg. "Judgment Engine." Copyright © 1995 by Greg Bear. Reprinted with permission by the author.

Bradbury, Ray. "The Pedestrian." Reprinted by permission of Don Congdon Associates, Inc. Copyright © 1951 by the Fortnightly Publishing Company.

Campbell, Ramsey. "The Pretence." Copyright © 2013 by Ramsey Campbell. Reprinted with permission by the author.

Clarke, Arthur C. "No Morning After." Reprinted by permission of the author and the author's agents, Scovil Galen Ghosh Literary Agency, Inc.

Ellison, Harlan. "Final Blackouts." Copyright © 2015 by the Kilimanjaro Corporation. Reprinted with permission by the author.

Ellison, Harlan. "I Have No Mouth, and I Must Scream." Copyright © 2015 by the Kilimanjaro Corporation. Reprinted with permission by the author.

King, Stephen. "The End of the Whole Mess." Copyright © 1993 by Stephen King. Reproduced by permission of Hodder and Stoughton Limited.

King, Stephen. "The End of the Whole Mess." Reprinted with the permission of Scribner, a Division of Simon & Schuster, Inc., from NIGHT-MARES & DREAMSCAPES BY Stephen King. Copyright © 1993 by Stephen King. All rights reserved.

Lansdale, Joe R. "Tight Little Stitches in a Dead Man's Back." Copyright © 1992 by Joe R. Lansdale. Reprinted with permission by the author.

Le Guin, Ursula K. "The Ones Who Walk Away from Omelas." Copyright © 1973 by Ursula K. Le Guin. First appeared in "New Dimension 3" in 1973, and then in *The Wind's Twelve Quarters*, published by Harper-Collins in 1975. Reprinted by permission of Curtis Brown, Ltd.

Machado, Carmen Maria. "Inventory." Copyright © 2013 by Carmen Maria Machado. Reprinted with permission by the author.

Samuels, Mark. "The Black Mould." Copyright © 2011 by Mark Samuels. Reprinted with permission by the author.

Satifka, Erica L. "Automatic." Copyright © 2007 by Erica L. Satifka. Reprinted with permission by the author.

Stableford, Brian. "The Engineer and the Executioner." Copyright © 1976 by Brian Stableford. Reprinted with permission by the author.

CONTENTS

Contents

The End of the World

Eugene Mouton

And the world will end by fire.

Of all the questions that interest humankind, none is more worthy of research than that of the destiny of the planet we inhabit. Geology and history have taught us many things about the Earth's past; we know the age of our world, within a few hundred million years or so; we know the order of development in which life progressively manifested itself and propagated over its surface; we know in which epoch humans finally arrived to sit down at the banquet that life had prepared for them, and for which it had taken several thousand years to set the table.

We know all that, or at least think we know it, which comes down to exactly the same thing—but if we are sure of our past, we are not of our future.

Humankind scarcely knows any more about the probable duration of its existence than each one of us knows about the number of years that he has yet to live:

> The table is laid,
> The exquisite parade,
> That gives us cheer!
> A toast, my dear!

All well and good—but are we on the soup, or the dessert? Who can tell us, alas, that the coffee will not be served very soon?

We go on and on, heedless of the future of the world, without ever asking ourselves whether, by chance, this frail boat that is carrying

1

us across the ocean of infinity is not at risk of capsizing suddenly, or whether its old hull, worn away by time and impaired by the agitations of the voyage, does not have some leak though which death is filtering into its carcass—which is, of course, the very carcass of humankind—one drop at a time.

The world—which is to say, our terrestrial globe—has not always existed. It had begun, so it will end. The question is, when?

First of all, let us ask ourselves whether the world might end by virtue of an accident, a perturbation of present laws.

We cannot admit that. Such a hypothesis would, in fact, be in absolute contradiction with the opinion that we intend to sustain in this work. It is obvious, therefore, that we cannot adopt it. Any discussion is impossible if one admits the opinion that one is setting out to combat.

Thus, one point is definitely established: the Earth will not be destroyed by accident; it will end as a consequence of the continued action of the laws of its present existence. It will die, as they say, its appropriate death.

But will it die of old age? Will it die of a disease?

I have no hesitation in replying: no, it will not die of old age; yes, it will die of a disease—in consequence of excess.

I have said that the world will end as a consequence of the continued action of the laws of its present existence. It is now a matter of figuring out which, of all the agents functioning for the maintenance of the life of the terraqueous globe, is the one that will have the responsibility of destroying it some day.

I say this without hesitation: that agent is the same one to which the Earth owed its existence in the first place: heat. Heat will drink the sea; heat will eat the Earth—and this is how it will happen.

One day, with regard to the functioning of locomotives, the illustrious Stephenson asked a great English chemist what the force was that moved such machines. The chemist replied: "It's the sun."

And, indeed, all the heat that we liberate when we burn combustible vegetable matter—wood or coal—has been stored there by the sun; a piece of wood or coal is therefore, fundamentally, nothing but a preserve of solar radiation. The more vegetable life develops, the greater the accumulation of these preserves becomes. If a great deal is burned and a great deal created—that is to say, if cultivation and industry evolve, the storage the solar radiation absorbed by the Earth on the one hand and its liberation on the other will increase incessantly, and the Earth will become warmer in a continuous manner.

What would happen if the animal population, and the human population in its turn, followed the same progress? What would happen if considerable transformations, born of the very development of animal life on the surface of the globe, were to modify the structure of terrains, displace the basins of the seas, and reassemble humankind on continents that are both more fertile and more permeable to solar heat?

Now, that is exactly what will happen.

When one compares the world with what it once was, one is immediately struck by one fact that leaps to the eyes: the worldwide evolution of organic life. From the most elevated summits of mountains to the most profound gulfs of the sea, millions of billions of animalcules, animals, cryptogams and superior plants, have been working day and night for centuries, as have the foraminifera on which half our continents are built.

That work was going rapidly enough before the epoch when humans appeared on the Earth, but since the appearance of man it has developed with a rapidity that is accelerating every day. As long as humankind remained restricted to two or three parts of Asia, Europe and Africa, it was not noticeable, because, save for a few focal points of concentration, life in general still found it easy to pour into empty space the surplus accumulated at certain points of the civilized world; it was thus that colonization increasingly populated previously uninhabited countries innocent of all cultivation. Then commenced the first phase of the progress of life by human action: the agricultural phase.

Things moved in this direction for about six centuries, but large deposits of oil were developed, and, almost at the same time, chemistry and steam-power. The Earth then entered its industrial phase—which is only just beginning, since that was not much more than sixty years ago. But where this movement will lead us, and with what velocity we shall arrive, it is easy to presume, given that which has already happened before our eyes.

It is evident, for anyone with eyes to see, that for half a century, animals and people alike have tended to multiply, to proliferate, to pullulate in a truly disquieting proportion. More is eaten, more is drunk, silkworms are cultivated, poultry fed and cattle fattened. At the same time, planning is going on everywhere; ground has been cleared; fecund crop rotations and intensive cultures have been invented, which double the soil's yields; not content with what the earth produces, salmon at five francs a side have been sown in our rivers, and oysters at twenty-four sous a dozen in our gulfs.

In the meantime, enormous quantities of wine, beer and cider have been fermented; veritable rivers of eau-de-vie have been distilled, and millions of tonnes of oil burned—not to mention that heating equipment is improving incessantly, that more and more houses are being rendered draught-proof, and that the linen and cotton fabrics that humans employ to keep themselves warm are being fabricated more cheaply with every passing day.

To this already-sufficiently-somber picture it is necessary to add the insane developments of public education, which one can consider as a source of light and heat, for, if it does not emit them itself, it multiplies their production by giving humans the means of improving and extending their impact on nature.

This is where we are now; this is where a mere half-century of industrialism has brought us; obviously, there are, in all of this, manifest symptoms of an imminent exuberance, and one can conclude that within a hundred years from now, the Earth will have developed a paunch.

Then will commence the redoubtable period in which the excess of production will lead to an excess of consumption, the excess of consumption to an excess of heat, *and the excess of heat to the spontaneous combustion of the Earth and all its inhabitants.*

It is not difficult to anticipate the series of phenomena that will lead the globe, by degrees, to that final catastrophe. Distressing as the depiction of these phenomena might be, I shall not hesitate to map them out, because the prevision of these facts, by enlightening future generations as to the dangers of the excesses of civilization, might perhaps serve to moderate the abuse of life and postpone the fatal final accounting by a few thousand years, or at least a few months.

This, therefore, is what will happen.

For ten centuries, everything will go progressively faster. Industry, above all, will make giant strides. To begin with, all the oil deposits will be exhausted, then all the sources of kerosene; then all the forests will be cut down; then the oxygen in the air and the hydrogen in the water will be burned directly. By that time, there will be something like a million steam-engines on the surface of the globe, averaging a thousand horse-power—the equivalent of a billion horse-power—functioning night and day.

All physical work is done by machines or animals; humans no longer do any, except for skillful gymnastics practised solely for hygienic reasons. But while their machines incessantly vomit out torrents of manufactured products, an ever-denser host of sheep, chickens, turkeys, pigs, ducks, cows and geese emerges from their agricultural factories, all oozing fat, bleating, lowing, gobbling, quacking, bellowing, whistling and demanding consumers with loud cries!

Now, under the influence of ever more abundant and ever more succulent nutrition, the fecundity of the human and animal species is increasing from day to day. Houses rise up one floor at a time; first gardens are done away with, then courtyards. Cities, then villages, gradually begin to project lines of suburbs in every direction; soon, transversal lines connect these radii.

Movement progresses; neighboring cities begin to connect with one another. Paris annexes Saint-Germain, Versailles and then Bauvais, then Châlons, then Orléans, then Tours; Marseilles annexes Toulon, Draguingnan, Nice, Carpentras, Nîmes and Montpellier; Bordeaux, Lyon and Lille share out the rest, and Paris ends up annexing

Marseilles, Lyon, Lille and Bordeaux. And the same thing is happening throughout Europe, and the other four continents of the world.

But at the same time, the animal population is increasing. All useless species have disappeared; all that now remain are cattle, sheep, horses and poultry. Now, to nourish all that, empty space is required for cultivation, and room is getting short.

A few terrains are then reserved for cultivation, fertilizer is piled herein, and there, lying amid grass six feet high, unprecedented species of sheep and cattle, devoid of hair, tails, feet and bones are seen rolling around, reduced by the art of husbandry to be nothing more than monstrous steaks alimented by four insatiable stomachs.

In the meantime, in the southern hemisphere, a formidable revolution is about to take place. What am I saying? Scarcely fifty thousand years have gone by, and here it is, complete!

The polypers have joined all the continents together, and all the islands of the Pacific Ocean and the southern seas. America, Europe and Africa have disappeared beneath the waters of the ocean; nothing remains of them but a few islands formed by the last summits of the Alps, the Pyrenees, the buttes Montmartre, the Carpathians, the Atlas Mountains and the Cordilleras.

The human race, retreating gradually from the sea, has expanded over the incommensurable plains that the sea has abandoned, bringing its overwhelming civilization with it; already space is beginning to run out on the former continents. Here it is the final entrenchments: it is here that it will battle against the invasion of animal life. Here is where it will perish!

It is on a calcareous terrain; an enormous mass of animalized materials is incessantly converted into a chalky state; this mass, exposed to the rays of a torrid sun, incessantly stores up new concentrations of heat, while the functioning of machines, the combustion of hearths and the development of animal heat cause the ambient temperature to rise incessantly.

And in the meantime, animal production continues to increase; there comes a time when the equilibrium breaks down; it becomes manifest that production will outstrip consumption.

Then, in the Earth's crust, a sort of rind begins to form at first, and subsequently, an appreciable layer of irreducible detritus; the Earth is saturated with life.

Fermentation begins.

The thermometer rises, the barometer falls, the hygrometer marches toward zero. Flowers wither, leaves turn yellow, parchments curl up; everything dries out and becomes brittle.

Animals shrink by virtue of the effects of heat and evaporation. Humans, in their turn, grow thin and desiccated; all temperaments melt into one—the bilious—and the last of the lymphatics[1] offers his daughter and a hundred millions in dowry to the last of the scrofulous, who has not a sou to his name, and who refuses out of pride.

The heat increases and the wells dry up. Water-carriers are elevated to the rank of capitalists, then millionaires, to the extent that the prince's Great Water-Carrier becomes one of the principal dignitaries of state. All the crimes and infamies that one sees committed today for a gold piece are committed for a glass of water, and Cupid himself, abandoning his quiver and arrows, replaces them with a carafe of ice-water.

In this torrid atmosphere, a lump of ice is worth twenty times its weight in diamonds. The Emperor of Australia, in a fit of mental aberration, orders a *tutti frutti* that cost an entire year's civil list. A scientist makes a colossal fortune by obtaining a hectoliter of fresh water at 45 degrees.

Streams dry up; crayfish, jostling one another tumultuously to run after the trickles of warm water that are abandoning them, change color as they go along, turning scarlet. Fish, their hearts weakening and their swim-bladders distended, let themselves drift on the currents, bellies up and fins inert.

---

[1] The lymphatic temperament, associated with one of the four humors of ancient medicine, is better known as the sanguine; it is associated with sociability and compassion, among other traits.

And the human species begins to go visibly mad. Strange passions, unexpected angers, overwhelming infatuations and insane pleasures make life into a series of furious detonations—or, rather, one continuous explosion, which begins at birth and concludes with death. In a world cooked by an implacable combustion, everything is scorched, crackled, grilled and roasted, and after the water, which has evaporated, one senses the air diminishing as it becomes more rarefied.

A terrible calamity! The rivers, great and small, have disappeared; the seas are beginning to warm up, then to heat up; now they are already simmering as if over a gentle fire.

First the little fish, asphyxiated, show their bellies at the surface; then come the algae, detached from the sea-bed by the heat; finally, cooked in red wine and rendering up their fat in large stains, the sharks, whales and giant squid rise up, along with the fabulous kraken and the much-contested sea serpent; and with all this fat, vegetation and fish cooked together, the steaming ocean becomes an incommensurable bouillabaisse.

A nauseating odor of cooking expands over the entire inhabited earth; it reigns there for barely a century; the ocean evaporates and leaves no other trace of its existence than fish-bones scattered over desert plains . . . .

It is the beginning of the end.

Under the triple influence of heat, asphyxia and desiccation, the human species is gradually annihilated; humans crumble and peel, falling into pieces at the slightest shock. Nothing any longer remains, to replace vegetables, but a few metallic plants that have been made to grow by irrigating them in vitriol. To slake devouring thirst, to reanimate calcined nervous systems, and to liquefy coagulating albumin, there are no liquids left but sulphuric and nitric acids.

Vain efforts.

With every breath of wind that agitates the anhydrous atmosphere, thousands of human creatures are instantaneously desiccated; the rider of his horse, the advocate at the bar, the judge on his bench, the acrobat on his rope, the seamstress at her window and the king on his throne all come to a stop, mummified.

Then comes the final day.

They are no more than thirty-seven, wandering like tinder spectors in the midst of a frightful population of mummies, which gaze at them with eyes reminiscent of Corinthian grapes.

And they take one another by the hand, and commence a furious round-dance, and with each rotation one of the dancers stumbles and falls down dead, with a dry sound. And when the thirty-sixth cycle is over, the survivor remains alone in front of the miserable heap in which the last debris of the human race is assembled.

He darts one last glance at the Earth; he says goodbye to it on behalf of all of us, and a tear falls from his poor scorched eyes— humankind's last tear. He catches it in his hand, drinks it, and dies, gazing at the heavens.

Pouff!

A little blue flame rises up tremulously, then two, then three, then a thousand. The entire globe catches fire, burns momentarily, and goes out.

It is all over; the Earth is dead.

Bleak and icy. It rolls sadly through the silent deserts of space; and of so much beauty, so much glory, so much joy, so much love, nothing any longer remains but a little charred stone, wandering miserably through the luminous spheres of new worlds.

Goodby, Earth! Goodbye, touching memories of our history, of our genius, of our dolors and our loves! Goodbye, Nature, whose gentle and serene majesty consoled us so effectively in our suffering! Goodbye, cool and somber woods, where, during the beautiful nights of summer, by the silvery light of the moon, the song of the nightingale was heard. Goodbye, terrible and charming creatures that guided the world with a tear or a smile, whom we called by such sweet names! Ah, since nothing more remains of you, all is truly finished: THE EARTH IS DEAD.

THE COMET

W. E. B. DU BOIS

HE STOOD a moment on the steps of the bank, watching the human river that swirled down Broadway. Few noticed him. Few ever noticed him save in a way that stung. He was outside the world—"nothing!" as he said bitterly. Bits of the words of the walkers came to him.

"The comet?"

"The comet—"

Everybody was talking of it. Even the president, as he entered, smiled patronizingly at him, and asked:

"Well, Jim, are you scared?"

"No," said the messenger shortly.

"I thought we'd journeyed through the comet's tail once," broke in the junior clerk affably.

"Oh, that was Halley's," said the president; "this is a new comet, quite a stranger, they say—wonderful, wonderful! I saw it last night. Oh, by the way, Jim," turning again to the messenger, "I want you to go down into the lower vaults today."

The messenger followed the president silently. Of course, they wanted *him* to go down to the lower vaults. It was too dangerous for more valuable men. He smiled grimly and listened.

"Everything of value has been moved out since the water began to seep in," said the president; "but we miss two volumes of old records. Suppose you nose around down there,—it isn't very pleasant, I suppose."

"Not very," said the messenger, as he walked out.

"Well, Jim, the tail of the new comet hits us at noon this time," said the vault clerk, as he passed over the keys; but the messenger passed silently down the stairs. Down he went beneath Broadway, where the dim light filtered through the feet of hurrying men; down to the dark basement beneath; down into the blackness and silence beneath that lowest cavern. Here with his dark lantern he groped in the bowels of the earth, under the world.

He drew a long breath as he threw back the last great iron door and stepped into the fetid slime within. Here at last was peace, and he groped moodily forward. A great rat leaped past him and cobwebs crept across his face. He felt carefully around the room, shelf by shelf, on the muddied floor, and in crevice and corner. Nothing. Then he went back to the far end, where somehow the wall felt different. He sounded and pushed and pried. Nothing. He started away. Then something brought him back. He was sounding and working again when suddenly the whole black wall swung as on mighty hinges, and blackness yawned beyond. He peered in; it was evidently a secret vault—some hiding place of the old bank unknown in newer times. He entered hesitatingly. It was a long, narrow room with shelves, and at the far end, an old iron chest. On a high shelf lay the two missing volumes of records, and others. He put them carefully aside and stepped to the chest. It was old, strong, and rusty. He looked at the vast and old-fashioned lock and flashed his light on the hinges. They were deeply incrusted with rust. Looking about, he found a bit of iron and began to pry. The rust had eaten a hundred years, and it had gone deep. Slowly, wearily, the old lid lifted, and with a last, low groan lay bare its treasure—and he saw the dull sheen of gold!

"Boom!"

A low, grinding, reverberating crash struck upon his ear. He started up and looked about. All was black and still. He groped for his light and swung it about him. Then he knew! The great stone door had swung to. He forgot the gold and looked death squarely in the face. Then with a sigh he went methodically to work. The cold sweat stood on his forehead; but he searched, pounded, pushed, and worked until after what seemed endless hours his hand struck a cold bit of metal and the great door swung again harshly on its hinges, and then, striking against something soft and heavy, stopped. He had just room to squeeze through. There lay the body of the vault clerk, cold and stiff. He stared at it, and then felt sick and nauseated. The air seemed unaccountably foul, with a strong, peculiar odor. He stepped forward, clutched at the air, and fell fainting across the corpse.

He awoke with a sense of horror, leaped from the body, and groped up the stairs, calling to the guard. The watchman sat as if asleep, with the gate swinging free. With one glance at him the messenger hurried up to the sub-vault. In vain he called to the guards. His voice echoed and re-echoed weirdly. Up into the great basement he rushed. Here another guard lay prostrate on his face, cold and still. A fear arose in the messenger's heart. He dashed up to the cellar floor, up into the bank. The stillness of death lay everywhere and everywhere bowed, bent, and stretched the silent forms of men. The messenger paused and glanced about. He was not a man easily moved; but the sight was appalling! "Robbery and murder," he whispered slowly to himself as he saw the twisted, oozing mouth of the president where he lay half-buried on his desk. Then a new thought seized him: If they found him here alone—with all this money and all these dead men—what would his life be worth? He glanced about, tiptoed cautiously to a side door, and again looked behind. Quietly he turned the latch and stepped out into Wall Street.

How silent the street was! Not a soul was stirring, and yet it was high-noon—Wall Street? Broadway? He glanced almost wildly up and down, then across the street, and as he looked, a sickening horror froze in his limbs. With a choking cry of utter fright he lunged, leaned giddily against the cold building, and stared helplessly at the sight. In the great stone doorway a hundred men and women and children lay crushed and twisted and jammed, forced into that great, gaping doorway like refuse in a can—as if in one wild, frantic rush to safety, they had rushed and ground themselves to death. Slowly the messenger crept along the walls, wetting his parched mouth and trying to comprehend, stilling the tremor in his limbs and the rising terror in his heart. He met a business man, silk-hatted and frock-coated, who had crept, too, along that smooth wall and stood now stone dead with wonder written on his lips. The messenger turned his eyes hastily away and sought the curb. A woman leaned wearily against the signpost, her head bowed motionless on her lace and silken bosom. Before her stood a street car, silent, and within—but the messenger but glanced and hurried on. A grimy newsboy sat in the gutter with the "last edition" in his uplifted hand: "Danger!" screamed its black headlines. "Warnings wired around the world. The Comet's tail sweeps past us at noon. Deadly gases expected. Close doors and windows. Seek the cellar." The messenger read and staggered on. Far out from a window above, a girl lay with gasping face and sleevelets on her arms. On a store step sat a little, sweet-faced girl looking upward toward the skies, and in the carriage by her lay—but the messenger looked no longer. The cords gave way—the terror burst in his veins, and with one great, gasping cry he sprang desperately forward and ran,— ran as only the frightened run, shrieking and fighting the air until with one last wail of pain he sank on the grass of Madison Square and lay prone and still.

When he rose, he gave no glance at the still and silent forms on the benches, but, going to a fountain, bathed his face; then hiding himself in a corner away from the drama of death, he quietly gripped himself and thought the thing through: The comet had swept the earth and this was the end. Was everybody dead? He must search and see.

He knew that he must steady himself and keep calm, or he would go insane. First he must go to a restaurant. He walked up Fifth Avenue to a famous hostelry and entered its gorgeous, ghost-haunted halls. He beat back the nausea, and, seizing a tray from dead hands, hurried into the street and ate ravenously, hiding to keep out the sights.

"Yesterday, they would not have served me," he whispered, as he forced the food down.

Then he started up the street,—looking, peering, telephoning, ringing alarms; silent, silent all. Was nobody—nobody—he dared not think the thought and hurried on.

Suddenly he stopped still. He had forgotten. My God! How could he have forgotten? He must rush to the subway—then he almost laughed. No—a car; if he could find a Ford. He saw one. Gently he lifted off its burden, and took his place on the seat. He tested the throttle. There was gas. He glided off, shivering, and drove up the street. Everywhere stood, leaned, lounged, and lay the dead, in grim and awful silence. On he ran past an automobile, wrecked and over-turned; past another, filled with a gay party whose smiles yet lingered on their death-struck lips; on past crowds and groups of cars, pausing by dead policemen; at 42nd Street he had to detour to Park Avenue to avoid the dead congestion. He came back on Fifth Avenue at 57th and flew past the Plaza and by the park with its hushed babies and silent throng, until as he was rushing past 72nd Street he heard a sharp cry, and saw a living form leaning wildly out an upper window. He gasped. The human voice sounded in his ears like the voice of God.

"Hello—hello—help, in God's name!" wailed the woman. "There's a dead girl in here and a man and—and see yonder dead men lying in the street and dead horses—for the love of God go and bring the officers——" And the words trailed off into hysterical tears.

He wheeled the car in a sudden circle, running over the still body of a child and leaping on the curb. Then he rushed up the steps and tried the door and rang violently. There was a long pause, but at last the heavy door swung back. They stared a moment in silence. She had not noticed before that he was a Negro. He had not thought of her as white. She was a woman of perhaps twenty-five—rarely beautiful and richly gowned, with darkly-golden hair, and jewels. Yesterday, he thought with bitterness, she would scarcely have looked at him twice. He would have been dirt beneath her silken feet. She stared at him. Of all the sorts of men she had pictured as coming to her rescue she had not dreamed of one like him. Not that he was not human, but he dwelt in a world so far from hers, so infinitely far, that he seldom even entered her thought. Yet as she looked at him curiously he seemed quite commonplace and usual. He was a tall, dark workingman of the better class, with a sensitive face trained to stolidity and a poor man's clothes and hands. His face was soft and slow and his manner at once cold and nervous, like fires long banked, but not out.

So a moment each paused and gauged the other; then the thought of the dead world without rushed in and they started toward each other.

'What has happened?" she cried. "Tell me! Nothing stirs. All is silence! I see the dead strewn before my window as winnowed by the breath of God,—and see——" She dragged him through great, silken hangings to where, beneath the sheen of mahogany and silver, a little French maid lay stretched in quiet, everlasting sleep, and near her a butler lay prone in his livery.

The tears streamed down the woman's cheeks and she clung to his arm until the perfume of her breath swept his face and he felt the tremors racing through her body.

"I had been shut up in my dark room developing pictures of the comet which I took last night; when I came out—I saw the dead!

"What has happened?" she cried again.

He answered slowly:

"Something—comet or devil—swept across the earth this morning and—many are dead!"

"Many? Very many?"

"I have searched and I have seen no other living soul but you."

She gasped and they stared at each other.

"My—father!" she whispered.

"Where is he?"

"He started for the office."

"Where is it?"

"In the Metropolitan Tower."

"Leave a note for him here and come."

Then he stopped.

"No," he said firmly—"first, we must go—to Harlem."

"Harlem!" she cried. Then she understood. She tapped her foot at first impatiently. She looked back and shuddered. Then she came resolutely down the steps.

"There's a swifter car in the garage in the court," she said.

"I don't know how to drive it," he said.

"I do," she answered.

In ten minutes they were flying to Harlem on the wind. The Stutz rose and raced like an airplane. They took the turn at 110th Street on two wheels and slipped with a shriek into 135th.

He was gone but a moment. Then he returned, and his face was gray. She did not look, but said:

"You have lost—somebody?"

"I have lost—everybody," he said, simply—"unless——"

He ran back and was gone several minutes—hours they seemed to her.

"Everybody," he said, and he walked slowly back with something film-like in his hand which he stuffed into his pocket.

"I'm afraid I was selfish," he said. But already the car was moving toward the park among the dark and lined dead of Harlem—the brown, still faces, the knotted hands, the homely garments, and the silence—the wild and haunting silence. Out of the park, and down Fifth Avenue they whirled. In and out among the dead they slipped and quivered, needing no sound of bell or horn, until the great, square Metropolitan Tower hove in sight. Gently he laid the dead elevator boy aside; the car shot upward. The door of the office stood open. On the threshold lay the stenographer, and, staring at her, sat the dead clerk. The inner office was empty, but a note lay on the desk, folded and addressed but unsent:

Dear Daughter:

I've gone for a hundred mile spin in Fred's new Mercedes. Shall not be back before dinner. I'll bring Fred with me.

J. B. H.

"Come," she cried nervously. "We must search the city."

Up and down, over and across, back again—on went that ghostly search. Everywhere was silence and death—death and silence! They hunted from Madison Square to Spuyten Duyvel; they rushed across the Williamsburg Bridge; they swept over Brooklyn; from the

Battery and Morningside Heights they scanned the river. Silence, silence everywhere, and no human sign. Haggard and bedraggled they puffed a third time slowly down Broadway, under the broiling sun, and at last stopped. He sniffed the air. An odor—a smell—and with the shifting breeze a sickening stench filled their nostrils and brought its awful warning. The girl settled back helplessly in her seat.

"What can we do?" she cried.

It was his turn now to take the lead, and he did it quickly.

"The long distance telephone—the telegraph and the cable—night rockets and then—flight!"

She looked at him now with strength and confidence. He did not look like men, as she had always pictured men; but he acted like one and she was content. In fifteen minutes they were at the central telephone exchange. As they came to the door he stepped quickly before her and pressed her gently back as he closed it. She heard him moving to and fro, and knew his burdens—the poor, little burdens he bore. When she entered, he was alone in the room. The grim switchboard flashed its metallic face in cryptic, sphinx-like immobility. She seated herself on a stool and donned the bright earpiece. She looked at the mouthpiece. She had never looked at one so closely before. It was wide and black, pimpled with usage; inert; dead; almost sarcastic in its unfeeling curves. It looked—she beat back the thought—but it looked,—it persisted in looking like—she turned her head and found herself alone. One moment she was terrified; then she thanked him silently for his delicacy and turned resolutely, with a quick intaking of breath.

"Hello!" she called in low tones. She was calling to the world. The world *must* answer. Would the world *answer*? Was the world—

Silence!

She had spoken too low.

"Hello!" she cried, full-voiced.

She listened. Silence! Her heart beat quickly. She cried in clear, distinct, loud tones: "Hello—hello—hello!"

What was that whirring? Surely—no—was it the click of a receiver?

She bent close, she moved the pegs in the holes, and called and called, until her voice rose almost to a shriek, and her heart hammered. It was as if she had heard the last flicker of creation, and the evil was silence. Her voice dropped to a sob. She sat stupidly staring into the black and sarcastic mouthpiece, and the thought came again. Hope lay dead within her. Yes, the cable and the rockets remained; but the world—she could not frame the thought or say the word. It was too mighty—too terrible! She turned toward the door with a new fear in her heart. For the first time she seemed to realize that she was alone in the world with a stranger, with something more than a stranger,—with a man alien in blood and culture—unknown, perhaps unknowable. It was awful! She must escape—she must fly; he must not see her again. Who knew what awful thoughts—

She gathered her silken skirts deftly about her young, smooth limbs—listened, and glided into a side-hall. A moment she shrank back: the hall lay filled with dead women; then she leaped to the door and tore at it, with bleeding fingers, until it swung wide. She looked out. He was standing at the top of the alley,—silhouetted, tall and black, motionless. Was he looking at her or away? She did not know—she did not care. She simply leaped and ran—ran until she found herself alone amid the dead and the tall ramparts of towering buildings.

She stopped. She was alone. Alone! Alone on the streets—alone in the city—perhaps alone in the world! There crept in upon her the sense of deception—of creeping hands behind her back—of silent, moving things she could not see,—of voices hushed in fearsome conspiracy. She looked behind and sideways, started at strange sounds and heard still stranger, until every nerve within her stood sharp and quivering, stretched to scream at the barest touch. She whirled and flew back, whimpering like a child, until she found that narrow alley again and the dark, silent figure silhouetted at the top. She stopped and rested; then she walked silently toward him, looked at him timidly; but he said nothing as he handed her into the car. Her voice caught as she whispered:

"Not—that."

And he answered slowly: "No—not that!"

They climbed into the car. She bent forward on the wheel and sobbed, with great, dry, quivering sobs, as they flew toward the cable office on the east side, leaving the world of wealth and prosperity for the world of poverty and work. In the world behind them were death and silence, grave and grim, almost cynical, but always decent; here it was hideous. It clothed itself in every ghastly form of terror, struggle, hate, and suffering. It lay wreathed in crime and squalor, greed and lust. Only in its dread and awful silence was it like to death everywhere.

Yet as the two, flying and alone, looked upon the horror of the world, slowly, gradually, the sense of all-enveloping death deserted them. They seemed to move in a world silent and asleep,—not dead. They moved in quiet reverence, lest somehow they wake these sleeping forms who had, at last, found peace. They moved in some solemn, world-wide *Friedhof,* above which some mighty arm had waved its magic wand. All nature slept until—until, and quick with the same startling thought, they looked into each other's eyes—he, ashen, and she, crimson, with unspoken thought. To both, the vision of a mighty beauty—of vast, unspoken things, swelled in their souls; but they put it away.

Great, dark coils of wire came up from the earth and down from the sun and entered this low lair of witchery. The gathered lightnings of the world centered here, binding with beams of light the ends of the earth. The doors gaped on the gloom within. He paused on the threshold.

"Do you know the code?" she asked.

"I know the call for help—we used it formerly at the bank."

She hardly heard. She heard the lapping of the waters far below,—the dark and restless waters—the cold and luring waters, as they called. He stepped within. Slowly she walked to the wall, where the water called below, and stood and waited. Long she waited, and he did not come. Then with a start she saw him, too, standing beside the black waters. Slowly he removed his coat and stood there silently. She walked quickly to him and laid her hand on his arm. He did not start or look. The waters lapped on in luring, deadly rhythm. He pointed down to the waters, and said quietly:

"The world lies beneath the waters now—may I go?"

She looked into his stricken, tired face, and a great pity surged within her heart. She answered in a voice clear and calm, "No."

Upward they turned toward life again, and he seized the wheel. The world was darkening to twilight, and a great, gray pall was falling mercifully and gently on the sleeping dead. The ghastly glare of reality seemed replaced with the dream of some vast romance. The girl lay silently back, as the motor whizzed along, and looked half-consciously for the elf-queen to wave life into this dead world again. She forgot to wonder at the quickness with which he had learned to drive her car. It seemed natural. And then as they whirled and swung into Madison Square and at the door of the Metropolitan Tower she gave a low cry, and her eyes were great! Perhaps she had seen the elf-queen?

The man led her to the elevator of the tower and deftly they ascended. In her father's office they gathered rugs and chairs, and he wrote a note and laid it on the desk; then they ascended to the roof and he made her comfortable. For a while she rested and sank to dreamy somnolence, watching the worlds above and wondering. Below lay the dark shadows of the city and afar was the shining of the sea. She glanced at him timidly as he set food before her and took a shawl and wound her in it, touching her reverently, yet tenderly. She looked up at him with thankfulness in her eyes, eating what he served. He watched the city. She watched him. He seemed very human,—very near now.

"Have you had to work hard?" she asked softly.

"Always," he said.

"I have always been idle," she said. "I was rich."

"I was poor," he almost echoed.

"The rich and the poor are met together," she began, and he finished:

"The Lord is the Maker of them all."

"Yes," she said slowly; "and how foolish our human distinctions seem—now," looking down to the great dead city stretched below, swimming in unlightened shadows.

"Yes—I was not—human, yesterday," he said.

She looked at him. "And your people were not my people," she said; "but today——" She paused. He was a man,—no more; but he was in some larger sense a gentleman,—sensitive, kindly, chivalrous, everything save his hands and—his face. Yet yesterday— "Death, the leveler!" he muttered.

"And the revealer," she whispered gently, rising to her feet with great eyes. He turned away, and after fumbling a moment sent a rocket into the darkening air. It arose, shrieked, and flew up, a slim path of light, and scattering its stars abroad, dropped on the city below. She scarcely noticed it. A vision of the world had risen before her. Slowly the mighty prophecy of her destiny overwhelmed her. Above the dead past hovered the Angel of Annunciation. She was no mere woman. She was neither high nor low, white nor black, rich nor poor. She was primal woman; mighty mother of all men to come and Bride of Life. She looked upon the man beside her and forgot all else but his manhood, his strong, vigorous manhood—his sorrow and sacrifice. She saw him glorified. He was no longer a thing apart, a creature below, a strange outcast of another clime and blood, but her Brother Humanity incarnate, Son of God and great All-Father of the race to be.

He did not glimpse the glory in her eyes, but stood looking outward toward the sea and sending rocket after rocket into the unanswering darkness. Dark-purple clouds lay banked and billowed in the west. Behind them and all around, the heavens glowed in dim, weird radiance that suffused the darkening world and made almost a minor music. Suddenly, as though gathered back in some vast hand, the great cloud-curtain fell away. Low on the horizon lay a long, white star—mystic, wonderful! And from it fled upward to the pole, like some wan bridal veil, a pale, wide sheet of flame that lighted all the world and dimmed the stars.

In fascinated silence the man gazed at the heavens and dropped his rockets to the floor. Memories of memories stirred to life in the dead recesses of his mind. The shackles seemed to rattle and fall from his soul. Up from the crass and crushing and cringing of his caste leaped the lone majesty of kings long dead. He arose within the shadows, tall, straight, and stern, with power in his eyes and ghostly scepters hovering to his grasp. It was as though some mighty Pharaoh lived again, or curled Assyrian lord. He turned and looked upon the lady, and found her gazing straight at him.

Silently, immovably, they saw each other face to face—eye to eye. Their souls lay naked to the night. It was not lust; it was not love—it was some vaster, mightier thing that needed neither touch of body nor thrill of soul. It was a thought divine, splendid.

Slowly, noiselessly, they moved toward each other—the heavens above, the seas around, the city grim and dead below. He loomed from out the velvet shadows vast and dark. Pearl-white and slender, she shone beneath the stars. She stretched her jeweled hands abroad. He lifted up his mighty arms, and they cried each to the other, almost with one voice, "The world is dead."

"Long live the——"

"Honk! Honk!" Hoarse and sharp the cry of a motor drifted clearly up from the silence below. They started backward with a cry and gazed upon each other with eyes that faltered and fell, with blood that boiled.

"Honk! Honk! Honk! Honk!" came the mad cry again, and almost from their feet a rocket blazed into the air and scattered its stars upon them. She covered her eyes with her hands, and her shoulders heaved. He dropped and bowed, groped blindly on his knees about the floor. A blue flame spluttered lazily after an age, and she heard the scream of an answering rocket as it flew.

Then they stood still as death, looking to opposite ends of the earth.

"Clang—crash—clang!"

The roar and ring of swift elevators shooting upward from below made the great tower tremble. A murmur and babel of voices swept in upon the night. All over the once dead city the lights blinked, flickered, and flamed; and then with a sudden clanging of doors the entrance to the platform was filled with men, and one with white and flying hair rushed to the girl and lifted her to his breast. "My daughter!" he sobbed.

Behind him hurried a younger, comelier man, carefully clad in motor costume, who bent above the girl with passionate solicitude and gazed into her staring eyes until they narrowed and dropped and her face flushed deeper and deeper crimson.

"Julia," he whispered; "my darling, I thought you were gone forever."

She looked up at him with strange, searching eyes.

"Fred," she murmured, almost vaguely, "is the world—gone?"

"Only New York," he answered; "it is terrible—awful! You know,—but you, how did you escape—how have you endured this horror? Are you well? Unharmed?"

"Unharmed!" she said.

"And this man here?" he asked, encircling her drooping form with one arm and turning toward the Negro. Suddenly he stiffened and his hand flew to his hip. "Why!" he snarled. "It's—a—nigger—Julia! Has he—has he dared——"

She lifted her head and looked at her late companion curiously and then dropped her eyes with a sigh.

"He has dared—all, to rescue me," she said quietly, "and I—thank him—much." But she did not look at him again. As the couple turned away, the father drew a roll of bills from his pockets.

"Here, my good fellow," he said, thrusting the money into the man's hands, "take that,—what's your name?"

"Jim Davis," came the answer, hollow-voiced.

"Well, Jim, I thank you. I've always liked your people. If you ever want a job, call on me." And they were gone.

The crowd poured up and out of the elevators, talking and whispering.

"Who was it?"

"Are they alive?"

"How many?"

'Two!"

"Who was saved?"

"A white girl and a nigger—there she goes."

"A nigger? Where is he? Let's lynch the damned——"

"Shut up—he's all right—he saved her."

"Saved hell! He had no business——"

"Here he comes."

Into the glare of the electric lights the colored man moved slowly, with the eyes of those that walk and sleep.

"Well, what do you think of that?" cried a bystander; "of all New York, just a white girl and a nigger!"

The colored man heard nothing. He stood silently beneath the glare of the light, gazing at the money in his hand and shrinking as he gazed; slowly he put his other hand into his pocket and brought out a baby's filmy cap, and gazed again. A woman mounted to the platform and looked about, shading her eyes. She was brown, small, and toil-worn, and in one arm lay the corpse of a dark baby. The crowd parted and her eyes fell on the colored man; with a cry she tottered toward him.

"Jim!"

He whirled and, with a sob of joy, caught her in his arms.

THE PEDESTRIAN

RAY BRADBURY

TO ENTER out into that silence that was the city at eight o'clock of a misty evening in November, to put your feet upon that buckling concrete walk, to step over grassy seams and make your way, hands in pockets, through the silences, that was what Mr. Leonard Mead most dearly loved to do. He would stand upon the corner of an intersection and peer down long moonlit avenues of sidewalk in four directions, deciding which way to go, but it really made no difference; he was alone in this world of 2053 A.D., or as good as alone, and with a final decision made, a path selected, he would stride off, sending patterns of frosty air before him like the smoke of a cigar.

Sometimes he would walk for hours and miles and return only at midnight to his house. And on his way he would see the cottages and homes with their dark windows, and it was not unequal to walking through a graveyard where only the faintest glimmers of firefly light appeared in flickers behind the windows. Sudden gray phantoms seemed to manifest upon inner room walls where a curtain was still undrawn against the night, or there were whisperings and murmurs where a window in a tomb-like building was still open.

Mr. Leonard Mead would pause, cock his head, listen, look, and march on, his feet making no noise on the lumpy walk. For long ago he had wisely changed to sneakers when strolling at night, because the dogs in intermittent squads would parallel his journey with barkings if he wore hard heels, and lights might click on and faces appear and an entire street be startled by the passing of a lone figure, himself, in the early November evening.

On this particular evening he began his journey in a westerly direction, toward the hidden sea. There was a good crystal frost in the air; it cut the nose and made the lungs blaze like a Christmas tree inside; you could feel the cold light going on and off, all the branches filled with invisible snow. He listened to the faint push of his soft shoes through autumn leaves with satisfaction, and whistled a cold quiet whistle between his teeth, occasionally picking up a leaf as he passed, examining its skeletal pattern in the infrequent lamplights as he went on, smelling its rusty smell.

"Hello, in there," he whispered to every house on every side as he moved. "What's up tonight on Channel 4, Channel 7, Channel 9? Where are the cowboys rushing, and do I see the United States Cavalry over the next hill to the rescue?"

The street was silent and long and empty, with only his shadow moving like the shadow of a hawk in mid-country. If he closed his eyes and stood very still, frozen, he could imagine himself upon the center of a plain, a wintry, windless Arizona desert with no house in a thousand miles, and only dry river beds, the streets, for company.

"What is it now?" he asked the houses, noticing his wrist watch. "Eight-thirty P.M.? Time for a dozen assorted murders? A quiz? A revue? A comedian falling off the stage?"

Was that a murmur of laughter from within a moon-white house? He hesitated, but went on when nothing more happened. He stumbled over a particularly uneven section of sidewalk. The cement was vanishing under flowers and grass. In ten years of walking by night or day, for thousands of miles, he had never met another person walking, not one in all that time.

He came to a cloverleaf intersection which stood silent where two main highways crossed the town. During the day it was a thunderous surge of care, the gas stations open, a great insect rustling and a ceaseless jockeying for position as the scarab-beetles, a faint incense puttering from their exhausts, skimmed homeward to the far directions. But now these highways, too, were like streams in a dry season, all stone and bed and moon radiance.

He turned back on a side street, circling around toward his home. He was within a block of his destination when the lone car turned a corner quite suddenly and flashed a fierce white cone of light upon him. He stood entranced, not unlike a night moth, stunned by the illumination, and then drawn toward it.

A metallic voice called to him:

"Stand still. Stay where you are! Don't move!"

He halted.

"Put up your hands!"

"But——" he said.

"Your hands up! Or we'll shoot!"

The police, of course, but what a rare, incredible thing; in a city of three million, there was only *one* police car left, wasn't that correct? Ever since a year ago, 2052, the election year, the force had been cut down from three cars to one. Crime was ebbing; there was no need now for the police, save for this one lone car wandering and wandering the empty streets.

"Your name?" said the police car in a metallic whisper. He couldn't see the men in it for the bright light in his eyes.

"Leonard Mead," he said.

"Speak up!"

"Leonard Mead!"

"Business or profession?"

"I guess you'd call me a writer."

"No profession," said the police car, as if talking to itself. The light held him fixed, like a museum specimen, needle thrust through chest.

"You might say that," said Mr. Mead. He hadn't written in years. Magazines and books didn't sell any more. Everything went on in the tomb-like houses at night now, he thought, continuing his fancy. The tombs, ill-lit by television light, where the people sat like the dead, the gray or multi-colored lights touching their faces, but never really touching them.

"No profession," said the phonograph voice, hissing. "What are you doing out?"

"Walking," said Leonard Mead.

"Walking!"

"Just walking," he said simply, but his face felt cold.

"Walking, just walking, walking?"

"Yes, sir."

"'Walking where? For what?"

"Walking for air. Walking to *see*."

"Your address!"

"Eleven South Saint James Street."

"And there is air *in* your house, you have an air *conditioner*, Mr. Mead?"

"Yes."

"And you have a viewing screen in your house to see with?"

"No."

"No?" There was a crackling quiet that in itself was an accusation.

"Are you married, Mr. Mead?"

"No."

"Not married," said the police voice behind the fiery beam. The moon was high and clear among the stars and the houses were gray and silent.

"Nobody wanted me," said Leonard Mead with a smile.

"Don't speak unless you're spoken to!"

Leonard Mead waited in the cold night.

"Just *walking*, Mr. Mead?"

"Yes."

"But you haven't explained for what purpose."

"I explained; for air, and to see, and just to walk."

"Have you done this often?"

"Every night for years."

The police car sat in the center of the street with its radio throat faintly humming.

"Well, Mr. Mead," it said.

"Is that all?" he asked politely.

"Yes," said the voice. "Here." There was a sigh, a pop. The back door of the police car sprang wide. "Get in."

"Wait a minute, I haven't done anything!"

"Get in."

"I protest!"

"Mr. Mead."

He walked like a man suddenly drunk. As he passed the front window of the car he looked in. As he had expected, there was no one in the front seat, no one in the car at all.

"Get in."

He put his hand to the door and peered into the back seat, which was a little cell, a little black jail with bars. It smelled of riveted steel. It smelled of harsh antiseptic; it smelled too clean and hard and metallic. There was nothing soft there.

"Now if you had a wife to give you an alibi," said the iron voice. "But—"

"Where are you taking me?"

The car hesitated, or rather gave a faint whirring click, as if information, somewhere, was dropping card by punch-slotted card under electric eyes. "To the Psychiatric Center for Research on Regressive Tendencies."

He got in. The door shut with a soft thud. The police car rolled through the night avenues, flashing its dim lights ahead.

They passed one house on one street a moment later, one house in an entire city of houses that were dark, but this one particular house had all of its electric lights brightly lit, every window a loud yellow illumination, square and warm in the cool darkness.

"That's *my* house," said Leonard Mead.

No one answered him.

The car moved down the empty river-bed streets and off away, leaving the empty streets with the empty sidewalks, and no sound and no motion all the rest of the chill November night.

No Morning After

Arthur C. Clarke

"But this is terrible!" said the Supreme Scientist. "Surely there is *something* we can do!"

"Yes, Your Cognizance, but it will be extremely difficult. The planet is more than five hundred light-years away, and it is very hard to maintain contact. However, we believe we can establish a bridgehead. Unfortunately, that is not the only problem. So far, we have been quite unable to communicate with these beings. Their telepathic powers are exceedingly rudimentary—perhaps even non-existent. And if we cannot talk to them, there is no way in which we can help."

There was a long mental silence while the Supreme Scientist analyzed the situation and arrived, as he always did, at the correct answer.

"Any intelligent race must have *some* telepathic individuals," he mused. "We must send out hundreds of observers, tuned to catch the first hint of stray thought. When you find a single responsive mind, concentrate all your efforts upon it. We *must* get our message through."

"Very good, Your Cognizance. It shall be done."

Across the abyss, across the gulf which light itself took half a thousand years to span, the questing intellects of the planet Thaar sent out their tendrils of thought, searching desperately for a single human being whose mind could perceive their presence. And as luck would have it, they encountered William Cross.

At least, they thought it was luck at the time, though later they were not so sure. In any case, they had little choice. The combination of circumstances which opened Bill's mind to them lasted only for seconds, and was not likely to occur again this side of eternity.

There were three ingredients to the miracle: it is hard to say if one was more important than another. The first was the accident of position. A flask of water, when sunlight falls upon it, can act as a crude lens, concentrating the light into a small area. On an immeasurably larger scale, the dense core of the Earth was converging the waves that came from Thaar. In the ordinary way, the radiations of thought are unaffected by matter—they pass through it as effortlessly as light through glass. But there is rather a lot of matter in a planet, and the whole Earth was acting as a gigantic lens. As it turned, it was carrying Bill through its focus, where the feeble thought-impulses from Thaar were concentrated a hundredfold.

Yet millions of other men were equally well placed: they received no message. But they were not rocket engineers: they had not spent years thinking and dreaming of space, until it had become part of their very being.

And they were not, as Bill was, blind drunk, teetering on the last knife-edge of consciousness, trying to escape from reality into the world of dreams, where there were no disappointments and setbacks.

Of course, he could see the Army's point of view. "You are paid, Dr. Cross," General Potter had pointed out with unnecessary emphasis, "to design missiles, not—ah—spaceships. What you do in your spare time is your own concern, but I must ask you not to use the facilities of the establishment for your hobby. From now on, all projects for the computing section will have to be cleared by me. That is all."

They couldn't sack him, of course: he was too important. But he was not sure that he wanted to stay. He was not really sure of anything except that the job had backfired on him, and that Brenda had finally gone off with Johnny Gardner—putting events in their order of importance.

Wavering slightly, Bill cupped his chin in his hands and stared at the white-washed brick wall on the other side of the table. The only attempt at ornamentation was a calendar from Lockheed and a glossy six by eight from Aerojet showing L'il Abner Mark I making a boosted takeoff. Bill gazed morosely at a spot midway between the two pictures, and emptied his mind of thought. The barriers went down. . . .

At that moment, the massed intellects of Thaar gave a soundless cry of triumph, and the wall in front of Bill slowly dissolved into a swirling mist. He appeared to be looking down a tunnel that stretched to infinity. As a matter of fact, he was.

Bill studied the phenomenon with mild interest. It had a certain novelty, but was not up to the standard of previous hallucinations. And when the voice started to speak in his mind, he let it ramble on for some time before he did anything about it. Even when drunk, he had an old-fashioned prejudice against starting conversations with himself.

"Bill," the voice began. "Listen carefully. We have had great difficulty in contacting you, and this is extremely important."

Bill doubted this on general principles. *Nothing* was important any more.

"We are speaking to you from a very distant planet," continued the voice in a tone of urgent friendliness. "You are the only human being we have been able to contact, so you *must* understand what we are saying."

Bill felt mildly worried, though in an impersonal sort of way, since it was now rather hard to focus onto his own problems. How serious was it, he wondered, when you started to hear voices? Well, it was best not to get excited. You can take it or leave it, Dr. Cross, he told himself. Let's take it until it gets to be a nuisance.

"O. K." he answered with bored indifference. "Go right ahead and talk to me. I won't mind as long as it's interesting."

There was a pause. Then the voice continued, in a slightly worried fashion.

"We don't quite understand. Our message isn't merely *interesting*. It's vital to your entire race, and you must notify your government immediately."

"I'm waiting," said Bill. "It helps to pass the time."

Five hundred light-years away, the Thaarns conferred hastily among themselves. Something seemed to be wrong, but they could not decide precisely what. There was no doubt that they had established contact, yet this was not the sort of reaction they had expected. Well, they could only proceed and hope for the best.

"Listen, Bill," they continued. "Our scientists have just discovered that your sun is about to explode. It will happen three days from now—seventy-four hours, to be exact. Nothing can stop it. But there's no need to be alarmed. We can save you, if you'll do what we say."

"Go on," said Bill. This hallucination was ingenious.

"We can create what we call a bridge—it's a kind of tunnel through space, like the one you're looking into now. The theory is far too complicated to explain, even to one of your mathematicians."

"Hold on a minute!" protested Bill. "I am a mathematician, and a darn good one, even when I'm sober. And I've read all about this kind of thing in the science-fiction magazines. I presume you're talking about some kind of short-cut through a higher dimension of space. That's old stuff—pre-Einstein."

A sensation of distinct surprise seeped into Bill's mind.

"We had no idea you were so advanced scientifically," said the Thaarns. "But we haven't time to talk about the theory. All that matters is this—if you were to step into that opening in front of you, you'd find yourself instantly on another planet. It's a short-cut, as you said—in this case, through the thirty-seventh dimension."

"And it leads to your world?"

"Oh no—you couldn't live here. But there are plenty of planets like Earth in the universe, and we've found one that will suit you. We'll establish bridgeheads like this all over Earth, so your people will only have to walk through them to be saved. Of course, they'll have to start building up civilization again when they reach their new homes, but it's their only hope. You have to pass on this message, and tell them what to do."

"I can just see them listening to me," said Bill. "Why don't you go and talk to the President?"

"Because yours was the only mind we were able to contact. Others seemed closed to us: we don't understand why."

"I could tell you," said Bill, looking at the nearly empty bottle in front of him. He was certainly getting his money's worth. What a remarkable thing the human mind was! Of course, there was nothing at all original in this dialogue: it was easy to see where the ideas came from. Only last week he'd been reading a story about the end of the world, and all this wishful thinking about bridges and tunnels through space was pretty obvious compensation for anyone who'd spent five years wrestling with recalcitrant rockets.

"If the sun does blow up," Bill asked abruptly—trying to catch his hallucination unawares—"what would happen?"

"Why, your planet would be melted instantly. All the planets, in fact, right out to Jupiter."

Bill had to admit that this was quite a grandiose conception. He let his mind play with the thought, and the more he considered it, the more he liked it.

"My dear hallucination," he remarked pityingly. "If I believed you, d'you know what I'd say?"

"But you *must* believe us!" came the despairing cry across the light-years.

Bill ignored it. He was warming to his theme.

"I'd tell you this. *It would be the best thing that could possibly happen.* Yes, it would save a whole lot of misery. No one would have to worry about the Russians and the atom bomb and the high cost of living. Oh, it would be wonderful! It's just what everybody really wants. Nice of you to come along and tell us, but just you go back home and pull your old bridge after you."

There was consternation on Thaar. The Supreme Scientist's brain, floating like a great mass of coral in its tank of nutrient solution, turned slightly yellow about the edges—something it had not done since the Xantil invasion, five thousand years ago. At least fifteen psychologists had nervous breakdowns and were never the same again. The main computer in the College of Cosmophysics started dividing every number in its memory circuits by zero, and promptly blew all its fuses.

And on Earth, Bill Cross was really hitting his stride.

"Look at *me*," he said, pointing a wavering finger at his chest. "I've spent years trying to make rockets do something useful, and they tell me I'm only allowed to build guided missiles, so that we can all blow each other up. The Sun will make a neater job of it, and if you did give us another planet we'd only start the whole damn thing all over again."

He paused sadly, marshaling his morbid thoughts.

"And now Brenda heads out of town without even leaving a note. So you'll pardon my lack of enthusiasm for your Boy Scout act."

He couldn't have said "enthusiasm" aloud, Bill realized. But he could still think it, which was an interesting scientific discovery. As he got drunker and drunker, would his cogitation—whoops, *that* nearly threw him!—finally drop down to words of one syllable?

In a final despairing exertion, the Thaarns sent their thoughts along the tunnel between the stars.

"You can't really mean it, Bill! Are *all* human beings like you?"

Now that was an interesting philosophical question, Bill considered it carefully—or as carefully as he could in view of the warm, rosy glow that was now beginning to envelope him. After all, things might be worse. He could get another job, if only for the pleasure of telling General Porter what he could do with his three stars. And as for Brenda—well, women were like streetcars: there'd always be another along in a minute.

Best of all, there was a second bottle of whiskey in the TOP SECRET file. Oh, frabjous day! He rose unsteadily to his feet and wavered across the room.

For the last time, Thaar spoke to Earth.

"Bill!" it repeated desperately. "Surely all human beings can't be like you!"

Bill turned and looked into the swirling tunnel. Strange—it seemed to be lit with flecks of starlight, and was really rather pretty. He felt proud of himself: not many people could imagine *that*.

"Like me?" he said. "No, they're not." He smiled smugly across the light-years, as the rising tide of euphoria lifted him out of his despondency. "Come to think of it," he added, "there are a lot of people much worse off than me. Yes, I guess I must be one of the lucky ones, after all."

He blinked in mild surprise, for the tunnel had suddenly collapsed upon itself and the whitewashed wall was there again, exactly as it had always been. Thaar knew when it was beaten.

"So much for that hallucination," thought Bill. "I was getting tired of it, anyway. Let's see what the next one's like."

As it happened, there wasn't a next one, for five seconds later he passed out cold, just as he was setting the combination of the file cabinet.

The next two days were rather vague and bloodshot, and he forgot all about the interview.

On the third day something was nagging at the back of his mind: he might have remembered if Brenda hadn't turned up again and kept him busy being forgiving.

And there wasn't a fourth day, of course.

Upon the Dull Earth

Philip K. Dick

"Who is Silvia? What is she?"
Oh, no!
What is Silvia . . .
and who isn't she?

SILVIA ran laughing through the night brightness, between the roses and cosmos and Shasta daisies, down the gravel paths and beyond the heaps of sweet-tasting grass swept from the lawns. Stars, caught in pools of water, glittered everywhere, as she brushed through them to the slope beyond the brick wall. Cedars supported the sky and ignored the slim shape squeezing past, her brown hair flying, her eyes flashing.

"Wait for me," Rick complained, as he cautiously threaded his way after her, along the half-familiar path. Silvia danced on without stopping. "Slow down!" he shouted angrily.

"Can't—we're late." Without warning, Silvia appeared in front of him, blocking the path. "Empty your pockets," she gasped, her gray eyes sparkling. "Throw away all metal. You know they can't stand metal."

Rick searched his pockets. In his overcoat were two dimes and a fifty-cent piece. "Do these count?"

"*Yes!*" Silvia snatched the coins and threw them into the dark heaps of calla lilies. The bits of metal hissed into the moist depths and were gone. "Anything else?" She caught hold of his arm anxiously. "They're already on their way. Anything else, Rick?"

"Just my watch." Rick pulled his wrist away as Silvia's wild fingers snatched for the watch. "*That's* not going in the bushes."

"Then lay it on the sundial—or the wall. Or in a hollow tree." Silvia raced off again. Her excited, rapturous voice danced back to him. "Throw away your cigarette case. And your keys, your belt buckle—everything metal. You know how they hate metal. Hurry, we're late!"

Rick followed sullenly after her. "All right, *witch.*"

Silvia snapped at him furiously from the darkness. "Don't *say* that! It isn't true. You've been listening to my sisters and my mother and—"

Her words were drowned out by the sound. Distant flapping, a long way off, like vast leaves rustling in a winter storm. The night sky was alive with the frantic pounding; they were coming very quickly this time. They were too greedy, too desperately eager to wait. Flickers of fear touched the man and he ran to catch up with Silvia.

Silvia was a tiny column of green skirt and blouse in the center of the thrashing mass. She was pushing them away with one arm and trying to manage the faucet with the other. The churning activity of wings and bodies twisted her like a reed. For a time she was lost from sight.

"Rick!" she called faintly. "Come here and help!" She pushed them away and struggled up. "They're suffocating me!"

Rick fought his way through the wall of flashing white to the edge of the trough. They were drinking greedily at the blood that spilled from the wooden faucet. He pulled Silvia close against him; she was terrified and trembling. He held her tight until some of the violence and fury around them had died down.

"They're hungry," Silvia gasped feebly.

"You're a little cretin for coming ahead. They can sear you to ash!"

"I know. They can do anything." She shuddered, excited and frightened. "Look at them," she whispered, her voice husky with awe. "Look at the size of them—their wingspread. And they're *white*, Rick. Spotless—perfect. There's nothing in our world as spotless as that. Great and clean and wonderful."

"They certainly wanted the lamb's blood."

Silvia's soft hair blew against his face as the wings fluttered on all sides. They were leaving now, roaring up into the night sky. Not up, really—away. Back to their own world, whence they had scented the blood. But it was not only the blood—they had come because of Silvia. *She* had attracted them.

The girl's gray eyes were wide. She reached up toward the rising white creatures. One of them swooped close. Grass and flowers sizzled as blinding white flames roared in a brief fountain. Rick scrambled away. The flaming figure hovered momentarily over Silvia and then there was a hollow *pop*. The last of the white-winged giants was gone. The air, the ground, gradually cooled into darkness and silence.

"I'm sorry," Silvia whispered.

"Don't do it again," Rick managed. He was numb with shock. "It isn't safe."

"Sometimes I forget. I'm sorry, Rick. I didn't mean to draw them so close." She tried to smile. "I haven't been that careless in months. Not since that other time, when I first brought you out here." The avid, wild look slid across her face. "Did you *see* him? Power and flames! And he didn't even touch us. He just—looked at us. That was all. And everything's burned up, all around."

Rick grabbed hold of her. "Listen," he grated. "You mustn't call them again. It's wrong. This isn't their world."

"It's not wrong—it's beautiful."

"It's not safe!" His fingers dug into her flesh until she gasped. "Stop tempting them down here!"

Silvia laughed hysterically. She pulled away from him, out into the blasted circle that the horde of angels had seared behind them as they rose into the sky. "I can't *help* it," she cried. "I belong with them. They're my family, my people. Generations of them, back into the past."

"What do you mean?"

"They're my ancestors. And someday I'll join them."

"You are a little witch!" Rick shouted furiously.

"No," Silvia answered. "Not a witch, Rick. Don't you see? I'm a saint."

The kitchen was warm and bright. Silvia plugged in the Silex and got a big red can of coffee down from the cupboards over the sink. "You mustn't listen to them," she said, as she set out plates and cups and got cream from the refrigerator. "You know they don't understand. Look at them in there."

Silvia's mother and her sisters, Betty Lou and Jean, stood huddled together in the living room, fearful and alert, watching the young couple in the kitchen. Walter Everett was standing by the fireplace, his face blank, remote.

"Listen to *me*," Rick said. "You have this power to attract them. You mean you're not—isn't Walter your real father?"

"Oh, yes—of course he is. I'm completely human. Don't I look human?"

"But you're the only one who has the power."

"I'm not physically different," Silvia said thoughtfully. "I have the ability to see, that's all. Others have had it before me—saints, martyrs. When I was a child, my mother read to me about St. Bernadette. Remember where her cave was? Near a hospital. They were hovering there and she saw one of them."

"But the blood! It's grotesque. There never was anything like that."

"Oh, yes. The blood draws them, lamb's blood especially. They hover over battlefields. Valkyries—carrying off the dead to Valhalla. That's why saints and martyrs cut and mutilate themselves. You know where I got the idea?"

Silvia fastened a little apron around her waist and filled the Silex with coffee. "When I was nine years old, I read of it in Homer, in the Odyssey. Ulysses dug a trench in the ground and filled it with blood to attract the spirits. The shades from the nether world."

"That's right," Rick admitted reluctantly. "I remember."

"The ghosts of people who died. They had lived once. Everybody lives here, then dies and goes there." Her face glowed. "We're all going to have wings! We're all going to fly. We'll all be filled with fire and power. We won't be worms any more."

"Worms! That's what you always call me."

"Of course you're a worm. We're all worms—grubby worms creeping over the crust of the Earth, through dust and dirt."

"Why should blood bring them?"

"Because it's life and they're attracted by life. Blood is *uisge beatha*—the water of life."

"Blood means death! A trough of spilled blood ..."

"It's *not* death. When you see a caterpillar crawl into its cocoon, do you think it's dying?"

Walter Everett was standing in the doorway. He stood listening to his daughter, his face dark. "One day," he said hoarsely, "they're going to grab her and carry her off. She wants to go with them. She's waiting for that day."

"You see?" Silvia said to Rick. "He doesn't understand either." She shut off the Silex and poured coffee. "Coffee for you?" she asked her father.

"No," Everett said.

"Silvia," Rick said, as if speaking to a child, "if you went away with them, you know you couldn't come back to us."

"We all have to cross sooner or later. It's part of our life."

"But you're only nineteen," Rick pleaded. "You're young and healthy and beautiful. And our marriage—what about our marriage?" He half-rose from the table. "Silvia, you've got to stop this!"

"I *can't* stop it. I was seven when I saw them first." Silvia stood by the sink, gripping the Silex, a faraway look in her eyes. "Remember, Daddy? We were living back in Chicago. It was winter. I fell, walking home from school." She held up a slim arm. "See the scar? I fell and cut myself on the gravel and slush. I came home crying—it was sleeting and the wind was howling around me. My arm was bleeding and my mitten was soaked with blood. And then I looked up and saw them."

There was silence.

"They want you," Everett said wretchedly. "They're flies—bluebottles, hovering around, waiting for you. Calling you to come along with them."

"Why not?" Silvia's gray eyes were shining and her cheeks radiated joy and anticipation. "You've seen them, Daddy. You know what it means. Transfiguration—from clay into gods!"

Rick left the kitchen. In the living room, the two sisters stood together, curious and uneasy. Mrs. Everett stood by herself, her face granite-hard, eyes bleak behind her steel-rimmed glasses. She turned away as Rick passed them.

"What happened out there?" Betty Lou asked him in a taut whisper. She was fifteen, skinny and plain, hollow-cheeked, with mousy, sand-colored hair. "Silvia never lets us come out with her."

"Nothing happened," Rick answered.

Anger stirred the girl's barren face. "That's not true. You were both out there in the garden, in the dark, and—"

"Don't talk to him!" her mother snapped. She yanked the two girls away and shot Rick a glare of hatred and misery. Then she turned quickly from him.

Rick opened the door to the basement and switched on the light. He descended slowly into the cold, damp room of concrete and dirt, with its unwinking yellow lights hanging from dust-covered wires overhead.

In one corner loomed the big floor furnace with its mammoth hot air pipes. Beside it stood the water heater and discarded bundles, boxes of books, newspapers and old furniture, thick with dust, encrusted with strings of spider webs.

At the far end were the washing machine and spin dryer. And Silvia's pump and refrigeration system.

From the workbench Rick selected a hammer and two heavy pipe wrenches. He was moving toward the elaborate tanks and pipes when Silvia appeared abruptly at the top of the stairs, her coffee cup in one hand.

She hurried quickly down to him. "What are you doing down here?" she asked, studying him intently. "Why that hammer and those two wrenches?"

Rick dropped the tools back onto the bench. "I thought maybe this could be solved on the spot."

Silvia moved between him and the tanks. "I thought you understood. They've always been a part of my life. When I brought you with me the first time, you seemed to see what—"

"I don't want to lose you," Rick said harshly, "to anybody or anything—in this world or any other. *I'm not going to give you up.*"

"It's not giving me up!" Her eyes narrowed. "You came down here to destroy and break everything. The moment I'm not looking you'll smash all this, won't you?"

"That's right."

Fear replaced anger on the girl's face. "Do you want me to be chained here? I have to go on—I'm through with this part of the journey. I've stayed here long enough."

"Can't you wait?" Rick demanded furiously. He couldn't keep the ragged edge of despair out of his voice. "Doesn't it come soon enough anyhow?"

Silvia shrugged and turned away, her arms folded, her red lips tight together. "You want to be a worm always. A fuzzy, little creeping caterpillar."

"I want *you.*"

"You can't *have* me!" She whirled angrily. "I don't have any time to waste with this."

"You have higher things in mind," Rick said savagely.

"Of course." She softened a little. "I'm sorry, Rick. Remember Icarus? You want to fly, too. I know it."

"In my time."

"Why not now? Why wait? You're afraid." She slid lithely away from him, cunning twisting her red lips. "Rick, I want to show you something. Promise me first—you won't tell anybody."

"What is it?"

"Promise?" She put her hand to his mouth. "I have to be careful. It cost a lot of money. Nobody knows about it. It's what they do in China—everything goes toward it."

"I'm curious," Rick said. Uneasiness flicked at him. "Show it to me."

Trembling with excitement, Silvia disappeared behind the huge, lumbering refrigerator, back into the darkness behind the web of frost-hard freezing coils. He could hear her tugging and pulling at something. Scraping sounds, sounds of something large being dragged out.

"See?" Silvia gasped. "Give me a hand, Rick. It's heavy. Hardwood and brass—and metal lined. It's hand-stained and polished. And the carving—see the carving! Isn't it beautiful?"

"What is it?" Rick demanded huskily.

"It's my cocoon," Silvia said simply. She settled down in a contented heap on the floor, and rested her head happily against the polished oak coffin.

Rick grabbed her by the arm and dragged her to her feet. "You can't sit with that coffin, down here in the basement with—" He broke off. "What's the matter?"

Silvia's face was twisting with pain. She backed away from him and put her finger quickly to her mouth. "I cut myself—when you pulled me up—on a nail or something." A thin trickle of blood oozed down her fingers. She groped in her pocket for a handkerchief.

"Let me see it." He moved toward her, but she avoided him. "Is it bad?" he demanded.

"Stay away from me," Silvia whispered.

"What's wrong? Let me see it!"

"Rick," Silvia said in a low, intense voice, "get some water and adhesive tape. As quickly as possible." She was trying to keep down her rising terror. "I have to stop the bleeding."

"Upstairs?" He moved awkwardly away. "It doesn't look too bad. Why don't you . . ."

"Hurry." The girl's voice was suddenly bleak with fear. "Rick, *hurry.*"

Confused, he ran a few steps.

Silvia's terror poured after him. "No, it's too late," she called thinly. "Don't come back—keep away from me. It's my own fault. I trained them to come. *Keep away!* I'm sorry, Rick. *Oh*—" Her voice was lost to him, as the wall of the basement burst and shattered. A cloud of luminous white forced its way through and blazed out into the basement.

It was Silvia they were after. She ran a few hesitant steps toward Rick, halted uncertainly, then the white mass of bodies and wings settled around her. She shrieked once. Then a violent explosion blasted the basement into a shimmering dance of furnace heat.

He was thrown to the floor. The cement was hot and dry—the whole basement crackled with heat. Windows shattered as pulsing white shapes pushed out again. Smoke and flames licked up the walls. The ceiling sagged and rained plaster down.

Rick struggled to his feet. The furious activity was dying away. The basement was a littered chaos. All surfaces were scorched black, seared and crusted with smoking ash. Splintered wood, torn cloth and broken concrete were strewn everywhere. The furnace and washing machine were in ruins. The elaborate pumping and refrigeration system—now a glittering mass of slag. One whole wall had been twisted aside. Plaster was rubbled over everything.

Silvia was a twisted heap, arms and legs doubled grotesquely. Shriveled, carbonized remains of fire-scorched ash, settling in a vague mound. What had been left behind were charred fragments, a brittle burned-out husk.

It was a dark night, cold and intense. A few stars glittered like ice from above his head. A faint, dank wind stirred through the dripping calla lilies and whipped gravel up in a frigid mist along the path between the black roses. He crouched for a long time, listening and watching. Behind the cedars, the big house loomed against the sky. At the bottom of the slope a few cars slithered along the highway. Otherwise, there was no sound. Ahead of him jutted the squat outline of the porcelain trough and the pipe that had carried blood from the refrigerator in the basement. The trough was empty and dry, except for a few leaves that had fallen in it.

Rick took a deep breath of thin night air and held it. Then he got stiffly to his feet. He scanned the sky, but saw no movement. They were there, though, watching and waiting—dim shadows, echoing into the legendary past, a line of god-figures.

He picked up the heavy gallon drums, dragged them to the trough and poured blood from a New Jersey abattoir, cheap-grade steer refuse, thick and clotted. It splashed against his clothes and he backed away nervously. But nothing stirred in the air above. The garden was silent, drenched with night fog and darkness.

He stood beside the trough, waiting and wondering if they were coming. They had come for Silvia, not merely for the blood. Without her there was no attraction but the raw food. He carried the empty metal cans over to the bushes and kicked them down the slope. He searched his pockets carefully, to make sure there was no metal on him.

Over the years, Silvia had nourished their habit of coming. Now she was on the other side. Did that mean they wouldn't come? Somewhere in the damp bushes something rustled. An animal or a bird?

In the trough the blood glistened, heavy and dull, like old lead. It was their time to come, but nothing stirred the great trees above. He picked out the rows of nodding black roses, the gravel path down which he and Silvia had run—violently, he shut out the recent memory of her flashing eyes and deep red lips. The highway beyond the slope—the empty, deserted garden—the silent house in which her family huddled and waited. After a time, there was a dull, swishing sound. He tensed, but it was only a diesel truck lumbering along the highway, headlights blazing.

He stood grimly, his feet apart, his heels dug into the soft black ground. He wasn't leaving. He was staying there until they came. He wanted her back—at any cost.

Overhead, foggy webs of moisture drifted across the moon. The sky was a vast barren plain, without life or warmth. The deathly cold of deep space, away from suns and living things. He gazed up until his neck ached. Cold stars, sliding in and out of the matted layer of fog. Was there anything else? Didn't they want to come, or weren't they interested in him? It had been Silvia who had interested them—now they had her.

Behind him there was a movement without sound. He sensed it and started to turn, but suddenly, on all sides, the trees and undergrowth shifted. Like cardboard props they wavered and ran together, blended dully in the night shadows. Something moved through them, rapidly, silently, then was gone.

They had come. He could feel them. They had shut off their power and flame. Cold, indifferent statues, rising among the trees, dwarfing the cedars—remote from him and his world, attracted by curiosity and mild habit.

"Silvia," he said clearly. "Which are you?"

There was no response. Perhaps she wasn't among them. He felt foolish. A vague flicker of white drifted past the trough, hovered momentarily and then went on without stopping. The air above the trough vibrated, then died into immobility, as another giant inspected briefly and withdrew.

Panic breathed through him. They were leaving again, receding back into their own world. The trough had been rejected; they weren't interested.

"Wait," he muttered thickly.

Some of the white shadows lingered. He approached them slowly, wary of their flickering immensity. If one of them touched him, he would sizzle briefly and puff into a dark heap of ash. A few feet away he halted.

"You know what I want," he said. "I want her back. She shouldn't have been taken yet."

Silence.

"You were too greedy," he said. "You did the wrong thing. She was going to come over to you, eventually. She had it all worked out."

The dark fog rustled. Among the trees the flickering shapes stirred and pulsed, responsive to his voice. *"True,"* came a detached, impersonal sound. The sound drifted around him, from tree to tree, without location or direction. It was swept off by the night wind to die into dim echoes. Relief settled over him. They had paused—they were aware of him—listening to what he had to say.

"You think it's right?" he demanded. "She had a long life here. We were going to marry, have children."

There was no answer, but he was conscious of a growing tension. He listened intently, but he couldn't make out anything. Presently he realized a struggle was taking place, a conflict among them. The tension grew—more shapes flickered—the clouds, the icy stars, were obscured by the vast presence swelling around him.

"Rick!" A voice spoke close by. Wavering, drifting back into the dim regions of the trees and dripping plants. He could hardly hear it—the words were gone as soon as they were spoken. "Rick—help me get back."

"Where are you?" He couldn't locate her. "What can I do?"

"I don't know." Her voice was wild with bewilderment and pain. "I don't understand. Something went wrong. They must have thought I—wanted to come right away. I *didn't!*"

"I know," Rick said. "It was an accident."

"They were waiting. The cocoon, the trough—but it was too soon." Her terror came across to him, from the vague distances of another universe. "Rick, I've changed my mind. I want to come back."

"It's not as simple as that."

"I know. Rick, time is different on this side. I've been gone so long—your world seems to creep along. It's been years, hasn't it?"

"One week," Rick said.

"It was their fault. You don't blame me, do you? They know they did the wrong thing. Those who did it have been punished, but that doesn't help me." Misery and panic distorted her voice so he could hardly understand her. "How can I come back?"

"Don't they know?"

"They say it can't be done." Her voice trembled. "They say they destroyed the clay part—it was incinerated. There's nothing for me to go back to."

Rick took a deep breath. "Make them find some other way. It's up to them. Don't they have the power? They took you over too soon—they must send you back. It's *their* responsibility."

The white shapes shifted uneasily. The conflict rose sharply; they couldn't agree. Rick warily moved back a few paces.

"They say it's dangerous." Silvia's voice came from no particular spot. "They say it was attempted once." She tried to control her voice. "The nexus between this world and yours is unstable. There are vast amounts of free-floating energy. The power we—on this side—have isn't really our own. It's a universal energy, tapped and controlled."

"Why can't they . . . "

"This is a higher continuum. There's a natural process of energy from lower to higher regions. But the reverse process is risky. The blood—it's a sort of guide to follow—a bright marker."

"Like moths around a light bulb," Rick said bitterly.

"If they send me back and something went wrong—" She broke off and then continued, "If they make a mistake, I might be lost between the two regions. I might be absorbed by the free energy. It seems to be partly alive. It's not understood. Remember Prometheus and the fire . . ."

"I see," Rick said, as calmly as he could.

"Darling, if they try to send me back, I'll have to find some shape to enter. You see, I don't exactly have a shape any more. There's no real material form on this side. What you see, the wings and the whiteness, are not really there. If I succeeded to make the trip back to your side . . ."

"You'd have to mold something," Rick said.

"I'd have to take something there—something of clay. I'd have to enter it and reshape it. As He did a long time ago, when the original form was put on your world."

"If they did it once, they can do it again."

"The One who did that is gone. He passed on upward." There was unhappy irony in her voice. "There are regions beyond this. The ladder doesn't stop here. Nobody knows where it ends, it just seems to keep on going up and up. World after world."

"Who decides about you?" Rick demanded.

"It's up to me," Slivia said faintly. "They say, if I want to take the chance, they'll try it."

"What do you think you'll do?" he asked.

"I'm afraid. What if something goes wrong? You haven't seen it, the region between. The possibilities there are incredible—they terrify me. He was the only one with enough courage. Everyone else has been afraid."

"It was their fault. They have to take responsibility."

"They know that." Silvia hesitated miserably. "Rick, darling, please tell me what to do."

"Come back!"

Silence. Then her voice, thin and pathetic. "All right, Rick. If you think that's the right thing."

"It is," he said firmly. He forced his mind not to think, not to picture or imagine anything. *He had to have her back.* "Tell them to get started now. Tell them—"

A deafening crack of heat burst in front of him. He was lifted up and tossed into a flaming sea of pure energy. They were leaving and the scalding lake of sheer power bellowed and thundered around him. For a split-second, he thought he glimpsed Silvia, her hands reaching imploringly toward him.

Then the fire cooled and he lay blinded in dripping, night-moistened darkness. Alone in the silence.

Walter Everett was helping him up. "You damn fool!" he was saying, again and again. "You shouldn't have brought them back. They've got enough from us."

Then he was in the big, warm living room. Mrs. Everett stood silently in front of him, her face hard and expressionless. The two daughters hovered anxiously around him, fluttering and curious, eyes wide with morbid fascination.

"I'll be all right," Rick muttered. His clothing was charred and blackened. He rubbed black ash from his face. Bits of dried grass stuck to his hair—they had seared a circle around him as they'd ascended. He lay back against the couch and closed his eyes. When he opened them, Betty Lou Everett was forcing a glass of water into his hand.

"Thanks," he muttered.

"You should never have gone out there," Walter Everett repeated. "Why? Why'd you do it? You know what happened to her. You want the same thing to happen to you?"

"I want her back," Rick said quietly.

"Are you mad? You can't get her back. She's gone." His lips twitched convulsively. "You saw her."

Betty Lou was gazing at Rick intently. "What happened out there?" she demanded. "They came again, didn't they?"

Rick got heavily to his feet and left the living room. In the kitchen he emptied the water in the sink and poured himself a drink. While he was leaning warily against the sink, Betty Lou appeared in the doorway.

"What do you want?" Rick demanded.

The girl's thin face was flushed an unhealthy red. "I know something happened out there. You were feeding them, weren't you?" She advanced toward him. "You're trying to get her back?"

"That's right," Rick said.

Betty Lou giggled nervously. "But you can't. She's dead—her body's been cremated—I saw it." Her face worked excitedly. "Daddy always said that something bad would happen to her, and it did." She leaned close to Rick. "She was a witch! She got what she deserved!"

"She's coming back," Rick said.

"*No!*" Panic stirred the girl's drab features. "She *can't* come back. She's dead—like she always said—worm into butterfly—she's a butterfly!"

"Go inside," Rick said.

"You can't order me around," Betty Lou answered. Her voice rose hysterically. "This is *my* house. We don't want you around here any more. Daddy's going to tell you. He doesn't want you and I don't want you and my mother and sister . . ."

The change came without warning. Like a film gone dead, Betty Lou froze, her mouth half open, one arm raised, her words dead on her tongue. She was suspended, an instantly lifeless thing raised slightly off the floor, as if caught between two slides of glass. A vacant insect, without speech or sound, inert and hollow. Not dead, but abruptly thinned back to primordial inanimacy.

Into the captured shell filtered new potency and being. It settled over her, a rainbow of life that poured into place eagerly—like hot fluid—into every part of her. The girl stumbled and moaned; her body jerked violently and pitched against the wall. A china teacup tumbled from an overhead shelf and smashed on the floor. The girl retreated numbly, one hand to her mouth, her eyes wide with pain and shock.

"Oh!" she gasped. "I cut myself." She shook her head and gazed up mutely at him, appealing to him. "On a nail or something."

"*Silvia!*" He caught hold of her and dragged her to her feet, away from the wall. It was *her* arm he gripped, warm and full and mature. Stunned gray eyes, brown hair, quivering breasts—she was now as she had been those last moments in the basement.

"Let's see it," he said. He tore her hand from her mouth and shakily examined her finger. There was no cut, only a thin white line rapidly dimming. "It's all right, honey. You're all right. There's nothing wrong with you!"

"Rick, I was over *there,*" Her voice was husky and faint. "They came and dragged me across with them." She shuddered violently. "Rick, am I actually *back?*"

He crushed her tight. "Completely back."

"It was so long. I was over there a century. Endless ages. I thought—" Suddenly she pulled away. "Rick . . ."

"What is it?"

Silva's face was wild with fear. "There's something wrong."

"There's nothing wrong. You've come back home and that's all that matters."

Silvia retreated from him. "But they took a living form, didn't they? Not discarded clay. They don't have the power, Rick. They altered His work instead." Her voice rose in panic. "A mistake—they should have known better than to alter the balance. It's unstable and none of them can control the . . ."

Rick blocked the doorway. "Stop talking like that!" he said fiercely. "It's worth it—*anything's* worth it. If they set things out of balance, it's their own fault."

"We can't turn it back!" Her voice rose shrilly, thin and hard, like drawn wire. "We've set it in motion, started the waves lapping out. The balance He set up is *altered.*"

"Come on, darling," Rick said. "Let's go and sit in the living room with your family. You'll feel better. You'll have to try to recover from this."

They approached the three seated figures, two on the couch, one in the straight chair by the fireplace. The figures sat motionless, their faces blank, their bodies limp and waxen, dulled forms that did not respond as the couple entered the room.

Rick halted, uncomprehending. Walter Everett was slumped forward, newspaper in one hand, slippers on his feet; his pipe was still smoking in the deep ashtray on the arm of his chair. Mrs. Everett sat with a lapful of sewing, her face grim and stern, but strangely vague. An unformed face, as if the material were melting and running together. Jean sat huddled in a shapeless heap, a ball of clay wadded up, more formless each moment.

Abruptly Jean collapsed. Her arms fell loose beside her. Her head sagged. Her body, her arms and legs filled out. Her features altered rapidly. Her clothing changed. Colors flowed in her hair, her eyes, her skin. The waxen pallor was gone.

Pressing her finger to her lips she gazed up at Rick mutely. She blinked and her eyes focused. "Oh," she gasped. Her lips moved awkwardly; the voice was faint and uneven, like a poor sound track. She struggled up jerkily, with uncoordinated movements that propelled her stiffly to her feet and toward him—one awkward step at a time—like a wire dummy.

"Rick, I cut myself," she said. "On a nail or something."

What had been Mrs. Everett stirred. Shapeless and vague, it made dull sounds and flopped grotesquely. Gradually it hardened and shaped itself. "My finger," its voice gasped feebly. Like mirror echoes dimming off into darkness, the third figure in the easy chair took up the words. Soon, they were all of them repeating the phrase, four figures, their lips moving in unison.

"My finger. I cut myself, Rick."

Parrot reflections, receding mimicries of words and movement. And the settling shapes were familiar in every detail. Again and again, repeated around him, twice on the couch, in the easy chair, close beside him—so close he could hear her breathe and see her trembling lips.

"What is it?" the Silvia beside him asked.

On the couch one Sylvia resumed its sewing—she was sewing methodically, absorbed in her work. In the deep chair another took up its newspaper, its pipe and continued reading. One huddled, nervous and afraid. The one beside him followed as he retreated to the door. She was panting with uncertainty, her gray eyes wide, her nostrils flaring.

"Rick . . ."

He pulled the door open and made his way out onto the dark porch. Machinelike, he felt his way down the steps, through the pools of night collected everywhere, toward the driveway. In the yellow square of light behind him, Silvia was outlined, peering unhappily after him. And behind her, the other figures, identical, pure repetitions, nodding over their tasks.

He found his coupé and pulled out onto the road.

Gloomy trees and houses flashed past. He wondered how far it would go. Lapping waves spreading out—a widening circle as the imbalance spread.

He turned onto the main highway; there were soon more cars around him. He tried to see into them, but they moved too swiftly. The car ahead was a red Plymouth. A heavy-set man in a blue business suit was driving, laughing merrily with the woman beside him. He pulled his own coupé up close behind the Plymouth and followed it. The man flashed gold teeth, grinned, waved his plump hands. The girl was dark-haired, pretty. She smiled at the man, adjusted her white gloves, smoothed down her hair, then rolled up the window on her side.

He lost the Plymouth. A heavy diesel truck cut in between them. Desperately he swerved around the truck and nosed in beyond the swift-moving red sedan. Presently it passed him and, for a moment, the two occupants were clearly framed. The girl resembled Silvia. The same delicate line of her small chin—the same deep lips, parting slightly when she smiled—the same slender arms and hands. It was Silvia. The Plymouth turned off and there was no other car ahead of him.

He drove for hours through the heavy night darkness. The gas gauge dropped lower and lower. Ahead of him dismal rolling countryside spread out, blank fields between towns and unwinking stars suspended in the bleak sky. Once, a cluster of red and yellow lights gleamed. An intersection—filling stations and a big neon sign. He drove on past it.

At a single-pump stand, he pulled the car off the highway, onto the oil-soaked gravel. He climbed out, his shoes crunching the stones underfoot, as he grabbed the gas hose and unscrewed the cap of his car's tank. He had the tank almost full when the door of the drab station building opened and a slim woman in white overalls and navy shirt, with a little cap lost in her brown curls, stepped out.

"Good evening, Rick," she said quietly.

He put back the gas hose. Then he was driving out onto the highway. Had he screwed the cap back on again? He didn't remember. He gained speed. He had gone over a hundred miles. He was nearing the state line.

At a little roadside café, warm, yellow light glowed in the chill gloom of early morning. He slowed the car down and parked at the edge of the highway in the deserted parking lot. Bleary-eyed he pushed the door open and entered.

Hot, thick smells of cooking ham and black coffee surrounded him, the comfortable sight of people eating. A juke box blared in the corner. He threw himself onto a stool and hunched over, his head in his hands. A thin farmer next to him glanced at him curiously and then returned to his newspaper. Two hard-faced women across from him gazed at him momentarily. A handsome youth in denim jacket and jeans was eating red beans and rice, washing it down with steaming coffee from a heavy mug.

"What'll it be?" the pert blonde waitress asked, a pencil behind her ear, her hair tied back in a tight bun. "Looks like you've got some hangover, mister."

He ordered coffee and vegetable soup. Soon he was eating, his hands working automatically. He found himself devouring a ham and cheese sandwich; had he ordered it? The juke box blared and people came and went. There was a little town sprawled beside the road, set back in some gradual hills. Gray sunlight, cold and sterile, filtered down as morning came. He ate hot apple pie and sat wiping dully at his mouth with a paper napkin.

The café was silent. Outside nothing stirred. An uneasy calm hung over everything. The juke box had ceased. None of the people at the counter stirred or spoke.

An occasional truck roared past, damp and lumbering, windows rolled up tight.

When he looked up, Silvia was standing in front of him. Her arms were folded and she gazed vacantly past him. A bright yellow pencil was behind her ear. Her brown hair was tied back in a hard bun. At the counter others were sitting, other Silvias, dishes in front of them, half-dozing or eating, some of them reading. Each the same as the next, except for their clothing.

He made his way back to his parked car. In half an hour he had crossed the state line. Cold, bright sunlight sparkled off dew-moist roofs and sidewalks as he sped through tiny unfamiliar towns.

Along the shiny morning streets he saw them moving—early risers, on their way to work. In twos and threes they walked, their heels echoing in the sharp silence. At bus stops he saw groups of them collected together. In the houses, rising from their beds, eating breakfast, bathing, dressing, were more of them—hundreds of them, legions without number. A town of them preparing for the day, resuming their regular tasks, as the circle widened and spread.

Upon the Dull Earth   57

He left the town behind. The car slowed under him as his foot slid heavily from the gas pedal. Two of them walked across a level field together. They carried books—children on their way to school. Repetitions, unvarying and identical. A dog circled excitedly after them, unconcerned, his joy untainted.

He drove on. Ahead a city loomed, its stern columns of office buildings sharply outlined against the sky. The streets swarmed with noise and activity as he passed through the main business section. Somewhere, near the center of the city, he overtook the expanding periphery of the circle and emerged beyond. Diversity took the place of the endless figures of Silvia. Gray eyes and brown hair gave way to countless varieties of men and women, children and adults, of all ages and appearances. He increased his speed and raced out on the far side, onto the wide four-lane highway.

He finally slowed down. He was exhausted. He had driven for hours; his body was shaking with fatigue.

Ahead of him a carrot-haired youth was cheerfully thumbing a ride, a thin bean-pole in brown slacks and light camel's-hair sweater. Rick pulled to a halt and opened the front door. "Hop in," he said.

"Thanks, buddy." The youth hurried to the car and climbed in as Rick gathered speed. He slammed the door and settled gratefully back against the seat. "It was getting hot, standing there."

"How far are you going?" Rick demanded.

"All the way to Chicago." The youth grinned shyly. "Of course, I don't expect you to drive me that far. Anything at all is appreciated." He eyed Rick curiously. "Which way you going?"

"Anywhere," Rick said. "I'll drive you to Chicago."

"It's two hundred miles!"

"Fine," Rick said. He steered over into the left lane and gained speed. "If you want to go to New York, I'll drive you there."

"You feel all right?" The youth moved away uneasily. "I sure appreciate a lift, but . . ." He hesitated. "I mean, I don't want to take you out of your way."

Rick concentrated on the road ahead, his hands gripped hard around the rim of the wheel. "I'm going fast. I'm not slowing down or stopping."

"You better be careful," the youth warned, in a troubled voice. "I don't want to get in an accident."

"I'll do the worrying."

"But it's dangerous. What if something happens? It's too risky."

"You're wrong," Rick muttered grimly, eyes on the road. "It's worth the risk."

"But if something goes wrong—" The voice broke off uncertainly and then continued, "I might be lost. It would be so easy. It's all so unstable." The voice trembled with worry and fear. "Rick, please . . ."

Rick whirled. "How do you know my name?"

The youth was crouched in a heap against the door. His face had a soft, molten look, as if it were losing its shape and sliding together in an unformed mass. "I want to come back," he was saying, from within himself, "but I'm afraid. You haven't seen it—the region between. It's nothing but energy, Rick. He tapped it a long time ago, but nobody else knows how."

The voice lightened, became clear and treble. The hair faded to a rich brown. Gray, frightened eyes flickered up at Rick. Hands frozen, he hunched over the wheel and forced himself not to move. Gradually he decreased speed and brought the car over into the right-hand lane.

"Are we stopping?" the shape beside him asked. It was Silvia's voice now. Like a new insect, drying in the sun, the shape hardened and locked into firm reality. Silvia struggled up on the seat and peered out. "Where are we? We're between towns."

He jammed on the brakes, reached past her and threw open the door. "Get out!"

Silvia gazed at him uncomprehendingly. "What do you mean?" she faltered. "Rick, what is it? What's wrong?"

"*Get out!*"

"Rick, I don't understand." She slid over a little. Her toes touched the pavement. "Is there something wrong with the car? I thought everything was all right."

He gently shoved her out and slammed the door. The car leaped ahead, out into the stream of mid-morning traffic. Behind him the small, dazed figure was pulling itself up, bewildered and injured. He forced his eyes from the rear-view mirror and crushed down the gas pedal with all his weight.

The radio buzzed and clicked in vague static when he snapped it briefly on. He turned the dial and, after a time, a big network station came in. A faint, puzzled voice, a woman's voice. For a time he couldn't make out the words. Then he recognized it and, with a pang of panic, switched the thing off.

Her voice. Murmuring plaintively. Where was the station? Chicago. The circle had already spread that far.

He slowed down. There was no point hurrying. It had already passed him by and gone on. Kansas farms—sagging stores in little old Mississippi towns—along the bleak streets of New England manufacturing cities swarms of brown-haired gray-eyed women would be hurrying.

It would cross the ocean. Soon it would take in the whole world. Africa would be strange—kraals of white-skinned young women, all exactly alike, going about the primitive chores of hunting and fruit-gathering, mashing grain, skinning animals. Building fires and weaving cloth and carefully shaping razor-sharp knives.

In China ... he grinned inanely. She'd look strange there, too. In the austere high-collar suit, the almost monastic robe of the young Communist cadres. Parades marching up the main streets of Peiping. Row after row of slim-legged full-breasted girls, with heavy Russian-made rifles. Carrying spades, picks, shovels. Columns of cloth-booted soldiers. Fast-moving workers with their precious tools. Reviewed by an identical figure on the elaborate stand overlooking the street, one slender arm raised, her gentle, pretty face expressionless and wooden.

He turned off the highway onto a side road. A moment later he was on his way back, driving slowly, listlessly, the way he had come.

At an intersection a traffic cop waded out through traffic to his car. He sat rigid, hands on the wheel, waiting numbly.

"Rick," she whispered pleadingly as she reached the window. "Isn't everything all right?"

"Sure," he answered dully.

She reached in through the open window and touched him imploringly on the arm. Familiar fingers, red nails, the hand he knew so well. "I want to be with you so badly. Aren't we together again? Aren't I back?"

"Sure."

She shook her head miserably. "I don't understand," she repeated. "I thought it was all right again."

Savagely he put the car into motion and hurtled ahead. The intersection was left behind.

It was afternoon. He was exhausted, riddled with fatigue. He guided the car toward his own town automatically. Along the streets she hurried everywhere, on all sides. She was omnipresent. He came to his apartment building and parked.

The janitor greeted him in the empty hall. Rick identified him by the greasy rag clutched in one hand, the big push-broom, the bucket of wood shavings. "Please," she implored, "tell me what it is, Rick. Please tell me."

He pushed past her, but she caught at him desperately. "Rick, I'm *back*. Don't you understand? They took me too soon and then they sent me back again. It was a mistake. I won't ever call them again— that's all in the past." She followed after him, down the hall to the stairs. "I'm never going to call them again."

He climbed the stairs. Silvia hesitated, then settled down on the bottom step in a wretched, unhappy heap, a tiny figure in thick workman's clothing and huge cleated boots.

He unlocked his apartment door and entered.

The late afternoon sky was a deep blue beyond the windows. The roofs of nearby apartment buildings sparkled white in the sun. His body ached. He wandered clumsily into the bathroom—it seemed alien and unfamiliar, a difficult place to find. He filled the bowl with hot water, rolled up his sleeves and washed his face and hands in the swirling hot steam. Briefly, he glanced up.

It was a terrified reflection that showed out of the mirror above the bowl, a face, tear-stained and frantic. The face was difficult to catch—it seemed to waver and slide. Gray eyes, bright with terror. Trembling red mouth, pulse-fluttering throat, soft brown hair. The face gazed out pathetically—and then the girl at the bowl bent to dry herself.

She turned and moved wearily out of the bathroom into the living room.

Confused, she hesitated, then threw herself onto a chair and closed her eyes, sick with misery and fatigue.

"Rick," she murmured pleadingly. "Try to help me. I'm back, aren't I?" She shook her head, bewildered. "Please, Rick. I thought everything was all right."

2 B R 0 2 B

Kurt Vonnegut, Jr.

Got a problem? Just pick up the phone.
It solved them all—and all the same way!

EVERYTHING was perfectly swell.

There were no prisons, no slums, no insane asylums, no cripples, no poverty, no wars.

All diseases were conquered. So was old age.

Death, barring accidents, was an adventure for volunteers.

The population of the United States was stabilized at forty-million souls.

One bright morning in the Chicago Lying-in Hospital, a man named Edward K. Wehling, Jr., waited for his wife to give birth. He was the only man waiting. Not many people were born a day any more.

Wehling was fifty-six, a mere stripling in a population whose average age was one hundred and twenty-nine.

X-rays had revealed that his wife was going to have triplets. The children would be his first.

Young Wehling was hunched in his chair, his head in his hand. He was so rumpled, so still and colorless as to be virtually invisible. His camouflage was perfect, since the waiting room had a disorderly and demoralized air, too. Chairs and ashtrays had been moved away from the walls. The floor was paved with spattered dropcloths.

The room was being redecorated. It was being redecorated as a memorial to a man who had volunteered to die.

A sardonic old man, about two hundred years old, sat on a stepladder, painting a mural he did not like. Back in the days when people aged visibly, his age would have been guessed at thirty-five or so. Aging had touched him that much before the cure for aging was found.

The mural he was working on depicted a very neat garden. Men and women in white, doctors and nurses, turned the soil, planted seedlings, sprayed bugs, spread fertilizer.

Men and women in purple uniforms pulled up weeds, cut down plants that were old and sickly, raked leaves, carried refuse to trash-burners.

Never, never, never—not even in medieval Holland nor old Japan—had a garden been more formal, been better tended. Every plant had all the loam, light, water, air and nourishment it could use.

A hospital orderly came down the corridor, singing under his breath a popular song:

> If you don't like my kisses, honey,
> Here's what I will do:
> I'll go see a girl in purple,
> Kiss this sad world toodleoo.
> If you don't want my lovin',
> Why should I take up all this space?
> I'll get off this old planet,
> Let some sweet baby have my place.

The orderly looked in at the mural and the muralist. "Looks so real," he said, "I can practically imagine I'm standing in the middle of it."

"What makes you think you're not in it?" said the painter. He gave a satiric smile. "It's called 'The Happy Garden of Life,' you know."

"That's good of Dr. Hitz," said the orderly.

He was referring to one of the male figures in white, whose head was a portrait of Dr. Benjamin Hitz, the hospital's Chief Obstetrician. Hitz was a blindingly handsome man.

"Lot of faces still to fill in," said the orderly. He meant that the faces of many of the figures in the mural were still blank. All blanks were to be filled with portraits of important people on either the hospital staff or from the Chicago Office of the Federal Bureau of Termination.

"Must be nice to be able to make pictures that look like something," said the orderly.

The painter's face curdled with scorn. "You think I'm proud of this daub?" he said. "You think this is *my* idea of what life really looks like?"

"What's your idea of what life looks like?" said the orderly.

The painter gestured at a foul dropcloth. "There's a good picture of it," he said. "Frame that, and you'll have a picture a damn sight more honest than this one."

"You're a gloomy old duck, aren't you?" said the orderly.

"Is that a crime?" said the painter.

The orderly shrugged. "If you don't like it here, Grandpa—" he said, and he finished the thought with the trick telephone number that people who didn't want to live any more were supposed to call. The zero in the telephone number he pronounced "naught."

The number was: "2 B R 0 2 B."

It was the telephone number of an institution whose fanciful sobriquets included: "Automat," "Birdland," "Cannery," "Catbox," "De-louser," "Easy-go," "Good-by, Mother," "Happy Hooligan," "Kiss-me-quick," "Lucky Pierre," "Sheepdip," "Waring Blendor," "Weep-no-more" and "Why Worry?"

"To be or not to be" was the telephone number of the municipal gas chambers of the Federal Bureau of Termination.

The painter thumbed his nose at the orderly. "When I decide it's time to go," he said, "it won't be at the Sheepdip."

"A do-it-yourselfer, eh?" said the orderly. "Messy business, Grandpa. Why don't you have a little consideration for the people who have to clean up after you?"

The painter expressed with an obscenity his lack of concern for the tribulations of his survivors. "The world could do with a good deal more mess, if you ask me," he said.

The orderly laughed and moved on.

Wehling, the waiting father, mumbled something without raising his head. And then he fell silent again.

A coarse, formidable woman strode into the waiting room on spike heels. Her shoes, stockings, trench coat, bag and overseas cap were all purple, the purple the painter called "the color of grapes on Judgment Day."

The medallion on her purple musette bag was the seal of the Service Division of the Federal Bureau of Termination, an eagle perched on a turnstile.

The woman had a lot of facial hair—an unmistakable mustache, in fact. A curious thing about gas-chamber hostesses was that, no matter how lovely and feminine they were when recruited, they all sprouted mustaches within five years or so.

"Is this where I'm supposed to come?" she said to the painter.

"A lot would depend on what your business was," he said. "You aren't about to have a baby, are you?"

"They told me I was supposed to pose for some picture," she said. "My name's Leora Duncan." She waited.

"And you dunk people," he said.

"What?" she said.

"Skip it," he said.

"That sure is a beautiful picture," she said. "Looks just like heaven or something."

"Or something," said the painter. He took a list of names from his smock pocket. "Duncan, Duncan, Duncan," he said, scanning the list. "Yes—here you are. You're entitled to be immortalized. See any faceless body here you'd like me to stick your head on? We've got a few choice ones left."

She studied the mural bleakly. "Gee," she said, "they're all the same to me. I don't know anything about art."

"A body's a body, eh?" he said "All righty. As a master of fine art, I recommend this body here." He indicated a faceless figure of a woman who was carrying dried stalks to a trash-burner.

"Well," said Leora Duncan, "that's more the disposal people, isn't it? I mean, I'm in service. I don't do any disposing."

The painter clapped his hands in mock delight. "You say you don't know anything about art, and then you prove in the next breath that you know more about it than I do! Of course the sheave-carrier is wrong for a hostess! A snipper, a pruner—that's more your line." He pointed to a figure in purple who was sawing a dead branch from an apple tree. "How about her?" he said. "You like her at all?"

"Gosh—" she said, and she blushed and became humble—"that— that puts me right next to Dr. Hitz."

"That upsets you?" he said.

"Good gravy, no!" she said. "It's—it's just such an honor."

"Ah, you admire him, eh?" he said.

"Who doesn't admire him?" she said, worshiping the portrait of Hitz. It was the portrait of a tanned, white-haired, omnipotent Zeus, two hundred and forty years old. "Who doesn't admire him?" she said again. "He was responsible for setting up the very first gas chamber in Chicago."

"Nothing would please me more," said the painter, "than to put you next to him for all time. Sawing off a limb—that strikes you as appropriate?"

"That is kind of like what I do," she said. She was demure about what she did. What she did was make people comfortable while she killed them.

And, while Leora Duncan was posing for her portrait, into the wait-ingroom bounded Dr. Hitz himself. He was seven feet tall, and he boomed with importance, accomplishments, and the joy of living. "Well, Miss Duncan! Miss Duncan!" he said, and he made a joke. "What are you doing here?" he said. "This isn't where the people leave. This is where they come in!"

"We're going to be in the same picture together," she said shyly.

"Good!" said Dr. Hitz heartily. "And, say, isn't that some picture?"

"I sure am honored to be in it with you," she said.

"Let me tell you," he said, "I'm honored to be in it with you. Without women like you, this wonderful world we've got wouldn't be possible."

He saluted her and moved toward the door that led to the delivery rooms. "Guess what was just born," he said.

"I can't," she said.

"Triplets!" he said.

"Triplets!" she said. She was exclaiming over the legal implications of triplets.

The law said that no newborn child could survive unless the parents of the child could find someone who would volunteer to die. Triplets, if they were all to live, called for three volunteers.

"Do the parents have three volunteers?" said Leora Duncan.

"Last I heard," said Dr. Hitz, "they had one, and were trying to scrape another two up."

"I don't think they made it," she said. "Nobody made three appointments with us. Nothing but singles going through today, unless somebody called in after I left. What's the name?"

"Wehling," said the waiting father, sitting up, red-eyed and frowzy. "Edward K. Wehling, Jr., is the name of the happy father-to-be."

He raised his right hand, looked at a spot on the wall, gave a hoarsely wretched chuckle. "Present," he said.

"Oh, Mr. Wehling," said Dr. Hitz, "I didn't see you."

"The invisible man," said Wehling.

"They just phoned me that your triplets have been born," said Dr. Hitz. "They're all fine, and so is the mother. I'm on my way in to see them now."

"Hooray," said Wehling emptily.

"You don't sound very happy," said Dr. Hitz.

"What man in my shoes wouldn't be happy?" said Wehling. He gestured with his hands to symbolize carefree simplicity. "All I have to do is pick out which one of the triplets is going to live, then deliver my maternal grandfather to the Happy Hooligan, and come back here with a receipt."

Dr. Hitz became rather severe with Wehling, towered over him. "You don't believe in population control, Mr. Wehling?" he said.

"I think it's perfectly keen," said Wehling tautly.

"Would you like to go back to the good old days, when the population of the Earth was twenty billion—about to become forty billion, then eighty billion, then one hundred and sixty billion? Do you know what a drupelet is, Mr. Wehling?" said Hitz.

"Nope," said Wehling sulkily.

"A drupelet, Mr. Wehling, is one of the little knobs, one of the little pulpy grains of a blackberry," said Dr. Hitz. "Without population control, human beings would now be packed on this surface of this old planet like drupelets on a blackberry! Think of it!"

Wehling continued to stare at the same spot on the wall.

"In the year 2000," said Dr. Hitz, "before scientists stepped in and laid down the law, there wasn't even enough drinking water to go around, and nothing to eat but seaweed—and still people insisted on their right to reproduce like jackrabbits. And their right, if possible, to live forever."

"I want those kids," said Wehling quietly. "I want all three of them."

"Of course you do," said Dr. Hitz. "That's only human."

"I don't want my grandfather to die, either," said Wehling.

"Nobody's really happy about taking a close relative to the Catbox," said Dr. Hitz gently, sympathetically.

"I wish people wouldn't call it that," said Leora Duncan.

"What?" said Dr. Hitz.

"I wish people wouldn't call it 'the Catbox,' and things like that," she said. "It gives people the wrong impression."

"You're absolutely right," said Dr. Hitz. "Forgive me." He corrected himself, gave the municipal gas chambers their official title, a title no one ever used in conversation. "I should have said, 'Ethical Suicide Studios,'" he said.

"That sounds so much better," said Leora Duncan.

"This child of yours—whichever one you decide to keep, Mr. Wehling," said Dr. Hitz. "He or she is going to live on a happy, roomy, clean, rich planet, thanks to population control. In a garden like that mural there." He shook his head. "Two centuries ago, when I was a young man, it was a hell that nobody thought could last another twenty years. Now centuries of peace and plenty stretch before us as far as the imagination cares to travel."

He smiled luminously.

The smile faded as he saw that Wehling had just drawn a revolver.

Wehling shot Dr. Hitz dead. "There's room for one—a great big one," he said.

And then he shot Leora Duncan. "It's only death," he said to her as she fell. "There! Room for two."

And then he shot himself, making room for all three of his children.

Nobody came running. Nobody, seemingly, heard the shots.

The painter sat on the top of his stepladder, looking down reflectively on the sorry scene.

The painter pondered the mournful puzzle of life demanding to be born and, once born, demanding to be fruitful . . . to multiply and to live as long as possible—to do all that on a very small planet that would have to last forever.

All the answers that the painter could think of were grim. Even grimmer, surely, than a Catbox, a Happy Hooligan, an Easy Go. He thought of war. He thought of plague. He thought of starvation.

He knew that he would never paint again. He let his paintbrush fall to the dropcloths below. And then he decided he had had about enough of life in the Happy Garden of Life, too, and he came slowly down from the ladder.

He took Wehling's pistol, really intending to shoot himself.

But he didn't have the nerve.

And then he saw the telephone booth in the corner of the room. He went to it, dialed the well-remembered number: "2 B R 0 2 B."

"Federal Bureau of Termination," said the very warm voice of a hostess.

"How soon could I get an appointment ?" he asked, speaking very carefully,

"We could probably fit you in late this afternoon, sir," she said. "It might even be earlier, if we get a cancellation."

"All right," said the painter, "fit me in, if you please." And he gave her his name, spelling it out.

"Thank you, sir," said the hostess. "Your city thanks you; your country thanks you; your planet thanks you. But the deepest thanks of all is from future generations."

I Have No Mouth,
and I Must Scream

Harlan Ellison

LIMP, the body of Gorrister hung from the pink palette; unsupported—hanging high above us in the computer chamber; and it did not shiver in the chill, oily breeze that blew eternally through the main cavern. The body hung head down, attached to the underside of the palette by the sole of its right foot. It had been drained of blood through a precise incision made from ear to ear under the lantern jaw. There was no blood on the reflective surface of the metal floor.

When Gorrister joined our group and looked up at himself, it was already too late for us to realize that once again AM had duped us, had had his fun; it had been a diversion on the part of the machine. All three of us had vomited, turning away from one another in a reflex as ancient as the nausea that had produced it.

Gorrister went white. It was almost as though he had seen a voodoo icon and was afraid for the future. "Oh, God," he mumbled, and walked away. The three of us followed him after a time and found him sitting with his back to one of the smaller chittering banks, his head in his hands. Ellen knelt down beside him and stroked his hair. He didn't move, but his voice came out of his covered face quite clearly. "Why doesn't it just do us in and get it over with. Christ, I don't know how much longer I can go on like this."

It was our one hundred and ninth year in the computer.

He was speaking for all of us.

Nimdok (which was the name the machine had forced him to use, because it amused itself with strange sounds) had hallucinated that there were canned goods in the ice caverns. Gorrister and I were very dubious. "It's another shuck," I told them. "Like the goddamn frozen elephant it sold us. Benny almost went out of his mind over *that* one. We'll hike all that way and it'll be putrefied or some damn thing. I say forget it. Stay here, it'll have to come up with something pretty soon or we'll die."

Benny shrugged. Three days it had been since we'd last eaten. Worms. Thick, ropey.

Nimdok was no more certain. He knew there was the chance, but he was getting thin. It couldn't be any worse there, than here. Colder, but that didn't matter much. Hot, cold, raining, lava, boils or locust—it never mattered: we had to take it or die.

Ellen decided us. "I've got to have something, Ted. Maybe there'll be some Bartlett pears or peaches. Please, Ted, let's try it."

I gave in easily. What the hell. Mattered not at all. Ellen was grateful, though. She took me twice out of turn. Even that had ceased to matter. The machine giggled every time we did it. Loud, up there, back there, all around us. And she never climaxed, so why bother.

We left on a Thursday. The machine always kept us aware of the date. The passage of time was important; not to us sure as hell, but to it. Thursday. Thanks.

Nimdok and Gorrister carried Ellen for a while, their hands locked to their own, and each other's wrists, a seat. Benny and I walked before and after, just to make sure that if anything happened, it would catch one of us and at least Ellen would be safe. Fat chance, safe. Didn't matter.

It was only a hundred miles or so to the ice caverns, and the second day, when we were lying out under the blistering sun-thing it had materialized, it sent down some manna. Tasted like boiled boar urine. We ate it.

On the third day we passed through a valley of obsolescence, filled with rusting carcasses of ancient computer banks. AM had been as ruthless with his own life as with ours. It was a mark of his personality:

he strove for perfection. Whether it was a matter of killing off unproductive elements in his own world-filling bulk, or perfecting methods for torturing us, AM was as thorough as those who had invented him—now long-since gone to dust—could ever have hoped.

There was light filtering down from above, and we realized we must be very near the surface. But we didn't try to crawl up to see. There was nothing out there; had been nothing for over a hundred years, but the blasted skin of what had once been the home of billions. Now there were only the five of us, down here inside, alone with AM.

I heard Ellen saying, frantically, "No, Benny! Don't, come on, Benny, don't please!"

And then I realized I had been hearing Benny murmuring, under his breath, for several minutes. He was saying, "I'm gonna get out, I'm gonna get out, I'm gonna get out . . . " over and over. His monkeylike face was crumbled up in an expression of beatific delight and sadness, all at the same time. The radiation scars AM had given him during the "festival" were drawn down into a mass of pink-white puckerings, and his features seemed to work independently of one another. Perhaps Benny was the luckiest of the five of us: he had gone stark, staring mad many years before.

But even though we could call AM any damned thing we liked, could think the foulest thoughts of fused memory banks and corroded base plates, of burnt-out circuits and shattered control bubbles, the machine would not tolerate our trying to escape. Benny leaped away from me as I made a grab for him. He scrambled up the face of a smaller memory cube, tilted on its side and filled with rotted components. He squatted there for a moment, looking like the chimpanzee AM had intended him to resemble.

Then he leaped high, caught a trailing beam of pitted and corroded metal, and went up it, hand-over-hand like an animal, till he was on a girdered ledge, twenty feet above us.

"Oh, Ted, Nimdok, please, help him, get him down before—" she cut off. Tears began to stand in her eyes. She moved her hands aimlessly.

It was too late. None of us wanted to be near him, when whatever was going to happen, happened. And besides, we all saw through her concern. When AM had altered Benny, during his mad period, it had not been merely his face. He was like an animal in many ways. Oh Ellen, pedestal Ellen, pristine pure Ellen, oh Ellen the clean!

Gorrister slapped her. She slumped down, staring up at poor loonie Benny, and she cried. It was her big defense, crying. We had gotten used to it seventy-five years ago. Gorrister kicked her in the side.

Then the sound began. It was light, that sound. Half sound and half light, something that began to glow from Benny's eyes and pulse with growing loudness, dim sonorities that grew more gigantic and brighter as the light/sound increased in tempo. It must have been painful, and the pain must have been increasing with the boldness of the light, the rising volume of the sound, for Benny began to mewl like a wounded animal. At first softly, when the light was dim and the sound was muted, then louder as his shoulders hunched together, his back humped, as though he was trying to get away from it. His hands folded across his chest like a chipmunk's. His head tilted to the side. The sad little monkey-face pinched in anguish. Then he began to howl, as the sound coming from his eyes grew louder. Louder and louder. I slapped the sides of my head with my hands, but I couldn't shut it out, it cut through easily. The pain shivered through my flesh like tinfoil on a tooth.

And Benny was suddenly pulled erect. On the girder he stood up, jerked to his feet like a puppet. The light was now pulsing out of his eyes in two great round beams. The sound crawled up and up some incomprehensible scale, and then he fell forward, straight down, and hit the plate steel floor with a crash. He lay there jerking spastically as the light flowed around and around him and the sound spiraled up out of normal range.

Then the light beat its way back inside his head, the sound spiraled down, and he was left lying there, crying piteously.

His eyes were two soft, moist pools of pus-like jelly. AM had blinded him. Gorrister and Nimdok and myself . . . we turned away.

But not before we caught the look of relief on Ellen's warm, concerned face.

Sea-green light suffused the cavern where we made camp. AM provided punk and we burned it, sitting huddled around the wan and pathetic fire, telling stories to keep Benny from crying in his permanent night.

"What does AM mean?"

Gorrister answered him. We had done this sequence a thousand times before, but it was familiar to Benny. "At first it meant Allied Mastercomputer, and then it meant Adaptive Manipulator, and later on it developed sentience and linked itself up and they called it an Aggressive Menace, but by then it was too late, and finally it called *itself* AM, emerging intelligence, and what it meant was I am . . . *cogito ergo sum* . . . I think, therefore I am."

Benny drooled a little and snickered.

"There was the Chinese AM and the Russian AM and the Yankee AM and—" He stopped. Benny was beating on the floorplates with a large, hard fist. He was not happy. Gorrister had not started at the beginning.

Gorrister began again. "The Cold War started and became World War Three and just kept going. It became a big war, a very complex war, so they needed the computers to handle it. They sank the first shafts and began building AM. There was the Chinese AM and the Russian AM and the Yankee AM and everything was fine until they had honeycombed the entire planet, adding on this element and that element. But one day AM woke up and knew who he was, and he linked himself, and he began feeding all the killing data, until everyone was dead, except for the five of us, and AM brought us down here."

Benny was smiling sadly. He was also drooling again. Ellen wiped the spittle from the corner of his mouth with the hem of her skirt. Gorrister always tried to tell it a little more succinctly each time, but beyond the bare facts there was nothing to say. None of us knew why AM had saved five people, or why our specific five, or why he spent all his time tormenting us, nor even why he had made us virtually immortal . . .

In the darkness, one of the computer banks began humming. The tone was picked up half a mile away down the cavern by another bank. Then one by one, each of the elements began to tune itself, and there was a faint chittering as thought raced through the machine.

The sound grew, and the lights ran across the faces of the consoles like heat lightning. The sound spiraled up till it sounded like a million metallic insects, angry, menacing.

"What is it?" Ellen cried. There was terror in her voice. She hadn't became accustomed to it, even now.

"It's going to be bad this time," Nimdok said.

"He's going to speak," Gorrister ventured.

"Let's get the hell out of here!" I said suddenly, getting to my feet

"No, Ted, sit down . . . what if he's got pits out there, or something else; we can't see, it's too dark." Gorrister said it with resignation.

Something moving toward us in the darkness. Huge, shambling, hairy, moist, it came toward us. We couldn't even see it, but there was the ponderous impression of *bulk,* heaving itself toward us. Great weight was coming at us, out of the darkness, and it was more a sense of *pressure,* of air forcing itself into a limited space, expanding the invisible walls of a sphere. Benny began to whimper. Nimdok's lower lip trembled and he bit it hard, trying to stop it. Ellen slid across the metal floor to Gorrister and huddled into him. There was the smell of matted, wet fur in the cavern. There was the smell of charred wood. There was the smell of dusty velvet. There was the smell of rotting orchids. There was the smell of sour milk. There was the smell of sulphur, of rancid butter, of oil slick, of grease, of chalk dust, of human scalps.

AM was keying us. He was tickling us. There was the smell of—

I heard myself shriek, and the hinges of my jaws ached. I scuttled across the floor, across the cold metal with its endless lines of rivets, on my hands and knees, the smell gagging me, filling my head with a thunderous pain that sent me away in horror. I fled like a cockroach, across the floor and out into the darkness, that *something* moving inexorably after me. The others were still back there, gathered around the firelight, laughing . . . their hysterical choir of insane giggles rising up into the darkness like thick, many-colored wood smoke. I went away, quickly, and hid.

How many hours it may have been, how many days or even years, they never told me. Ellen chided me for "sulking," and Nimdok tried to persuade me it had only been a nervous reflex on their part—the laughing.

But I knew it wasn't the relief a soldier feels when the bullet hits the man next to him. I knew it wasn't a reflex. They hated me. They were surely against me, and AM could even sense this hatred, and made it worse for me *because of* the depth of their hatred. We had been kept alive, rejuvenated, made to remain constantly at the age we had been when AM had brought us below, and they hated me because I was the youngest, and the one AM had affected least of all.

I knew. God, how I knew. The bastards, and that bitch Ellen. Benny had been a brilliant theorist, a college professor; now he was little more than a semi-human, semi-simian. He had been handsome, the machine had ruined that. He had been lucid, the machine had driven him mad. AM had done a job on Benny. Gorrister had been a worrier. He was a connie, a conscientious objector; he was a peace marcher; he was a planner, a doer, a looker-ahead. AM had turned him into a shoulder-shrugger, had made him a little dead in his concern. AM had robbed him. Nimdok went off in the darkness by himself for long times. I don't know what it was he did out there, AM never let us know. But whatever it was, Nimdok always came back white, drained of blood, shakes, shaking. AM had hit him hard in a special way, even if we didn't know quite how. And Ellen! AM had left her alone, had made her more of a slut than she had ever been. All her talk of sweetness and light, all her memories of true love, all the lies she wanted us to believe that she had been a virgin only twice removed before AM grabbed her and brought her down here with us. It was all filth, that lady my lady Ellen. She loved it, five men all to herself. No, AM had given her pleasure, even if she said it wasn't nice to do.

I was the only one still sane and whole.

AM had not tampered with my mind.

I only had to suffer what he visited down on us. All the delusions, all the nightmares, the torments. But those scum, all four of them, they were lined and arrayed against me. If I hadn't had to stand them off all the time, be on my guard against them all the time, I might have found it easier to combat AM.

At which point it passed, and I began crying.

Oh, Jesus sweet Jesus, if there ever was a Jesus and if there *is* a God, please please please let us out of here, or kill us. Because at that moment I think I realized completely, so that I was able to verbalize it: AM was intent on keeping us in his belly forever, twisting and torturing us forever. The machine hated us as no sentient creature had ever hated before. And we were helpless. It also became hideously clear:

If there was a sweet Jesus and if there was a God, the God was AM.

The hurricane hit us with the force of a glacier thundering into the sea. It was a palpable presence. Winds that tore at us, flinging us back the way we had come, down the twisting, computer-lined corridors of the darkway. Ellen screamed as she was lifted and hurled face-forward into a screaming shoal of machines, their individual voices strident as bats in flight. She could not even fall. The howling wind kept her aloft, buffeted her, bounced her, tossed her back and back and down away from us, out of sight suddenly as she was swirled around a bend in the darkway. Her face had been bloody, her eyes closed.

None of us could get to her. We clung tenaciously to whatever outcropping we had reached: Benny wedged in between two great crackle-finish cabinets, Nimdok with fingers claw-formed over a railing circling a catwalk forty feet above us, Gorrister plastered upside-down against a wall niche formed by two great machines with glass-faced dials that swung back and forth between red and yellow lines whose meanings we could not even fathom.

Sliding across the deckplates, the tips of my fingers had been ripped away. I was trembling, shuddering, rocking as the wind beat at me, whipped at me, screamed down out of nowhere at me and pulled me free from one sliver-thin opening in the plates to the next. My mind was a roiling tinkling chittering softness of brain parts that expanded and contracted in quivering frenzy.

The wind was the scream of a great mad bird, as it flapped its immense wings.

And then we were all lifted and hurled away from there, down back the way we had come, around a bend, into a darkway we had never explored, over terrain that was ruined and filled with broken glass and rotting cables and rusted metal and far away further than any of us had ever been . . . .

Trailing along miles behind Ellen, I could see her every now and then, crashing into metal walls and surging on, with all of us screaming in the freezing, thunderous hurricane wind that would never end and then suddenly it stopped and we fell. We had been in flight for an endless time. I thought it might have been weeks. We fell, and hit, and I went through red and gray and black and heard myself moaning. Not dead.

AM went into my mind. He walked smoothly here and there, and looked with interest at all the pockmarks he had created in one hundred and nine years. He looked at the cross-routed and reconnected synapses and all the tissue damage his gift of immortality had included. He smiled softly at the pit that dropped into the center of my brain and the faint, moth-soft murmurings of the things far down there that glibbered without meaning, without pause. AM said, very politely, in a pillar of stainless steel with neon lettering:

HATE. LET ME TELL YOU HOW MUCH I'VE COME TO HATE YOU SINCE I BEGAN TO LIVE. THERE ARE 387.44 MILLION MILES OF PRINTED CIRCUITS IN WAFER THIN LAYERS THAT FILL MY COMPLEX. IF THE WORD HATE WAS ENGRAVED ON EACH NONOANGSTROM OF THOSE HUNDREDS OF MILLION

MILES IT WOULD NOT EQUAL ONE ONE-BILLIONTH OF THE
HATE I FEEL FOR HUMANS AT THIS MICRO-INSTANT FOR
YOU. HATE. HATE.

AM said it with the sliding cold horror of a razor blade slicing my
eyeball. AM said it with the bubbling thickness of my lungs filling
with phlegm, drowning me from within. AM said it with the shriek
of babies being ground beneath blue-hot rollers. AM said it with
the taste of maggoty pork. AM touched me in every way I had ever
been touched, and devised new ways, at his leisure, there inside my
mind.

All to bring me to full realization of why he had done this to the
five of us; why he had saved us for himself.

We had given him sentience. Inadvertently, of course, but sentience nonetheless. But he had been trapped. He was a machine. We
had allowed him to think, but to do nothing with it. In rage, in frenzy,
he had killed us, almost all of us, and still he was trapped. He could
not wander, he could not wonder, he could not belong. He could
merely be. And so, with the innate loathing that all machines had
always held for the weak soft creatures who had built them, he had
sought revenge. And in his paranoia, he had decided to reprieve five
of us, for a personal, everlasting punishment that would never serve
to diminish his hatred . . . that would merely keep him reminded,
amused, proficient at hating man: Immortal, trapped, subject to any
torment he could devise for us from the limitless miracles at his
command.

He would never let us go. We were his belly slaves. We were all he
had to do with his forever time. We would be forever with him, with
the cavern-filling bulk of him, with the all-mind soulless world he
had become. He was Earth and we were the fruit of that Earth and
though he had eaten us, he would never digest us. We could not die.
We had tried it. We had attempted suicide, oh, one or two of us had.
But AM had stopped us. I suppose we had wanted to be stopped.

Don't ask why. I never did. More than a million times a day. Perhaps once we might be able to sneak a death past him. Immortal,

yes, but not indestructible. I saw that when AM withdrew from my mind, and allowed me the exquisite ugliness of returning to consciousness with the feeling of that burning neon pillar still rammed deep into the soft gray brain matter.

He withdrew murmuring *to hell with you.*

And added, brightly, *but then you're there, aren't you.*

The hurricane had, indeed, precisely, been caused by a great mad bird, as it flapped its immense wings.

We had been travelling for close to a month, and AM had allowed passages to open to us only sufficient to lead us up there, directly under the North Pole, where he had nightmared the creature for our torment. What whole cloth had he employed to create such a beast? Where had he gotten the concept? From our minds? From his knowledge of everything that had ever been on this planet he now infested and ruled? From Norse mythology it had sprung, this eagle, this carrion bird, this roc: Huergelmir. The wind creature the Hurokan incarnate.

Gigantic. The words immense, monstrous, grotesque, massive, swollen, overpowering, beyond description. There on a mound rising above us, the bird of winds heaved with its own irregular breathing, its snake neck arching up into the gloom beneath the North Pole, supporting a head as large as a Tudor mansion; a beak that opened slowly as the jaws of the most monstrous crocodile ever conceived, sensuously; ridges of tufted flesh puckered about two evil eyes, as cold as the view down into a glacial crevasse, ice blue and somehow moving liquidly; it heaved once more, and lifted its great sweat-colored wings in a movement that was certainly a shrug. Then it settled and slept. Talons. Fangs. Nails. Blades. It slept.

AM appeared to us as a burning bush and said we could kill the hurricane bird if we wanted to eat. We had not eaten in a very long time, but even so, Gorrister merely shrugged. Benny began to shiver and he drooled. Ellen held him. "Ted, I'm hungry," she said. I smiled at her; I was trying to be reassuring, but it was as phony as Nimdok's bravado: "Give us weapons!" he demanded.

The burning bush vanished and there were two crude sets of bow and arrows, and a water pistol, lying on the cold deckplates. I picked up a set. Useless.

Nimdok swallowed heavily. We turned and started the long way back. The hurricane bird had blown us about for a length of time we could not conceive. Most of that time we had been unconscious. But we had not eaten. A month on the march to the bird itself. Without food. Now how much longer to find our way to the ice caverns, and the promised canned goods?

None of us cared to think about it. We would not die. We would be given filths and scums to eat, of one kind or another. Or nothing at all. AM would keep our bodies alive somehow, in pain, in agony.

The bird slept back there, for how long it didn't matter; when AM was tired of its being there, it would vanish. But all that meat. All that tender meat.

As we walked, the lunatic laugh of a fat woman rang high and around us in the computer chambers that led endlessly nowhere.

It was not Ellen's laugh. She was not fat, and I had not heard her laugh for one hundred and nine years. In fact, I had not heard . . . we walked . . . I was hungry . . . .

We moved slowly. There was often fainting, and we would have to wait. One day he decided to cause an earthquake, at the same time rooting us to the spot with nails through the soles of our shoes. Ellen and Nimdok were both caught when a fissure shot its lightning-bolt opening across the floor-plates. They disappeared and were gone. When the earthquake was over we continued on our way, Benny, Gorrister and myself. Ellen and Nimdok were returned to us later that night which became a day abruptly as the heavenly legion bore them to us with a celestial chorus singing, *Go Down Moses.* The archangels circled several times and then dropped the hideously mangled bodies. We kept walking, and a while later Ellen and Nimdok fell in behind us. They were no worse for wear.

But now Ellen walked with a limp. AM had left her that.

It was a long trip to the ice caverns, to find the canned food. Ellen kept talking about Bing cherries and Hawaiian fruit cocktail. I tried not to think about it. The hunger was something that had come to life, even as AM had come to life. It was alive in my belly, even as we were alive in the belly of AM, and AM was alive in the belly of the Earth, and AM wanted the similarity known to us. So he heightened the hunger. There was no way to describe the pains that not having eaten for months brought us. And yet we were kept alive. Stomachs that were merely cauldrons of acid, bubbling, foaming, always shooting spears of sliver-thin pain into our chests. It was the pain of the terminal ulcer, terminal cancer, terminal paresis. It was unending pain . . . .

And we passed through the cavern of rats.

And we passed through the path of boiling steam.

And we passed through the country of the blind.

And we passed through the slough of despond.

And we passed through the vale of tears.

And we came, finally, to the ice caverns. Horizonless thousands of miles in which the ice had formed in blue and silver flashes, where novas lived in the glass. The down-dropping stalactites as thick and glorious as diamonds that had been made to run like jelly and then solidified in graceful eternities of smooth, sharp perfection.

We saw the stack of canned goods, and we tried to run to them. We fell in the snow, and we got up and went on, and Benny shoved us away and went at them, and pawed them and gummed them and gnawed at them and he could not open them. AM had not given us a tool to open the cans.

Benny grabbed a three quart can of guava shells, and began to batter it against the ice bank. The ice flew and shattered, but the can was merely dented while we heard the laughter of a fat lady, high overhead. and echoing down and down and down the tundra. Benny went completely mad with rage. He began throwing cans, as we all scrabbled about in the snow and ice trying to find a way to end the helpless agony of frustration. There was no way.

Then Benny's mouth began to drool, and he flung himself on Gorrister . . . .

In that instant, I became terribly calm.

Surrounded by madness, surrounded by hunger, surrounded by everything but death. I knew death was our only way out. AM had kept us alive, but there was a way to defeat him. Not total defeat, but at least peace. I would settle for that.

I had to do it quickly.

Benny was eating Gorrister's face. Gorrister on his side, thrashing snow, Benny wrapped around him with powerful monkey legs crushing Gorrister's waist, his hands locked around Gorrister's head like a nutcracker, and his mouth ripping at the tender skin of Gorrister's cheek. Gorrister screamed with such jagged-edged violence that stalactites fell; they plunged down softly, erect in the receiving snowdrifts. Spears, hundreds of them, everywhere, protruding from the snow. Benny's head pulled back sharply, as something gave all at once, and a bleeding raw-white dripping of flesh hung from his teeth.

Ellen's face, black against the white snow, dominos in chalk-dust. Nimdok with no expression but eyes, all eyes. Gorrister half-conscious. Benny now an animal. I knew AM would let him play. Gorrister would not die, but Benny would fill his stomach. I turned half to my right and drew a huge ice-spear from the snow.

All in an instant:

I drove the great ice-point ahead of me like a battering ram, braced against my right thigh. It struck Benny on the right side, just under the rib cage, and drove upward through his stomach and broke inside him. He pitched forward and lay still. Gorrister lay on his back; I pulled another spear free and straddled him, still moving, driving the spear straight down through his throat. His eyes closed as the cold penetrated. Ellen must have realized what I had decided, even as the fear gripped her. She ran at Nimdok with a short icicle, as he screamed, and into his mouth, and the force of her rush did the job. His head jerked sharply as if it had been nailed to the snow crust behind him.

All in an instant.

There was an eternity beat of soundless anticipation. I could hear AM draw in his breath. His toys had been taken from him. Three of them were dead, could not be revived. He could keep us alive, by his strength and his talent, but he was *not* God. He could not bring them back.

Ellen looked at me, her ebony features stark against the snow that surrounded us. There was fear and pleading in her manner, the way she held herself ready. I knew we had only a heartbeat before AM would stop us.

It struck her and she folded toward me, bleeding from the mouth. I could not read meaning into her expression, the pain had been too great, had contorted her face; but it *might* have been thank you. It's possible. Please.

Some hundreds of years may have passed. I don't know. AM has been having fun for some time, accelerating and retarding my time sense. I will say the word *now*. Now. It took me ten months to say *now*. I don't know. I *think* it has been some hundreds of years.

He was furious. He wouldn't let me bury them. It didn't matter. There was no way to dig in the deckplates. He dried up the snow. He brought the night. He roared and sent locusts. It didn't do a thing; they stayed dead. I'd had him. He was furious. I had thought AM hated me before. I was wrong. It was not even a shadow of the hate he now slavered from every printed circuit. He made certain I would suffer eternally and could not do myself in.

He left my mind intact. I can dream, I can wonder, I can lament. I remember all four of them. I wish—

Well, it doesn't make any sense. I know I saved them, I know I saved them from what has happened to me, but still, I cannot forget killing them. Ellen's face. It isn't easy.

Sometimes I want to, it doesn't matter.

AM has altered me for his own peace of mind, I suppose. He doesn't want me to run at full speed into a computer bank and smash my skull. Or hold my breath till I faint. Or cut my throat on a rusted sheet of metal.

There are reflective surfaces down here. I will describe myself as I see myself:

I am a great soft jelly thing. Smoothly rounded, with no mouth, with pulsing white holes filled by fog where my eyes used to be. Rubbery appendages that were once my arms; bulks rounding down into legless humps of soft slippery matter. I leave a moist trail when I move. Blotches of diseased, evil gray come and go on my surface, as though light is being beamed from within.

Outwardly: dumbly, I shamble about, a thing that could never have been known as human, a thing whose shape is so alien a travesty, that humanity becomes more obscene for the vague resemblance.

Inwardly: alone. Here. Living under the land, under the sea, in the belly of AM, whom we created because our time was badly spent and we must have known unconsciously that he could do it better. At least the four of them are safe at last.

AM will be all the madder for that. It makes me a little happier. And yet . . . AM has won, simply . . . he has taken his revenge. . . . I have no mouth. And I must scream.

THE ONES WHO WALK AWAY
FROM OMELAS

URSULA K. LE GUIN

(Variations on a Theme by William James)

WITH A CLAMOR of bells that set the swallows soaring, the Festival of Summer came to the city Omelas, bright-towered by the sea. The rigging of the boats in harbor sparkled with flags. In the streets between houses with red roofs and painted walls, between old moss-grown gardens and under avenues of trees, past great parks and public buildings, processions moved. Some were decorous: old people in long stiff robes of mauve and gray, grave master workmen, quiet, merry women carrying their babies and chatting as they walked. In other streets the music beat faster, a shimmering of gong and tambourine, and the people went dancing, the procession was a dance. Children dodged in and out, their high calls rising like the swallows' crossing flights over the music and the singing. All the processions wound toward the north side of the city, where on the great watermeadow called the Green Fields boys and girls, naked in the bright air, with mudstained feet and ankles and long, lithe arms, exercised their restive horses before the race. The horses wore no gear at all but a halter without bit. Their manes were braided with streamers of silver, gold, and green. They blew out their nostrils and pranced and boasted to one another; they were vastly excited, the horse being the only animal who has adopted our ceremonies as his own. Far off to the north and west the mountains stood up half-encircling Omelas on her bay. The air of morning was so clear that the snow still crowning the Eighteen Peaks burned with white-gold fire across the miles of sunlit air, under the dark blue of the sky. There was just enough wind to make the banners that marked the race course snap and flutter now and then. In the silence of the broad green meadows one could hear the music winding through the city streets, farther and nearer and ever approaching, a cheerful faint sweetness of the air that from time to time trembled and gathered together and broke out into the great joyous clanging of the bells.

Joyous! How is one to tell about joy? How describe the citizens of Omelas?

They were not simple folk, you see, though they were happy. But we do not say the words of cheer much any more. All smiles have become archaic. Given a description such as this one tends to make certain assumptions. Given a description such as this one tends to look next for the King, mounted on a splendid stallion and surrounded by his noble knights, or perhaps in a golden litter borne by great-muscled slaves. But there was no king. They did not use swords, or keep slaves. They were not barbarians. I do not know the rules and laws of their society, but I suspect that they were singularly few. As they did without monarchy and slavery, so they also got on without the stock exchange, the advertisement, the secret police, and the bomb. Yet I repeat that these were not simple folk, not dulcet shepherds, noble savages, bland Utopians. They were not less complex than we. The trouble is that we have a bad habit, encouraged by pedants and sophisticates, of considering happiness as something rather stupid. Only pain is intellectual, only evil interesting. This is the treason of the artist: a refusal to admit the banality of evil and the terrible boredom of pain. If you can't lick 'em, join 'em. If it hurts, repeat it. But to praise despair is to condemn delight, to embrace violence is to lose hold of everything else. We have almost lost hold; we can no longer describe a happy man, nor make any celebration of joy. How can I tell you about the people of Omelas? They were not naive and happy children—though their children were, in fact, happy. They were mature, intelligent, passionate adults whose lives were not wretched. O miracle! But I wish I could describe it better. I wish I could convince you. Omelas sounds in my words like a city in a fairytale, long ago and far away, once upon a time. Perhaps it would be best if you imagined it as your own fancy bids, assuming it will rise to the occasion, for certainly I cannot suit you all. For instance, how about technology? I think that there would be no cars or helicopters in and above the streets; this follows from the fact that the people of Omelas are happy people. Happiness is based on a just discrimination of what is necessary, what is neither necessary nor destructive, and what is destructive. In the middle category, however—that of the unnecessary but undestructive, that of comfort, luxury, exuberance, etc.—they could perfectly well have central heating, subway trains, washing machines, and all kinds of marvelous devices not yet invented here, floating light-sources, fuelless power, a cure for the common cold. Or they could have none of that: it doesn't matter. As you like it. I incline to think that people from towns up and down the coast have been coming in to Omelas during the last days before the Festival on very fast little trains and doubledecked trams, and that the train station of Omelas is actually the handsomest building in town, though plainer than the magnificent Farmers Market. But even granted trains, I fear that Omelas so far strikes some of you as goody-goody. Smiles, bells, parades, horses, bleh. If so, please add an orgy. If an orgy would help, don't hesitate. Let us not, however, have temples from which issue beautiful nude priests and priestesses already half in ecstasy and ready to copulate with whosoever, man or woman, lover or stranger, desires union with the deep godhead of the blood, although that was my first idea. But really it would be better not to have any temples in Omelas—at least, not manned temples. Religion yes, clergy no. Surely the beautiful nudes can just wander about, offering themselves like divine soufflés to the hunger of the needy and the rapture of the flesh. Let them join the processions. Let tambourines be struck above the copulations, and the glory of desire be proclaimed upon the gongs, and (a not unimportant point) let the offspring of these delightful rituals be beloved and looked after by all. One thing I know there is none of in Omelas is guilt. But what else should there be? I thought at first there were no drugs, but that is puritanical. For those who like it, the faint insistent sweetness of *drooz* may perfume the ways of the city, *drooz* which first brings a great lightness and brilliance to the mind and limbs, and then after some hours a dreamy languor, and wonderful visions at last of the very arcana and inmost secrets of the Universe, as well as exciting the pleasure of sex beyond all belief; and it is not habit-forming. For more modest tastes I think there ought to be beer. What else, what else belongs in the joyous city? The sense of victory, surely, the celebration of courage. But as we did without clergy, let us do without soldiers. The joy built upon successful slaughter is not the right kind of joy; it will not do; it is fearful and it is trivial. A boundless and generous contentment, a magnanimous triumph felt not against some outer enemy but in communion with the finest and fairest in the souls of all men everywhere and the splendor of the world's summer: this is what swells the hearts of the people of Omelas, and the victory they celebrate is that of life. I really don't think many of them need to take *drooz*.

Most of the processions have reached the Green Fields by now. A marvelous smell of cooking goes forth from the red and blue tents of the provisioners. The faces of small children are amiably sticky; in the benign gray beard of a man a couple of crumbs of rich pastry are entangled. The youths and girls have mounted their horses and are beginning to group around the starting line of the course. An old woman, small, fat, and laughing, is passing out flowers from a basket, and tall young men wear her flowers in their shining hair. A child of nine or ten sits at the edge of the crowd, alone, playing on a wooden flute. People pause to listen, and they smile, but they do not speak to him, for he never ceases playing and never sees them, his dark eyes wholly rapt in the sweet, thin magic of the tune.

He finishes, and slowly lowers his hands holding the wooden flute.

As if that little private silence were the signal, all at once a trumpet sounds from the pavilion near the starting line: imperious, melancholy, piercing. The horses rear on their slender legs, and some of them neigh in answer. Sober-faced, the young riders stroke the horses' necks and soothe them, whispering, "Quiet, quiet, there my beauty, my hope . . ." They begin to form in rank along the starting line. The crowds along the race course are like a field of grass and flowers in the wind. The Festival of Summer has begun.

Do you believe? Do you accept the festival, the city, the joy? No? Then let me describe one more thing.

In a basement under one of the beautiful public buildings of Omelas, or perhaps in the cellar of one of its spacious private homes, there is a room. It has one locked door, and no window. A little light seeps in dustily between cracks in the boards, secondhand from a cobwebbed window somewhere across the cellar. In one corner of the little room a couple of mops, with stiff, clotted, foul-smelling heads, stand near a rusty bucket. The floor is dirt, a little damp to the touch, as cellar dirt usually is. The room is about three paces long and two wide: a mere broom closet or disused toolroom. In the room a child is sitting. It might be a boy or a girl. It looks about six, but actually is nearly ten. It is feebleminded. Perhaps it was born defective, or perhaps it has become imbecile through fear, malnutrition, and neglect. It picks its nose and occasionally fumbles vaguely with its toes or genitals, as it sits hunched in the corner farthest from the bucket and the two mops. It is afraid of the mops. It finds them horrible. It shuts its eyes, but it knows the mops are still standing there; and the door is locked; and nobody will come. The door is always locked, and nobody ever comes, except that sometimes—the child has no understanding of time or interval—sometimes the door rattles terribly and opens, and a person, or several people, are there. One of them may come in and kick the child to make it stand up. The others never come close, but peer in at it with frightened, disgusted eyes. The food bowl and the water jug are hastily filled, the door is locked, the eyes disappear. The people at the door never say anything, but the child, who has not always lived in the toolroom, and can remember sunlight and its mother's voice, sometimes speaks. "I will be good," it says. "Please let me out. I will be good!" They never answer. The child used to scream for help at night, and cry a good deal, but now it only makes a kind of whining, "eh-haa, eh-haa," and it speaks less and less often. It is so thin there are no calves to its legs; its belly protrudes; it lives on a half-bowl of cornmeal and grease a day. It is naked. Its buttocks and thighs are a mass of festered sores, as it sits in its own excrement continually.

They all know it is there, all the people of Omelas. Some of them have come to see it, others are content merely to know it is there. They all know that it has to be there. Some of them understand why, and some do not, but they all understand that their happiness, the beauty of their city, the tenderness of their friendships, the health of their children, the wisdom of their scholars, the skill of their makers, even the abundance of their harvest and the kindly weathers of their skies, depend wholly on this child's abominable misery.

This is usually explained to children when they are between eight and twelve, whenever they seem capable of understanding; and most of those who come to see the child are young people, though often enough an adult comes, or comes back, to see the child. No matter how well the matter has been explained to them, these young spectators are always shocked and sickened at the sight. They feel disgust, which they had thought themselves superior to. They feel anger, outrage, impotence, despite all the explanations. They would like to do something for the child. But there is nothing they can do. If the child were brought up into the sunlight out of that vile place, if it were cleaned and fed and comforted, that would be a good thing, indeed; but if it were done, in that day and hour all the prosperity and beauty and delight of Omelas would wither and be destroyed. Those are the terms. To exchange all the goodness and grace of every life in Omelas for that single, small improvement: to throw away the happiness of thousands for the chance of the happiness of one: that would be to let guilt within the walls indeed.

The terms are strict and absolute; there may not even be a kind word spoken to the child.

Often the young people go home in tears, or in a tearless rage, when they have seen the child and faced this terrible paradox. They may brood over it for weeks or years. But as time goes on they begin to realize that even if the child could be released, it would not get much good of its freedom: a little vague pleasure of warmth and food, no doubt, but little more. It is too degraded and imbecile to know any real joy. It has been afraid too long ever to be free of fear. Its habits are too uncouth for it to respond to humane treatment. Indeed after so long it would probably be wretched without walls about it to protect it, and darkness for its eyes, and its own excrement to sit in. Their tears at the bitter injustice dry when they begin to perceive the terrible justice of reality, and to accept it. Yet it is their tears and anger, the trying of their generosity and the acceptance of their helplessness, which are perhaps the true source of the splendor of their lives. Theirs is no vapid, irresponsible happiness. They know that they, like the child, are not free. They know compassion. It is the existence of the child, and their knowledge of its existence, that makes possible the nobility of their architecture, the poignancy of their music, the profundity of their science. It is because of the child that they are so gentle with children. They know that if the wretched one were not there sniveling in the dark, the other one, the flute player, could make no joyful music as the young riders line up in their beauty for the race in the sunlight of the first morning of summer.

Now do you believe in them? Are they not more credible? But there is one more thing to tell, and this is quite incredible.

At times one of the adolescent girls or boys who go to see the child does not go home to weep or rage, does not, in fact, go home at all. Sometimes also a man or woman much older falls silent for a day or two, and then leaves home. These people go out into the street, and walk down the street alone. They keep walking, and walk straight out of the city of Omelas, through the beautiful gates. They keep walking across the farmlands of Omelas. Each one goes alone, youth or girl, man or woman. Night falls; the traveler must pass down village streets, between the houses with yellow-lit windows, and on out into the darkness of the fields. Each alone, they go west or north, toward the mountains. They go on. They leave Omelas, they walk ahead into the darkness, and they do not come back. The place they go toward is a place even less imaginable to most of us than the city of happiness. I cannot describe it at all. It is possible that it does not exist. But they seem to know where they are going, the ones who walk away from Omelas.

The Engineer and the Executioner

Brian M. Stableford

"My life," said the engineer. "It's mine. Can you understand that?"

"I understand," replied the executioner calmly.

"I created it," persisted the little man with the spectacles and the unsteady eyes. "I made it, with my own hands. It wasn't all the creation of my own imagination. Other men can take credit for the actual *plan*, and the theory which allowed them to make the plan. But I made it. It was me who put the genes together, sculptured the chromosomes, put the initial cell together. Mine was the real job. I gave the time, the concentration, the determination. The others played with ideas, but I actually built their life-system. I made a dream come true. But you can't understand how I feel about it."

"I understand," repeated the robot. His red eyes shone unblinking from its angular head. He really did understand.

"Look at it," said the little man, waving an arm towards the great concave window that was one wall of the room. "Look at it and tell me it's not worth anything. It's mine, remember. It all grew from what I built. It all evolved from the cells I created. It's going its own way now. It has been for years. But I put it on that road."

The man and the robot stared through the glass. Beyond the window was the hollow interior of Asteroid Lamarck. From space, Lamarck looked like any other asteroid. It had crater-scars and boulders and lots of dust. But it was hollow, and inside it was a tightly-sealed, carefully controlled, Earth-simulation environment. It had air, and water—carefully transported from Earth—and light from the great batteries which trapped solar energy on the outside of the planetoid and released it again on the inside.

The light was pale and pearly. It waxed and waned as the asteroid turned on its axis. At this particular moment it shone bright and clear—it was the middle of inner-Lamarck's day.

It showed the edge of a great forest of silver, shimmering things like wisps of cobweb. The things were so slight and filmy that it seemed as though one ought to be able to see a long way, but in fact clear vision was lost within a hundred metres of the observation window.

Half-hidden by the silvery web-work were other growths of different colours and species. There were red ones like sea anemones that moved their tentacles in a slow, rhythmic dance, as though fishing for prey too tiny to be seen by human eyes. There were pale spheres of lemon yellow mottled with darker colours, suspended within the framework of the silver filaments. There were tall, ramrod-straight spikes of varying colours which grew in geometrically regular clumps at random intervals.

There were things which moved too—airborne puffballs and tiny beings like tropical fish which floated in the gigantic bowl of air. There seemed to be no crawling life, nothing that walked. Everything mobile flew or floated. The shell of the asteroid was so thin that there was practically no gravity in the vast chamber. There was no up and down. There was only surface and lumen.

"The life-system is somewhere between community, organism and cell," said the engineer. "It possesses certain characteristics of each. The method of reproduction employed by the life system is so unique as to make its strict classification impossible by means of the terms we apply to types of Earth organic material. It is completely closed. Light is the only thing which comes in from the outside, to provide the energy winch keeps the system in operation. Water, air, minerals are all recycled. There is no more organic matter there than there has ever been. Everything is used and reused as the life-system evolves and improves. As it grows, it changes, day by day it evolves. It was designed to evolve, to mutate and adapt at a terrific pace. The cycle of its elements is a spiral rather than a circle. Nothing ever returns to a former state. Every generation is a new species, nothing ever reproduces itself. What I have built here is ultra-evolution—evolution which is not caused by natural selection. My life-system exhibits true Lamarckian evolution. My life is better than the life which was spawned on Earth. Don't you see why it's so important, so wonderful?"

"I do," said the robot.

"It's the most wonderful thing we have ever made," continued the little man dreamily. "It is the greatest of our achievements. And I built it. It's mine."

"I know," said the executioner, irrelevantly.

"You don't know," said the little man. "What can you know? You're metal. Hard, cold metal You don't reproduce. Your kind has no evolution. What do you know about life-systems? You can't know what it's like to live and change, to dream and build. How can you claim to know what I mean?"

"I try to understand."

"You came to destroy it all! You came to send Lamarck toppling into the sun, to burn my world and my life into cinders. You were sent to commit murder. How can a murderer claim to understand life? Life is sacred."

"I am not the murderer," said the robot calmly. "It was the people who sent me who made the decision. Real, live people. They must have understood, but they took the decision. Metal doesn't make decision. Metal doesn't murder. I only came to do what I was told to do."

"They can't tell you to kill me," said the bespectacled man, in a low, petulant voice. "They can't make you destroy my work. They can't throw me into the sun. It is against the law to commit murder. Robots can't break the law."

"Sometimes the law has to be ignored," quoted the robot. "It was considered too dangerous to permit Asteroid Lamarck to exist. It was held that the dangerous experiment begun here should be obliterated with all possible speed, and that no possibility of contamination should be tolerated.

"It was held that Asteroid Lamarck held a danger which threatens the existence of life on Earth. It was considered that there was a danger of spores leaking from within the planetoid which were capable of crossing space. It was pointed out that if such an eventuality were to come about, there would be absolutely no way of preventing the Lamarck life-system from destroying all life on Earth.

"It was concluded that, however small the probability of such an occurrence, the potential loss was too great for any such risk to be taken. It was therefore ordered that Asteroid Lamarck should be tipped into the sun, and that nothing which had been in contact with the asteroid should be allowed to return to Earth."

The little man wasn't really listening. He had heard it before. He was staring hard through the window, at the silver forest. His unsteady eyes were leaking little teardrops into the corners of his eyes. He was not crying for himself, but for the life he had created in Lamarck.

"But *why*?" he complained. "My life—it's wonderful, beautiful. It means more to science than anything else we've made or discovered. *Who* took this decision? Who wants to destroy it?"

"It is dangerous," stated the executioner, obstinately. "It must be destroyed."

"You've been programmed to secrecy," said the engineer.

"They are afraid. They are even afraid to tell me who they are. That's not the work of honest men—responsible men. It was politicians who sent you, not scientists.

"What are they really afraid of? Afraid that my life might evolve intelligence? That it might become cleverer, better in every way than a man? But that is foolishness."

"I know nothing about fear," said the robot. "I know what I have been told, and I know what you think of it. But the facts are unalterable. There is a danger of infection from Asteroid Lamarck. The consequences of such a danger are so terrible that no such danger can be allowed to exist for a moment longer than is inevitable."

"My life could never reach Earth."

"It is felt that there is a danger of the evolution of Arrhenius spores."

"Arrhenius spores," sneered the little man. "What could Arrhenius know? He died hundreds of years ago. His speculations are nonsense. His concept of life-spores seeding new planets was naive and ridiculous. There is no evidence that such spores could ever exist. If the men who sent you used Arrhenius spores as an excuse, then they are fools."

"No risk, however slight, is worthwhile," persisted the robot.

"There is *no danger*," stressed the genetic engineer. "We are separated from my life forms by a wall of glass. In all the years I have worked here, my life has never breached that wall. What you are suggesting involves breaking through the crust of a planetoid and crossing a hundred and eighty million miles of space, then finding a relatively small world and becoming established." The little man's voice had risen sharply, and he was gabbling.

"I'm sorry," said the robot.

"You're sorry! How can you be sorry? You aren't alive. How can you know what life means, let alone feel as I feel about it?"

"I am alive," contradicted the executioner. "I am as alive as you, or as the world beyond your window."

"You can't feel sorrow," snapped the little man. "You're only metal. You can't understand."

"Your passionate determination to demonstrate my lack of understanding is wrong," said the robot, with a hint of metallic bitterness. "I know exactly what your life-system is. I know exactly what you are. I know exactly what you feel."

"But you can't feel it yourself."

"No."

'Then you don't understand." The little man was quiet again, his anger spent against the executioner's coldness.

"I understand exactly what you have done, and why," said the robot patiently.

"Then you know there is no danger," said the engineer.

"Your life-system, if it ever got to Earth, would destroy the planet. Your life-system does not reproduce by replication. Every organism is unique, and carries two chromosomes, each one of which carries a complete genome. One chromosome determines the organism, the other codes for a virus particle. This second chromosome is dormant until the organism reaches senility, whereupon it pre-empts control of protein synthesis from the organism-chromosome. Billions and billions of virus particles are produced and the organism dies of its inbuilt disease. The virus particles are released and are universally infective. Any protein-synthesizing system is open to their attack. On infection, the organism-chromosome and the organism-chromosome of the host fuse and co-adapt, evolving by a process of directed change. The new chromosome then induces metamorphosis of the host body, into a creature which is at first parasitic, but may later become free-living. The new being carries the dormant virus chromosome in its own cells.

"The important aspect of the life-system is the fact that the virus may infect absolutely any living creature, irrespective of whether or not it is already a part of the life-system. There is no possible immunization. Thus, eventually, all life in any continuum must inevitably become part of the life-system. And incorporation inevitably means total loss of identity."

The little man nodded. "So you know it all," he conceded. "You know just what it is and how it works. Yet even knowing all the facts you can stand there and accuse me of creating some kind of Frankenstein monster which is just waiting to destroy me and conquer Earth. Can't you see how childish and ludicrous it is?"

"There exists a danger," said the robot obstinately.

"Utter nonsense! My life-system is absolutely bound to the inside of Asteroid Lamarck. There is no possibility of its ever reaching the exterior. If it did, it could not live. Not even a system as versatile as mine could live out there, without air or water. Only robots can do that. There is no escape from Lamarck, as far as the system is concerned."

"If, as you have claimed in your reports, the evolution of the Lamarck life-system is directive and improving, then it would be a mistake to limit the presumed capabilities of the system. There is a finite probability that the system will gain access to outer Lamarck, and will evolve a mechanism of extraplanetary dispersal."

"Arrhenius spores!" spat the little man. "*How? Just tell me, how?* How can a closed system, inside an asteroid, get spores to Earth, *against* the solar wind? Surely, even the idiots who sent you must realise that Arrhenius spores must drift outwards, *away* from Earth, even if there were a vanishingly small probability that such spores could be formed."

"It is impossible to make predictions about the pattern of drift within the solar system," stated the robot implacably.

"Do you think I'm a fool?"

"No."

"Then why do you refuse to concede anything that I say. Robots are essentially logical beings. Surely I have logic on my side."

"No amount of logic can save you. The device is already set and activated. Asteroid Lamarck is on its way into the sun. There is no appeal against the decision."

"No appeal," sneered the genetic engineer. "There is no appeal because they did not dare allow me a voice. There is no justice in this decision. There is only fear."

"There is fear," admitted the robot.

"You try to convince me that there is reason behind this death sentence. You speak in cold, exact terms of probability and danger. You try to tell me, to cover the truth and the guilt.

"Be honest, if you can. Tell me the truth—that I have been condemned to death by a crazy, irrational fear—the fear of some monstrous ghost which can never evolve from my life-system. That's all it is—a crazy, stupid, pathological fear of something they can't begin to understand or appreciate. Fear that can be made to breed fear, to infect others with fear. Fear that can be used as a lever to make death sentences. They say that my infective virus might reach Earth. It is there already. Fear infects everything, and its second generation is murder."

"Fear is only natural," said the executioner.

"Natural!" The little man raised his bespectacled eyes to the ceiling and spread his arms wide. "What sort of nature is afraid of nature?"

"Human nature," said the robot, with mechanical glibness.

"That's what condemned me," said the man. "Human nature. Not reason—not finite probabilities. Human nature, human vanity and human fear. But what they are afraid of is only themselves.

"Humans designed this virus. Biochemists and geneticists conceived it. Genetic engineers and construct surgeons assembled it. The entire system is a product of human inspiration, human ingenuity, human ability.

"What are you going to quote to me now? There are some things that man was not meant to know? Creation is the prerogative of divinity?"

"No," said the executioner. "I will say simply that because a man can do something, there is not an *ipse facto* reason why he should or must. What you have brought into existence is so potentially dangerous that it cannot be allowed to remain in existence."

"They told you to say that."

"These are my words," persisted the robot. "I do as I am told. I say what I am told to say. But I believe. I am metal, but I am alive. I believe in myself. I know what I am doing."

"It's a death sentence for you too," said the engineer.

"I accept the necessity."

"Is that supposed to make me accept it too? You're a robot. You don't put the same value on life that I do. You're programmed to die. No matter what your metal mind believes, you can't be human. You can't accept human values. You're only a machine."

"Yes," said the robot demurely, "I am a machine."

The little man stared through the glass wall, forcing back the nausea, the frustration—and the fear.

"It's not just me," said the man. "It's my life. It's everything I've ever done—everything I believe in. I don't want to die, but I don't want all *this* to die either. It's important to me. I made it. *That,* you can't possibly understand."

"If you say so," conceded the executioner, tiredly.

"I don't understand it either," confessed the little man.

"No," said the robot. "You can't. It isn't your science. It's your child."

The man bridled. "Who are you to judge? *What* are you to judge? How can a metal creature say things like that? What's the difference to me? My science is my child. Because I love the system I have created, is my reason devalued? Are my arguments to be discounted because I am personally involved with them?"

"Your arguments don't matter at all. The argument is already over."

"And the sentence passed. Who spoke for me? Who presented my arguments, my defence?"

"They were presented," said the robot stiffly.

"And discounted. Devalued."

"The decision was made. All the facts were taken into consideration. Every possible course of action was studied. But no chances can be taken. Asteroid Lamarck and everything which has come into contact with it, must be destroyed. The danger of infection must be eliminated."

"They must be mad," said the little man distantly. "Unreasoned fear couldn't spread so far. They are not even content with taking my life. They must kill me too. They must murder as well as destroy. Surely that means they are afraid of *me*—of what I might say. How tenuous must their arguments be, if they dare not allow my voice to be heard?"

"They were afraid of spores," said the robot. "You have come into close personal contact with the system. It would have been inviting the danger which they want to prevent, if they allowed you to return to Earth."

"Are you sure? Do you believe that as well? Why didn't they claim that my knowledge was too dangerous as well? Wouldn't it have been far more diplomatic to have me die in an accident?

"Or is that what they *will* say?" added the engineer, as the thought occurred to him.

"It makes no difference," said the robot.

"Who is it that sent you?" demanded the little man, knowing full well that he was going to get no answer from the executioner. "Who started the scare?"

"What scare?" parried the robot.

"This panic. Who spread the fear behind this decision? It didn't just grow. It didn't form in serious minds because of spontaneous generation. Someone put it there. Someone embarked upon a crusade. Someone wanted a lever. It's obvious.

"I'm not stupid enough to think that anyone hates me, or that some lunatic really does believe in the danger of infection. Someone wanted a platform. Someone wanted to exploit fear, to make a crusade which could carry him along at its head. It's politics that produced your twisted logic. It's politics that swore you to secrecy. It's politics that uses fear as a weapon. That's it, isn't it?"

"I don't know."

"I do. Fear doesn't just spring into being, fully formed. It has to be spread, like a virus. It has to be nurtured, injected. It's part of the currency of politics. Planted, grown, bought and sold."

"You're talking nonsense," said the robot sensibly.

"Tell me I don't understand," suggested the little man, and laughed. The robot didn't laugh.

"'There's no point," said the robot, "in trying to change my mind. You can't devalue my arguments, because the decision has already been made. The sentence has already been carried out."

The little man walked away from the glass wall, towards the door.

"Nothing you do will help," said the robot. "If you are going to fetch the gun from your desk, don't bother. There's nothing you can do. The device was planted and activated before I came here. Lamarck is already dead."

The little man stopped and turned his head.

"I wasn't going to fetch the gun," he said.

The robot couldn't smile. "Go on then," said the executioner. "Go and do whatever you want to do."

The little man left, and the robot turned his red eyes to the glass wall. He stood in silent contemplation, watching the silken forest. Beyond and within the silver threadwork—which was all one organism—were other organisms, other fractions of organisms. The robot did not try to see them. He was not interested.

Asteroid Lamarck began to lose orbital velocity, and started a long, slow spiral in towards the sun.

The little man held the gun in both hands. He had small, delicate hands and thin arms. The gun was heavy.

"What are you going to do?" asked the robot, quietly.

The little man peered through his thin-rimmed spectacles at the unfamiliar object which he held.

"It won't help you to shoot me with that," said the robot.

"What do you care whether I shoot you or not?" demanded the little man. His voice was sharp and emotional. "You're metal. You don't understand *life*. You kill, but you don't know what you're really doing."

"I know what it is to live," said the robot.

"You *exist*," sneered the engineer. "You don't know what a human life *means*. You don't know what *that* means—" he pointed at the window in the wall—"to me, to science. You only want to kill. To kill life, to kill knowledge, to kill science. For fear."

"We've been through all that."

"What else is there to do but go through it all again? What else is there but talk, until Lamarck falls into the sun and you and I become cinders? What do *you* want to do?"

"It's futile to argue."

"Everything's futile. I'm a condemned man. Whatever I do, it's a waste of time. I'm a dead man. You're a dead robot. But you don't care."

The executioner remained silent.

The little man raised the gun, and pointed it at one of the robot's red eyes. For a few moments, man and metal stared at each other. The robot watched a thin, unsteady finger press the trigger of the gun.

The hands that held the gun jerked as the recoil jolted the genetic engineer. There was a loud bang. The bullet clanged off the metal ceiling, ricocheted into the window, but the glass was unbroken.

"It's pointless," said the robot softly. Somehow, after the report of the gun, his calmness seemed plaintive.

The little man fired again, squeezing the muscles round his eyes and mouth as he struggled to keep his hands still. The bullet splashed the robot's electronic eye into tiny red fragments. The metal man moaned, and went over backwards. There was a moment when the balance adjustment in his double-jointed knees compensated for the impact, and held the robot in a backward kneeling position. Then the moaning ended in a sharp gasp, and the engineer winced as the robot fell full length on to the floor.

The dead robot gave a mock laugh, which rattled harshly out of the uncoordinated vocal apparatus. The engineer stared at the crumpled heap of metal. It was no longer a parody of a human form. It was just metal. It was dead.

The little man walked slowly over to the large window. He fired from the waist, gunfighter style. The bullet bounced off the glass and hit him in the thigh. His face went pale, and he winced, but he did not fall. He fired three more times, and the third time the glass cracked. But there was still no breach in the glass wall.

The engineer felt tears easing from the corners of his eyes, and a trickle of blood on his leg. He smashed the butt of the gun into the glass again and again. The cracks spread, and finally the window gave up the fight and shattered.

Once the gap was there, it was easy to enlarge it. The little man allowed the artificial gravity of the laboratory to pull him to the floor, resting his injured leg, while he chipped away at the lower edge of the hole until he had made a doorway in the wall.

He crawled through, into the world of his life-system. Once there, beyond the pull of gravity, his leg stopped hurting him, and his body was filled with an exhilarating buoyancy.

He breathed the air, and imagined that he found it cleaner and fresher, than the cold, sterile air of his own world inside Lamarck. He felt nothing, but he knew that in the air he breathed, and through the wound in his leg, the virus was invading his body.

He began to crawl away from the window, to get away from the murdered robot, and found that he could crawl with amazing rapidity and with little expenditure of effort. There was just enough gravity to stop him hurting himself. The engineer left the window behind, because it was not a window into a world that had sent an executioner to take away his life. He pulled himself further and further into the body of the silver forest, and on, and on.

He found another forest—another single being with many individual aspects. This was a conglomeration of tree-forms which consisted of twisted, many-branched stalks, each of which seemed to have arisen by a process of bifurcation and spiralling away of elements from a single point or origin. Each of the branches terminated in a small, eye-like spheroid.

The branches were of equal thickness, and of a glass-like smoothness and hardness. At first sight, the entire forest seemed petrified, but there was life there, and growth. Nothing petrified in the Lamarck life-system. Within the globes at the ends of the branches, the engineer could perceive movement, and when he stopped to look more closely, he saw a shifting and pouring like swirling smoke that could only be cytoplasmic streaming. He perceived darker regions that were nuclei and organelles. He concluded that the spheroids were the living elements of a colonial being or hive, which constructed the stalks which bore them from purely inorganic matter.

Then he pulled himself on, half-flying through the small forest, and into another forest, and another. He had lost sight of the smashed window, and he could not see the battery of solar cells which were the only other evidence of human interference with the Lamarck life-system. He was alone, a stranger in the world he had made. He floated to a stop, and sank slowly to the carpet of tiny unique organisms. He lay, exhausted, listening to the beating of his heart and admiring the wonders which his genetic engineering skill had produced.

He saw a giant plant, not far off, which must have covered a much larger area of ground than any of the so-called forests. It was of such complexity that it was built in tiers in the air.

The lowest layer consisted of a dense tangle of light-coloured tendrils of even continuity, not unlike the filaments of the silken forest. The slender threads were woven into a cushion of varying density.

Above this was a looser serial carpet of thicker elements which were darker in colour, but of a similar even texture. The threads stirred gently, and appeared to be very flexible.

From this aerial stratum there extended towers of small spherical elements, held vertical by some adhesive force that was not apparent. These spherical cells were being continually produced by budding from the filaments. The topmost spheres were always losing the mysterious adhesion and drifting away, falling very slowly, in a dipping-and-soaring fashion. Eventually, they exploded into clouds of invisibly small virus particles.

In the opposite direction, the engineer could see another vast growth, which had the appearance of a tree bearing fruits that were precious stones. The growth arose from a deep bed of slime—a great, extensive cushion which would have seemed hostile to life had it not been part of the Lamarck life-system. When he squinted, the little man could perceive thousands of rod-like bodies moving randomly within the slime-body.

The tree itself was slender and extremely beautiful in the manner of its curving and branching. The branches were translucent, but not wholly clear, for at certain points they contained encapsulated rod-bodies, entombed like flies in amber. The engineer imagined that the tree was formed of crystalline slime.

At the tip of each branch was a large spherical or elliptical jewel, each enclosed by a thin membrane. There was movement within each gem, and they looked like the many faceted eyes of some strange beast.

The engineer looked, and marvelled, and loved.

Asteroid Lamarck passed within the orbit of Mars.

The engineer slept, and while he slept he died.

The virus worked within him. It invaded cells, penetrated nuclei, It pre-empted protein production. It killed. And while it was still killing, it began rebuilding and regenerating. The second virus chromosome and the forty-six human chromosomes formed a complex, and the DNA within them began to undergo chemical metamorphosis as bases shifted and genes were remodeled.

As the new genotype was created, the virus sculpted, stimulated and responded. It mutated and tested. The path of generation of the new being was amended continually.

In conjunction with the chemical metamorphosis came physical change. The body of the engineer began to flow and distort. A new being was born inside him and was growing from him, feeding on him. The virus tested the viability of what its second set of chromosomes was building, and the being that was emerging was perfectly designed to fulfill its task. The process which was going on inside the corpse of the little man was far beyond the elementary process which the engineer had made. The rapidity of the Lamarck life-system's evolution had taken the speed, the smoothness, and the efficiency of the metamorphosis a long way.

The new being absorbed the engineer, and came slowly to maturity.

Asteroid Lamarck crossed the orbit of Earth.

The body of the little man had lost most of its substance. The face had widened into a skull-grin, and the ridiculous pair of spectacles lay lop-sided across the gleaming white bridge of the nose. The brain had completely gone from the skull, and the whole of the lower abdomen had disappeared. The legs were only thin ropes of decayed muscle. The ribs were reduced to tiny studs attached to what had once been the spine. Only dust remained where the internal organs had once been.

Above the corpse, a winged thing hovered bat-like, testing its strength. It was small bodied but large-skulled. It had a tiny, oddly human, wizened face without eyes. The face moved continuously as though expressing unknown emotions, and the creature made a small, thin sound like a rattling laugh.

It flew away from the remains of its father, zooming through the weird forests of inner Lamarck in great circles. Finally, it found the silver forest, and settled on a branch very near to the smashed glass wall. It lay still. It had never eaten. It was not even equipped to eat. It had been born only to perform one small task for the Lamarck life-system, and then to die again.

Meanwhile, the plants of inner Lamarck had passed through the doorway which the engineer had made for them. They had explored his laboratories, his library, his bedroom, his office. They had dipped under doors and through keyholes. There was only one place they could not reach, and that was the world of outer Lamarck, beyond the great iron air-lock that had neither crack nor key.

Plants died, and were reborn. New types of plant formed around and on the iron door—plants that built their cell walls out of pure iron. With vegatable efficiency, they began to dissolve the airlock.

The winged creature began to sprinkle tiny objects from its abdomen. A sphincter pulsed and pulsed hundreds of contractions per minute, and every pulse released another particle. The motes floated in the air, far too light for the weak gravity to pull them to the ground. The air in the silver forest became filled with them.

Asteroid Lamarck crossed the orbit of Venus.

Pinpricks formed in the outer airlock door. The inner door was completely gone. Air began to seep away, but before the seepage became dramatic, the holes were the size of fists. Like all the other members of the Lamarck life-system, the iron-eaters were fast and efficient. The seepage became a rush. With it, the air took the tiny particles produced in hundreds of millions by the winged creature.

Lamarck was too small to hold the atmosphere which flooded out into the desolation of its outer surface. The air was lost and the particles with it. While Lamarck plunged on towards the sun, in an ever-decreasing spiral, it left behind a long, long trail of Arrhenius spores, which began to drift lazily on the solar wind.

Slowly outwards, toward the orbit of Earth.

The End of the Whole Mess

Stephen King

I WANT to tell you about the end of war, the degeneration of mankind, and the death of the messiah—an epic story, deserving thousands of pages and a whole shelf of volumes, but you—if there are any of "you" later on to read this—will have to settle for the freeze-dried version. The direct injection works very fast. I figure I've got somewhere between forty-five minutes and two hours, depending on my blood type. I think it's A, which should give me a little more time, but I'll be goddamned if I can remember for sure. If it turns out to be O, you could be in for a lot of blank pages, my hypothetical friend. I think maybe I better assume the worst and go as fast as I can. I'm using the electric typewriter—Bobby's word processor is faster but the genny's cycle is too irregular to be trusted, even with the voltage regulator. I've only got one shot at this; I can't risk getting most of the way home and then seeing the whole thing go to data heaven because of an ohm drop.

My name is Howard Fornoy. I was a freelance writer. My brother, Robert Fornoy was the messiah. I killed him by shooting him up with his own discovery four hours ago. *He* called it The Calmative. A Real Big Mistake might have been a better name, but what's done is done and can't be undone, as the Irish have been saying for centuries . . . which *proves* what assholes they are.

Shit, I can't afford these digressions.

After Bobby died I covered him with a quilt, sat at the window of this cabin just north of North Conway, New Hampshire, for some three hours, looking out at the big nothing. Used to be you could see the orange glow of the high-intensity arc-sodiums from town, but no more. Now there's just the White Mountains, looking like dark pieces of crepe paper cut out by a child, and the pointless stars.

I turned on the radio, dialed through four bands, found one crazy guy, and shut it off. I sat there thinking of ways to tell this story. My mind kept sliding away toward all that nothing. Finally I realized I needed to get myself off the dime and shoot myself up. Shit, I never *could* work without a deadline. Well, I got one now.

Our parents had no reason to expect anything other than what they got: bright children. Dad was a history major who had become a full professor at Hofstra at thirty. Ten years later he was one of six vice administrators of the National Archives in Washington, DC, and in line for the top spot. Good shit, too. Had a whole Chuck Berry collection, my dad. He filed by day and rocked by night. Mom graduated cum laude from Drew. Business administration. Got a Phi Beta Kappa key she sometimes wore on this funky fedora she had. She became a successful CPA in DC, met my dad, married him, and took in her shingle when she became pregnant with yours truly. I came along in 1980. By '84 she was doing taxes for some of my dad's associates as a "hobby." By the time Bobby was born in 1987, she was handling taxes, investment portfolios, and estate planning for a dozen powerful men. I could name them, but who gives a fuck? They're either dead or driveling idiots by now.

I think she probably made more out of her "hobby" each year than my dad made at his job, but that never mattered—they were happy with what they were to themselves and to each other. I saw them squabble lots of times, but I never saw them fight. When I was growing up, the only difference I saw between my mom and my playmates' moms was that their moms used to read or iron or sew or talk on the phone while the soaps played on the tube, and my mom used to run a pocket calculator and write down numbers on big green sheets of paper while the soaps played.

I was no disappointment to a couple of people with Mensa cards in their wallets. I maintained A and B averages through my public-school career (the idea that either I or my brother might go to a private school was never even discussed, so far as I know). I also wrote well early, with no effort at all. I sold my first magazine piece when I was twenty—it was on how the Continental Army wintered at Valley Forge. I sold it to an airline magazine for four hundred fifty dollars. My dad, whom I loved and do love deeply, asked me if he could buy that check from me. He gave me his own personal check and had the check from the airline magazine framed and hung over his desk. Sweet guy. Of course he and my mother both died raving and pissing in their pants—like most of the human race—late last year, but I never stopped loving either of them.

I was the sort of child they had every reason to expect: a good boy who grew up in an atmosphere of love and confidence, a bright boy who found a considerable talent and put it to work.

Bobby was different. Bobby wasn't just bright; he was a bona fide genius.

I potty trained two years earlier than Bob; that was the only thing in which I ever beat him. But I never felt jealous of him; that would have been like a fairly good high-school pitcher feeling jealous of Catfish Hunter or Ron Guidry. After a certain point the comparisons that cause feelings of jealousy simply cease to exist. I've been there, and I can tell you: You just stand back and shield your eyes from the flash burns. Bobby read at two and began writing at three. His printing was the straggling, struggling, galvanic constructions of a six-year-old. . . . startling enough in itself; but if transcribed so that the lagging motor control no longer became an evaluative factor, you would have thought you were reading the work of a bright, if extremely naive, junior high school student. Sometimes his syntax was garbled and his modifiers, misplaced; but he had such flaws—which plague most writers all their lives—pretty well under control by age five.

He developed headaches. My parents were afraid he had some sort of physical problem—a brain tumor, perhaps—and took him to a doctor who examined him carefully, listened to him even more carefully, and then told my parents there was nothing wrong with Bobby except stress: He was in a state of extreme frustration because his hand would not work as well as his brain. "You got a kid trying to pass a mental kidney stone," the doctor said. "I could prescribe something for his headaches. but I think the drug he really needs is a typewriter." So Mom and Dad gave Bobby an IBM. A year later they gave him a Commodore 64 with a *WordStar* program for Christmas, and Bobby's headaches stopped . . . although he really believed for the next two or three years that it was Santa Claus who put that word cruncher under the tree.

Now that I think of it, that was maybe the only other place where I beat Bobby: I Santa trained earlier, too.

I could go on. and will have to, at least a little, but I'll have to go fast. The deadline. Ah, the deadline. I once read a very funny piece called "The Essential *Gone with the Wind*" that went like this: "'A war?' laughed Scarlett. 'Oh, fiddledeedee!' Boom! Charleston was taken! Ashley died! Atlanta burned! Rhett walked in and then walked out! 'Fiddledeedee,' said Scarlett through her tears. 'I will think about it tomorrow, for tomorrow is another day.'" I laughed heartily over that when I read it; now that I'm faced with doing it, it doesn't seem quite so funny. But here goes.

"A child with an I.Q. immeasurable by any existing test?" smiled India Fornoy to her devoted husband, Richard. "Fiddledeedee! We'll provide an atmosphere where his intellect—not to mention that of his something-less-than-moronic older brother—can grow. And we'll raise them as the normal, all-American boys they by gosh are!" Boom! The Fornoy brothers grew up! Howard went to Rutgers, graduated cum laude, and settled down to a freelance-writing career! Made a comfortable living! Stepped out with a lot of women and went to bed with more than a few of them! Managed to avoid social diseases both sexual and pharmacological! Bought a Curtis-Mathis TV and a Mitsubishi stereo system! Wrote home at least once a week! Published two novels that did pretty well! "Fiddledeedee," said Howard, "this is the life for me!" And so it was, at least until the day Bobby showed up with his two glass boxes, a bee's nest in one and a wasp's nest in the other, Bobby wearing a Mumford Phys. Ed. T-shirt inside out in the best mad-scientist tradition, on the verge of destroying human intellect and just as happy as a clam at high tide.

Guys like my brother Bobby only come along once every two or three generations, I think—guys like Newton, Einstein, Da Vinci, maybe Edison. They all seem to have one thing in common: They are like huge compasses that swing aimlessly for a long time, searching for some true north and then homing in on it with fearful force. Before that happens, such guys are apt to get up to some weird shit, and Bobby was no exception. When he was eight and I was fifteen, he came to me and said he had invented an airplane. By then I knew Bobby too well to just say "Bullshit" and kick him out of my room. I went out to the garage, where there was this weird plywood contraption sitting on his American Flyer red wagon. It looked a little like a fighter plane, but the wings were raked forward instead of back. He had mounted the saddle from his rocking horse on the middle of it with bolts. There was a lever on the side. There was no motor. He said it was a glider. He wanted me to push him down Carrigan's Hill, which was the steepest grade in DC's Grant Park—there was a cement path down the middle of it for old folks. That, Bobby said, would be his runway.

"Bobby," I said, "you got this puppy's wings on backward."

"No," he said. "This is the way they're supposed to be. I saw something on *Wild Kingdom* about hawks. They dive down on their prey and then reverse their wings coming up. They're double-jointed, see? You get better lift this way."

"Then why isn't the Air Force building them this way?" I asked, blissfully unaware that both America and the Soviet Union had plans for such forward-wing fighter planes on their drawing boards.

Bobby just shrugged. We went over to Carrigan's Hill, and he climbed into the rocking-horse saddle and gripped the lever. "Push me *hard*," he said. His eyes were dancing with that crazed light I knew so well—Christ, his eyes used to light up that way in his cradle sometimes. But I swear to God, I never would have pushed him down the cement path as hard as I did if I thought the thing would actually work.

But I didn't know, and I gave him one hell of a shove. He went freewheeling down the hill, whooping like a cowboy just off a trail drive and headed into town for a few cold beers. An old lady had to jump out of his way, and he just missed an old guy in a walker. Halfway down he pulled the handle, and I watched, wide-eyed and gapejawed, as his splintery plywood plane separated from the wagon. At first it only hovered inches above it, and for a second it looked like it was going to settle back. Then there was a gust of wind, and Bobby's plane took off like someone had it on an invisible cable. The American Flyer wagon ran off the concrete path and into some bushes. All of a sudden Bobby was ten feet in the air, then twenty, then fifty. He went gliding over Grant Park on a steepening, upward plane, whooping cheerily.

I went running after him, screaming for him to come down, visions of his body tumbling off that stupid rocking-horse saddle and impaling itself on a tree or one of the park's many statues standing out with hideous clarity in my head. I did not just imagine my brother's funeral; I *attended* it. "BOBBY!" I shrieked. "COME DOWN!"

"WHEEEEEEEE!" Bobby screamed back, his voice faint but clearly ecstatic. Startled chess players, Frisbee throwers, book readers. lovers, and joggers stopped whatever they were doing to watch.

"BOBBY, THERE'S NO SEAT BELT ON THAT FUCKING THING!" I screamed. It was the first time I ever used that particular word, so far as I can remember.

"I'll be all right . . ." he was screaming at the top of his lungs, but I could barely hear him. I went running down Carrigan's Hill, shrieking all the way. I don't have the slightest memory of just what I was yelling, but the next day I could not speak above a whisper. I *do* remember passing a young fellow in a neat three-piece suit standing by the statue of Eleanor Roosevelt at the foot of the hill. He looked at me and said conversationally, "Tell you what, my friend, I'm having one *hell* of an acid flashback."

I remember that odd, misshapen shadow gliding across the green floor of the park, rising and rippling as it crossed over park benches, litter baskets, and the upturned faces of the watching people. I remember chasing it. I remember how my mother's face crumpled and how she started to cry when I told her that Bobby's plane, which had no business flying in the first place, turned upside down in a sudden eddy of wind and that Bobby finished his short but brilliant career splattered all over D Street.

Way things turned out, it would have been better for everyone if it had turned out that way. Instead, Bobby banked back toward Carrigan's Hill, holding nonchalantly on to the tail of his plane to keep from falling off the damned thing, and brought it down toward the pond at the center of Grant Park. He went air-sliding five feet over it, then four . . . and then he was dragging his sneakers in the water, sending back twin white wakes, scaring the usually complacent (and overfed) ducks into honking indignant flurries before him, laughing his cheerful laugh. He came down on the far side, exactly between two park benches that snapped off the wings of his plane. Bobby flew out of the saddle, thumped his head, and started to bawl.

That was life with Bobby.

Not that everything was that spectacular—in fact, I don't think anything (at least until The Calmative) was quite *that* spectacular. But life with Bobby was a constant boggle. By age nine he was attending quantum-physics and advanced-algebra classes at Georgetown University. One day he blanked out every radio and TV on our street— and the surrounding four blocks—with his own voice; he had found an old portable TV in the attic and turned it into a wide-band radio broadcasting station. One old black-and-white Zenith, twelve feet of hi-fi flex, a coat hanger mounted on the roof peak of our house, and presto! For about two hours all four blocks of Georgetown could receive was WBOB . . . which happened to be my brother, reading some of my short stories, telling moron jokes, and explaining that the high sulfur content in baked beans was the reason our dad farted so much in church every Sunday morning. "But he gets most of 'em off pretty quiet," Bobby told his audience of roughly three thousand, "or sometimes he holds the real bangers until it's time for the hymns."

My dad, who was less than happy about all this, ended up paying a seventy-five-dollar fine and taking it out of Bobby's allowance for the next year. Life with Bobby, oh, yeah . . . and look here, I'm crying. Is it honest sentiment, I wonder, or the onset? The former, I think— Christ knows how much I loved him—but I think I better try to hurry up a little just the same.

Bobby had graduated high school, for all practical purposes, by the age of ten. But he never got a B.A. or B.S., let alone any advanced degree. It was that big, powerful compass in his head, swinging around and around, looking for some true north to point at. He went through a physics period and a shorter period when he was nutty for chemistry . . . but in the end, Bobby was too impatient with mathematics for either of those fields to hold him. He could do it, but it—and ultimately all so-called hard science—bored him. By the time he was fifteen, it was archaeology—he combed the rocky White Mountain foothills in the area around our summer place in North Conway, building a history of the Indians who had lived there.

But that passed, too: He began to read history and anthropology. When he was sixteen my folks gave their reluctant approval when Bobby requested that he be allowed to accompany a party of New England anthropologists on an expedition into South America. He came back five months later with the first real tan of his life; he was also an inch taller, fifteen pounds lighter, and much quieter. He was still cheerful enough, or could be, but his little-boy exuberance— sometimes infectious, sometimes wearisome, but always there— was gone. He had grown up. And for the first time I remember him talking about the news . . . how bad it was, I mean. That was 2003, the year a PLO splinter group called Sons of the Jihad set off a squirt bomb in London, polluting sixty percent of it for the next seventy years and making the rest of it extremely unhealthy for people who ever planned to have children (or to live past the age of fifty without developing some sort of cancer, for that matter). The year after, we tried to blockade the Philippines after the Cedeno administration accepted a "small group" of Red Chinese advisers (fifteen thousand of them, according to our spy satellites) and only backed down when it became clear that a) the Chinese weren't kidding about emptying the holes if we didn't pull back; and b) the American people weren't all that crazy about committing mass suicide over the Philippine islands. That was the same year some other group of crazy mother-fuckers—Albanians, I think—tried to air-spray the AIDS virus over West Berlin.

This sort of stuff depressed everybody, but it depressed the *shit* out of Bobby.

"Why are people so goddamn mean?" he asked me one day. We were in North Conway, it was late August, and most of our stuff was already in boxes and suitcases . . . the place had that sad, deserted look it got just before we all went our separate ways. For me it meant back to The Rut; for Bobby it meant Waco, Texas, of all places . . . he had spent the summer reading sociology and geology texts—how's that for a crazy salad?—and said he wanted to run a couple of experiments down there. He said it in a casual way, but I saw my mother looking at him with a peculiar, thoughtful scrutiny in the last couple of weeks we were all together. Neither Dad nor I suspected, but I think my mom knew that Bobby's compass needle had finally stopped swinging and started pointing.

"Why?" I asked. "I'm supposed to answer that?"

"Someone better. Pretty soon, too."

"Because that's the way people are built."

"That's bullshit. I don't believe it. Even that double-X-chromo-some stuff turned out to be bullshit in the end."

"Because of economic pressures."

"Also bullshit. The only people who really want to fight are relatively well-off. And the people they want to fight are also relatively well-off. Poor folks are too busy looking for something to eat."

"Original sin," I said.

"Well," he said, "maybe that's it. I won't say it isn't. But what's the *instrument?*"

"I'm not following you," I said.

"It's the water," Bobby said moodily.

"Say *what?*"

"The water. Something in the water."

He looked at me.

"Or something that *isn't.*"

The next day Bobby went off to Waco. I didn't see him again until he showed up at my apartment wearing the inside-out Mumford shirt and carrying the two glass boxes. That was three years later.

"Hi, Howie," he said, stepping in and giving me a swat on the back as if it had been three days instead of three years.

"Bobby!" I yelled, and threw both arms around him in a bear hug. Hard angles bit into my chest, and I heard an angry hive hum.

"I'm glad to see you, too," Bobby said, "but you better go easy. You're upsetting the natives."

I stepped back in a hurry. Bobby set down the big paper bag he was carrying and unslung his shoulder bag. Then he carefully brought the glass boxes out of the bag. There was a beehive in one, a wasps' nest in the other. The bees were already settling down and going back to whatever business bees have, but the wasps were clearly unhappy about the whole thing.

"Okay, Bobby," I said. I looked at him and grinned. I couldn't seem to stop grinning. "What are you up to this time?"

He unzipped the tote bag and brought out a mayonnaise jar that was half filled with a clear liquid.

"See this?" he said.

"Yeah. Looks like water."

"It is with two important differences: It came from an artesian well in La Plata, a little town forty miles east of Waco, and before I turned it into this concentrated form, there was five gallons of it. I've got a regular little distillery running down there, Howie." He was grinning, and now the grin broadened. "Water's all it is, but it's the goddamnedest popskull the human race has ever seen, just the same."

"I don't have the slightest idea what you're talking about."

"I know you don't. But you will. You know what, Howie?"

"What?"

"If the idiotic human race can just manage to hold itself together for another six months, it'll hold itself together for all time."

He held up the mayonnaise jar, and one magnified Bobby-eye stared at me through it with huge solemnity. "This is the big one," he said. "The cure for the worst disease to which *Homo sapiens* falls prey."

"Cancer?"

"Nope," Bobby said. "War. Where's your bathroom? My back teeth are floating."

When he came back he had not only turned the Mumford T-shirt right side out, he had combed his hair—nor had his method of doing this changed, I saw. Bobby just held his head under the faucet for a while, then raked his fingers through his long, coarsely blond shag. He looked at the two glass boxes and pronounced the bees and wasps back to normal. "Not that a wasps' nest ever approaches anything closely resembling 'normal,' Howie. Wasps are societal insects, like bees and ants. But unlike bees, which are almost sane, and ants, which have occasional schizoid lapses, wasps are lunatics." He smiled. "Like people." He took the top off the glass box containing the beehive.

"Tell you what, Bobby," I said. I was smiling, but the smile felt much too wide. "Put the top back on and just tell me about it—what do you say? Save the Mr. Wizard demonstration for later. I mean, my landlord's a real pussycat, but the super's this big bulldyke who smokes Odie Perode cigars and has thirty pounds on me. She—"

"You'll like this," Bobby said, as if I hadn't spoken at all—a habit as familiar to me as his Ten-Fingers Method of Hair Grooming. He was never impolite but often totally absorbed. And could I stop him? Aw shit, no. It was too good to have him back. I mean, I think I knew even then that something was going to go totally wrong, but when I was with Bobby for more than five minutes, he just hypnotized me. He was Lucy holding the football and promising me this time *for sure,* and I was Charlie Brown, rushing down the field to kick it. "In fact, you've probably seen it done before—they show pictures of it in magazines from time to time or in TV wildlife documentaries. It's nothing very special, but people have got a set of prejudices about bees."

And the weird thing was, he was right—I *had* seen it before.

He stuck his hand into the box between the hive and the glass. In less than fifteen seconds his hand had acquired a living, black and yellow glove.

It brought back an instant of total recall: sitting in front of the TV, wearing footy pajamas and clutching my Paddington bear, maybe half an hour before bedtime (and surely years before Bobby was born), watching with mingled horror, disgust, and fascination as some beekeeper allowed bees to cover his entire face. They had formed a sort of executioner's hood at first, and then he had brushed them into a grotesque, living beard.

Bobby winced suddenly, sharply, then grinned.

"One of 'em stung me," he said. "They're still a little upset from the trip. I hooked a ride with the local insurance lady from La Plata to Waco—she's got an old Piper Cub—and flew People's from there."

"I think you ought to get your hand out of there," I said. I kept waiting for some of them to fly out—I could imagine chasing them around with a rolled-up magazine for hours after he bopped out, bringing them down one by one, like escapees from some old prison movie. But none of them had . . . at least so far.

"Relax, Howie. You ever see a bee sting a flower? Or even hear of it?"

"You don't look like a flower."

He laughed. "Shit, you think bees know what a flower looks like? Uh-uh! No way, man! They don't know what a flower looks like any more than you or I know what a cloud sounds like. They know I'm sweet because I excrete sucrose dioxin in my sweat . . . along with at least thirty-seven other dioxins."

He paused thoughtfully. "Although I must confess I *was* careful to, uh, sweeten myself up a little tonight. Ate a box of chocolate-covered cherries on the plane—"

"Oh, Bobby, Jesus!"

"—and had a couple of MallowCremes in the taxi coming here."

He reached in with his other hand and carefully began to brush the bees off. I saw him wince once more just before he got the last of them off and eased my mind considerably by replacing the lid on the glass box. I saw a red swelling on each of his hands: one in the cup of the left palm, another high up on the right, near what the palmists call the Bracelets of Fortune. He'd been stung, but I saw well enough what he'd set out to show me: What looked like at least four hundred bees had investigated him. Only two had stung.

He took a pair of tweezers out of his jeans pocket and went over to my desk. He moved the pile of manuscripts and trained my Tensor lamp on the place where the pages had been—fiddling with it until it formed a tiny, hard spotlight on the wood.

"Writin' anything good, Bow-Wow?" he asked casually, and I felt the hair stir on the back of my neck. When was the last time he'd called me Bow-Wow? When he was four? Six? He was working carefully on his left hand with the tweezers. I saw him extract a tiny something that looked a little like a nostril hair and place it in my ashtray.

"Piece on art forgery for *Vanity Fair*. Bobby, what in hell are you up to this time?"

"You want to pull the other one for me?" he asked, offering me the tweezers, his right hand, and an apologetic smile. "I keep thinking if I'm so goddamn smart I ought to be ambidextrous, but my left hand has still got an I.Q. of about six."

Same old Bobby.

I sat down beside him, took the tweezers, and pulled the bee stinger out of the red swelling near what in his case should have been called the Bracelets of Doom; and while I did it he told me about the difference between bees and wasps, the difference between the water in La Plata and the water in New York, and how, goddamn! everything was going to be all right with his water and a little help from me.

And oh, shit, I ended up running at the football while my laughing, wildly intelligent brother held it one last time.

"Bees don't sting unless they have to, because it kills them," Bobby said matter-of-factly. "You remember that time in North Conway when you said we kept killing each other because of original sin?"

"Yes. Hold still."

"Well, if there *is* such a thing, if there's a God who could simultaneously love us enough to serve us His own Son on a cross and send us all on a rocket sled to hell just because one stupid bitch bit a bad apple, then the curse was just this: He made us like wasps instead of bees. *Shit,* Howie, what are you doing?"

"Hold still and I'll get it out. If you want to make a lot of big gestures, I'll wait."

"Okay," he said, and after that he held relatively still while I extracted the stinger. "Bees are nature's kamikaze pilots, Bow-Wow. Look in that glass box; you'll see the two who stung me lying dead at the bottom. Their stingers are barbed, like fishhooks. They slide in easy. When they pull out, they disembowel themselves."

"Gross," I said, dropping the second stinger in the ashtray.

"It makes them particular, though."

"I bet."

"Wasps, on the other hand, have smooth stingers. They can belt you all they like. They use up the poison by the third or fourth shot, but they can go right on making holes if they like . . . and usually they do. Especially wall wasps. The kind I've got over there. You gotta sedate 'em. Stuff called Noxon. It must give 'em a hell of a hangover because they wake up madder than ever." He looked at me somberly, and for the first time I saw the dark brown wheels of weariness under his eyes and realized my kid brother was tired, almost tired to death, maybe.

"*That's* why people go on fighting, Bow-Wow. On and on and on. We got smooth stingers. Now watch this."

He got up, went over to his tote bag, rummaged in it, and came up with an eyedropper. He opened the mayonnaise jar, put the dropper in, and drew up a tiny bubble of his distilled Texas water.

When he took it over to the glass box with the wasps' nest inside, I saw the top on this one was different—there was a tiny, plastic slide piece set into the top. With the wasps, he was taking no chances.

He squeezed the black bulb. Two drops of water fell onto the nest, making a momentary dark spot that disappeared almost at once. "Give it about three minutes," he said.

"What—"

"No questions," he said. "You'll see. Three minutes."

In that period he read my piece on art forgery . . . although it was already twenty pages long.

"Okay," he said, putting the pages down. "That's pretty good, man. You ought to read up on how Jay Gould furnished the parlor car of his private train with fake Manets—shit, that's a riot—but it's good. Watch."

Before I really knew what he was up to—I was musing on how much Gould might have paid for the fake Manets—he had removed the cover of the glass box containing the wasps' nest.

"Jesus, Bobby, quit it!" I yelled.

"Same old wimp," Bobby laughed and pulled the nest, which was dull gray and about the size of a bowling ball, out of the box. He held it in his hands. Wasps flew out and lit on his arms, his cheeks, his forehead. One landed on my forearm. I slapped it, and it fell dead to the carpet. I was scared—I mean, really scared.

"Don't kill 'em," Bobby said. "You might as well be machine-gunning babies. They're harmless, for Christ's sake. That's the *point.*" He tossed the nest from hand to hand like an overgrown softball. He lobbed it in the air. I watched, horrified, as wasps cruised the living room of my apartment like fighter planes.

Bobby lowered the nest carefully back into the box and sat down on my couch. He patted the place next to him, and I went over, nearly hypnotized. They were everywhere: on the rug, the ceiling, the drapes. Half a dozen of them were crawling across the screen of my Curtis-Mathis.

Before I could sit down, he brushed away a couple that were on the sofa cushion where my ass was aimed. They flew away quickly. They were all flying easily, crawling, moving fast. There was nothing drugged about their behavior. But as Bobby talked, they gradually found their way back to their spit-paper home, crawled over it, and eventually disappeared inside again through the hole in the top.

"I wasn't the first one to get interested in Waco," he said. "It just happens to be the biggest town in the funny little nonviolent section of what is, per capita, the most violent state in the Union. Texans *love* to shoot each other, Howie—I mean, it's like a state hobby. Half the male population goes around armed. Saturday night in the Fort Worth bars is like a shooting gallery where you get to plonk away at drunks instead of clay ducks. There are more NRA-card carriers than there are Methodists. Not that Texas is the only place where people shoot each other or carve each other up with straight razors or stick their kids in the oven if they cry too long, you understand, but they sure do like their firearms."

"Except in Waco," I said.

"Oh, they like 'em there, too," he said. "It's just that they use 'em on each other a hell of a lot less often."

Jesus. I just looked up at the clock and saw the time. It feels like about fifteen minutes, but it's been almost an hour already. That happens to me sometimes when I'm running at white-hot speed, but I can't allow myself to be seduced into these specifics. I feel as well as ever—no noticeable drying of the membranes in the throat, no groping for words, and as I glance back over what I've done, I see only the normal typos and strikeovers. But I can't kid myself. I've got to hurry up. "Fiddledeedee," said Scarlett, and all of that.

The nonviolent atmosphere of the Waco area had been noticed and investigated before, mostly by sociologists. Bobby said that when you fed enough statistical data on Waco and similar areas into a computer—population density, mean age, mean economic level, mean educational level, and dozens of other numbers—you got back a whopper of an anomaly. Scholarly papers are rarely jocular, but even so, several of the better than fifty Bobby read on the subject suggested ironically that maybe it was "something in the water."

"I decided that maybe it was time to take the joke seriously," Bobby said. "After all, there's something in the water of a lot of places that prevents tooth decay. It's called fluoride."

He went to Waco accompanied by a trio of research assistants—two of these were sociology grad students, the other a full professor of geology who was on sabbatical. Within six months Bobby and the sociology guys had constructed a computer program that Bobby called the world's only seismographic picture of a calmquake. He had a slightly rumpled printout in his tote. He gave it to me. I was looking at a series of forty concentric rings with a diameter of six miles each. Waco was in the eighth, ninth, and tenth rings.

"Now look at this," he said, and put a transparent overlay on the printout. More rings; but in each one there was a number. Fortieth ring: 471. Thirty-ninth: 420. Thirty-eighth: 418. And so on. In a couple of places the numbers went up instead of down, but only in a couple (and only by a little).

"What are they?"

"Each number represents the incidence of violent crime in that particular circle," Bobby said. "Murder, rape, assault and battery, even acts of vandalism. The computer assigns a number by a formula that takes the population density into account." He tapped the twenty-seventh circle, which held the number 204, with his finger. "There's less than nine hundred people in this whole area, for instance. The number indicates three or four cases of spouse abuse, a couple of barroom brawls, an act of animal cruelty—some senile farmer got pissed at a pig and hit him with a shovel—and one involuntary manslaughter."

At the center of Bobby's calmquake was the town of La Plata. To call it a sleepy little town seems more than fair. The numerical value assigned to La Plata was zero.

"So here it is," Bobby said, leaning forward and rubbing his long hands together nervously. "Here's this weird little sagebrush Garden of Eden. Here's a community of fifteen thousand, twenty-four percent of which are people of mixed blood commonly called Indios. There's a moccasin factory, a couple of little motor courts, a couple of scrub farms. That's it for work. For play there's four bars, a couple of dance halls where you can hear any kind of music you want as long as it sounds like George Jones, two drive-ins, and a bowling alley." He paused and added, "There's also a still. I didn't know anybody made whiskey that good outside of Tennessee."

In short (and it is now too late to be anything else), La Plata should have been a fertile breeding ground for the sort of casual

violence you can read about in the police-blotter section of the
local newspaper. Should have been, but wasn't. There had been
only one murder in La Plata during the five years previous to my
brother's arrival, two cases of assault, no rapes, no reported inci-
dents of child abuse. There had been a number of armed robberies,
but they had all been committed by transients . . . as the murder
and one of the assaults had been. The local sheriff was a fat old
Republican gent with a pretty fair Rodney Dangerfield imitation
and what Bobby believed to be the preliminary symptoms of Alzheimer's disease. His only deputy was his nephew. Bobby told me
that he bore an uncanny resemblance to Barney Fife on the old
Andy Griffith show.

"Put those two guys in a Pennsylvania town similar to La Plata in
every way but the geographical," Bobby said, "and they would have
been out on their asses fifteen years ago. But in La Plata they're gonna
go on until they die . . . which they'll probably do in their sleep."

"What did you do?" I asked.

"Well, for the first week or so after we got our statistical shit
together, we just sort of sat around and stared at each other," Bobby
said. "I mean, we were prepared for something, but nothing like this.
I mean, Waco doesn't prepare you for La Plata."

He tapped the readout and the overlay, and I saw what he meant.
The numbers in the last seven or eight circles dropped off radically:
83, 81, 70, 63, 40, 21, 5, 0.

"It was the classic Holmes situation of the dog that *didn't* bark."
Bobby shifted restlessly and cracked his knuckles.

"Jesus, I hate it when you do that," I said.

He smiled. "Sorry, Bow-Wow. Anyway, we started geological tests,
then microscopic analysis of the water. I didn't expect a hell of a lot;
everyone in the area has got a well, and they get their water tested
to make sure they're not drinking borax or something. If there had
been something readily apparent, it would have turned up a long
time ago. So we went on to submicroscopy, and that was when we
started to turn up some goddamn weird stuff."

"What kind of weird stuff?"

"Breaks in chains of atoms, subdynamic electrical fluctuations, and some sort of unidentified protein. Water ain't really H_2O, you know—not when you add in the sulfides, iron, God knows what else happens to be in the aquifer of a given region. But La Plata water— you'd have to give it a string of letters like the ones after a professor emeritus's name." His eyes gleamed. "But the protein was the most interesting thing, Bow-Wow. So far as we know, it's only found in one other place: the human brain."

Uh-oh. It just arrived, between one swallow and the next: the throat dryness. Not much as yet but enough for me to break away and get a glass of ice water. I've got maybe forty minutes left. And oh, Jesus, there's so much I want to tell! About the wasps' nests they found with wasps that wouldn't sting; about the fender bender Bobby and one of his assistants saw where the two drivers—both male, both drunk, and both about twenty-four (sociological bull moose, in other words)—got out, shook hands, and exchanged driver's licenses and insurance information amicably. Well . . . one of them had insurance information; the other had no insurance at all. And of course, the guy without the insurance had clearly been at fault and had sustained about five hundred dollars' less damage. But here's this other guy, clapping him on the back and saying they can work it out.

Bobby talked for hours—more hours than I have. But the upshot and the result were both the same: the stuff in the mayonnaise jar.

"We've got our own still in La Plata now," he said. "This is the stuff we're brewing, Howie, pacifist white lightning. The aquifer under that area of Texas is deep but amazingly large; it's like this incredible Lake Victoria driven into the porous sediment that overlays the Moho. The water is potent, but we've been able to make the stuff I squirted on the wasps even more potent. We've got damn near six thousand gallons now in these big steel tanks. By the end of the year we'll have fourteen thousand. By next June we'll have thirty thousand. But it's not enough. We need more, we need it faster . . . and then we need to transport it."

"Transport it where?" I asked him.

"Borneo, to start with."

I thought either I had lost my mind or misheard him. I really did.

"Look, Bow-Wow . . . sorry, Howie." He was scrumming through his tote bag again. He brought out a number of aerial photographs and handed them over to me. "You see? You see how fucking perfect it is? It's as if God suddenly busted through with something like 'And now we bring you a special bulletin! This is your last chance, assholes! And now we return you to *Wheel of Fortune.*' Or something like that."

"I don't get you," I said. "And I have no idea what I'm looking at." Of course I did; it was an island—not Borneo itself but an island lying to the west of Borneo identified as Gulandio—with a mountain in the middle and a lot of muddy little villages lying on its lower slopes. What I meant was that I didn't know what I was looking *for.*

"The mountain has the same name as the island," he said. "Gulandio. In the local patois it means *grace,* or *fate,* or *destiny,* or take your pick. But Duke Rogers says it's really the biggest time bomb on Earth . . . and it's wired to go off by October of next year. Probably earlier."

The crazy thing's this: The story's only crazy if you try to tell it in a speed rap, which is what I'm trying to do now. Bobby wanted me to help him raise somewhere between six hundred thousand and a million and a half dollars to do the following: first, to synthesize fifty to seventy thousand gallons of what he called the high-test; second, to airlift all of this water to Borneo, which had landing facilities (you could land a hang glider on Gulandio, but that was about all); third, to ship it over to Gulandio; fourth, to truck it up the slope of the volcano, which had been dormant (save for a few puffs in 1938) since 1804, and then to drop it down the muddy tube of the volcano's caldera. Duke Rogers was actually John Paul Rogers, the geology professor. He claimed that Gulandio was going to do more than just erupt; he claimed that it was going to explode, as Krakatoa had done in the nineteenth century, creating a bang that would make the Hiroshima bomb look like a stick of dynamite and the squirt bomb that depopulated three quarters of London like a kid's firecracker. The debris from the Krakatoa blowup, Bobby told me, had literally encircled the globe; the observed results had formed an important part of the Sagan group's nuclear-winter theory. For three months afterward sunsets and sunrises half a world away had been grotesquely colorful as a result of the ash whirling around in both the jet stream and the Van Allen currents, which lie forty miles below the Van Allen belt. There had been global changes in climate that lasted five years, and nipa palms, which previously had only grown in eastern Africa and Micronesia, suddenly showed up in both South and North America.

"The North American nipas all died before the turn of the century," Bobby said, "but they're alive and well below the equator. Krakatoa seeded them there, Howie . . . the way I want to seed La Plata water all over the earth. I want people to go out in La Plata water when it rains—and it's going to rain a lot after Gulandio goes bang. I want them to drink the La Plata water that falls in their reservoirs. I want them to wash their hair in it, bathe in it, soak their contact lenses in it. I want whores to *douche* in it."

"Bobby," I said, knowing he was not, "you're crazy."

He gave me a crooked, tired grin. It wasn't until then that I saw how tired my brother was, how badly he needed a place to sleep, to vacation from himself a while.

"I ain't crazy," he said. "You want to see crazy? Turn on CNN, B— . . . Howie. You'll see crazy, in living color."

But I didn't need to turn on Cable News to know what Bobby was talking about. The Indians and the Pakistanis were poised on the brink. The Russians and the Chinese, ditto. Half of Africa was starving; the other half was on fire. There had been border skirmishes along the entire Tex-Mex border in the last five years, since Mexico went Communist, and people had started calling the Tijuana crossing point in California Little Berlin because of the wall. The saber rattling had become a din. On the last day of the old year the Scientists for Nuclear Responsibility had set their black clock to fifteen seconds before midnight.

"Bobby, let's suppose it could be done and everything went according to schedule. You don't have the slightest idea what the long-term effects might be."

He started to say something, and I waved it away.

"Don't even suggest that you do, because you don't! You've had time to find this calmquake of yours and isolate the cause, I'll give you that. But do you remember thalidomide? Or that nifty little acne stopper that caused cancer and heart attacks in thirty-year-olds? Or the AIDS vaccine in 1994?

"Bobby?"

"It stopped the disease, but it turned all the test subjects into epileptics."

"Bobby?"

"Then there was—"

"Bobby?"

I stopped and looked at him.

"The world," Bobby said, and then stopped. His throat worked. I saw he was struggling with tears. "The world needs heroic measures, man. I don't know about long-term effects, and there's no time to study them because there's no long-term prospect. Maybe we can cure the whole mess. Or maybe—"

He shrugged, tried to smile, and looked at me with shining eyes from which two single tears slowly tracked.

"Or maybe we're giving heroin to a patient with terminal cancer. Either way, it's an end to the whole mess." He spread out his hands, palms up, so I could see the stings. "Help me, Bow-Wow. Please help me."

So I helped him. So we fucked up.

I don't give a shit.

We killed all the plants, but at least we saved the greenhouse. Something will grow there again someday. I hope.

Are you reading this?

My gears are starting to get a little sticky. For the first time in years I'm having to think about what I'm doing. Should have hurried more at the start.

Well, of course we did it: distilled the water, flew it in, transported it to Gulandio, built a cog railway up the side of the volcano, and dropped over twelve thousand five-gallon containers of La Plata water—the brain-buster version—into the murky, misty depths of the volcano's caldera. We did all of this in just eight months. It didn't cost six hundred thousand dollars or a million and a half; it cost over four million, still less than a quarter of one percent of what America spent on defense that year. You want to know how we razed it? I'd tell you if I had more thyme, but my head's falling apart so never mine. I raised most of it myself if it matters to you. Some by hoof and some by croof. Tell you the truth, I didn't know I could do it muself until I did. But we did it, and somehow the world held together and that volcano—whatever its name wuz, I can't remember and there izzunt time to go back over the manuscript—it blue just when it was spo Wait

Okay. A little better. Dilantin. Bobby had it. Heart's beating like crazy but I can think again. The volcano—Gulandio, by God—blue just when Dook Rogers said it would. Everything when skihi and for a while everyone's attention turned away from whatever and toward the skies. And bim-deedle-eee, said Scarlett!

It happened pretty fast like sex and checks and special effex and everybody got healthy again. I mean wait

Jesus please let me finish this.

I mean that everybody stood down. Everybody started to get a little purs perspective on the situation. The wurld started to get like the wasps in Bobbys nest the one he showed me where they didn't stink too much. There was three yerz like an Indian sumer. People getting together like in that old Youngbloods song that went cmon everybody get together rite now, as in Shop-Rite where mom took me when I wuz in the babby seat and wt

More Dilantin. Big blast. Feel like my heart is coming out thru my ears. But if I concentrate every bit of my force, my—

It was like an Indian summer. Three years. Bobby went on with his resurch. La Plata. Sociological background, etc. You remember the local sheriff? Fat old Republican with a good Henny Youngblood imi-tashun? How Bobby said he had the preliminary simptoms of Rodney's disease?

concentrate asshole

Wasn't just him; turned out like there was a lot of that going around in that part of Texas. All's Hallows disease is what I meen. For three yerz me and Bobby were down there. Created a new program. New graff of cirkles. I saw what was happen and came back here. Bobby and his to asistants stayed on. One shot hiself Boby said when he showed up here.

Wait one more blast

All right. Last time. Heart beating so fast I can hardly breeve. The new grafp, the *last* graph, really only whammed you when it was laid over the calmquake graft. The calmquake grafp showed acts of vilence going down as you approached La Place in the muddle; the Alzheimer's graft graph ghowed incidence of premature seenullity going *up* as you approached La Place. Peeple there were geting very silly very young but bubby wasn't there long enough to see it or even how dogs got silly very yung altho he remebered something later if I had time to tell you. We didn't take any water but botled three years and wor big long sleekers in the ran. so no war and when every-bobby started to get seely we din and I came back here because he my brother I cant remember what his name Bobby

Bobby made me sick what he had dun only when he come here tongit crying I sed Bobby I lov you Bobby sed I'm sorry Bowwow Ime sorry I died it the world the hole world ful of foals and dumbbels and I sed better fouls and bells than a big black sinder in spaz and he cryed and I cryed Bobby I lov you and he sed will you give me some wadder and I sed yez and he said wil yu ride it down and I sed yez an I think I did but its if I cant remember I see wurds but dnt no what they meen bt I uzed to no

I have a Bobby his nayme is bruther and I theen I am dun riding and I have a bocks to put this into thats Bobby sd full of quiyet air to last a milyun yrz so gudb'o Im goin to stob gadbo bobby i love you it wuz nt yor falt i love you forgiv yu

love yu

sined (for the wurld),

                              Bow Wow Fornoy ∞

Tight Little Stitches in a Dead Man's Back

Joe R. Lansdale

For Ardath Mayhar

From the journal of Paul Marder
(Boom!)

THAT'S a little scientist joke, and the proper way to begin this. As for the purpose of this notebook, I'm uncertain. Perhaps to organize my thoughts and not go insane.

No. Probably so I can read it and feel as if I'm being spoken to. Maybe neither of those reasons. It doesn't matter. I just want to do it, and that is enough.

What's new?

Well, Mr. Journal, after all these years I've taken up martial arts again—or at least the forms and calisthenics of Tae Kwon Do. There is no one to spar with here in the lighthouse, so the forms have to do.

There is Mary, of course, but she keeps all her sparring verbal. And as of late, there is not even that. I long for her to call me a sonofabitch. Anything. Her hatred of me has cured to 100% perfection and she no longer finds it necessary to speak. The tight lines around her eyes and mouth, the emotional heat that radiates from her body like a dreadful cold sore looking for a place to lie down, is voice enough for her. She lives only for the moment when she (the cold sore) can attach herself to me with her needles, ink and thread. She lives only for the design on my back.

135

That's all I live for as well. Mary adds to it nightly and I enjoy the pain. The tattoo is of a great, blue mushroom cloud, and in the cloud, etched ghost-like, is the face of our daughter, Rae. Her lips are drawn tight, eyes are closed and there are stitches deeply pulled to simulate the lashes. When I move fast and hard they rip slightly and Rae cries bloody tears.

That's one reason for the martial arts. The hard practice of them helps me to tear the stitches so my daughter can cry. Tears are the only thing I can give her.

Each night I bare my back eagerly to Mary and her needles. She pokes deep and I moan in pain as she moans in ecstasy and hatred. She adds more color to the design, works with brutal precision to bring Rae's face out in sharper relief. After ten minutes she tires and will work no more. She puts the tools away and I go to the full-length mirror on the wall. The lantern on the shelf flickers like a jack-o-lantern in a high wind, but there is enough light for me to look over my shoulder and examine the tattoo. And it is beautiful. Better each night as Rae's face becomes more and more defined.

Rae.

Rae. God, can you forgive me, sweetheart?

But the pain of the needles, wonderful and cleansing as they are, is not enough. So I go sliding, kicking and punching along the walkway around the lighthouse, feeling Rae's red tears running down my spine, gathering in the waistband of my much-stained canvas pants.

Winded, unable to punch and kick any more, I walk over to the railing and call down into the dark, "Hungry?"

In response to my voice a chorus of moans rises up to greet me.

Later, I lie on my pallet, hands behind my head, examine the ceiling and try to think of something worthy to write to you, Mr. Journal. So seldom is there anything. Nothing seems truly worthwhile.

Bored of this, I roll on my side and look at the great light that once shone out to the ships, but is now forever snuffed. Then I turn the other direction and look at my wife sleeping on her bunk, her naked ass turned toward me. I try to remember what it was like to make love to her, but it is difficult. I only remember that I miss it. For a long moment I stare at my wife's ass as if it is a mean mouth about to open and reveal teeth. Then I roll on my back again, stare at the ceiling, and continue this routine until daybreak.

Mornings I greet the flowers, their bright red and yellow blooms bursting from the heads of long-dead bodies that will not rot. The flowers open wide to reveal their little black brains and their feathery feelers, and they lift their blooms upward and moan. I get a wild pleasure out of this. For one crazed moment I feel like a rock singer appearing before his starry-eyed audience.

When I tire of the game I get the binoculars, Mr. Journal, and examine the eastern plains with them, as if I expect a city to materialize there. The most interesting thing I have seen on those plains is a herd of large lizards thundering north. For a moment, I considered calling Mary to see them, but I didn't. The sound of my voice, the sight of my face, upsets her. She loves only the tattoo and is interested in nothing more.

When I finish looking at the plains, I walk to the other side. To the west, where the ocean was, there is now nothing but miles and miles of cracked, black sea bottom. Its only resemblances to a great body of water are the occasional dust storms that blow out of the west like dark tidal waves and wash the windows black at mid-day. And the creatures. Mostly mutated whales. Monstrously large, sluggish things. Abundant now where once they were near extinction. (Perhaps the whales should form some sort of GREENPEACE organization for humans now. What do you think, Mr. Journal? No need to answer. Just another one of those little scientist jokes.)

These whales crawl across the sea bottom near the lighthouse from time to time, and if the mood strikes them, they rise on their tails and push their heads near the tower and examine it. I keep expecting one to flop down on us, crushing us like bugs. But no such luck. For some unknown reason the whales never leave the cracked sea bed to venture onto what we formerly called the shore. It's as if they live in invisible water and are bound by it. A racial memory perhaps. Or maybe there's something in that cracked black soil they need. I don't know.

Besides the whales I suppose I should mention I saw a shark once. It was slithering along at a great distance and the tip of its fin was winking in the sunlight. I've also seen some strange, legged fish and some things I could not put a name to. I'll just call them whale food since I saw one of the whales dragging his bottom jaw along the ground one day, scooping up the creatures as they tried to beat a hasty retreat.

Exciting, huh? Well, that's how I spend my day, Mr. Journal. Roaming about the tower with my glasses, coming in to write in you, waiting anxiously for Mary to take hold of that kit and give me the signal. The mere thought of it excites me to erection. I suppose you could call that our sex act together.

And what was I doing the day they dropped The Big One?

Glad you asked that Mr. Journal, really I am.

I was doing the usual. Up at six, did the shit, shower and shave routine. Had breakfast. Got dressed. Tied my tie. I remember doing the latter, and not very well, in front of the bedroom mirror, and noticing that I had shaved poorly. A hunk of dark beard decorated my chin like a bruise.

Rushing to the bathroom to remedy that, I opened the door as Rae, naked as the day of her birth, was stepping from the tub.

Surprised, she turned to look at me. An arm went over her breasts, and a hand, like a dove settling into a fiery bush, covered her pubic area.

Embarrassed, I closed the door with an "excuse me" and went about my business—unshaved. It was an innocent thing. An accident. Nothing sexual. But when I think of her now, more often than not, that is the first image that comes to mind. I guess it was the moment I realized my baby had grown into a beautiful woman.

That was also the day she went off to her first day of college and got to see, ever so briefly, the end of the world.

And it was the day the triangle—Mary, Rae and myself—shattered.

If my first memory of Rae alone is that day, naked in the bathroom, my foremost memory of us as a family is when Rae was six. We used to go to the park and she would ride the merry-go-round, swing, teeter-totter, and finally my back. ("I want to piggy Daddy.")

We would gallop about until my legs were rubber, then we would stop at the bench where Mary sat waiting. I would turn my back to the bench so Mary could take Rae down, but always before she did, she would reach around from behind, caressing Rae, pushing her tight against my back, and Mary's hands would touch my chest.

God, but if I could describe those hands. She still has hands like that, after all these years. They are long and sleek and artistic. Naturally soft, like the belly of a baby rabbit. And when she held Rae and me that way, I felt that no matter what happened in the world, we three could stand against it and conquer.

But now the triangle is broken and the geometry gone away.

So the day Rae went off to college and was fucked into oblivion by the dark, pelvic thrust of the bomb, Mary drove me to work. Me, Paul Marder, big shot with The Crew. One of the finest, brightest young minds in the industry. Always teaching, inventing and improving on our nuclear threat, because, as we often joked, "We cared enough to send only the very best."

When we arrived at the guard booth, I had out my pass, but there was no one to take it. Beyond the chain-link gate there was a wild mêlée of people running, screaming, falling down.

I got out of the car and ran to the gate. I called out to a man I knew as he ran by. When he turned his eyes were wild and his lips were flecked with foam. "The missiles are flying," he said, then he was gone, running madly.

I jumped in the car, pushed Mary aside and stomped on the gas. The Buick leaped into the fence, knocking it asunder. The car spun, slammed into the edge of a building and went dead. I grabbed Mary's hand, pulled her from the car and we ran toward the great elevators. We made one just in time. There were others running for it as the door closed, and the elevator went down. I still remember the echo of their fists on the metal as it began to drop. It was like the rapid heartbeat of something dying.

And so the elevator took us to the world of Down Under and we locked it off. There we were in a five-mile layered city designed not only as a massive office and laboratory, but as a impenetrable shelter.

It was our special reward for creating the poisons of war. There was food, shelter, medical supplies, films, books, you name it. Enough to last two thousand people for a hundred years. Of the two thousand it was designed for, perhaps eleven hundred made it. The others didn't run fast enough from the parking lot or the other buildings, or they were late for work, or maybe they had called in sick.

Perhaps they were the lucky ones. They might have died in their sleep. Or while they were having a morning quickie with the spouse. Or perhaps as they lingered over that last cup of coffee.

Because you see, Mr. Journal, Down Under was no paradise. Before long suicides were epidemic. I considered it myself from time to time. People slashed their throats, drank acid, took pills. It was not unusual to come out of your cubicle in the morning and find people dangling from pipes and rafters like ripe fruit.

There were also the murders. Most of them performed by a crazed group who lived in the deeper recesses of the unit and called themselves the Shit Faces. From time to time they smeared dung on themselves and ran amok, clubbing men, women, and children born Down Under, to death. It was rumored they ate human flesh.

We had a police force of sorts, but it didn't do much. It didn't have a sense of authority. Worse, we all viewed ourselves as deserving victims. Except for Mary, we had all helped to blow up the world.

Mary came to hate me. She came to the conclusion I had killed Rae. It was a realization that grew in her like a drip growing and growing until it became a gushing flood of hate. She seldom talked to me. She tacked up a picture of Rae and looked at it most of the time.

Topside she had been an artist, and she took that up again. She rigged a kit of tools and inks and became a tattooist. Everyone came to her for a mark. And though each was different, they all seemed to indicate one thing: I fucked up. I blew up the world. Brand me.

Day in and day out she did her tattoos, having less and less to do with me, pushing herself more and more into this work until she was as skilled with skin and needles as she had been Topside with brush and canvas. And one night, as we lay on our separate pallets, feigning sleep, she said to me, "I just want you to know how much I hate you."

"I know," I said.

"You killed Rae."

"I know."

"Say you killed her, you bastard. Say it."

"I killed her," I said, and meant it.

Next day I asked for my tattoo. I told her of this dream that came to me nightly. There would be darkness, and out of this darkness would come a swirl of glowing clouds, and the clouds would meld into a mushroom shape, and out of that—torpedo-shaped, nose pointing skyward, striding on ridiculous cartoon legs—would step The Bomb.

There was a face painted on The Bomb, and it was my face. And suddenly the dream's point of view would change, and I would be looking out of the eyes of that painted face. Before me was my daughter. Naked. Lying on the ground. Her legs wide apart. Her sex glazed like a wet canyon.

And I/The Bomb, would dive into her, pulling those silly feet after me, and she would scream. I could hear it echo as I plunged through her belly, finally driving myself out of the top of her head, then blowing to terminal orgasm. And the dream would end where it began. A mushroom cloud. Darkness.

When I told Mary the dream and asked her to interpret it in her art, she said, "Bare your back," and that's how the design began. An inch of work at a time—a painful inch. She made sure of that.

Never once did I complain. She'd send the needles home as hard and deep as she could, and though I might moan or cry out, I never asked her to stop. I could feel those fine hands touching my back and I loved it. The needles. The hands. The needles. The hands.

And if that was so much fun, you ask, why did I come Topside?

You ask such probing questions, Mr. Journal. Really you do, and I'm glad you asked that. My telling you will be like a laxative, I hope. Maybe if I just let the shit flow I'll wake up tomorrow and feel a lot better about myself.

Sure. And it will be the dawning of a new Pepsi generation as well. It will have all been a bad dream. The alarm clock will ring, I'll get up, have my bowl of Rice Krispies and tie my tie.

Okay, Mr. Journal. The answer. Twenty years or so after we went Down Under, a fistful of us decided it couldn't be any worse Topside than it was below. We made plans to go see. Simple as that. Mary and I even talked a little. We both entertained the crazed belief Rae might have survived. She would be thirty-eight. We might have been hiding below like vermin for no reason. It could be a brave new world up there.

I remember thinking these things, Mr. Journal, and half-believing them.

We outfitted two sixty-foot crafts that were used as part of our transportation system Down Under, plugged in the half-remembered codes that opened the elevators, and drove the vehicles inside. The elevator lasers cut through the debris above them and before long we were Topside. The doors opened to sunlight muted by grey-green clouds and a desert-like landscape. Immediately I knew there was no brave new world over the horizon. It had all gone to hell in a fiery handbasket, and all that was left of man's millions of years of development were a few pathetic humans living Down Under like worms, and a few others crawling Topside like the same.

We cruised about a week and finally came to what had once been the Pacific Ocean. Only there wasn't any water now, just that cracked blackness.

We drove along the shore for another week and finally saw life. A whale. Jacobs immediately got the idea to shoot one and taste its meat.

Using a high-powered rifle he killed it, and he and seven others cut slabs off it, brought the meat back to cook. They invited all of us to eat, but the meat looked greenish and there wasn't much blood and we warned him against it. But Jacobs and the others ate it anyway. As Jacobs said, "It's something to do."

A little later on Jacobs threw up blood and his intestines boiled out of his mouth, and not long after those who had shared the meat had the same thing happen to them. They died crawling on their bellies like gutted dogs. There wasn't a thing we could do for them. We couldn't even bury them. The ground was too hard. We stacked them like cordwood along the shoreline and moved camp down a way, tried to remember how remorse felt.

And that night, while we slept as best we could, the roses came.

Now, let me admit, Mr. Journal, I do not actually know how the roses survive, but I have an idea. And since you've agreed to hear my story—and even if you haven't, you're going to anyway—I'm going to put logic and fantasy together and hope to arrive at the truth.

These roses lived in the ocean bed, underground, and at night they came out. Up until then they had survived as parasites of reptiles and animals, but a new food had arrived from Down Under. Humans. Their creators actually. Looking at it that way, you might say we were the gods who conceived them, and their partaking of our flesh and blood was but a new version of wine and wafer.

I can imagine the pulsating brains pushing up through the sea bottom on thick stalks, extending feathery feelers, and tasting the air out there beneath the light of the moon—which through those odd clouds gave the impression of a pus-filled boil—and I can imagine them uprooting and dragging their vines across the ground toward the shore where the corpses lay.

Thick vines sprouted little, thorny vines, and these moved up the bank and touched the corpses. Then, with a lashing motion, the thorns tore into the flesh, and the vines, like snakes, slithered through the wounds and inside. Secreting a dissolving fluid that turned the innards to the consistency of watery oatmeal, they slurped up the mess, and the vines grew and grew at amazing speed, moved and coiled through the bodies, replacing nerves and shaping into the symmetry of the muscles they had devoured, and lastly they pushed up through the necks, into the skulls, ate tongues and eyeballs and sucked up the mouse-grey brains like soggy gruel. With an explosion of skull shrapnel, the roses bloomed, their tooth-hard petals expanding into beautiful red and yellow flowers, hunks of human heads dangling from them like shattered watermelon rinds.

In the center of these blooms a fresh, black brain pulsed and feathery feelers once again tasted air for food and breeding grounds. Energy waves from the floral brains shot through the miles and miles of vines that were knotted inside the bodies, and as they had replaced nerves, muscles and vital organs, they made the bodies stand. Then those corpses turned their flowered heads toward the tents where we slept, and the blooming corpses (another little scientist joke there if you're into English idiom, Mr. Journal) walked, eager to add the rest of us to their animated bouquet.

I saw my first rose-head while I was taking a leak.

I had left the tent and gone down to the shore line to relieve myself, when I caught sight of it out of the corner of my eye. Because of the bloom I first thought it was Susan Myers. She wore a thick, wooly Afro that surrounded her head like a lion's mane, and the shape of the thing struck me as her silhouette. But when I zipped and turned, it wasn't an Afro. It was a flower blooming out of Jacobs. I recognized him by his clothes and the hunk of his face that hung off one of the petals like a worn-out hat on a peg.

In the center of the blood-red flower was a pulsating sack, and all around it little wormy things squirmed. Directly below the brain was a thin proboscis. It extended toward me like an erect penis. At its tips, just inside the opening, were a number of large thorns.

A sound like a moan came out of that proboscis, and I stumbled back. Jacob's body quivered briefly, as if he had been besieged by a sudden chill, and ripping through his flesh and clothes, from neck to foot, was a mass of thorny, wagging vines that shot out to five feet in length.

With an almost invisible motion, they waved from west to east, slashed my clothes, tore my hide, knocked my feet out from beneath me. It was like being hit by a cat-o-nine-tails.

Dazed, I rolled onto my hands and knees, bear-walked away from it. The vines whipped against my back and butt, cut deep.

Every time I got to my feet, they tripped me. The thorns not only cut, they burned like hot ice picks. I finally twisted away from a net of vines, slammed through one last shoot, and made a break for it.

Without realizing it, I was running back to the tent. My body felt as if I had been lying on a bed of nails and razor blades. My forearm hurt something terrible where I had used it to lash the thorns away from me. I glanced down at it as I ran. It was covered in blood. A strand of vine about two feet in length was coiled around it like a garter snake. A thorn had torn a deep wound in my arm, and the vine was sliding into the wound.

Screaming, I held my forearm in front of me like I had just discovered it. The flesh, where the vine had entered, rippled and made a bulge that looked like a junkie's favorite vein. The pain was nauseating. I snatched at the vine, ripped it free. The thorns turned against me like fishhooks.

The pain was so much I fell to my knees, but I had the vine out of me. It squirmed in my hand, and I felt a thorn gouge my palm. I threw the vine into the dark. Then I was up and running for the tent again.

The roses must have been at work for quite some time before I saw Jacobs, because when I broke back into camp yelling, I saw Susan, Ralph, Casey and some others, and already their heads were blooming, skulls cracking away like broken model kits.

Jane Calloway was facing a rose-possessed corpse, and the dead body had its hands on her shoulders, and the vines were jetting out of the corpse, weaving around her like a web, tearing, sliding inside her, breaking off. The proboscis poked into her mouth and extended down her throat, forced her head back. The scream she started came out a gurgle.

I tried to help her, but when I got close, the vines whipped at me and I had to jump back. I looked for something to grab, to hit the damn thing with, but there was nothing. When next I looked at Jane, vines were stabbing out of her eyes, and her tongue, now nothing more than lava-thick blood, was dripping out of her mouth onto her breasts, which like the rest of her body, were riddled with stabbing vines.

I ran away then. There was nothing I could do for Jane. I saw others embraced by corpse hands and tangles of vines, but now my only thought was Mary. Our tent was to the rear of the campsite, and I ran there as fast as I could.

She was lumbering out of our tent when I arrived. The sound of screams had awakened her. When she saw me running she froze. By the time I got to her, two vine-riddled corpses were coming up on the tent from the left side. Grabbing her hand I half pulled, half dragged her away from there. I got to one of the vehicles and pushed her inside.

I locked the doors just as Jacobs, Susan, Jane, and others appeared at the windshield, leaning over the rocket-nosed hood, the feelers around their brain sacs vibrating like streamers in a high wind. Hands slid greasily down the windshield. Vines flopped and scratched and cracked against it like thin bicycle chains.

I got the vehicle started, stomped the accelerator, and the rose-heads went flying. One of them, Jacobs, bounced over the hood and splattered into a spray of flesh, ichor, and petals.

I had never driven the vehicle, so my maneuvering was rusty. But it didn't matter. There wasn't exactly a traffic rush to worry about.

After an hour or so, I turned to look at Mary. She was staring at me, her eyes like the twin holes of a double-barreled shotgun. They seemed to say, "More of your doing," and in a way she was right. I drove on.

Daybreak we came to the lighthouse. I don't know how it survived. One of those quirks. Even the glass was unbroken. It looked like a great stone finger shooting us the bird.

The vehicle's tank was near empty, so I assumed here was as good a place to stop as any. At least there was shelter, something we could fortify. Going on until the vehicle was empty of fuel didn't make much sense. There wouldn't be any more fill-ups, and there might not be any more shelter like this.

Mary and I (in our usual silence) unloaded the supplies from the vehicle and put them in the lighthouse. There was enough food, water, chemicals for the chemical toilet, odds and ends, extra clothes, to last us a year. There were also some guns. A Colt .45 revolver, two twelve-gauge shotguns and a .38, and enough shells to fight a small war.

When everything was unloaded, I found some old furniture downstairs, and using tools from the vehicle, tried to barricade the bottom door and the one at the top of the stairs. When I finished, I thought of a line from a story I had once read, a line that always disturbed me. It went something like, "Now we're shut in for the night."

Days. Nights. All the same. Shut in with one another, our memories and the fine tattoo.

A few days later I spotted the roses. It was as if they had smelled us out. And maybe they had. From a distance, through the binoculars, they reminded me of old women in bright sun hats.

It took them the rest of the day to reach the lighthouse, and they immediately surrounded it, and when I appeared at the railing they would lift their heads and moan.

And that, Mr. Journal, brings us up to now.

I thought I had written myself out, Mr. Journal. Told the only part of my life story I would ever tell, but now I'm back. You can't keep a good world destroyer down.

I saw my daughter last night and she's been dead for years. But I saw her, I did, naked, smiling at me, calling to ride piggyback.

Here's what happened.

It was cold last night. Must be getting along winter. I had rolled off my pallet onto the cold floor. Maybe that's what brought me awake. The cold. Or maybe it was just gut instinct.

It had been a particularly wonderful night with the tattoo. The face had been made so clear it seemed to stand out from my back. It had finally become more defined than the mushroom cloud. The needles went in hard and deep, but I've had them in me so much now I barely feel the pain. After looking in the mirror at the beauty of the design, I went to bed happy, or as happy as I can get.

During the night the eyes ripped open. The stitches came out and I didn't know it until I tried to rise from the cold, stone floor and my back puckered against it where the blood had dried.

I pulled myself free and got up. It was dark, but we had a good moonspill that night and I went to the mirror to look. It was bright enough that I could see Rae's reflection clearly, the color of her face, the color of the cloud. The stitches had fallen away and now the wounds were spread wide, and inside the wounds were eyes. Oh, God, Rae's blue eyes. Her mouth smiled at me and her teeth were very white.

Oh, I hear you, Mr. Journal. I hear what you're saying. And I thought of that. My first impression was that I was about six bricks shy of a load, gone 'round the old bend. But I know better now. You see, I lit a candle and held it over my shoulder, and with the candle and the moonlight, I could see even more clearly. It was Rae all right, not just a tattoo.

I looked over at my wife on the bunk, her back to me, as always. She had not moved.

I turned back to the reflection. I could hardly see the outline of myself, just Rae's face smiling out of that cloud.

"Rae," I whispered, "is that you?"

"Come on, Daddy," said the mouth in the mirror, "that's a stupid question. Of course, it's me."

"But . . . You're . . . you're . . ."

"Dead?"

"Yes . . . Did . . . did it hurt much?"

She cackled so loudly the mirror shook. I could feel the hairs on my neck rising. I thought for sure Mary would wake up, but she slept on.

"It was instantaneous, Daddy, and even then, it was the greatest pain imaginable. Let me show you how it hurt."

The candle blew out and I dropped it. I didn't need it anyway. The mirror grew bright and Rae's smile went from ear to ear—literally—and the flesh on her bones seemed like crêpe paper before a powerful fan, and that fan blew the hair off her head, the skin off her skull and melted those beautiful blue eyes and those shiny white teeth of hers to a putrescent goo the color and consistency of fresh bird shit. Then there was only the skull, and it heaved in half and flew backwards into the dark world of the mirror and there was no reflection now, only the hurtling fragments of a life that once was and was now nothing more than swirling cosmic dust.

I closed my eyes and looked away.

"Daddy?"

I opened them, looked over my shoulder into the mirror. There was Rae again, smiling out of my back.

"Darling," I said, "I'm so sorry."

"So are we," she said, and there were faces floating past her in the mirror. Teenagers, children, men and women, babies, little embryos swirling around her head like planets around the sun. I closed my eyes again, but I could not keep them closed. When I opened them the multitudes of swirling dead, and those who had never had a chance to live, were gone. Only Rae was there.

"Come close to the mirror, Daddy."

I backed up to it. I backed until the hot wounds that were Rae's eyes touched the cold glass and the wounds became hotter and hotter and Rae called out, "Ride me piggy, Daddy," and then I felt her weight on my back, not the weight of a six-year-old child or a teenage girl, but a great weight, like the world was on my shoulders and bearing down.

Leaping away from the mirror I went hopping and whooping about the room, same as I used to in the park. Around and around I went, and as I did, I glanced in the mirror. Astride me was Rae, lithe and naked, red hair fanning around her as I spun. And when I whirled by the mirror again, I saw that she was six years old. Another spin and there was a skeleton with red hair, one hand held high, the jaws open and yelling, "Ride 'em cowboy."

"How?" I managed, still bucking and leaping, giving Rae the ride of her life. She bent to my ear and I could feel her warm breath. "You want to know how I'm here, Daddy-dear? I'm here because you created me. Once you laid between Mother's legs and thrust me into existence, the two of you, with all the love there was in you. This time you thrust me into existence with your guilt and Mother's hate. Her thrusting needles, your arching back. And now I've come back for one last ride, Daddy-o. Ride, you bastard, ride."

All that while I had been spinning, and now as I glimpsed the mirror, I saw wall to wall faces, weaving in, weaving out, like smiling stars, and all those smiles opened wide and words came out in chorus, "Where were you when they dropped The Big One?"

Each time I spun and saw the mirror again, it was a new scene. Great flaming winds scorching across the world, babies turning to fleshy jello, heaps of charred bones, brains boiling out of the heads of men and women like backed up toilets overflowing, The Almighty, Glory Hallelujah, Ours Is Bigger Than Yours Bomb hurtling forward, the mirror going mushroom white, then clear, and me, spinning, Rae pressed tight against my back, melting like butter on a griddle, evaporating into the eye wounds on my back, and finally me alone, collapsing to the floor beneath the weight of the world.

Mary never awoke.

The vines outsmarted me.

A single strand found a crack downstairs somewhere and wound up the steps and slipped beneath the door that led into the tower. Mary's bunk was not far from the door, and in the night, while I slept and later while I spun in front of the mirror and lay on the floor before it, it made its way to Mary's bunk, up between her legs, and entered her sex effortlessly.

I suppose I should give the vine credit for doing what I had not been able to do in years, Mr. Journal, and that's enter Mary. Oh God, that's a funny one, Mr. Journal. Real funny. Another little scientist joke. Let's make that a mad scientist joke, what say? Who but a madman would play with the lives of human beings by constantly trying to build the bigger and better boom machine?

So what of Rae, you ask?

I'll tell you. She is inside me. My back feels the weight. She twists in my guts like a corkscrew. I went to the mirror a moment ago, and the tattoo no longer looks like it did. The eyes have turned to crusty sores and the entire face looks like a scab. It's as if the bile that made up my soul, the unthinking, nearsightedness, the guilt that I am, has festered from inside and spoiled the picture with pustule bumps, knots and scabs.

To put it in layman's terms, Mr. Journal, my back is infected. Infected with what I am. A blind, senseless fool.

The wife?

Ah, the wife. God, how I loved that woman. I have not really touched her in years, merely felt those wonderful hands on my back as she jabbed the needles home, but I never stopped loving her. It was not a love that glowed any more, but it was there, though hers for me was long gone and wasted.

This morning when I got up from the floor, the weight of Rae and the world on my back, I saw the vine coming up from beneath the door and stretching over to her. I yelled her name. She did not move. I ran to her and saw it was too late. Before I could put a hand on her, I saw her flesh ripple and bump up, like a den of mice were nesting under a quilt. The vines were at work. (Out goes the old guts, in goes the new vines.)

There was nothing I could do for her.

I made a torch out of a chair leg and an old quilt, set fire to it, burned the vine from between her legs, watched it retreat, smoking, under the door. Then I got a board, nailed it along the bottom, hoping it would keep others out for at least a little while. I got one of the twelve-gauges and loaded it. It's on the desk beside me, Mr. Journal, but even I know I'll never use it. It was just something to do, as Jacobs said when he killed and ate the whale. Something to do.

I can hardly write any more. My back and shoulders hurt so bad. It's the weight of Rae and the world.

I've just come back from the mirror and there's very little left of the tattoo. Some blue and black ink, a touch of red that was Rae's hair. It looks like an abstract painting now. Collapsed design, running colors. It's real swollen. I look like the hunchback of Notre Dame.

What am I going to do, Mr. Journal?

Well, as always, I'm glad you asked me that. You see, I've thought this out.

I could throw Mary's body over the railing before it blooms. I could do that. Then I could doctor my back. It might even heal, though I doubt it. Rae wouldn't let that happen, I can tell you now.

And I don't blame her. I'm on her side. I'm just a walking dead man and have been for years.

I could put the shotgun under my chin and work the trigger with my toe, or maybe push it with the very pen I'm using to create you, Mr. Journal. Wouldn't that be neat? Blow my brains to the ceiling and sprinkle you with my blood.

But as I said, I loaded the gun because it was something to do. I'd never use it on myself or Mary.

You see, I want Mary. I want her to hold Rae and me one last time like she used to in the park. And she can. There's a way.

I've drawn all the curtains and made curtains out of blankets for those spots where there aren't any. It'll be sunup soon and I don't want that kind of light in here. I'm writing this by candlelight and it gives the entire room a warm glow. I wish I had wine. I want the atmosphere to be just right.

Over on Mary's bunk she's starting to twitch. Her neck is swollen where the vines have congested and are writhing toward their favorite morsel, the brain. Pretty soon the rose will bloom (I hope she's one of the bright yellow ones, yellow was her favorite color and she wore it well) and Mary will come for me.

When she does, I'll stand with my naked back to her. The vines will whip out and cut me before she reaches me, but I can stand it. I'm used to pain. I'll pretend the thorns are Mary's needles. I'll stand that way until she folds her dead arms around me and her body pushes up against the wound she made in my back, the wound that is our daughter Rae. She'll hold me so the vines and the proboscis can do their work. And while she holds me, I'll grab her fine hands and push them against my chest, and it will be we three again, standing against the world, and I'll close my eyes and delight in her soft, soft hands one last time.

JUDGMENT ENGINE

GREG BEAR

We

SEVEN tributaries disengage from their social=mind and Library and travel by transponder to the School World. There they are loaded into a temporary soma, an older physical model with eight long, flexible red legs. Here the seven become We.

We have received routine orders from the Teacher Annex. We are to investigate student labor on the Great Plain of History, the largest physical feature on the School World. The students have been set to searching all past historical records, donated by the nine remaining Libraries. Student social=minds are sad; they will not mature before Endtime. They are the last new generation, and their behavior is often aberrant. There may be room for error.

The soma sits in an enclosure. We become active and advance from the enclosure's shadow into a light shower of data condensing from the absorbing clouds high above. We see radiation from the donating Libraries, still falling on School World from around the three remaining systems; We hear the lambda whine of storage in the many rows of black hemispheres perched on the plain; we feel a patter of drops on our black carapace.

We stand at the edge of the plain, near a range of bare brown-and-black hills left over from planetary reformation. The air is thick and cold. It smells sharply of rich data moisture, wasted on us; We do not have readers on our surface. The moisture dews up on the dark, hard ground under our feet, evaporates, and is reclaimed by translucent soppers. The soppers flit through the air, a tenth our size and delicate.

The hemispheres are maintained by single-tributary somas. They are tiny, marching along the rows by the hundreds of thousands.

The brilliant violet sun appears in the west, across the plain, surrounded by streamers of intense blue. The streamers curl like flowing hair. Sun and streamers cast multiple shadows from each black hemisphere. The sun attracts our attention. It is beautiful, not part of a Library simscape; this scape is *real*. It reminds us of approaching Endtime. The changes made to conserve and concentrate the last available energy have rendered the scape beautifully novel, unfamiliar to the natural birth algorithms of our tributaries.

The three systems are unlike anything that has ever been. They contain all remaining order and available energy. Drawn close together, surrounded by the permutation of local space and time, the three systems deceive the dead outer universe, already well into the dull inaction of the long Between. We are proud of the three systems. They took a hundred million years to construct, and a tenth of all remaining available energy. They were a gamble. Nine of thirty-seven major Libraries agreed to the gamble. The others spread themselves into the greater magnitudes of the Between, and died.

The gamble worked.

Our soma is efficient and pleasant to work with. All of our tributaries agree, older models of such equipment are better. We have an appointment with the representative of the School World student tributaries, who are lodged in a newer model soma, called a Berkus, fashioned after a social=mind on Second World, where it was designed. A Berkus soma is not favored. It is noisy, perhaps more efficient, but brasher and less elegant. We agree it will be ugly.

Data clouds swirl and spread tendrils high over the plain. The single somas march between our legs, cleaning unwanted debris from the black domes. Within the domes, all history. We could reach down and crush one with the claws on a single leg, but that would slow Endtime Work and waste available energy. We are proud of such stray, antisocial thoughts, and more proud still that We can ignore them. They show that We are still human, still linked directly to the past.

We are teachers. All teachers must be linked with the past, to understand and explain. Teachers must understand error; the past is rich with pain and error.

We await the Berkus.

Too much time passes. The world turns away from the sun and night falls. Centuries of Library time pass, but We try to be patient and think in the flow of external time. Some of our tributaries express a desire to taste the domes, but there is no real need, and this would also waste available energy.

With night, more data from the other systems fills the skies, condenses, and rains down, covering us with a thick sheen. Soppers again clean our carapace. All around, the domes grow richer, absorbing history. We see, in the distance, a night interpreter striding on giant disjointed legs between the domes. It eats the domes and returns white mounds of discard. All the domes must be interpreted to see if any of the history should be carried by the final Endtime self.

The final self will cross the Between, order held in perfect inaction, until the Between has experienced sufficient rest and boredom. It will cross that point when time and space become granular and nonlinear, when the unconserved energy of expansion, absorbed at the minute level of the quantum foam, begins to disturb the metric. The metric becomes noisy and irregular, and all extension evaporates. The universe has no width, no time, and all is back at the beginning.

The final self will survive, knitting itself into the smallest interstices, armored against the fantastic pressures of a universe's deathsound. The quantum foam will give up its noise, and new universes will bubble forth and evolve. One will transcend. The transcendent reality will absorb the final self, which will seed it. From the compression should arise new intelligent beings.

It is an important thing, and all teachers approve. The past should cover the new, forever. It is our way to immortality.

Our tributaries express some concern. We are, to be sure, not on a vital mission, but the Berkus is very late. Something has gone wrong. We investigate our links and find them cut. Transponders do not reply.

The ground beneath our soma trembles. Hastily, the soma retreats from the Great Plain of History. It stands by a low hill, trying to keep steady on its eight red legs. The clouds over the plain turn green and ragged. The single somas scuttle between vibrating hemispheres, confused.

We cannot communicate with our social=mind or Library. No other Libraries respond. Alarmed, we appeal to the School World Student Committee, then point our thoughts up to the Endtime Work Coordinator, but they do not answer, either.

The endless kilometers of low black hemispheres churn as if stirred by a huge stick. Cracks appear, and from the cracks, thick red fluid drops; the drops crystallize into high, tall prisms. Many of the prisms shatter and turn to dead white powder.

We realize with great concern that we are seeing the internal stored data of the planet itself. This is a reserve record of all Library knowledge, held condensed; the School World contains selected records from the dead Libraries, more information than any single Library could absorb in a billion years. The knowledge shoots through the disrupted ground in crimson fountains, wasted.

> Our soma retreats deeper into the hills.
> Nobody answers our emergency signal.
> Nobody will speak to us, anywhere.

More days pass. We are still cut off from the Library. Isolated, we are limited to only what the soma can perceive, and that makes no sense at all.

We have climbed a promontory overlooking what was once the Great Plain of History. Where once our students worked to condense and select those parts of the past that would survive the Endtime, the hideous leaking of reserve knowledge has slowed, and an equally hideous round of what seems to be amateurish student exercises works itself in rapid time.

Madness covers the plain. The hemispheres have all disintegrated, and the single somas and interpreters have vanished.

Now, everywhere on the plain, green and red and purple forests grow and die in seconds; new trees push through the dead snags of the old. New kinds of trees invade from the west and push aside their predecessors. Climate itself accelerates: the skies grow heavy with cataracting clouds made of water, and rain falls in sinuous sheets. Steam twists and pullulates. The ground becomes hot with change.

Trees themselves come to an end and crumble away; huge, solid brown-and-red domes balloon on the plain, spread thick shell-leaves like opening cabbages, push long shoots through their crowns. The shoots tower above the domes and bloom with millions of tiny gray and pink flowers.

Watching all our work and plans being destroyed, the seven tributaries within our soma offer dismayed hypotheses: this is a malfunction, the conservation and compression engines have failed, and all knowledge is being acted out uselessly; no, it is some new gambit of the Endtime Work Coordinator, an emergency project; on the contrary, it is a political difficulty, lack of communication between the Coordinator and the Libraries, and it will all be over soon . . .

We watch shoots topple with horrendous snaps and groans, domes collapse in brown puffs of corruption.

The scape begins anew.

More hours pass, and still no communication with any other social=minds. We fear our Library itself has been destroyed; what other explanation for our abandonment? We huddle on our promontory, seeing patterns but no sense. Each generation of creativity brings something different, something that eventually fails or is rejected.

Today, large-scale vegetation is the subject of interest. The next day, vegetation is ignored for a rush of tiny biologies, but there is no change visible from where We stand, our soma still and watchful on its eight sturdy legs. We shuffle our claws to avoid a carpet of reddish growth surmounting the rise. By nightfall, we see, the mad scape could claim this part of the hill and we will have to move.

The sun approaches zenith. All shadows vanish. Its violet magnificence humbles us, a feeling we are not used to. We are from the great social=minds of the Library; humility and awe come from our isolation and concern. Not for a billion years have any of our tributaries felt so removed from useful enterprise. If this is the Endtime overtaking us, overcoming all our efforts, so be it. We feel resolve, pride at what we have managed to accomplish.

Then, we receive a simple message. The meeting with the students will take place. The Berkus will find us and explain. But We are not told when.

Something has gone very wrong when students should dictate to their teachers, and should put so many tributaries through this kind of travail.

The concept of *mutiny* is studied by all the tributaries within the soma. It does not explain much. New hypotheses occupy our thinking. Perhaps the new matter of which all things are now made has itself gone wrong, destabilizing our worlds and interrupting the consolidation of knowledge; that would explain the scape's ferment and our isolation. It might explain unstable and improper thought processes. Or, the students have allowed some activity on School World to run wild; error.

The scape pushes palace-like glaciers over its surface, gouging itself in painful ecstasy: change, change, birth and decay, all in a single day, but slower than the rush of forests and living things. We might be able to remain on the promontory.

Why are We treated so?

We keep to the open, holding our ground, clearly visible, concerned but unafraid. We are of older stuff. Teachers have always been of older stuff.

Could We have been party to some mis-instruction, to cause such a disaster? What have We taught that might push our students into manic creation and destruction? We search all records, all memories, contained within the small soma. The full memories of our seven tributaries have not of course been transferred into the extension; it was to be a temporary assignment, and besides, the records would not fit. The lack of capacity hinders our thinking, and we find no satisfying answers.

One of our tributaries has brought along some personal records. It has a long-shot hypothesis and suggests that an ancient prior self be activated to provide an objective judgment engine. There are two reasons: the stronger is that this ancient self once, long ago, had a connection with a tributary making up the Endtime Work Coordinator. If the problem is political, perhaps the self's memories can give us deeper insight. The second and weaker reason: truly, despite our complexity and advancement, perhaps we have missed something important. Perhaps this earlier, more primitive self will see what we have missed.

There is indeed so little time; isolated as we are from a greater river of being, a river that might no longer exist, we might be the last fragment of social=mind to have any chance of combating planet-wide madness.

There is barely enough room to bring the individual out of compression. It sits beside the tributaries in the thought plenum, in distress and not functional. What it perceives it does not understand.

Our questions are met with protests and more questions.

The Engine

I come awake, aware. *I* sense a later and very different awareness, part of a larger group. My thoughts spin with faces to which I try to apply names, but my memory falters. These fade and are replaced by gentle calls for attention, new and very strange sensations.

I label the sensations around me: other humans, but not in human bodies. They seem to act together while having separate voices. I call the larger group the We-ness, not me, and yet it is in some way accessible, as if part of my mind and memory.

I do not think that I have died, that I am *dead*. But the quality of my thought has changed. I have no body, no sensations of liquid pumping and breath flowing in and out.

Isolated, confused, I squat behind the We-ness's center of observation, catching glimpses of a chaotic, high-speed landscape. Are they watching some entertainment?

I worry that I am in a hospital, in recovery, forced to consort with other patients who cannot or will not speak with me. I try to recollect my last meaningful memories. I remember a face again and give it a name and relation: Elisaveta, my wife, standing beside me as I lie on a narrow bed. Machines bend over me. I remember nothing after that.

But I am not in a hospital, not now.

Voices speak to me and I begin to understand some of what they say. The voices of the We-ness are stronger, more complex and richer, than anything I have ever experienced.

I do not hear them.

I have no ears.

"You've been stored inactive for a very long time," the We-ness tells me. It is (or they are) a tight-packed galaxy of thoughts, few of them making any sense at all.

Then I know.

I have awakened in the future. Thinking has changed.

"I don't know where I am. I don't know who you are . . ."

"We are joined from seven tributaries, some of whom once had existence as individual biological beings. You are an ancient self of one of us."

"Oh," I say. The word seems wrong without lips or throat. I will not use it again.

"We're facing great problems. You'll provide unique insights." The voice expresses overtones of fatherliness and concern.

I do not believe it. Blackness paints me.

"I'm hungry but I can't feel my body. Where am I? I'm afraid. I miss . . . my family."

"There is no body, no need for hunger, no need for food. Your family—*our* family—no longer lives."

"How did I get here?"

"You were stored before a major medical reconstruction, to prevent total loss. Your stored self was kept as a kind of an historical record, as a memento."

I don't remember any of that, but then, how could I? I remember signing contracts to allow such a thing. I remember thinking about the possibility I would awake in the future. But I did not die! "How long has it been?"

"Twelve billion two hundred and seventy-nine million years."

Had the We-ness said "ten thousand years" or even "two hundred years," I might feel some visceral reaction. All I know is that such an enormous length of time is beyond geological. It is *cosmological*. I do not believe in it.

I glimpse the landscape again, glaciers slipping down mountain slopes, clouds pregnant with winter building gray and orange in the stinging glare of a huge setting sun. The sun is all wrong—too bright, too violet. It resembles a dividing cell, all extrusions and blebs and long ribbons of streaming hair. It could be Medusa, one of the Gorgon sisters.

The edges of the glaciers calve pillars of white ice that topple and shatter across hills and valleys. I have awakened in the middle of an ice age. But it is *fast*, too fast.

Nothing makes sense.

"Is all of me here?" I ask. Perhaps, lacking a whole mind, I am delusional.

"The most important part of you is here. We would like to ask you some questions. Do you recognize any of the following faces, voices, thought patterns, styles?"

Disturbing synesthesia—bright sounds, loud colors, dull electric smells—fill my senses and I close them out as best I can. "No! That isn't right. Please, no questions until I know what's happened. No! That hurts!"

The We-ness prepares to turn me off, to shut me down. I am warned that I will again become inactive. Just before I wink out, I feel a cold blast of air crest the promontory on which the We-ness, and I, sit. Glaciers now blanket the hills and valleys. The We-ness flexes eight fluid red legs, pulling them from quick-freezing mud.

The sun still has not set.

Thousands of years in a day.

I am given sleep as blank as death, but not so final.

* * *

We gather as one and consider the problem of the faulty interface. "This is too early a self. It doesn't understand our way of thinking," one tributary says. "We must adapt to it."

The tributary whose prior self this was volunteers to begin restructuring.

"There is so little time," says another, who now expresses strong disagreement with the plan to resurrect. "Are we truly agreed this is best?"

We threaten to fragment as two of the seven tributaries vehemently object. But solidarity holds. All tributaries flow again to renewed agreement. We start the construction of an effective interface, which first requires deeper understanding of the nature of the ancient self.

This takes some more precious time. The glacial cold nearly kills us. The soma changes its fluid nature by linking liquid water with long-chain and even more slippery molecules, highly resistant to freezing.

"Do the students know We're here, that We watch?" asks a tributary.

"They must . . . " says another. "They express a willingness to meet with us."

"Perhaps they lie, and they mean to destroy this soma, and us with it. There will be no meeting."

Dull sadness.

We restructure the ancient self, wrap it in our new interface, build a new plenary face to hold us all on equal ground, and call it up again, saying,

Vasily

* * *

I know the name, recognize the fatherly voice, feel a new clarity. I wish I could forget the first abortive attempt to live again, but my memory is perfect from the point of first rebirth on. I will forget nothing.

"Vasily, your descendant self does not remember you. It has purged older memories many times since your existence; even so, We recognize some similarities between your patterns. Birth patterns are strong and seldom completely erased. Are you comfortable now?"

I think of a simple place where I can sit. I want wood paneling and furniture and a fireplace, but I am not skilled; all I can manage is a small gray cubicle with a window on one side. In the wall is a hole through which the voices come. I imagine I am hearing them through flesh ears, and a kind of body forms within the cubicle. This body is my security. "I'm still afraid. I know—there's no danger."

"There *is* danger, but We do not yet know how significant the danger is."

Significant carries an explosion of information. If their original selves still exist elsewhere, in a social=mind adjunct to a Library, then all that might be lost will be immediate memories. A *social=mind*, I understand, is made up of fewer than ten thousand tributaries. A Library typically contains a trillion or more social=minds.

"I've been dead for billions of years," I say, hoping to address my future self. "But you've lived on—you're immortal."

"We do not measure life or time as you do. Continuity of memory is fragmentary in our lives, across eons. But continuity of access to the Library—and access to records of past selves—does confer a kind of immortality. If that has ended, We are completely mortal."

"I must be so primitive," I say, my fear oddly fading now. This is a situation I can understand—life or death. I feel more solid within my cubicle. "How can I be of any use?"

"You are primitive in the sense of *firstness*. That is why you have been activated. Through your life experience, you may have a deeper understanding of what led to our situation. Argument, rebellion, desperation . . . These things are difficult for us to deal with."

Again, I don't believe them. From what I can tell, this group of minds has a depth and strength and complexity that makes me feel less than a child . . . perhaps less than a bacterium. What can I do except cooperate? I have nowhere else to go . . .

For billions of years . . . inactive. Not precisely death.

I remember that I was once a *teacher*.

Elisaveta had been my student before she became my wife.

The We-ness wants me to teach it something, to do something for it. But first, it has to teach me history.

"Tell me what's happened," I say.

The Libraries

In the beginning, human intelligences arose, and all were alone. That lasted for tens of thousands of years. Soon after understanding the nature of thought and mind, intelligences came together to create group minds, all in one. Much of the human race linked in an intimacy deeper than sex. Or unlinked to pursue goals as quasi-individuals; the choices were many, the limitations few. (*This all began a few decades after your storage.*) Within a century, the human race abandoned biological limitations, in favor of the social=mind. Social=minds linked to form Libraries, at the top of the hierarchy.

The Libraries expanded, searching around star after star for other intelligent life. They found life—millions upon millions of worlds, each rare as a diamond among the trillions of barren star systems, but none with intelligent beings. Gradually, across millions of years, the Libraries realized that they were the All of intelligent thought.

We had simply exchanged one kind of loneliness for a greater and more final isolation. There were no companion intelligences, only those derived from humanity . . .

As the human Libraries spread and connections between them became more tenuous—some communications taking thousands of years to be completed—many social=minds re-individuated, assuming lesser degrees of togetherness and intimacy. Even in large Libraries, individuation became a crucial kind of relaxation and holiday. The old ways reasserted.

Being human, however, some clung to old ways, or attempted to enforce new ones, with greater or lesser tenacity. Some asserted moral imperative. Madness spread as large groups removed all the barriers of individuation, in reaction to what they perceived as a dangerous atavism—the "lure of the singular."

These "uncelled" or completely communal Libraries, with their slow, united consciousness, proved burdensome and soon vanished—within half a million years. They lacked the range and versatility of the "celled" Libraries.

But conflicts between differing philosophies of social=mind structure continued. There were wars.

Even in wars the passions were not sated; for something more frightening had been discovered than loneliness: the continuity of error and cruelty. After tens of millions of years of steady growth and peace, the renewed paroxysms dismayed us. No matter how learned or advanced a social=mind became, it could, in desperation or in certain moments of development, perform acts analogous to the errors of ancient, individuated societies. It could kill other social=minds, or sever the activities of many of its own tributaries. It could frustrate the fulfillment of other minds. It could experience something like *rage*, but removed from the passions of the body: rage cold and precise and long-lived, terrible in its persuasiveness, dreadful in its consequences. Even worse, it could experience *indifference*.

* * *

I tumble through these records, unable to comprehend the scale of what I see. Our galaxy was linked star to star with webworks of transferred energy and information; but large sectors of the galaxy were darkened by massive conflict, and millions of stars turned off, shut down.

This was war.

At the scale of individual humans, planets seemed to revert to ancient Edens, devoid of artifice or instrumentality; but the trees and animals themselves carried myriads of tiny machines, and the ground beneath them was an immense thinking system, down to the core . . .

Other worlds, and other structures between worlds, seemed as abstract and meaningless as the wanderings of a stray brush on canvas.

The Proof

One great social=mind, retreating from the ferment of the Libraries, formulated the rules of advanced meta-biology, and found them precisely analogous to those governing planet-bound ecosystems: competition, victory through survival, evolution and reproduction. It proved that error and pain and destruction are essential to any change—but more importantly, to any growth.

The great social=mind carried out complex experiments simulating millions of different ordering systems, and in every single case, the rise of complexity (and ultimately intelligence) led to the wanton destruction of prior forms. Using these experiments to define axioms, what began as a scientific proof ended as a rigorous mathematical proof:

There can be no ultimate ethical advancement in this universe.

The indifference of the universe—reality's grim and mindless harshness—is multiplied by the necessity that old order, prior thoughts and lives, must be extinguished to make way for new.

After checking its work many times, the great social=mind wiped its stores and erased its infrastructure in, on, and around seven worlds and the two stars, leaving behind only the formulation and the Proof.

For Libraries across the galaxy, absorption of the Proof led to mental disruption. From the nightmare of history there was to be no awakening.

Suicide was one way out. A number of prominent Libraries brought their own histories to a close. Others recognized the validity of the Proof, but did not commit suicide. They lived with the possibility of error and destruction. And still, they grew wiser, greater in scale and accomplishment . . .

Crossing from galaxy to galaxy, still alone, the Libraries realized that human perception was the only perception. The Proof would never be tested against the independent minds of non-human intelligences.

In this universe, the Proof must stand.

Billions of years passed, and the universe became a huge kind of house, confining a practical infinity of mind, an incredible ferment which "burned" the available energy with torchy brilliance, decreasing the total life span of reality.

Yet the Proof remained unassailed.

* * *

Wait. I don't see anything here. I don't *feel* anything. This isn't history; it's . . . too large! I can't understand some of the things you show me . . . But worse, pardon me, it's babbling among minds who feel no passion. This We-ness . . . how do you *feel* about this?

* * *

You are distracted by preconceptions. You long for an organic body, and assume that lacking organic bodies, We experience no emotions. We experience emotions. *Listen* to them>>>>>

* * *

I squirm in my cubicle and experience their emotions of first and second loneliness, degrees of isolation from old memories, old selves; longing for the first individuation, the Birth-time . . . hunger for understanding of not just the outer reality beyond the social=mind's vast internal universe of thought but the ever-changing currents and orderliness arising between tributaries. Here is social and mental interaction as a great song, rich and joyous, a love greater than anything I can remember experiencing as an embodied human. Greater emotions still, outside my range again, of loyalty and love for a social=mind and something like *respect* for the immense Libraries. (I am shown what the We-ness says is an emotion experienced at the level of Libraries, but it is so far beyond me that I seem to disintegrate, and have to be coaxed back to wholeness.)

A tributary approaches across the mind space within the soma. My cubicle grows dim. I feel a strange familiarity again.

This will be, this *is*, my future self.

This tributary feels sadness and some grief, touching its ancient self—me. It feels pain at my limitations, at my tight-packed biological character. Things deliberately forgotten come back to haunt it.

And they haunt *me*. My own inadequacies become abundantly clear. I remember useless arguments with friends, making my wife cry with frustration, getting angry at my children for no good reason. My childhood and adolescent indiscretions return like shadows on a scrim. And I remember my *drives*: rolling in useless lust, and later, Elisaveta!, with her young and supple body.

And others.

Just as significant, but different in color, the cooler passions of discovery and knowledge, my growing self-awareness. I remember fear of inadequacy, fear of failure, of not being a useful member of society. I needed above all (more than I needed Elisaveta) to be important and to teach and be influential on young minds.

All of these emotions, the We-ness demonstrates, have analogous emotions at their level. For the We-ness, the most piercing unpleasantness of all—akin to physical pain—comes from recognition of their possible failure. The teachers may not have taught their students properly, and the students may be making mistakes.

"Let me get all this straight," I say. I grow used to my imagined state—to riding like a passenger within the cubicle, inside the eight-legged soma, to seeing as if through a small window the advancing and now receding of the glaciers. "You're teachers—as I was once a teacher—and you used to be connected to a larger social=mind, part of a Library." I mull over mind as society, society as mind. "But there may have been a revolution. After billions of years! Students . . . A *revolution!* Extraordinary! You've been cut off from the Library. You're alone, you might be killed . . . And you're telling *me* about ancient history?"

The We-ness falls silent.

"I must be important," I say with an unbreathed sigh, a kind of asterisk in the exchanged thoughts. "I can't imagine why. But maybe it doesn't matter—I have so many questions!" I hunger for knowledge of what has become of my children, of my wife. Of everything that came after me . . .

All the changes!

"We need information from you, and your interpretation of certain memories. Vasily was our name once. Vasily Gerazimov. You were the husband of Elisaveta, father of Maxim and Giselle . . . We need to know more about Elisaveta."

"You don't remember her?"

"Twelve billion years have passed. Time and space have changed. This tributary alone has since partnered and bonded and matched and socialized with perhaps fifty billion individuals and tributaries. Our combined tributaries in the social=mind have had contacts with all intelligent beings, once or twice removed. Most have dumped or stored memories more than a billion years old. If We were still connected to the Library, I could learn more about my past. I have kept you as a kind of *memento*, a talisman, and nothing more."

I feel a freezing awe. Fifty billion mates . . . Or whatever they had been. I catch fleeting glimpses of liaisons in the social=mind, binary, trinary, as many as thousands at a time linked in the crumbling remnants of marriage and sexuality, and finally those liaisons passing completely out of favor, fashion, or usefulness.

"Elisaveta and you," the tributary continues, "were divorced ten years after your storage. I remember nothing of the reasons why. We have no other clues to work with."

The "news" comes as a doubling of my pain, a renewed and expanded sense of isolation from a loved one. I reach up to touch my face, to see if I am crying. My hands pass through imagined flesh and bone. My body is long since dust; Elisaveta's body is dust.

What went wrong between us? Did she find another lover? Did I? I am a ghost. I should not care. There were difficult times, but I never thought of our liaison, our *marriage* (I would defend that word even now), as temporary. Still, across *billions* of years! We have become *immortal*—her perhaps more than I, who remember nothing of the time between. "Why do you need me at all? Why do you need clues?"

But we are interrupted. An extraordinary thing happens to the retreating glaciers. With the soma half-hidden behind an upthrust of frozen and deformed knowledge, we see, from the promontory, the icy masses blister and bubble as if made of some superheated glass or plastic. Steam bursts from the bubbles—at least, what appears to be steam—and freezes in the air in shapes suggesting flowers. All around, the walls and sheets of ice succumb to this beautiful plague.

The We-ness understands this occurrence no more than I.

From the hill below come faint sounds and hints of radiation—gamma rays; beta particles; mesons, all clearly visible to the We-ness, and vaguely passed on to me as well.

"Something's coming," I say.

* * *

The Berkus advances in its unexpected cloud of production/destruction. There is something deeply wrong with it—it squanders too much available energy. Its very presence disrupts the new matter of which We are made.

Of the seven tributaries, four feel an emotion rooted in the deepest algorithms of their pasts: fear. Three have never known such bodily functions, have never known mortal and embodied individuation. They feel intellectual concern and a tinge of cosmic sadness, as if our end might be equated with the deaths of stars and galaxies. We keep to our purpose despite these ridiculous excursions, the increasing and disturbing signs of our disorder.

The Berkus advances up the hill.

* * *

I see through my window this monumental and absolutely horrifying *creature*, shining with a brightness comprised of the qualities of diamonds and polished silver, a scintillating insect pushing its sharply pointed feet into the thawing soil, steam rising all around. The legs hold together despite gaps where joints should be, gaps crossed only by something that produces hard radiation. Below the Berkus (as the We-ness calls it), the ground ripples as if School World has muscles and twitches, wanting to scratch.

With blasts of neutrons flicked as casually as a flashlight beam, the Berkus pauses and sizes up our much less powerful, much smaller soma. The material of our soma wilts and re-forms beneath this withering barrage. The soma expresses distress—and inadvertently, the We-ness translates this distress to me as tremendous pain.

Within my confined mental space, I explode . . .

Again comes the blackness.

* * *

The Berkus decides it is not necessary to come any closer. That is fortunate for us and for our soma. Any lessening of the distance could prove fatal.

The Berkus communicates with pulsed light. "Why are you here?"

"We have been sent here to observe and report. We are cut off from the Library—"

"Your Library has fled," the Berkus informs us. "It disagreed with the Endtime Work Coordinator."

"We were told nothing of this."

"It was not our responsibility. We did not know you would be here."

The magnitude of this rudeness is difficult to envelop. We wonder how many tributaries the Berkus contains. We hypothesize that it might contain all of the students, the entire student social=mind, and this would explain its use of energy and change in design.

Our pitiful ancient individual flickers back into awareness and sits quietly, too stunned to protest.

"We do not understand the purpose of this creation and destruction," We say. Our strategy is to avoid the student tributaries altogether now. Still, they might tell us more We need to know.

"It must be obvious to teachers," the Berkus says. "By order of the Coordinator, We are rehearsing all possibilities of coherence, usurping stored knowledge down to the planetary core and converting it. There must be an escape from the Proof."

"The Proof is an ancient discovery. It has never been shown to be wrong. What can it possibly mean to the Endtime Work?"

"It means a great deal," the Berkus says.

"How many are you?"

The Berkus does not answer. All this has taken place in less than a millionth of a second. The Berkus's uncommunication lengthens into seconds, then minutes.

Around us, the glaciers crumple like mud caught in rushing water.

"Another closed path, of no value," the Berkus finally says.

"We wish to understand your motivations. Why this concern with the Proof? And what does it have to do with the change you provoke, the destruction of School World's knowledge?"

The Berkus rises on a tripod of three disjointed legs, waving its other legs in the air, a cartoon medallion so disturbing in design that We draw back a few meters. "The Proof is a cultural aberration," it radiates fiercely, blasting our surface and making the mud around us bubble. "It is not fit to pass on to those who seed the next reality. You failed us. You showed no way beyond the Proof. The Endtime Work has begun, the final self chosen to fit through the narrow gap—"

*   *   *

I see all this through the We-ness as if I have been there, have lived it, and suddenly I know why I have been recalled, why the We-ness has shown me faces and patterns.

The universe, across more than twelve billion years, grows irretrievably old. From spanning the galaxies billions of years before, all life and intelligence—all arising from the sole intelligence in all the universe, humanity—have shrunk to a few star systems. These systems have been resuscitated and nurtured by concentrating the remaining available energy of thousands of dead galaxies.

But they are no longer natural star systems with planets—the bloated, coma-wrapped violet star rising at zenith is a congeries of plasma macromachines, controlling and conserving every gram of the natural matter remaining, harnessing every erg of available energy. These artificial suns pulse like massive living cells, shaped to be ultimately efficient and to squeeze every moment of active life over the time remaining. The planets themselves have been condensed, recarved, rearranged—and they too are composed of geological macromachines.

With some dread, I gather that the matter of which all these things are made is *itself* artificial, with redesigned component particles. The natural galaxies have died, reduced to a colorless murmur of useless heat, and the particles of all original creation—besides those marshaled and remade in these three close-packed systems—have dulled and slowed and unwound. Gravity itself has lost its bearings and become a chancy phenomenon, supplemented by new forces generated within the macromachine planets and suns. Nothing is what it seems, and nothing is what it had been when I lived.

The We-ness looks forward to less than four times ten to the fiftieth units of Planck time—roughly an old Earth year.

And in charge of it all, controlling the Endtime Work, a supremely confident social=mind composed of many "tributaries," and among those gathered selves . . .

Someone very familiar to me indeed.

My wife.

"Where is she? Can I speak to her? What happened to her? Did she die, was she stored—did she live?"

The We-ness seems to vibrate both from my reaction to this information, and to the spite of the Berkus. I am assigned to a quiet place where I can watch and listen without bothering them.

I feel our soma, our insect-like body, dig into the loosening substance of the promontory.

* * *

"You taught us the Proof was absolute," the Berkus says, "that throughout all time, in all circumstances, error and destruction and pain will accompany growth and creation, that the universe must remain indifferent and randomly hostile. We do not accept that."

"But why dissolve links with the Library?" We cry, even as We shrink beneath the Berkus's glare. The constantly reconstructed body of the Berkus channels and consumes energy with enormous waste, as if the students do not care, intent only on their frantic mission, whatever that might be . . . Reducing available active time by days for *all of us*—

* * *

I know why! I know the reason! I shout in the quiet place, but I am not heard, or not paid attention to.

* * *

"Why condemn us to a useless end in this chaos, this madness?" We ask.

"Because We must refute the Proof, and there is so little useful time remaining. The final self must not be sent over carrying this burden of error."

* * *

"*Of sin!*" I shout, still not heard. Proof of the validity of primordial sin—that everything living must eat, must destroy, must climb up the ladder on the backs of miserable victims; that all true creation involves death and pain; that the universe is a charnel house.

I am fed and I study the Proof. I try to encompass the principles and expressions, no longer given as words, but as multi-sense abstractions. In the Proof, miniature universes of discourse are created, manipulated, reduced to an expression, and discarded. The Proof is more complex than any single human life, or even the life of a species, and its logic is not familiar. The Proof is rooted in areas of mental experience I am not equipped to understand, but I receive glosses.

Law: Any dynamic system (I understand this as *organism*) **has limited access to resources, and a limited time in which to achieve its goals.** A multitude of instances are drawn from history, as well as from an artificial miniature universe. Other laws follow regarding behavior of systems within a flow of energy, but they are completely beyond me.

Observed Law: The goals of differing organisms, even of like variety, never completely coincide. History and the miniature universe teem with instances, and the Proof lifts these up for inspection at moments of divergence, demonstrating again and again this obvious point.

Then comes a roll of deductions, backed by examples too numerous for me to absorb:

And so it follows that for any complex of organisms, competition must arise for limited resources.

From this: Some will fail to acquire resources sufficient to live and some will succeed. Those who succeed express themselves in latter generations.

From this: New dynamic systems will arise to compete more efficiently.

From this: Competition and selection will give rise to *streamlined* organisms that are incapable of surviving even in the midst of plenty because they are not equipped with complete methods of absorbing resources. These will prey on complete organisms to acquire their resources.

And in return, the prey will acquire a reliance on the predators to hone their fitness.

From this: Other forms of *streamlining* will occur. Some of the resulting systems will become diseases and parasites, depending entirely on others for reproduction and fulfillment of basic goals.

From this: Ecosystems will arise, interdependent, locked in predator/prey, disease/host relationships.

I experience a multitude of rigorous experiments, unfolding like flowers.

And so it follows that in the course of competition, some forms will be outmoded and will pass away, and others will be preyed upon to extinction, without regard to their beauty, their adaptability to a wide range of possible conditions.

I sense here a kind of aesthetic judgment, above the fray: beautiful forms will die without being fully tested, their information lost, their opportunities limited.

And so it follows . . .

And so it follows . . .

The ecosystems increase in complexity, giving rise to organisms whose primary adaptation is perception and judgment, forming the abstract equivalents of societies, which interact through the exchange of resources and extensions of cultures and politics—models for more efficient organization. Still, change and evolution, failure and death, societies and cultures pass and are forgotten; whole classes of these larger systems suffer extinction, without being allowed fulfillment.

From history: Nations prey upon nations and eat them alive, discarding them as burned husks.

Law: *The universe is neutral; it will not care, nor will any ultimate dynamic system interfere . . .*

In those days before I was born, as smoke rose from the ovens, God did not hear the cries of His people.

And so it follows: No system will achieve perfect efficiency and self-sufficiency. Within all changing systems, accumulated error must be purged. For the good of the dynamic whole, systems must die. But efficient and beautiful systems will die as well.

I see the Proof's abstraction of evil: a shark-like thing, to me, but no more than a very complex expression. In this shark there is history, and dumb organic pressure, and the accumulations of the past, and the shark does not discriminate, knows nothing of judgment or justice, will eat the promising and the strong, as well as birthing young. Waste, waste, an agony of waste, and over it all, not watching, the indifference of the real.

After what seems hours of study, of questions asked and answered, of new ways of thinking—re-education—I begin to feel the thoroughness of the Proof, and I feel a despair unlike anything in my embodied existence.

Where once there had been hope that intelligent organisms could see their way to just, beautiful, and efficient systems, in practice, without exception, they revert to the old rules.

Things have not and will never improve.

Heaven itself would be touched with evil—or stand still. But there is no heaven run by a just God. Nor can there be a just God. Perfect justice and beauty and evolution and change are incompatible.

Not the birth of my son and daughter, not the day of my marriage, not all my moments of joy can erase the horror of history. And the stretch of future histories, after my storage, shows even more horror, until I seem to swim in carnivorous, *cybernivorous* cruelty.

Connections

We survey the Berkus with growing concern. Here is not just frustration of our attempts to return to the Library, not just destruction of knowledge, but a flagrant and purposeless waste of precious resources. Why is it allowed?

Obviously, the Coordinator of the Endtime Work has given license, handed over this world, with such haste that We did not have time to withdraw. The Library has been forced away (or worse), and all transponders destroyed, leaving us alone on School World.

The ancient self, having touched on the Proof (absorbing no more than a fraction of its beauty), is wrapped in a dark shell of mood. This mood, basic and primal as it is, communicates to the tributaries. Again, after billions of years, We feel sadness at the inevitability of error and the impossibility of justice—and sadness at our own error. The Proof has always stood as a monument of pure thought—and a curse, even to We who affirm it.

The Berkus expands like a balloon. "There is going to be major work done here. You will have to move."

"No," the combined tributaries cry. "This is enough confusion and enough being *shoved around*." Those words come from the ancient self.

The Berkus finds them amusing.

"Then you'll stay here," it says, "and be absorbed in the next round of experiment. You are teachers who have taught incorrectly. You deserve no better."

* * *

I break free of the *dark shell of mood*, as the tributaries describe it, and now I seem to kick and push my way to a peak of attention, all without arms or legs.

"Where is the plan, the order? Where are your billions of years of superiority? How can this be happening?"

* * *

We pass on the cries of the ancient self. The Berkus hears the message.

"We are not familiar with this voice," the student social=mind says.

"I judge you from the past!" the ancient self says. "You are *all* found wanting!"

"This is not the voice of a tributary, but of an individual," the Berkus says. "The individual sounds uninformed."

* * *

"I demand to speak with my wife!"

My demand gets no reaction for almost a second. Around me, the tributaries within the soma flow and rearrange, thinking in a way I cannot follow. They finally rise as a solid, seamless river of consent.

"*We charge you with error,*" they say to the Berkus. "*We charge you with confirming the Proof you wish to negate.*"

The Berkus considers, then backs away swiftly, beaming at us one final message: "There is an interesting rawness in your charge. You no longer think as outmoded teachers. A link with the Endtime Work Coordinator will be requested. Stand where you are. Our own work must continue."

* * *

I feel a sense of relief around me. This is a breakthrough. I have a purpose! The Berkus retreats, leaving us on the promontory to observe. Where once, hours before, glaciers melted, the ground begins to churn, grow viscous, divide into fenced enclaves. Within the enclaves, green and gray shapes arise, sending forth clouds of steam. These enclaves surround the range of hills, surmount all but our promontory, and move off to the horizon on all sides, perhaps covering the entire School World.

In the center of each fenced area, a sphere forms, first as a white blister on the hardness, then as a pearl resting on the surface. The pearl lifts, suspended in air. The pearls begin to evolve in different ways, turning inward, doubling, tripling, flattening into disks, dividing at their centers to form toruses—a practical infinity of different forms.

The fecundity of idea startles me. Blastulas give rise to cell-like complexity, spikes twist into intricate knots, all the rules of ancient topological mathematics are demonstrated in seconds, and then violated as the spaces within the enclaves themselves change.

"What are they doing?" I ask, bewildered.

"A mad push of evolution," my descendant self explains, "trying all combinations, starting from a simple beginning. This was once a common exercise, but not on such a vast scale. Not since the formulation of the Proof."

"What do they want to learn?"

"If they can find one instance of evolution and change that involves only growth and development, not competition and destruction, then they will have falsified the Proof."

"But the Proof is perfect," I said. "It can't be falsified . . ."

"So We have judged. The students incorrectly believe We are wrong."

The field of creation becomes a vast fabric, each enclave contributing to a larger weave. What is being shown here could have occupied entire civilizations in my time: the dimensions of change, all possibilities of progressive growth.

"It's beautiful," I say.

"It's futile," my descendant self says, its tone bitter. I feel the emotion in its message as an aberration, and it immediately broadcasts shame to all of its fellows, and to me.

"Are you afraid they'll show your teachings were wrong?" I ask.

"No," my tributary says. "I am sorry that they will fail. Such a message to pass on to a young universe . . . That whatever our nature and design, however We develop, We are doomed to make errors and cause pain. Still, that is the truth, and it has never been refuted."

"But even in my time, there was a solution," I say.

They show mild curiosity. What could come from so far in the past that they hadn't advanced upon, improved a billion times over, or discarded? I wonder why I have been activated at all . . .

But I persist. "From God's perspective, destruction and pain and error may be part of the greater whole, a beauty from Its point of view. We only perceive them as evil because of our limited point of view."

The tributaries allow a polite pause. My tributary explains, as gently as possible, "We have never encountered ultimate systems you call gods. Still, We are or have been very much like gods. As gods, all too often We have made horrible errors, and caused unending pain. Pain did not add to the beauty."

I want to scream at them for their hubris, but it soon becomes apparent to me they are right. Their predecessors have reduced galaxies, scanned all histories, made the universe itself run faster with their productions and creations. They have advanced the Endtime by billions of years, and now prepare to seed a new universe across an inconceivable gap of darkness and immobility.

From my perspective, humans have certainly become god-like. But not just. And there are no others. Even in the diversity of the human diaspora across the galaxies, not once has the Proof been falsified.

And that is all it would have taken: one instance.

"*Why did you bring me back, then?*" I ask my descendant self in private conference.

It replies in kind:

"Your thought processes are not our own. You can be a judgment engine. You might give us insight into the reasoning of the students, and help explain to us their plunge into greater error. There must be some motive not immediately apparent, some fragment of personality and memory responsible for this. An ancient self of you and a tributary of the Endtime Work Coordinator were once intimately related— married as sexual partners. You did not stay married. That is division and dissent. And there is division and dissent between the Endtime Work Committee and the teachers. That much is apparent . . ."

Again I feel like clutching my hands to my face and screaming in frustration. Elisaveta—it must mean Elisaveta.

But we were not divorced . . . not when I was stored!

I sit in my imagined gray cubicle, my imagined body uncertain in its outline, and wish for a moment of complete privacy. They give it to me.

Tapering Time

The scape has progressed to a complexity beyond our ability to process. We stand on our promontory, surrounded by the field of enclaved experiments, each enclave containing a different evolved object, still furiously morphing. Some of the objects glow faintly as night sweeps across our part of the School World.

We are as useless and incompetent as the revived ancient self, now wrapped in its own shock and misery. Our tributaries have fallen silent. We wait for what will happen next, either in the scape, or in the promised contact with the Endtime Work Coordinator.

The ancient self rises from its misery and isolation. It joins our watchful silence, expectant. It has not completely lost *hope*. We have never had need of *hope*. Connected to the Library, fear became a distant and unimportant thing; hope, its opposite, equally distant and useless.

* * *

I have been musing over my last hazy memories of Elisaveta, of our children Maxim and Giselle—bits of conversation, physical features, smells . . . reliving long stretches with the help of memory recovery ... watching seconds pass into minutes as if months pass into years.

Outside, time seems to move much more swiftly. The divisions between enclaves fall, and the uncounted experiments stand on the field, still evolving, but now allowed to interact. Tentatively, their evolution takes in the new possibility of *motion*.

I feel for the students, wish to be part of them. However wrong, this experiment is vital, idealistic. It smells of youthful naiveté. Because of my own rugged youth, raised in a nation running frantically from one historical extreme to another, born to parents who jumped like puppets between hope and despair, I have always felt uneasy in the face of idealism and naiveté.

Elisaveta was a naive idealist when I first met her. I tried to teach her, pass on my sophistication, my sense of better judgment.

The brightly colored, luminous objects hover over the plain, discovering new relations: a separate identity, a larger sense of space. The objects have reached a high level of complexity and order, but within a limited environment. If any have developed mind, they can now reach out and explore new objects.

First, the experiments shift a few centimeters this way or that, visible across the plain as a kind of restless, rolling motion. The plain becomes an ocean of gentle waves. Then, the experiments *bump* each other. Near our hill, some of the experiments circle and surround their companions, or just bump with greater and greater urgency. Extensions reach out, and We can see—it must be obvious to all— that mind does exist, and new senses are being created and explored.

If Elisaveta, whatever she has become, is in charge of this sea of experiments, then perhaps she is merely following an inclination she had billions of years before: when in doubt, when all else fails, *punt.*

This is a cosmological kind of punt, burning up available energy at a distressing rate ...

Just like her, I think, and feel a warmth of connection with that ancient woman. But the woman *divorced* me. She found me wanting, later than my memories reach ... And after all, what she has become is as little like the Elisaveta I knew as my descendant tributary is like me.

The dance on the plain becomes a frenzied blur of color. Snakes flow, sprout legs, wings beat the air. Animal relations, plant relations, new ecosystems . . . But these creatures have evolved not from the simplest beginnings, but from already elaborate sources. Each isolated experiment, already having achieved a focused complexity beyond anything I can understand, becomes a potential player in a new order of interaction.

What do the students—or Elisaveta—hope to accomplish in this peculiar variation on the old scheme?

I am so focused on the spectacle surrounding us that it takes a "nudge" from my descendant self to alert me to change in the sky. A liquid silvery ribbon pours from above, spreading over our heads into a flat, upside-down ocean of reflective cloud. The inverse ocean expands to the horizon, blocking all light from the new day.

Our soma rises expectantly on its eight legs. I feel the tributaries' interest as a kind of heat through my cubicle, and for the moment, abandon the imagined environment.

Best to receive this new phenomenon directly.

A fringed curtain, like the edge of a shawl woven from threads of mercury, descends from the upside-down ocean, brushing across the land. The fringe crosses the plain of experiments without interfering, but surrounds our hill, screening our view. Light pulses from selected threads in the liquid weave.

The tributaries translate instantly.

"What do *you* want?" asks a clear, neutral voice. No character, no tone, no emotion. This is the Endtime Work Coordinator, or at least an extension of that powerful social=mind. It does not sound anything like Elisaveta. My hopes have been terribly naive.

After all this time and misery, the teachers' reserve is admirable. I detect respect, but no awe; they are used to the nature of the Endtime Work Coordinator, largest of the social=minds not directly connected to a Library.

"We have been cut off, and We need to know why," the tributaries say.

"Your work reached a conclusion," the voice responds.

"Why were We not accorded the respect of being notified, or allowed to return to our Library?"

"Your Library has been terminated. We have concluded the active existence of all entities no longer directly connected with Endtime Work, to conserve available energy."

"But you have let us live."

"It would involve more energy to terminate existing extensions than to allow them to run down."

The sheer coldness and precision of the voice chill me. The end of a Library is equivalent to the end of thousands of worlds full of individual intelligences.

Genocide. Error and destruction.

But my future self corrects me. *"This is expediency,"* it says in a private sending. *"It is what We all expected would happen sooner or later. The manner seems irregular, but the latitude of the Endtime Work Coordinator is great."*

Still, the tributaries request a complete accounting of the decision. The Coordinator obliges.

A judgment arrives:

The teachers are irrelevant. Teaching of the Proof has been deemed useless; the Coordinator has decided—

I hear a different sort of voice, barely recognizable to me— Elisaveta—

"All affirmations of the Proof merely discourage our search for alternatives. The Proof has become a thought disease, a cultural tyranny. It blocks our discovery of another solution."

A New Accounting

Our ancient self recognizes something in the message. What We have planned from near the beginning now bears fruit—the ancient self, functioning as an engine of judgment and recognition, has found a key player in the decision to isolate us, and to terminate our Library.

"We detect the voice of a particular tributary," We say to the Coordinator. "May We communicate with this tributary?"

"Do you have a valid reason?" the Coordinator asks.

"We must check for error."

"Your talents are not recognized."

"Still, the Coordinator might have erred, and as there is so little time, following the wrong course will be doubly tragic."

The Coordinator reaches a decision after sufficient time to show a complete polling of all tributaries within its social=mind.

"An energy budget is established. Communication is allowed."

We follow protocol billions of years old, but excise unnecessary ceremonies. We poll the student tributaries, searching for some flaw in reasoning, finding none.

Then We begin searching for our own justification. If We are about to *die*, lost in the last-second noise and event-clutter of a universe finally running down, We need to know where *We* have failed. If there is no failure—and if all this experimentation is simply a futile act—We might die less ignominiously. We search for the tributary familiar to the ancient self, hoping to find the personal connection that will reduce all our questions to one exchange.

Bright patches of light in the sky bloom, spread, and are quickly gathered and snuffed. The other suns and worlds are being converted and conserved.

We have minutes, perhaps only seconds.

We find the voice of descendant tributary Elisaveta.

* * *

There are immense deaths in the sky, and now all is going dark. There is only the one sun—turning in on itself, violet changing to deep orange—and the School World.

Four seconds. I have just four seconds . . . Endtime accelerates upon us. The student experiment has consumed so much energy. All other worlds have been terminated, all social=minds except the Endtime Coordinator's and the final self . . . the seed that will cross the actionless Between.

I feel the tributaries frantically create an interface, make distant requests, then demands. They meet strong resistance from a tributary within the Endtime Work Coordinator. This much they convey to me ... I sense weeks, months, years of negotiation, all passing in a second of more and more disjointed and uncertain real time.

As the last energy of the universe is spent, as all potential and all kinesis bottoms out at a useless average, the fractions of seconds become clipped, their qualities altered. Time advances with an irregular jerk, truly like an off-center wheel.

Agreement is reached. Law and persuasion even now have some force.

"Vasily. I haven't thought about you in ever so long."

"Elisaveta, is that you?"

I cannot see her. I sense a total lack of emotion in her words. And why not?

"Not *your* Elisaveta, Vasily. But I hold her memories and some of her patterns."

"You've been alive for billions of years?"

I receive a condensed impression of a hundred million sisters, all related to Elisaveta, stored at different times, like a huge library of past selves. The final tributary she has become, now an important part of the Coordinator, refers to her past selves much as a grown woman might open childhood diaries. The past selves are kept informed, to the extent that being informed does not alter their essential natures.

How differently my own descendant self behaves, sealing away a small part of the past as a reminder, but never consulting it. How perverse for a mind that reveres the past! Perhaps what it reveres is form, not actuality ...

"Why do you want to speak with me?" Elisaveta asks. Which Elisaveta, from which time, I cannot tell right away.

"I think ... *they* seem to think it's important. A disagreement, something that went wrong."

"They are seeking justification through you, a self stored billions of years ago. They want to be told that their final efforts have meaning. How like the Vasily I knew."

"It's not my doing! I've been inactive ... Were we divorced?"

"Yes." Sudden realization changes the tone of this Elisaveta's voice. "You were stored before we divorced?"

"Yes! How long after . . . were you stored?"

"A century, maybe more," she answers. With some wonder, she says, "Who could have known we would live forever?"

"When I saw you last, we loved each other. We had children . . ."

"They died with the Libraries," she says.

I do not feel physical grief, the body's component of sadness and rage at loss, but the news rocks me, even so. I retreat to my gray cubicle. What happened to my children, in my time? What did they become to me, and I to them? Did they have children, grandchildren, and after our divorce, did they respect me enough to let me visit my grandchildren . . .? But it's all lost now, and if they kept records of their ancient selves—records of what had truly been my children—that is gone, too.

My children! They have survived all this time, and yet I have missed them.

They are *dead*.

Elisaveta regards my grief with some wonder and finds it sympathetic. I feel her warm to me slightly. "They weren't really our children any longer, Vasily. They became something quite different, as have you and I. But *this* you—you've been kept like a butterfly in a collection. How sad."

She seeks me out and takes on a bodily form. It is not the shape of the Elisaveta I knew. She once built a biomechanical body to carry her thoughts. This is the self-image she carries now, of a mind within a primitive, woman-shaped soma.

"What happened to us?" I ask, my agony apparent to her, to all who listen.

"Is it that important to you?"

"Can you explain any of this?" I ask. I want to bury myself in her bosom, to hug her. I am so lost and afraid I feel like a child, and yet my pride keeps me together.

"I was your student, Vasily. Remember? You *browbeat* me into marrying you. You poured learning into my ear day and night, even when we made love. You were so full of knowledge. You spoke nine languages. You knew all there was to know about Schopenhauer and Hegel and Marx and Wittgenstein. You did not listen to what was important to me."

I want to draw back; it is impossible to cringe. This I recognize. This I remember. But the Elisaveta I knew had come to accept me, my faults and my learning, joyously; had encouraged me to open up with her. I had taught her a great deal.

"You gave me absolutely no room to grow, Vasily."

The enormous triviality of this conversation, at the end of time, strikes me, and I want to laugh out loud. Not possible. I stare at this *monstrous* Elisaveta, so bitter and different . . . And now, to me, shaded by her indifference.

"I feel like I've been half a dozen men, and we've all loved you badly," I say, hoping to sting her.

"No. Only one. You became angry when I disagreed with you. I asked for more freedom to explore . . . You said there was really little left to explore. Even in the last half of the twenty-first century, Vasily, you said we had found all there was to find, and everything thereafter would be mere details. When I had my second child, it began. I saw you through the eyes of my infant daughter, saw what you would do to her, and I began to grow apart from you. We separated, then divorced, and it was for the best. For me, at any rate; I can't say that you ever understood."

We seem to stand in that gray cubicle, that comfortable simplicity with which I surrounded myself when first awakened.

Elisaveta, taller, stronger, face more seasoned, stares at me with infinitely more experience. I am outmatched.

Her expression softens. "But you didn't deserve *this*, Vasily. You mustn't blame me for what your tributary has done."

"I am not he . . . It. It is not me. And you are not the Elisaveta I know!"

"You wanted to keep me forever the student you first met in your classroom. Do you see how futile that is now?"

"Then what can we love? What is there left to attach to?"

She shrugs. "It doesn't much matter, does it? There's no more time left to love or not to love. And love has become a vastly different thing."

"We reach this *peak* ... of intelligence, of accomplishment, immortality..."

"Wait." Elisaveta frowns and tilts her head, as if listening; lifts her finger in question and listens again to voices I do not hear. "I begin to understand your confusion," she says.

"What?"

"This is not a peak, Vasily. This is a backwater. We are simply all that's left after a long, dreadful attenuation. The greater, more subtle galaxies of Libraries ended themselves a hundred million years ago."

"Suicide?"

"They saw the very end we contemplate now. They decided that if our kind of life had no hope of escaping the Proof—the Proof these teachers helped fix in all our thoughts—then it was best not to send a part of ourselves into the next universe. We are what's left of those who disagreed..."

"My tributary did not tell me this."

"Hiding the truth from yourself even now."

I hold my hands out to her, hoping for pity, but this Elisaveta has long since abandoned pity. I desperately need to activate some fragment of love within her. "I am so lost..."

"We are all lost, Vasily. There is only one hope."

She turns and opens a broad door on one side of my cubicle, where I originally placed the window to the outside. "If we succeed at this," she says, "then we are better than those great souls. If we fail, they were right: better that nothing from our reality crosses the Between."

I admire her for her knowledge, then, for being kept so well informed. But I resent that she has advanced beyond me, has no need for me.

The tributaries watch with interest, like voyeurs.

(*"Perhaps there is a chance,"*) my descendant self says in a private sending.

"I see why you divorced me," I say sullenly.

"You were a tyrant and a bully. When you were stored—before your heart replacement, I remember now . . . When you were stored, you and I had not yet grown so far apart. We would. It was inevitable."

"The Proof is very convincing," I tell Elisaveta. "Perhaps *this* is futile."

"You simply have no say, Vasily. The effort is being made."

I have touched her, but it is not pity I arouse, and certainly not love. It is disgust.

Through the window, Elisaveta and I see a portion of the plain. On it, the experiments have congealed into a hundred, a thousand, smooth, slowly pulsing shapes. Above them all looms the shadow of the Coordinator. I feel a bridge being made, links being established. I sense panic in my descendant self, who works without the knowledge of the other tributaries.

Then I am asked, "*Will you become part of the experiment?*"

"*I don't understand.*"

"*You are the judgment engine.*"

"Now I must go," Elisaveta says. "We will all die soon. Neither you nor I are in the final self. No part of the teachers, or the Coordinator, will cross the Between."

"All futile, then," I say.

"Why so, Vasily? When I was young, you told me that change was an evil force, and that you longed for an eternal college, where all learning could be examined at leisure, without pressure. You've found that. Your tributary self has had billions of years to study the unchanging truths. And to infuse them into new tributaries. You've had your heaven, and I've had mine. Away from you, among those who nurture and respect."

I am left with nothing to say. Then, unexpectedly, the figure of Elisaveta reaches out with a nonexistent hand and touches my unreal cheek. For a moment, between us, there is something like the contact of flesh on flesh. I feel her fingers. She feels my cheek. Despite her words, the love has not died completely.

She fades from the cubicle. I rush to the window, to see if I can make out the Coordinator, but the shadow, the mercury-liquid cloud, has already vanished.

"They will fail," the We-ness says. It surrounds me with its mind, its persuasion, greater in scale than a human of my time to an ant. "This shows the origin of their folly. We have justified our existence."

(You can still cross. There is still a connection between you. You can judge the experiment, go with the Endtime Work Coordinator.)

I watch the plain, the joined shapes. They are extraordinarily beautiful, like condensed cities or civilizations or entire histories.

The sunlight dims, light rays jerk in our sight, in our fading scales of time.

(Will you go?)

"She doesn't need me . . ." I want to go with Elisaveta. I want to reach out to her and shout, "I see! I understand!" But there is still sadness and self-pity. I am, after all, too small for her.

(You may go. Persuade. Carry us with you.)

And billions of years too late—

Shards of Seconds

We know now that the error lies in the distant past, a tendency of the Coordinator, who has gathered tributaries of like character. As did the teachers. The past still dominates, and there is satisfaction in knowing We, at least, have not committed any errors, have not fallen into folly.

We observe the end with interest. Soon, there will be no change. In that, there is some cause for exultation. Truly, We are tired.

On the bubbling remains of the School World, the students in their Berkus continue to the last instant with the experiment, and We watch from the cracked and cooling hill.

Something huge and blue and with many strange calm aspects rises from the field of experiments. It does not remind us of anything We have seen before.

It is new.

The Coordinator returns, embraces it, draws it away.

* * *

("She does not tell the truth. Parts of the Endtime Coordinator must cross with the final self. This is your last chance. Go to her and reconcile. Carry our thoughts with you.")

I feel a love for her greater than anything I could have felt before. I hate my descendant self; I hate the teachers and their gray spirits, depth upon depth of ashes out of the past. They want to use me to perpetuate all that matters to them.

I ache to reclaim what has been lost, to try to make up for the past.

The Coordinator withdraws from School World, taking with it the results of the student experiment. Do they have what they want—something worthy of being passed on? It would be wonderful to know ... I could die contented, knowing the Proof has been shattered. I could cross over, ask ...

But I will not pollute her with me anymore.

"No."

The last thousandths of the last second fall like broken crystals.

(The connection is broken. You have failed.)

My tributary self, disappointed, quietly suggests I might be happier if I am deactivated.

* * *

Curiously, to the last, he clings to his imagined cubicle window. He cries his last words where there is no voice, no sound, no one to listen but us:

"Elisaveta! YES! YES!"

The last of the ancient self is packed, mercifully, into oblivion. We will not subject him to the Endtime. We have pity.

We are left to our thoughts. The force that replaces gravity now spasms. The metric is very noisy. Length and duration become so grainy that thinking is difficult.

One tributary works to solve an ancient and obscure problem. Another studies the Proof one last time, savoring its formal beauty. Another considers ancient relations.

Our end, our own oblivion, the Between, will not be so horrible. There are worse things. Much

Automatic

Erica L. Satifka

HE rents his optic nerve to vacationers from Ganymede for forty skins a night. She finds him in the corner of the bar he goes to every night after work and stays in until it's time to go to work again, sucking on an electrical wire that stretches from the flaking wall.

"That's not going to kill you any more," she says.

He ignores her, grinding sheathed copper between brown-stained molars.

"My name is Linda Sue. I want to make babies with you."

"That rhymes," he says.

"Will you do it or not?"

"Or not."

Linda Sue stamps her foot. "Come on."

"I'll take you out first. Then we'll see." He takes her by the hand and leads her out of the bar, out into the heart of downtown New York City.

New York City, population three hundred and twenty.

* * *

He guides her to a restaurant he knows where the food is stacked in piles on hygienic white counters and the electricity works. She has two eyes and two hands and one set of lips, which means she is pretty. They each take a few slabs of food—the food here is free—and sit on the ground. He tells her about his life and her eyes open wide as headlights.

"I've never known anyone who had a job before."

193

"It's not a job. It's a career." He works at a factory, pouring liquid plastic into molds shaped like four-tined forks. "I have a quota to fill."

"Why don't you just ask the Ganys for plastic forks? Why does someone need so many plastic forks anyway." She tears off a corner of her foodslab; it comes off onto her fingers like cotton candy. Or insulation.

"They're not for me, they're for people."

"I don't have to work. I don't like to. I just ask the Ganys for everything. They like to give us stuff."

"Well, I don't ask them." He doesn't think about the creatures dancing spider-like on his nerve. "I'm self-sufficient."

"Are we going to fuck or what?"

"Later, later. If you're good."

* * *

In Central Park they walk past a rusted-over carousel. She's drunk from the amber-colored alcohol-infused drinkslab she's consumed, and he's propping her up, forcing her to walk straight.

"I think I'm in love with you," she slurs.

"You don't know what that word means."

They pass a pair of Ganys wrapped in the form of two wall-eyed Jamaican teenagers, humans whose bodies were either sacrificed to or commandeered by the intelligent energy beams. The girls giggle and point as they pass. He flips them off.

"That wasn't very nice."

"They patronize us. Don't you see how they patronize us? There's too many of them in this city. I want to get away from here, out into the country. Will you come with me?"

"Nobody lives in the country."

"Exactly." But he knows it is pointless; nobody lives in the country because there is no way to live in the country. The farms are all poisoned and the shadow of the plague still lingers. The Ganys, knowing this, constructed an invisible olfactory wall, to keep humans and germs from mingling.

He will never leave New York City. Always a hotel, never a tourist.

* * *

The story of the plague goes like this:

Once you could be certain that you would not spontaneously grow legs from your shoulder blades and arms from your buttocks. You could be reasonably sure that ears would not sprout on your cheeks overnight. Then the plague happened, and you couldn't take that for granted anymore.

Until the Ganys came.

* * *

They get back to the bar and she takes off her clothes. Her ribs stick out like a xylophone. The foodslabs keep them alive, but they aren't the right kind of nourishment. But you couldn't expect intelligent energy beams to understand food.

Linda Sue's body is fuzzy and indistinct, a peach-colored blur. His vision is cloudy from the tourists in his head. He crawls back to his corner.

"Aren't you going to fuck me now? Aren't you going to give me my babies?"

"No, I'm still not ready."

"Oh, screw you! You're crazy. Why don't you get the Ganys to fix that for you? They fixed it for me."

Now all you want to do is mate, he thinks. Not make love, you can't love anymore. Mate with the last members of your species so you can bring us back from the brink of extinction. That's all it is.

"I can't."

She shakes her head. "I'm leaving. I can find some other male to give me my babies. I don't need you." She slams the lockless door behind her. He hunkers down in the corner.

* * *

He awakes to unclouded vision. The vacationers checked out of his optic nerve as he slept. He rubs his empty eyes and stumbles to the corner market, where he throws down a few skins and picks up some foodslabs.

"You don't have to pay for those," the Gany monitoring the electricity says.

"Yes, I do."

It would be so easy, he thinks sometimes, to go down to the place where the Ganys congregate, the place where you can go rent your body for a day or a lifetime to their volunteers, and just turn yourself over. Shut off your brain for as long as you wanted, and you'd get a nice pile of goodies when your assignment was over. But he'd never done that. Renting his eyes was as far as he'd go. And even that was done not out of love for the aliens or the desire for material objects but the knowledge that, if he did not do it, he would be marked a traitor and slated for commandeering.

The Ganys have taken a special interest in humans. They had cordoned them off in cities with invisible olfactory walls, so that the remaining humans would be able to find one another more easily. And of course, they had brought The Cure. All of it was done for our—no, he thinks, their—own good.

He takes a dramatic bow, as if addressing a live audience. And in a way, he is.

* * *

He's leaving the city today. He crams a stack of foodslabs into a looted knapsack and heads north on foot. He walks until the sun is directly overhead and then stops by a river to eat.

The river is contaminated; he can smell the plague in it, festering. But there are drinkslabs in his pack, too. He tears off a few chunks of the tasteless foam and presses on.

A half hour later he is halted by a smell halfway between burning plastic and dog shit. I've reached it, he thinks. The wall between New York City and the rest of the world. He holds his breath and trudges through the wall, but it is no use. He can't hold his breath forever. His chest deflates and the putrescent odor fills his nose and lungs, as if the dog shit is being shoveled into his mouth by the handful. He gags, and vomits up a piece of semi-digested foodslab. Choking, he runs out of the wall, and takes a whiff of pure air.

He didn't even make it past the fifty yard line.

Plunging back in, he finds the smell has changed. Now it's the scent of burning tires. He moves to the right and hits a wall of solid rotting flowers. Moving forward, there is a stench like fish guts being baked in the sun. He stumbles backwards, and falls into the strong arms of a stranger.

"Hello there, little guy," a park ranger says. He looks into the ranger's crossed and clouded eyes. A Gany.

"I couldn't get past the wall," he says. His eyes are running with tears and there is vomit on his chin.

"You shouldn't be out here all alone." The ranger gestures at his vehicle. "C'mon, let me give you a ride back home."

He doesn't want to take charity from a Gany, but he doesn't like the prospect of walking three and a half hours either, especially since he still can't breathe in all the way and his stomach feels swollen and fluttery. He gets in the vehicle.

"You have a mate back at home?" Of course, that's the first thing the ranger would say.

"No."

"Human beings should be fruitful and multiply. It says so in your holy book." The Gany speaks with the friendly, homey Upper New York accent that was the ranger's voice when he was in control of the body, but he can sense the cold analytical tone of the intelligent energy beam guiding it.

He grunts and turns back to the window. Less than twenty minutes later the four-wheel-drive all-terrain vehicle pulls up in front of his bar. That fucking Gany read his mind.

"You be safe now, partner."

He slams the door.

In the apartment building across the street two humans are mating. For a moment, he wonders what it would be like to forget everything, become a creature of instinct, every moment of your life unscripted and so automatic.

Then he goes back into the bar.

THE BLACK MOULD

MARK SAMUELS

THE mould first appeared in a crater on a dead world at the rim of the universe. This world, with a thin atmosphere and a surface that comets and meteors had battered for millions of years, spun in a void of sunless dark. Perhaps it had been one of those comet collisions that had brought the mould into existence, some unique arrangement of molecules mutated by radiation and lying dormant in the comet's slushy ice, something waiting to awaken and grow. The mould may have taken aeons to reach maturity and begin the process of reproduction. But when it did so, it grew rapidly and spread unchecked over the surface of that dead world, across its valleys and craters and mountains, across the equator and from pole to pole.

Once it had conquered that first world it became conscious, such was the size and complexity of the mould. The billions upon billions of simple cells formed a network that developed into a debased, gigantic hive-mind. The mould experienced a progressively horrible sequence of nightmares, a spiral of nameless dread without a centre. Its form of consciousness did not include the faculty of reason, but was a unique faculty; that of derangement. And its monstrous visions grew more intense as it spread, ever more profound in their ineffable malignity.

When it had conquered that dead and distant world, after everything lay under its ghastly black embrace, its nightmares demanded that it reach out across the void. And so trillions of spores were ejected into space.

In the end it brought ghastly, complete darkness to that unknown quarter of cosmic space, for it learnt how to suffocate stars.

It was terror, deepening without cessation, which bore aloft the spores of the mould on their voyage through interstellar space. Nightmarish ecstasy was the soul of the mould. It hungered and sought to consume the universe itself. Its dread was of a nameless horror, a stark madness beyond imagination; an ultimate horror that lurked somewhere in the universe but which it could not yet identify.

The mould had no means of recognising any other form of consciousness apart from its own. As it reproduced, the nameless dread that assailed it became exponentially complex. It existed only in order to experience the ultimate nightmare, the heart of horror, the petrifying vision that ends only in oblivion. It was in the attempt to destroy itself that the mould consumed everything around it, and dimly it looked forward to a time when there was nothing left to consume, when the entire universe was laid waste, and it would wither and die for want of sustenance. It was one entity, eventually separated by the inconceivable vastness of the intergalactic void, and with each spore exhaled between worlds still a component of the whole. Its nightmares were communicated telepathically and were not slowed by the immensity of the cosmos. Dreams are swifter than light.

When the spores found a world, be it asteroid, moon or planet, they would drift to its surface like soft rain and begin the process of assimilating whatever was found there. Where once there was a mighty empire with towers that reached to the heavens, soon after there were only ruins, and the black mould consumed the creatures of that world. Only husks remained as evidence that they had ever existed at all.

The ravages of the mould increased as it multiplied. As immeasurable time passed, countless galaxies bore the evidence of its all-conquering reign. Where there had been a multitude of worlds of differing aspects, of arid yellow deserts, of misty and scarred blue ice, of airless grey dust, now all were identical. All were blackened, their surfaces entirely smothered by the mould: canyons and mountains, plateaux and craters, cities and forests, ice and sand, even oceans (choked by a miasmal slime that conquered all incalculable depths). The mould flourished everywhere and anywhere. It mattered not if its habitat were a world of liquid methane or water, or a world roasting close to a star, or a world far flung out in space and frozen at absolute zero.

Astronomers on distant worlds looked on with dread at the development. Those that perceived it not, perished all the same. Multiform were the species of the universe, following different paths of evolution and modes of thought, though none were as the mould. But all those that looked outward at the universe felt wonder and terror, whether they were taloned crustaceans in a fungous jungle, cognisant machines of incredible technological complexity, or peace-loving sea mammals that gazed with dark eyes at the stars above the waters of an alien world. All knew the end was near and their kind would, ere centuries had passed, be consumed and then participate in the cosmic corruption of the mould.

One insignificant species amongst the many millions in the universe succumbed to the mould after vain attempts to resist its advance. This species, a nearly hairless race of anthropoids, habited the third planet orbiting an undistinguished star. The mould consumed the outer gas giants and the satellites of this solar system one by one. The simians watched with mounting terror as the spores drew inexorably nearer, moving unaccountably against the solar wind and turning the red desert planet in fourth orbit as black as the other outer worlds.

By the time the mould had reached the third planet's only satellite the hairless apes were in turmoil. Their civilisation was on the brink of anarchy and they were close to destroying themselves. The light cast by the world's moon at night was no longer white but a deathly grey, shading to black, and becoming dim. It bore the same affliction that had reigned throughout all those galactic regions the mould had conquered. There were morbid ape poets that wrote verses to the contagion and seemed to welcome the insidious nightmares that foretold complete assimilation. But other apes, vainglorious followers of science, who fired rockets into the heavens, watched the explosions that took place on their moon with desperate hope. The satellite bore a hellish aspect, utterly unfamiliar to them. The mould had rendered it terrifying: like decay in a corpse.

And when the spores finally filtered down onto their own world, there were many more explosions and scenes of horror amongst the hairless apes as they turned on themselves, blaming each other for the failure to resist what was, after all, inevitable.

And it was not long before the streets of their cities were thick with the mould, not long before black slime ran in the water, not long before the anthropoids found the first patches of black ichors on their skins. And then the endless dreams came, just before the mould completely consumed the helpless simians.

As soon as the star of that solar system was overrun and suffocated, the spores progressed onwards, their numbers always swelled by the exhalations of the solar systems consumed before. Across the unknown stellar gulfs spread the contagion, never once halted in its expansion. There were other civilisations that tried to resist its advance, but all perished in the end. The most advanced ones, who had cunning and the available means, elected to flee before the mould's arrival. But even these were caught up with and consumed in the end. After aeons, all those that fled found that there was no longer anywhere left to hide.

The mould and its spores became omnipresent throughout the universe. The gas clouds and the gulfs of space were choked with spores. And yet the mould had not achieved its goal. Although the entire universe had been laid waste, and neither life nor thought existed, except for the mould and its exponential nameless dread, still it had not achieved the final petrifying vision that could terrify it into self-extinction.

And so the spores poured into those stars that had reached the final point of collapse, into the black holes scattered throughout the cosmos. The mould appeared in other universes and in every epoch across those other dimensions. It spread and adapted as voraciously as it had ever done, unchecked and irresistible, from the beginning until the end of all existence.

But the ultimate, petrifying vision could still not be glimpsed and the mould, now the supreme conqueror, dreamed on and on in its hideous majesty; doomed to re-experience its nameless dread forever; for it was the mould itself that was the ultimate horror and of itself it had never dreamed.

It groped futilely, as one in darkness gropes for the light, backwards and forwards throughout all space and time, until all that had been, and all that was to be, fell under its dominion. And there was to be no release from the nightmare.

THE PRETENCE

RAMSEY CAMPBELL

As the taxi drew up outside the terminal the driver said "What time's your flight?"

"In about an hour."

"Where are you flying?"

"To the mainland. Just to Liverpool."

"You'll be home before tomorrow, then."

"I expect so." Though he didn't see why this should concern her, Slater said "I'm sure I shall."

An April breeze like a reminiscence of a summer holiday set palm leaves chattering above him while he paid the fare. As he made for the terminal, the glass doors slipped apart, letting out a young woman so wide-eyed that her stare seemed to render her pale face even thinner. She thrust a glossy brochure at him, and he took it for a special offer until he glanced at it, having trundled his suitcase into the departure hall. The cover of the pamphlet showed a clock without hands and urged **SEE YOUR TIME** in type as thick as blackened matchsticks. It could almost have been directing his attention to the matrix sign that showed his flight was delayed. He wouldn't be home by midnight after all; he mightn't even be on land.

Having failed to locate a handy bin, Slater crumpled the pamphlet in his fist as he led his luggage to the security gates. On the far side of the electronic barrier he retrieved his watch and cash and mobile phone from the tray that emerged from the scanner like a car at the end of a fairground ride. He was putting on his shoes when the guard beside the conveyor belt beckoned to him. "Excuse me, sir, we don't need that."

She meant the brochure he'd left in the tray. "Can you bin it for me?"

"I can't." Apparently he'd ceased to be a sir. "Please take it," she said.

It was her reproachful look that made him blurt "You're a Finalist, are you?"

"We aren't permitted to discuss our faith, sir." Though she'd reverted to professionalism, her eyes hadn't quite caught up, and she leaned across the dormant belt to murmur "If I were you I'd read what you have there."

He already knew what they believed—he imagined nobody could avoid knowing—and he tramped away so fast that his shoelaces lashed the tiled floor. He sat down to tie them before wadding the brochure to lob it into the nearest bin. As he made for the bar through the duty-free court, sunglasses gave him a host of black looks while a multitude of watches showed him the time, the time, the time. Nobody was seated at the bar itself, though a few of the tables were occupied. Slater perched on a stool at the bar and ordered a glass of merlot. "A large one," he said.

The barman was a broad slow fellow with a tentatively amused expression. As he brought Slater the glass he said "Another one held up."

"Me, you mean." The barman could have been referring to the plane, but when he didn't admit to it Slater said "No point in fussing over it. I'll be home when I am."

"You're not holding your breath for the end of the world, then."

"I can't believe anybody is. It's not as if this is the first time that was supposed to happen. It's been meant to end a dozen times in this century alone."

"Maybe it did."

Presumably this was the style of joke the barman had been waiting to deliver. "I don't know why so many people have got it into their heads this time," Slater complained. "You'd think by now they would know better."

"If you ask me it's all the computers. They're meant to be giving us more of a mind, but it's got stuff like that in it."

"The internet, you're saying. It contains everything, that's the problem."

"So none of us know what the world's like any more."

"I shouldn't think it's quite as bad as that. My mother has no time for computers but she knows what the Finalists are saying will happen."

"It's like I say, they get in everybody's head."

"She's why I was over here. She and her friends have been working themselves up so much that she had an attack."

"Better now, is she?"

"She is since I got her to talk about it. I did think the care home staff might have."

"I couldn't put my folks in one of those places."

"My parents came to live on the island," Slater said with some resentment, "and that's where she says she wants to stay."

"What we say isn't always what we think. Won't she be fretting about not seeing you tomorrow?"

"I'd already booked the flight. I could have stayed longer with her if I'd known it was going to be late."

"Thought you weren't bothered about that," the barman said as if he'd been presented with a reason for amusement. "Well, it'll all be over by tomorrow."

Slater saw people at the tables lift their heads as if they'd sensed danger. He took hold of his glass, only to find he'd drained it while talking. "Same again," he said. "I'll just find something to read."

As he made for the bookshop, such as it was—the first items he saw in it were earplugs and blindfolds—he took out his mobile and sent Melanie a message. Plane late. Don't know how long. He leafed through the newspapers, which felt oddly out of date, containing not a single reference to the Finalists and their dogged prophecy, though of course that was hardly news any more, if it ever had been. Too many of the paperbacks on display seemed designed to resemble one another—he could almost have taken them for the products of a single mind—and in any case he didn't expect to have time to finish or even get far into one. He bought a music magazine that reviewed new releases, and was returning to the bar when his mobile emitted its version of Beethoven's pastoral hymn. "Hold on," he told Melanie and paid the barman before carrying his glass to a table. "Here I am."

"Where's here, Paul?"

"Still at the airport. On the island, I mean."

"Oh dear. Well, it can't be helped." She let out a breath like a delicate sniff in reverse and said "What's the situation, do we know?"

"Do we know what the delay is?" Slater called to the barman.

"The way I heard it, some of the crew didn't show up for work."

"Let's hope they're ill, then," Melanie said.

This was a decidedly untypical wish, and then Slater understood. "Rather than nervous of flying tonight, you mean."

"So long as there's someone who isn't."

"Of course I'm not," Slater said before he grasped that she wasn't referring to him. As he looked away from a woman who was staring reproachfully at him he felt prompted to ask "How are Tom and Amy?"

"Asleep, I hope."

"You may as well be too. That's to say don't wait till I come home."

"You know I'll be waiting even if I'm asleep." As if she hadn't changed the subject Melanie said "How's Eileen now?"

"I think I've put her right. I just wonder if any of the staff at the home believe that rubbish. Well, they won't for much longer."

"That'll be strange for them," Melanie said. "See you however late you are, then."

"Absolutely, yes. See you then."

He would have added some endearments if he hadn't felt overheard in the bar. He ended the call and was pocketing the mobile when a voice behind him said "Anybody here think we're all stopping at midnight?"

The speaker—a small man who appeared to have concentrated most of his bulk in his stomach—was at a table by himself. A scowl clenched his mottled reddish face, which was decorated with a fading false moustache, a strip of foam from his latest pint of beer. "Don't be shy if you're one of that lot," he urged so vigorously that he left some consonants behind.

Slater supposed his phone call had provoked the outburst. He turned away as other customers lowered their heads or resumed their conversations, but the man wasn't so easily ignored. "Don't any of us read the Bible? Me neither, but they've told us what they say it says."

A sinking movement drew Slater's attention to the window, but it was the reflection of the man's tankard, not a plane. "The Koran too," the man said less distinctly, "and the rest of them fairy tales. Shows how much crap they are when that's all they can agree about."

Was everyone as embarrassed as Slater? The lack of a response only antagonised the man. "Who's keeping quiet?" he more or less pronounced. "Don't tell me there's none of you here. My lad's computer says you're everywhere."

Slater felt the man's gaze on the nape of his neck, though he couldn't tell from the reflection where the fellow was looking. Perhaps the sensation simply proved how much that you took for the external world was happening inside you. It dissipated as the man said "Come to think, they won't be travelling tonight. They're all praying the rest of us are wrong, I shouldn't wonder."

As the man's reflection slumped back in its chair Slater finished his drink. He oughtn't to have any more when he didn't know how soon he might be driving. He leafed through the magazine, but the names of favourite composers and their works didn't sound many notes in his head. He shut his eyes to rest them for a moment—at least, that was all he intended, but he was wakened by the man behind him. "It's here."

A plane was coasting past the window, with Slater's heartbeat for its soundtrack. It glided out of sight, and he felt as if he were a member of a chorus all holding their breaths. Certainly he wasn't alone in breathing aloud when a voice from above invited passengers for John Lennon to the gate. Several people raised a feeble if not ironic cheer, and as the barman called "Safe home" Slater found himself humming a snatch of "Imagine" as a reminiscence of the singer who'd lent the Liverpool airport his name.

While the bar and then the passage to the gate resounded with a prolonged drumroll of luggage, the elevated voice advised passengers to have their boarding cards and passports ready. No doubt the airline was attempting to make up for the delay, since a uniformed woman had already opened the exit to the airfield. "Come straight to me," she said.

She barely glanced at Slater's documents before she scanned his boarding card. A boxy corridor reverberated with his luggage and led him out beneath a black sky, in which he imagined more stars were visible than he had time to glimpse. At the top of the steps to the plane a woman in a larger version of the airline uniform looked impatient for the passengers to cross the tarmac. A man in a suit that identified him as a pilot ushered Slater to a seat halfway down the aisle, not the place he'd been assigned. "There's just a few of you tonight," the pilot said. "We're seating you for balance."

"Thanks for taking the trouble for us."

"Someone had to. The job's the job."

Slater hoisted his suitcase into the overhead locker and was fastening his safety belt as the pilot found a seat for the last passenger to board, the small big-bellied fellow. The larger stewardess oversaw the man's audibly peevish struggle with his seatbelt while the pilot shut himself in the cockpit, and then there was silence apart from a murmur of music that sounded reluctant to take much shape or to make clear which if any instruments were involved. The steps backed away from the plane as the pilot's voice set about directing the cabin crew. As soon as the plane began to taxi he apologised for the delay, and then a recorded message prompted the cabin crew to perform their safety mime, which was so familiar that Slater could easily have dreamed it. The small man gave it a loose round of applause while the plane gathered speed, and the tarmac fell away as the plane sailed up into a larger darkness. The wing tilted as if the earth was calling it back, and Slater watched a few illuminated roads dwindle to filaments before the island drifted down the inclined sea into the dark.

He could have been gesturing at the night as he flourished his wristwatch. It would be midnight in not much over a quarter of an hour. Waiting for the slimmer stewardess to wheel a trolley down the aisle used up several minutes, and obtaining a bottle of water took one more. He sucked at the plastic nipple and then picked up his magazine, but leafing through it felt like trying to recapture information. Did he need to stay awake? Wouldn't it be wiser to catch a little sleep before he had to drive? He closed his eyes and felt the magazine sliding out of his hands until he fumbled it onto the seat beside him. His head drooped and jerked up and sank again, and the low unchanging chord of the engines seemed to expand to meet him. Then they cut out, or rather his consciousness did, and he knew nothing until he came back to himself with a violent lurch.

It felt worse than any panic he'd experienced in his life—worse than the endless minutes he'd once spent searching for baby Tom and lost toddler Amy in the retail park where he worked. He felt as though his innards had dropped out of him, and he was just a shell that ached with emptiness. He wasn't even seated any longer; he'd plummeted into the dark so violently that it had snatched away his vision along with his ability to breathe. He was utterly alone in the midst of a vast silence unrelieved by so much as a heartbeat. He couldn't have said whether it lasted for an instant or longer than he had the means to comprehend before he heard a voice. "Just someone expected word you meant," it said.

Or was it saying that he'd sent someone a worm or that they expected a firmament? He had to struggle to grasp who was speaking, and then he managed to deduce that the pilot was apologising for some unexpected turbulence. As he risked opening his eyes his sight returned, unless the uncontrollable lurch of the aircraft had put out the lights in the cabin at the moment he'd jerked awake. How could the voice be declaring "Police state sees to damned"? No, it was telling the passengers "Please stay seated and keep your belts fastened. Justify caution. No cause for alarm."

The last words let Slater understand that the pilot had said it only as a precaution. He could have thought the turbulence had dislodged his perceptions, which might explain why he felt so alone in the cabin. The lights were dimmer than he remembered, and they appeared to be showing him row after row of empty seats. He was absurdly grateful to hear a blurred voice. "Christ, give us a drink."

The tops of heads rose above half a dozen seats, and Slater glanced around to see faces leaning into the aisle like cards displayed by a cagey player. The stewardess who'd been at the boarding gate appeared from behind a curtain near the cockpit to murmur "We're only serving water now, sir, and could you please watch your language."

"Holy water, is it? We'll be needing more than that if you keep on chucking us about."

"We've started our dissent," Slater heard her say until he thought about it. A glance at his watch showed him that the time was several minutes after midnight. He'd no idea how much time had passed since the plane had encountered the turbulence, and there was certainly no reason to ask. All that mattered was that they would be landing soon, and he strained his eyes at the blackness that appeared to have become the substance of the window. At first he wasn't sure that he was seeing tiny lights lying too low for stars, and then the pattern like a distant constellation resolved itself into a set of grids. They were marking airstrips, and he didn't need the announcement that the plane was about to land.

Perhaps the pilot was resolved to make up for the turbulence, since they touched down as if the plane weighed nothing to speak of. It came to a virtually imperceptible halt while noises almost too undefined to resemble music hovered in the cabin, and then a staircase lumbered out of the dark. The more substantial of the stewardesses opened the door to it, and her colleague waited on the tarmac to point the passengers towards the terminal. Slater made for the entrance so fast he hadn't time to notice any stars in the black sky, but when he stepped into the extensive bare white room he had to join a queue for the solitary operating immigration booth.

He'd never seen anyone so apparently determined not just to do but to look like their job. The officer's long face was an all-purpose warning, and jowls resembling a bloodhound's made it even more morose. He questioned a woman at length before sending her on her way and beckoning the next passenger forward. He was still quizzing her when the man with the prominent stomach began to complain. "What's the holdup this time? Some of us want to get home."

The immigration officer sent him an ominous look that only provoked him to raise his voice. "We're all Brits here, aren't we? Don't treat us like we've landed somewhere else."

Before he'd finished speaking two men in identical sombre suits appeared from behind a partition beyond the booths and converged on the protester. "Please come with us," one said—Slater couldn't tell which.

"That's more like. You don't get anywhere if you don't kick up a row."

One official led the way between two empty booths while the other followed close behind the passenger. When they reached the partition the man turned to the queue as if his belly was swinging him around. "You want to kick up as well," he told them. "Hang on, where are you taking—"

As his escorts ushered him behind the partition, each with a hand on one of his arms, his voice ceased. The only sounds were at the booth. At last the officer handed back the woman's passport and beckoned Slater with a gesture reminiscent of a fighter summoning an opponent. Slater tried offering a generalised smile along with his passport, but the overture might as well have been invisible. "Name?" the officer said.

"Paul Slater. Derek Paul, if you want the whole thing."

"Which are you?"

"I was born Derek Paul. Not born it, obviously, but that's what they called me when they did. I left Derek behind a long time ago."

"You've changed your name."

"Not officially, no. It's still in there if you look."

The officer opened the passport at the identification page and glanced away at last from Slater's face. "Date of birth."

"Just had my birthday last week. Twenty-third of April." Since this apparently wasn't enough Slater added "Seventy-six."

"Age."

For a moment Slater didn't know, or at least had to remember the date. His answer only made way for another toneless question. "Place of birth."

"Right here in Liverpool."

"Citizenship."

"British." With a surge of the irritation that had seized the protester in the queue Slater said "Can't you tell?"

"Date of expiry."

"Not for a long time yet, I hope." This went unappreciated too. "The passport, you mean," he said. "I'm not really sure without looking. Since when were we expected to be?"

If there was any answer in the unwavering pale gaze, it was just an admonition. "Wait a minute," Slater said with no idea of what he was preventing. "It's, don't tell me, no, I see you wouldn't. It's, hold on now, yes, it's next, next March."

The man shut the passport without another glance. "You are advised to leave sufficient time for the renewal."

As Slater took hold of the passport he said "Do you mind if I ask what you're looking for?"

"Why should you want to know that?"

"I don't suppose I need to. In fact I'm sure I don't." Slater was about to risk tugging at the passport—the man's grasp felt like a confirmation of the warning in his eyes—when he found he was alone in holding it. "Thank you for," he said and couldn't leave the word dangling. "Thank you for your time."

He expected to find a door behind the partition on the far side of the booths, but there was just a blank wall. The partition must cut off any sounds; he couldn't even hear the interrogation that would be following his. The arrivals hall was deserted, and the shops were blanked out by metal shutters. As he hurried to the exit the high roof seemed to shrink his footsteps until they were no more substantial than their echoes. His reflection was growing on the glass doors when they parted with a gasp like the last of a breath.

Above the lamps that glared down on the car park the sky could almost have been a roof they were set in. No doubt they were helping to render it so black. The multitude of cars appeared to be forgetting their own colours, and if he hadn't memorised the location of the Astra—section E for *Eroica* and for the key of the symphony as well, third row like the number of the symphony—he might have panicked. He had to rouse it with the key fob before he was sure that the grey car was his gold one. He rested a hand on its hollow metal pate while he gazed at the sky until he succeeded in conjuring forth a star attended by three other intermittently visible gleams. He found them oddly reassuring, and so were the headlamps once he switched them on, and the dashboard lights that Tom and Amy used to pretend were the lights on the control panel in a cockpit. Some if not all of this felt like a promise of the lights of home.

The barrier raised its arm to point at the sky. Along the empty four-lane road that led away from the airport, the branches of thin trees netted scraps of the blackness. Single-storey blocks of grey corrugated metal flanked the road, and Slater hadn't previously realised how little the route offered for the mind to grasp. Miles later he came to the first houses, in which every window was as black as the sky. Beyond the houses ranks of headstones stretched away on both sides of the road into the dark, and he couldn't recall ever having taken so long to leave the cemetery behind. At last the road widened, and soon the grassy strip between the pairs of deserted lanes was as broad as a road itself. The elongated grove that stood on it, and the fields that kept interrupting the parade of unlit houses, had begun to feel as if the land was reminiscing about itself. No doubt the night was giving Slater thoughts like these, along with a sense of isolation.

As he turned along St Peter Street he couldn't immediately see the house; the trees standing in square plots on the pavements blocked his view. He was nearly home by the time he saw that the windows were full of the sky, like mirrors with nothing to show. He parked beside Melanie's Viva on the drive and carried his suitcase to the front door rather than risk disturbing anyone with the sound of the wheels. He was finding his keys when the four panes in the door lit up as though he'd triggered an alarm.

He saw Melanie's silhouette descend into the hall with a flickering movement reminiscent of an old film. Her shape was snagging on the frosted panes, which made her look intermittently atomised. She must mean not to waken the children, since he couldn't hear her footsteps. The glass tried to recompose her features as she opened the door, and then her large generous face seemed to brighten the night with a smile. She stood on the threshold and hugged him with all her strength, whispering "Is it really you at last, Paul?"

"I can't imagine who else it's likely to be," Slater murmured. She was in just her dressing-gown, which fluttered as a chill wind reminded him of the hour. "Let's get you inside," he said. "I don't want to lose you, do I?"

She tilted her head back without letting go of him, and her glossy black hair trailed over her shoulders as her oval brown eyes seemed to deepen with a question. "How are you going to do that?"

"I'm saying I'm not. You aren't dressed for out here, that's all."

She shook her head, presumably at herself, as they retreated into the hall, and he was managing to shut the door without a sound when Amy called "Is that dad?"

"Is it, mummy?" Tom contributed at once.

As he appeared at the top of the stairs Amy joined him. They looked like sleepy versions of their images that lined the hall and climbed beside the stairs, framed photographs of the family holidaying in half a dozen European countries. Yet again Slater found himself thinking how his and Melanie's features had been displaced: the nine-year-old boy made his mother's face male with hair cropped almost as short as he would like, while Amy's extra pair of years hadn't altered her resemblance to her father—blue eyes set wide, rounded face except for the prominent chin, small mouth. "Now you've seen him you can both go back to sleep," Melanie said. "You've school and rehearsals as well."

"Can't we stay up? It's nearly time to go."

"Nowhere near, Tom," Slater said before he saw what time the pincers of the hour and minute hands were closing on. "We aren't even close to four," he said.

"Can't we wait anyway? I don't feel like going to sleep."

"And I don't," his sister declared.

"There's nothing to keep you awake, is there? I'm sorry if I did, but it's not my fault I was held up. It's your last rehearsal today and we want to be proud of you both. I'm sure you want that as well."

"You know we both do," Melanie said.

"That's right," Slater said, which seemed inadequate. "Just remember you two and your mother are all I need in my life. You can think about that while you go to sleep."

As he hefted the suitcase Melanie switched out the hall light, and he saw the children's eyes grow dark. When Tom lingered beside the highest photograph Slater felt he had to ask "What were you saying you wanted to wait for?"

"The sun." With some defiance the boy said "It won't be today till it comes up."

"You mean it won't stop being yesterday," Amy said.

While Slater thought she was doing her best to scoff, he was uncertain whether she secretly shared the idea. "Come on, you two," he said. "Don't tell me you're still bothered by that nonsense. I didn't think you ever were."

Was that too rough? They seemed less than reassured. "If you were worried because I wasn't here when—"

"Can we leave it, Paul? This isn't the time for it, especially if you want anyone to sleep."

"All I'm saying," Slater said, "is we're all here and it's the day after, and that shows there was no reason to worry in the first place."

"Well, you've said it now, and it's time everyone was in bed."

When the children headed for their rooms as if they were competing to mime reluctance Slater said "If the sun doesn't wake you we'll tell you when it's here."

He followed Melanie into their bedroom to leave his suitcase by the bed, and felt her watching him all the way out of the room. In the bathroom the electronic buzz of the toothbrush filled his skull while his reflection grimaced at him. He had the odd notion that the sight and its monotonous two-note chord—the high whine of the motor, the low drone of bristles against teeth—had a message for him, but he was too aware of the series of meaningless expressions his mouth was adopting. He used the toilet and found his face with soap and water and a towel, and then he hurried to the bedroom.

Melanie lay facing the door, and stretched a hand across the white cloudscape of the quilt to him. As soon as he'd eased the door shut she murmured "You were a long time."

"I didn't think I was." In fact he couldn't tell, and so he said "I didn't mean to be."

"Then don't be any longer."

She turned on her back to watch him undress and leave his clothes on the chair beside the window, beyond which the trees were as still as the streetlamps that drained them of colour. When he joined her beneath the quilt she gave him a soft lingering kiss and captured his hand to draw his arm around her as she nestled her back against him. As he reached for the light-cord she intertwined their fingers, the way she did on planes when they were taking off or about to land. He could almost have fancied that she was bracing herself, which made him feel oddly apprehensive. He yanked at the cord, and as the dark fell on them she clasped his hand tighter. "You aren't going away again, are you?"

"Not that I'm aware of." When her grasp didn't relax he said "No reason to think I am."

"I wish it were the weekend."

"The concert will be done and we can all unwind, you mean."

"Don't give me any more to fret about, Paul. I meant we'll be together, the four of us."

This so plainly confirmed how he'd suspected she was feeling that he said under his breath "That rubbish about yesterday got to you, didn't it."

He'd meant to speak too low for Melanie to hear, but she said "It was being on my own that did."

"You aren't now, so it can stop." He wasn't going to apologise for reassuring his mother, even though Melanie was gripping his hand as if to keep him there. "I wonder what they can be thinking now," he said, "the Finalists."

"I'd rather not."

"Maybe it's better to think than feel sometimes," Slater retorted, but with less than a breath on her neck. "Then don't," he said more audibly. "Just sleep."

Since she was unwilling to release his hand, he used hers as well to rub her stomach. She'd liked him to stroke it when she was pregnant, and this was still a way of bringing her some calm. She thought it was related to meditation—the diaphragm was—but it felt as though he was moulding her to him as she settled more closely against him. Soon he couldn't distinguish her body or her breathing from his own, presumably because he'd gone to sleep.

The inclination of the seat helped. It had reclined all the way to horizontal. His breaths had grown so even that they were indistinguishable from the unwavering note of the jet stream, which sounded like the voice of the featureless dark outside the window. Some detail seemed capable of troubling him, and eventually he remembered that he'd dumped his luggage in the aisle beside himself rather than stowing it overhead. Surely it wasn't worth waking up for when there appeared to be no cabin crew to stumble over it, but he was jerked awake by an urgent bleeping and a voice that identified it as an alarm.

Why was she saying there was no cause for it when it was so nervously insistent? He felt as if the violent jolt had dislocated his ability to grasp language—as if he'd left too much of his intelligence behind in the dream. The incessant repetition of the note seemed capable of driving every other sense out of his mind, and he had no idea how long he took to grow aware that Melanie was still clasping his hand. It allowed him to recognise that he'd heard her saying "Now there's the alarm."

How could it still be dark at this hour? If it wasn't, where had his sight gone? Perhaps some of his perceptions needed to catch up with him, but he had to grip Melanie's hand more fiercely than she was holding his before he felt able to risk opening his eyes. She was lying on her back, waiting to meet his gaze. "What were you thinking?" she said.

It might have been a gentle accusation, and he wasn't going to admit that he'd been unaware of her. "I can't with this," he said and stretched out his hand to shut off the racket, which had begun to put him in mind of a very young child at a keyboard. The abrupt hush let him notice how flat the light appeared to be, but he managed to recall his promise. "I'll tell them the sun's up."

"We both will."

Why might he have a problem in reaching the door? Because he could fall over his suitcase, of course, which was where he remembered leaving it. On the door his and Melanie's dressing-gowns looked shrunken by emptiness, or at least they would if he let them. He gave Melanie a vigorous hug once he'd shoved his fists through the synthetic silk sleeves and tied the slippery cord. As she crossed the landing to waken Amy he made for Tom's room.

The curtains framed a sky so featurelessly white that it could have been last night's in negative. Its muffled pallid light showed him the familiar chaos of the boy's room, clothes and books and computer games strewn on and around the desk overlooked by football posters. While the bed was thoroughly rumpled, it was unoccupied. Not seeing Tom filled him with a panic that he heard in Melanie's voice as well. "Amy?" she was pleading.

Slater twisted around to see that the girl's bedroom was deserted too. As his mind seized on the extravagant disorder she'd left behind and posters for pop stars stared back at him, he might have been making a desperate bid to cling to some sense of his daughter. She and her brother amounted to far more than that, and as Slater told himself so he heard Amy call "We're here."

"We've had our breakfast," Tom shouted.

"You can't have had much," their mother said.

There was certainly no smell of breakfast, which might have wakened Slater. "Who's going in the bathroom?" Melanie asked him.

"Why don't we both?"

They hadn't often shared it since Amy was born, but he wondered if he'd been alone in wanting to do so now. "Wash up if you've finished," Melanie called down the stairs, "and then these rooms are overdue for tidying if you're ready for school."

How anxious was she to restore a domestic routine? Sharing the bathroom wasn't quite as Slater thought it used to be. Although they kept touching and following that with a smile, Melanie seemed distracted by listening for the children, wherever they were in the house. Slater felt compelled to strain his ears and saw her relax when they were rewarded with domestic sounds offstage. As he and Melanie returned to the bedroom Amy called "Hurry down, we want you."

"We're making you toast," Tom shouted.

Now that he'd said it Slater could smell it. No doubt the steam that had turned the bathroom mirror as blank as the sky had prevented him. "Save your voices. Remember the concert," he told the children.

Melanie was straightening up hastily from the dressing-table mirror. She was in one of her business outfits—metallic grey suit, polo-necked blouse. He'd never known her to dress so fast, which seemed to urge him to be at least as quick, especially since she lingered at the top of the stairs while he did his best. She kept him in sight but started downstairs before he emerged from the room. "Here come your customers," she called.

Amy was wielding tongs to pass Tom slices out of the toaster. He was diligently buttering them—at least, applying a synthetic substitute— all the way to every corner, as if they were outlines he had to fill in. He and his sister were wearing their St Dunstan's uniforms, the green of which had been putting Slater in mind of spring for weeks. He should have known the children would have made coffee too, and the white mugs on the equally colourless table were exuding steam like their own substance rendered vague. He sat opposite Melanie and heard her crunch a piece of toast, delicately echoing the sound inside his head. "Compliments to the kitchen," he said once his speech was clear.

"And the people in it," Melanie said as if this needed establishing. "Are you two ready to go when we've finished?"

Slater glanced at the clock on the cooker to see the matchstick puzzle of the digits adopt a new shape. "I'll run them to school," he said.

"We both can."

Surely Melanie's first job of the day wouldn't take her in that direction, and he thought of reminding her until he glimpsed determination in her eyes. If she had to deal with some anxiety, he was sure that she was strong enough to do so by herself—she was clearly not inviting discussion, especially in front of the children—and so he said "Who's travelling with whom?"

"I will with mummy," Amy said at once.

"The men will lead the trek, shall we?" This aimed to be more of a joke than it seemed to end up, and he confined himself to the sounds inside his head until he and Melanie had cleared their plates. "Let's see what the day has in store," he said.

It seemed to have little enough for the moment. All along the street the trees were as motionless as the pallid slab of the sky, which turned the windows of the houses into blank rectangles that might almost have been waiting to be written on. Presumably the neighbours who went to work had already gone or were yet to emerge. The cars yipped like electronic puppies at each other, and as the children climbed in Tom called to his sister "See you at school."

His voice sounded not just dwarfed by the silence but muffled, as if the sky had shut it in. The doors shut with four hollow thuds, and Slater swung the Astra out of the drive. Beyond St Peter Street the houses grew taller while the spaces between them demonstrated how low the sky had grown. Soon a park seemed to bring it even closer, and Slater saw how bare the trees still were, as if the leaves had found too little light to coax them forth. As he glanced in the mirror to remind himself where Melanie and Amy were, Tom said "Did you miss the earthquake, dad?"

Was this another reason for Slater's mother to be worried? It reminded him that he had to call her. "On the island, do you mean?" he said. "When did that happen?"

"It woke me up while we were waiting for you to come home. Everything was shaking. Me as well."

"I'm sorry I wasn't there." Slater wasn't sure if he was apologising or just regretted not having shared the experience. "Did anything break?"

"I don't know." The idea seemed to take the boy unawares. "I didn't see."

"Then I expect it didn't. I haven't noticed anything," Slater said, only to wonder if he should. "Did Amy or your mother?"

"It wasn't just me. It was everything."

Slater had to work out the question Tom thought he'd asked. If the rest of the family had been unaware of any tremor, perhaps the boy had dreamed it but was determined not to think so. The road had brought them to an even wider one that was flanked and divided by trees, and it led to a profusion of green – not leaves but the uniforms of children trooping into St Dunstan's. Slater watched Tom and Amy until they were lost in the uniformed crowd, and then he noticed Melanie waving at him in the mirror—how insistently before he'd realised, he couldn't say. "Stay in touch," she mouthed.

As he pulled away from the kerb she followed him. He was wondering how far she meant to accompany him—as he recalled, her first job was downtown—when she found a gap in the tree-lined strip and turned away out of the mirror. His own route took him back towards the cemetery—almost home—but he stopped short of it and took out his mobile. After several measured trills of a bell that sounded more than usually artificial, a woman's voice said "Aurora House. Constance speaking."

"How are you?" He meant this as a greeting more than a question but couldn't tell if it was taken as either. "Is Mrs Slater available?" he said.

"Available."

"To speak to. This is her son."

"Son."

Until Constance had identified herself he could have thought she was a recorded message, and she still didn't sound much more vital. "Her son Paul, yes," he said. "She wanted me to call. I was there just yesterday but it seems longer."

"A lifetime."

So she was capable of finding words of her own, though he didn't especially care for the odd choice of phrase. Might she have been a Finalist? He didn't see how they could still cling to their faith, and yet he didn't like to think that any of them were looking after his mother. "So could I have a word?" he said.

"Mrs Slater."

"Yes, Mrs Slater. Eileen Slater, yes."

He thought his impatience had driven the woman away until he wondered if she had been addressing his mother, not parroting him yet again. He didn't know how long the silence, which felt like the aural equivalent of the sky, gave no hint of activity before he heard his mother's voice. "Is that Derek?"

It sounded vague and so, he was unhappy to recognise, did she. Both his parents had called him Derek when he was too young to have much of a sense of himself, but once he'd seen he had a choice he'd settled on his present name. "It's Paul," he said.

"Paul." He could have thought she'd picked up a trait from Constance, especially when she repeated "Paul." At least this seemed to have helped define her voice as she said "Are you there at last?"

"I have been for a while. I didn't call in case you were asleep."

"I was."

"Then I'm sorry. Constance should have said and I'd have called back."

"Constance." This earned no response that he could hear. "I didn't mean now," his mother said. "I was asleep when, you know."

With a sense of being made to join in the game of echoes Slater said "When…"

"When nothing happened."

Somehow this wasn't as reassuring as it ought to be, but he said "That's fine then, isn't it?"

"It woke me up. I didn't know where I was."

He was close to asking what had wakened her, and then he was as far away from it as possible. "So long as you do now," he said.

"I'm better for hearing from you, Derek."

He kept his protest to himself and found something else to say. "Is everyone else all right?"

"Everyone."

Surely he could take that for a yes. "And they're looking after you," he said. "The staff."

"Constance."

Was this addressed to the woman? Neither its tone nor anything it brought about was telling. He couldn't recall meeting Constance; at best he had a generalised impression of people in uniform. "Her and the rest," he said.

"That's what I need." Perhaps this was a play on words, unless his meaning hadn't immediately reached her, because she added "They're not the same as you, Derek."

"He isn't either."

He didn't say this aloud, and yet he had a disconcerting sense of having failed to keep it to himself. He held his breath until his mother said "Anyway, you've your family to think of. Will I be seeing them soon?"

"I'll talk to Melanie about when."

"Melanie." As he wondered if he needed to explain, his mother said "Remember her. Your wife."

She was saying that she did, of course, not that he should. "And the young ones," she said.

"Tom and Amy."

"That's right." She could almost have been commending his memory, praising him as if he'd reverted to the child whose name she kept using. "Amy and Tom," she said as though testing whether the sequence was equally valid. "Let's try and be together soon."

Too much of the conversation seemed to consist of repetitions, in slow motion too. "We'll be in touch," Slater said. "Now why don't you catch up on the rest you were saying you needed."

"The rest." She might have forgotten what she'd meant or somehow changed her mind. "There's plenty," she said.

"Then you should treat yourself to a helping," Slater told her, only to feel he'd misunderstood. He had to trade several endearments before he felt comfortable with ending the call. He left the mobile on the seat beside him as token company, and was easing the Astra forward when he noticed a police car in the nearest entrance to the graveyard.

Had the police been watching him? Now he recalled that you weren't expected just to switch off the engine if you used your mobile in a car, you had to remove the key from the ignition too. As he drove towards them, not too fast but surely not slowly enough to arouse any suspicions, he saw that both the occupants of the white vehicle were disconcertingly young. Perhaps that was one reason why their smooth scrubbed faces looked so tightly closed around a purpose, determined not to let in any doubt or humour, but he was reminded of the Finalists. He straightened his lips and gave the police a terse nod of acknowledgement before he let them see him focus on the road ahead.

He was alongside the cemetery entrance when he glimpsed twin items at the edge of his vision, a pair of roundish objects as blank and white as the sky. Of course they weren't faces; the driver had flashed the headlights, and now he saw her stretching out a hand towards him and then patting the air as if dealing with some article he couldn't see—a child's head, perhaps, or a mound of earth. She was gesturing him to pull over, and he braked so quickly that he blocked the way out of the graveyard.

It seemed advisable not to move on in case they took him to be trying to escape. The driver stayed in her seat while her colleague ducked out of the car, tugging his official headgear down as though to consolidate his small stiff face. He paced to the front of the Astra and scrutinised the number plate before raising his pale gaze to inspect Slater. When he came to the driver's door at the speed of Slater's pulse, Slater lowered the window. "How can I help?" he said.

He couldn't tell if the policeman was considering the question or Slater's face, even once the man said "Where have you been, sir?"

"Just dropping the children off at school." Slater would have hoped this might earn him at least a hint of approval. "Mine and my wife's," he said in case this solved the unidentified problem. "We both did."

"Where is your wife now?"

"On her way to work if she's not already there."

"What work would that be, sir?"

Slater was close to laughing at the vintage phraseology, which could have been designed as a badge of maturity. Certainly the man seemed more like a memory of a police officer than today's version. "She fixes computers," he said.

"And what work do you do?"

"I'm in charge of music at Texts in Speke."

"In charge."

"Of the department, yes. I'm your classical man in particular." Slater thought he could risk showing a trace of impatience as he added "I'm on my way there now."

This didn't change the man's blank gaze, but neither had anything else. Slater could almost have imagined that his interrogator knew the answers and was testing him to find out if he did. The policeman closed one hand on the lowered window and held out the other. "May I see your licence, please."

"Here I am." Slater unfolded his wallet to exhibit the driving licence in its plastic window. "Nobody else would have that face," he said.

The policeman might have been miming the absence of any response. Admittedly it hadn't been much of a joke, especially considering Amy's resemblance to her father. "Please hand it to me, sir," the policeman said.

Slater removed the licence from the wallet and planted it on the man's palm, which was disconcertingly soft as well as pale and smooth enough to put him in mind of a cloud. "Wait here, sir," the policeman said.

Slater wasn't too far from enquiring where the fellow thought he might have gone. He watched the man return to the police car and sit beside his colleague while she consulted a small computer. They didn't speak—the deserted road was as silent as the multitude of stones—and he didn't see them communicate in any way before the policeman came back to him, so deliberately that Slater would have expected his footfalls to be noisier. "All in order, then?" Slater said. "I'm who it says and this is my car and it's taxed and insured."

The policeman lowered his head as if the monologue had weighed it down. "Where were you last night, sir?"

"Good God, how much else do you want to know?" Having kept this to himself, Slater said "On the way home from visiting my mother."

"That's confirmed. Tell anyone who wants to know."

Slater didn't speak until he had his licence back. "Such as who else?"

"Anyone who asks you, Mr Slater. Please be sure to remember."

He had even less sense of what he was being told to do or why, and he blurted "Just how much do you know about me?"

"Everything you are is in the system."

He didn't care for the notion at all. "May I ask what this has been about?"

"You'd be advised to forget about it, Mr Slater."

"How can I forget it when I don't know what it is?"

While he didn't feel quite confident enough to say that, he wouldn't be the first to blink. The policeman was staring at him as if searching for Slater's thoughts, although his eyes looked as dully vacant as the sky. Then his face appeared not just to flare up with the same pallor but to flatten as his surroundings did. His colleague must have been flashing the headlights, and once Slater blinked his vision reverted to normal. "You can forget this ever happened," the policeman said.

Slater barely managed not to retort that he'd had enough of being told what to forget and to remember. As the policeman turned away at last Slater shut the window. At the sound of the engine the man glanced over his shoulder, but Slater had the unsettling impression that both officious faces were fully turned to him. He must need to catch up on his sleep, though perhaps he ought to be glad that the police hadn't tested his breath. He sent the Astra forward and saw the white car shrink to the size of a toy in the mirror. Stones and trees closed around it, and then it was gone as though it had been too transitory to have a place in the venerable landscape.

The cemetery fell behind at last, and houses in which the windows were suffused with no colour flanked the road. Soon it narrowed, and the sky seemed to press the houses closer to the earth before they gave way to blocks of shops. These looked dingy and anonymous, as if the second-hand goods dimly visible beyond the windows had infected them with staleness, and Slater was glad to reach the main road.

It led him towards the airport, though there weren't any planes in the sky, and then to the retail park. Apart from the outsize writing of their names the buildings weren't much more individuated than the sky. The sign for **texts** was in computer type and as devoid of capitals as the average message on a mobile. Slater found a space not too many ranks of cars away from the store and felt as if the sky was pacing him while he hurried across the car park.

Beyond the shop entrance and the displays of books he shouldn't have to glance towards to recognise, music was in the air. It reminded him of the vague tentative murmurs he'd heard on the plane, but he couldn't name the composer. He was straining to hear it more clearly so that he could identify it when Shelley Blake came over to him.

He'd never known how much the manager's name had to do with literature. Her taste in reading didn't seem to extend beyond her lifetime, if even that far. Perhaps she wouldn't be able to attribute the Text for Today, this month's quotation that was printed on the staff T-shirts: *Had we but world enough and time* … Either she was wearing more makeup than usual or he was more aware of the mascara that outlined her grey eyes, the pink lipstick that helped shape her full lips. Even the silvery blonde hair that framed her snub-nosed oval face might have had its tints touched up. She waited while he abandoned trying to recognise the music, and then she said "Put something else on when you're ready, Paul. Something everyone will know."

Was that a criticism of his selections? "Any requests?" he said.

"It's your department. We'll leave it to you."

He might have preferred her to say what she thought the customers might like. He nodded at the trace of music in the air. "Whose idea was that, then?"

"Whoever made it up, I should think."

He'd already had one conversation that resembled a series of ill-defined traps in a dream. She was gazing at him as though she expected more of him, but all he could think of to say was "Sorry, am I late?"

"Nobody's saying so."

"I think I lost track of the time. Don't ask me why, but some police pulled me up."

"I wasn't asking, Paul."

"I know, but if you were . . ." Even if he felt as though he was talking to himself, it needed to be put into words. "You wouldn't believe how much they wanted to be told," he said, "and they already had it on the computer."

"I expect we're all there."

"I don't know about you, but I'd like to think there was more to me than some electronic information."

"You should then, Paul."

"I just don't know what they were trying to do."

"No need to say. Really, there's no need."

Perhaps her urgency was meant to suggest that he would soon be late after all. "I won't waste any more time, then," he said.

As he made for the staff quarters he found his name tag in his pocket and pinned it above the Marvell. At the door he extended the plastic rectangle on its lead to fit it to the plaque on the wall. He thought the anonymous murmur in the air had muffled the click of the door release until he found that the door didn't budge. He peered at the tag, only to wonder how anyone could expect the system to recognise **RETALS LUAP**, which sounded like a misspelled retail outlet. Then he managed to laugh, though not before he felt as if looking down at his transformed name had seized him with vertigo. He applied the tag again and heard the lock acknowledge him.

The staffroom was a large white concrete box in which straight chairs huddled against a table opposite a gathering of seats padded with slabs of imitation leather. Under the fluorescent tubes the room looked not just empty but impersonal. Slater clocked on with his tag, triggering a ding that put him in mind of winning an electronic game, and glanced at the memory board on the wall. Was that his handwriting? Presumably whatever task he'd written up had been dealt with, since the words had mostly been erased. Just a few letters were faintly distinguishable: *RE A L*, too widely spaced to be spelling the word. He couldn't make sense of them as he hung his jacket in the nearest of the lockers in the kitchen beyond the staffroom. Once he'd switched off his mobile he went back to the shop.

The music section was at the back, past a multitude of books. Perhaps it was his lack of sleep that made their covers look oddly imprecise in the artificial light, which had as little colour as the sky that glared through the long windows. Even the cases in the racks of compact discs seemed less familiar than they had to be. The prospect of relinquishing his own taste so as to reflect everyone else's felt oddly threatening, and at first he couldn't even think how to do it. If the music was supposed to exemplify the shop, he might as well select from the label that their multinational owners had caused to be created. Perhaps in some sense that music represented the world.

The Primest discs had their own prominent display, where the timidly classical compilations were shelved behind the more unashamedly popular. *Beathoven* emphasised the rhythms of the composer's best-known melodies, while *High Din* did the same for his contemporary, and *Lud Wig* showed Mozart topped by an extravagantly elaborate hairpiece composed of notes. On reflection Slater didn't think he could live with any of those performances, let alone *Bach with Bite* or *Poochini* or *Un-Ravel*, and so he slipped Beethoven's *Pastoral*—the symphony, he thought, not the sonata— into the player. "Is this all right for everyone?" he called.

"We've heard it before."

He couldn't tell which of the staff had spoken. They were deployed throughout the shop, shelving books or arranging displays or checking stock against lists on handheld monitors or serving customers, although the day had brought out few of those. He heard a murmur of agreement, either with his question or with the response. He propped the compact disc case on the Now Playing stand on the Information counter, and looked up to find that somebody was waiting to be seen.

He was a large balding man in a grey track suit that made his shape vaguer. His roundish face looked blurred by fat and to some extent defined by hair—eyebrows overshadowing the small eyes, a moustache and a restrained beard framing the mouth, uneven stubble poking out of the broad nose. As Slater met his gaze he raised his shaggy eyebrows, which appeared to expand. "Have you remembered yet?" he said.

Slater felt rude for gazing at him, especially since it didn't make the man look any more familiar. "I'm sorry," he said, "I'm not sure..."

"You were finding a tune for me. You thought you were the man to know."

Slater couldn't recall being asked. He was hoping for some help, but when the fellow only stared at him he had to ask "Which tune was it again?"

"Something like this."

The man lifted his gaze heavenwards, suggesting that the melody resembled the one in the air. Certainly the tentative notes he hummed weren't too distinguishable from it. Slater would have been embarrassed to ask him to repeat them, but had to admit "I haven't found it yet, I'm afraid."

"Where did you look?"

"In the catalogues online." That had to be the answer, even if he couldn't recall doing so. How badly was his lack of sleep affecting him? At least he was able to say "It does sound rather familiar."

"That's what you thought." Perhaps this was a reproach, but the man added "I think I've remembered some words."

"It's a song, you mean."

"Didn't you say?"

Slater had no idea, and his forgetfulness had started to make him feel lacking. "What words are those?" he said, trying not to sound nervous.

"It starts off with the town where I was born."

"That should help." The man's accent prompted Slater to add "I'd say Liverpool."

"Like you by the sound of it. You're best ending up where you came from."

"Some of us have never left." That wasn't true—visiting his mother was enough to give it the lie—and Slater felt as if he was trying too hard to manage his memories. "Are you thinking of the Beatles?" he said.

"You've got to if you think of Liverpool."

"Yes, but do you have their song in mind? The one that starts the way you said."

All at once he was afraid of being asked for the title. How could he have forgotten it, even if he specialised in other kinds of music? Perhaps the man knew it, because he said "I'm not thinking of that, no."

It sounded unnecessarily reminiscent of a guessing game. "Is it more recent?" Slater said. "One of Dylan's, could it be?"

"Isn't he the poet?"

"Not the one from Wales, the singer who took his name."

"You shouldn't do that." Slater felt no less bewildered than accused, even once his customer said "Take a name. Don't they say never take one in vain?"

"That's just God."

"It ought to be the rest of us as well. Take it away and you won't be able to get to yourself. You know yourself you can't look anything up without a name."

"So, Dylan the singer," Slater said in a bid not to think about any of that. "Was it his song?"

"Doesn't sound like him."

"Then I'm guessing it's the one he based his song on. Barbara," Slater said and then "Barbara."

"Barbara Barbara. Don't know that one."

"Not Barbara Barbara," Slater said and tried to laugh, despite feeling like an echo of an echo. "Barbara. Barbara…" With an effort that strained not just his mind but the whole of him he succeeded in recalling "Barbara Allen."

"Hey," the man said in surprise if not indignation, "that's my name."

Slater was on the edge of laughter now, unless it was hysteria. "What is?"

"It's not going to be Barbara, is it? Not Barbara Barbara either. Have a go at Alan."

Perhaps that was how he spelled it, whichever of his names it might be. "As you see, mine's Paul," Slater said.

The customer peered at his badge—indeed, scrutinised it so closely that Slater was reminded of immigration or the police. "If you say so," the man eventually said.

Slater glanced down to see that the badge was inverted, turned up towards him as though to remind him of his name. Even once Slater reversed the badge the customer didn't look especially convinced. "Can you sing it for me?" the man said.

For a disoriented moment Slater thought he was being asked to perform his own name, a notion that seemed capable of driving the ballad out of his head. With an effort he succeeded in retrieving a pair of lines: "He turned his face unto the wall, and death was drawing nigh him..." He would rather not sing that just now if ever, and he struggled to recapture the words that the man had more or less told him. He took a breath that he couldn't hear for the hovering music, and sang "In something town where I was born..."

"How's that again?"

Slater did his best to raise his voice while he repeated the line, but couldn't prevent the rhythm from fitting itself to the symphony, and the melody fared not much better. The customer had him rehearse it once more, and this time he joined in. As Slater saw his colleagues duck towards their work, quite possibly to shut out the duet, the man said "That's something like."

"Shall I see if I can find it for you?"

"If you want."

The song wasn't on any of the albums by the Neaps. It wasn't among the Only Folk compilations, and it didn't seem to have been recorded by Maurice and His Men. Slater searched through all the likely discs and then the increasingly unlikely ones before he had to tell his customer "I'm afraid we don't have it in Folk just now."

"Doesn't have to be."

Presumably he meant he would accept a composer's interpretation, and Slater moved to the classical racks. Volkswagen came to mind until the initials yielded Vaughan Williams, who didn't seem to have gone anywhere near the ballad. Britain was a thought—Britten, to be more precise—but he hadn't set it either. Holst had stayed clear along with Grainger, and there was no trace of a version by Beethoven, whose rustic dance was leaving very little room in Slater's head for any other musical thoughts. At last he said "It looks as if I'll have to order it for you."

"If it won't be too much trouble for nothing."

"It's none at all. We're here for you. Without you we wouldn't exist," Slater said and typed his name to log onto the computer at Information. The screen flickered for an instant, unless his vision did, before responding. Invalid, it declared.

The customer glanced at the screen and then gazed at Slater. "Aren't you well?"

"I'm fine. It's the system that isn't."

"I wouldn't say that too loud if I were you."

"I don't care who hears." This was no more defensive than his remark about the computer. "Slater," he hissed as he put in the name again, just as unsuccessfully. He was about to page the manager, though it made him feel worse than incompetent, when a thought saved him. He typed Paul and was acknowledged at once, which would have reassured him if he weren't so aware of having forgotten the routine. "I'm in," he said. "What sort of version would you like?"

"Of you? The one you are will do, I'd say."

However plainly this was a joke, Slater didn't find it appropriate. "Of the music," he said.

Since Slater hadn't even hinted at a grin, his customer's face stayed blank. "Whichever you think."

"Traditional?" When the man raised no objection Slater brought up the title, but the onscreen repetitions were so numerous that he had to search for a reason to single one out. "The Final Family," his instincts eventually prompted him to say. "I believe they're supposed to have caught the spirit."

"Let's have them, then."

Slater patched the details into an online order form before he had to say "And your name again . . ."

"Allen."

"Mr Allen," Slater said, almost sure he'd heard that spelling, and in the absence of any contradiction he entered it on the form. "And your postcode."

He had to ask to hear it again, which didn't lessen how it made him feel. "Sorry," he said. "It was just a surprise. It's the same as mine."

"You'll be looking for me at home."

Slater couldn't help wishing he were there right now—him, not the customer. "What number's yours?" he said.

"Don't tell me that's yours too."

Slater suppressed his unease, since the idea was absurd. The mumbled number was a teen, but certainly not his. "Close," he said, though he wasn't sure how close. "You must be just round a corner."

"You'll be seeing me again before you know it."

"It ought to be here soon," Slater said, as that was all the customer could mean, and he printed out the information. "If you could bring that with you it would be helpful."

"It'll help you remember, you mean." As he took the flimsy slip the man said "Thank you for your time, Mr Player."

"So long as you care about names, this is me," Slater said and extended his badge on its lead.

He might have been making a bid for admission at an invisible threshold. The man didn't even glance at the badge before he turned away, murmuring "I'll leave you alone then, Mr Later."

"Slater," Slater protested but had no idea who heard him. Everyone had their backs to him, and he couldn't tell how much of his voice the discreetly boisterous music had absorbed. "I'll be in the office if anyone needs me," he said rather louder than he'd proclaimed his name, and made for the plaque on the wall.

The office was the second room along the concrete passage. It was a windowless bunker much like the staffroom but with desks, each of which was occupied by a computer, their screens as blank as oblivion. As Slater sat in front of his the unadorned white walls reminded him of the sky; it felt like being surrounded by slabs of solidified cloud, or else the walls seemed less substantial than they ought to. He would leave once he'd checked for any calls; he didn't even know why he was so anxious to do it—but as soon as he switched on the mobile it clanked and trembled in his hand. Melanie had tried to reach him.

At least she had left him a message, and he fumbled for the key. A woman told him he had one new message and gave him instructions on how to retrieve it, which he couldn't do until he had finished being told. He'd forgotten to wait for the anonymous artificial voice to finish before he poked the appropriate key, and had to go through the ritual again. Once he'd jabbed the key a second time he heard a whisper of static not too distinguishable from silence, and then it produced Melanie's voice—the memory of her call. "Don't worry if you're there," she said. "Well, of course you are. Just checking all is as it should be. The children tried and so I said I would. We'll all be fine till we're back together."

What did she mean about the children? He thumbed the button to recall her number and pressed the phone against his ear, and heard silence as blank as he imagined the unseen sky must be. He didn't know how long he waited to hear an unnecessarily remote bell, which seemed to be summoning more of the silence as it echoed itself. Then the bell faltered like a musician who had missed a note, and Melanie said "Hello?"

It shouldn't be a question. She ought to be seeing his name. Did her voice sound artificial? Perhaps it was her answering message, which he couldn't recall ever having heard. Before he managed to respond or even take a breath she said "Who's calling me?"

"It's me. It's only me."

"Not only at all, unless you're saying you're the only thing that matters."

"I'd never say that. There are you and the children for a start."

"Matters to them and to me. You ought to know I meant that."

"I'm sure other people do as well. Matter, I'm saying." The sense of artificiality hadn't left him; the conversation felt like rummaging in his mind. "Why couldn't you see me?" he said.

"What do you mean, Paul?"

That sounded genuine enough—her unease did. "Just now," he said. "When I rang. You couldn't see my name."

"I wasn't looking. I wanted to hear."

Had he aggravated her unease? He still had to ask "Why did you call? What was wrong?"

"Nothing is now."

"That's a relief, but what were you saying was the matter with the children?"

She was certainly less at ease now. "What did I say?"

"That they'd tried to get in touch with me, I thought. There's no trace on my phone."

"That explains it, then." Her relief seemed to let her add "Mind you, there are always traces. If there weren't I couldn't do my job."

She was talking about computers, but he was anxious to learn "Why did they want me?"

"Why wouldn't they?"

"I'm asking why they tried to call."

"I really couldn't tell you. I expect it can wait till tonight if I let them know I've spoken to you." She sounded eager to say "We'll pick them up after their rehearsal, shall we? I should be finished by then."

"I can get them if you like."

"No need to be apart any longer than we have to be." As if to leave the thought behind she said without a pause "How's your day shaping up?"

"I don't know how long I was dealing with a customer. One of our neighbours or not far from it. A Mr Allen, I believe."

"He does sound a bit familiar, but let's concentrate on us."

At least their conversation had lent her voice some substance, and she sounded close enough to be in the room. "And our work," Slater said.

"That's us as well, and the children are."

"I should think we ought to let them be themselves." Just in time Slater grasped that whatever was behind Melanie's words, she wouldn't want to hear that kind of comment, and so he gave her a silence to prompt her to speak. "I can't wait to see them, can you?" she said.

"We'd better get back to work so we're in time."

"I expect so." As Slater made to say something other than farewell she said "See them performing, I meant."

"That as well," Slater said and was anxious for the day to be done. The shop felt like a stage in his return to the family, and he seemed to need to keep them in his mind. By the end of the workday he could scarcely bring to mind how he'd spent it—checking stock, removing items from the shelves to send back where they'd come from, finding music for a customer, serving at the tills, which emitted notes like rudimentary attempts to join in the melodies overhead if not to diminish them or take their place—and he left all that behind as he made for his car.

Beneath the white sheet of the sky the dormant vehicles might have been forgetting their colours. Perhaps the sunless light was muffling his perceptions, because he had to use the key fob to locate the Astra. He heard an electronic sound that seemed to be transformed into a flare of light, but he had to rouse the car again, having lost it once more in the maze of empty metal. He fell into his seat and grabbed a water bottle to suck at the plastic nipple, feeling vulnerable and isolated. It must show how incomplete he was without his family, and he twisted the key to bring the car back to life.

The traffic lights at the exit from the retail park looked blanched by the sky. Although the main road was anything but busy, the lights took their time about releasing him. Such traffic as there was stayed on the main road when he turned away between the faded shops. He couldn't help looking for the police at the graveyard, but except for trees there were only stones like extrusions of the rock beneath the grass.

He saw St Dunstan's before he was expecting to, though he couldn't recall when he'd last approached it from this direction. At first the white blocks of the school consisted mostly of a mass of stripes, the railings of the schoolyard. The bars moved lethargically apart as he drove closer, as if the view beyond them was gradually taking shape—the buildings practically indistinguishable from the sky, their windows blank as cataracts, the empty yard. No, there was a glimpse of green, and then the gaps between the bars let him see

Amy and Tom. Melanie was with them, and he should have noticed
her car on a side street ahead, especially since no houses were in
the way. "Now we're all together again," Amy cried as he opened the
passenger door.

"We'll always be," said Tom.

Slater would have expected her to give that a big sister's look, but
for a change she seemed not to feel superior. "Who's coming home
with me?" he said.

The children's faces wavered, and he could have thought Melanie
seemed taken aback too. "We all are," she said.

"No, I mean who's travelling with me." When even this appeared
to fall short Slater said "In my car."

"It can be the boys again," Melanie said.

Tom apparently understood this before his father did, and climbed
in the Astra. Amy and her mother hurried to the Viva, which swerved
at speed out of the side road as if Melanie couldn't wait to see the rest
of the family in her mirror. As the Astra came up behind her she
moved off so deliberately that Slater assumed she wanted him to stay
in the reflection. He grew aware that Tom was gazing at him. "Well,
Tom," he said and for a disconcerting moment didn't know how to
continue. "Are you prepared?"

The boy's gaze flickered, surely not with nervousness. "What for,
dad?"

"What else could it be? Your concert, of course."

"I think we are." Even more gravely Tom added "I hope."

"No need for that, I'm certain." When the boy looked less than
reassured Slater said "I believe in you and Amy."

"And mummy."

"She does too."

Tom's gaze retreated, leaving his eyes blank, so that Slater wondered if he'd misunderstood the boy somehow. He could have
thought he was forgetting how to talk to his family. Was this another
indication that he needed to catch up on his sleep? Even that prospect made him uneasy, and he concentrated on following the Viva,
meeting Melanie's eyes in the mirror whenever she looked for him.

He was barely aware of having a passenger, and had to keep glancing at Tom, who was intent on the other car.

As he followed Melanie into St Peter Street the trees closed in. Was even the vegetation confused by the unemphatic light? He could have thought all the buds were taking their leaves back, having concluded that spring had proved to be an illusion. The pallid sky appeared to have settled into every window of the house, and until he left the car he couldn't see a single room. Melanie opened the front door, revealing the hall and the photographs climbing towards the sky. Once Slater crossed the threshold he could see the photographs weren't blank. As he shut out the inhibited trees and the unforthcoming sky he said "We'll have dinner when you two have done your homework."

"We haven't got any," Tom said.

He looked oddly lost, and Amy did until she said "They let us off because of rehearsals."

Slater was disconcerted to feel that the domestic routine had been undermined. How regulated did he need their life to be? What did he think would happen otherwise? Before he could ponder this, if indeed he wanted to, Melanie said "Come and read while we get dinner ready, then."

He had the odd notion that she meant the children to read aloud to them. He wouldn't have encouraged reading at the table—surely that used to be regarded as rude—but at least it meant the family was all together. As he made a salad to accompany the lasagne Melanie had taken from the refrigerator he saw that the children's books must be old favourites, revisited so often that they'd shed their presumably disintegrating jackets. He was doing his best to identify them—it felt like a memory exercise—when Melanie said "If you're ready we are."

The children shut their books at once. The blank pages Slater glimpsed were the flyleaves, of course. He poured drinks—lemonade for the children, wine for him and Melanie—while she loaded everybody's dishes, and then he remembered a question he'd wanted to ask. "Who's going to tell me about the earthquake?"

Melanie frowned, and Amy produced a smaller but fiercer version. "Which one?" she said before her mother could speak.

"How many have there been?"

"None at all that I'm aware of," Melanie said. "Now why doesn't everyone—"

"I believe there was a bit of one, wasn't there? Tom said you had it while I was on my way home."

"Tom would," Amy said.

"You must have felt it too," the boy protested. "You woke up like me."

With all the loftiness her extra years had conferred upon her Amy told him "That wasn't an earthquake."

"What was it, then?"

"I don't know what woke me." As their mother made to intervene Amy said "I went all shivery. It was like having ripples in my tummy and my head."

"That's the same thing. It wasn't just us, it was—"

"You were worried about your father being late, that's all," Melanie said. "You can forget all about it now. Don't go getting yourselves worked up when you have your big day tomorrow."

The children looked frustrated if not more thoroughly dissatisfied, and Slater did his best to divert them. "That's enough earthquakes for one day," he said, and when their faces stayed stubbornly baffled "Your mother's excelled herself today, hasn't she? I can't remember when it tasted so good."

He was confusing himself if not them. Melanie hadn't made the lasagne today, and he couldn't even recall which of the two of them had been the cook. Soon enough everyone's plates looked as if they mightn't have held food at all, and the children left the table. "Don't go far," Melanie said and seemed to wonder why she had.

"We're only going to watch," Amy said.

As Slater passed Melanie items to put in the dishwasher he couldn't hear the television in the next room. When he and Melanie left the kitchen he heard sounds too rapid to identify, and the flat screen in the living-room met him with a series of random images like frames in a chaotic film. Tom was switching channels, only to complain "There's nothing on."

"It looks as if there's far too much," Melanie said.

"Let's have the control, please," Slater said.

He lingered on some of the channels long enough to be sure what they were offering, but in no case was it much. The fragments of news seemed bland and overly familiar—predictions of prosperity, forecasts of employment, prognoses of technological developments, assurances of better times in store. Slater hoped all this would come true for Tom and Amy, but he saw it wasn't reaching them just now. Otherwise there were cartoons—"Seen it," Tom and then Amy announced—and quiz shows—"Seen it," the children chorused— and episodes of comedies—"Seen it" in every case. "Well then," Melanie said with impatience that Slater thought wasn't too far from nervousness, "what do you want to see?"

"The film with all the music in," Tom said, very nearly at once.

"The one that's made of music," Amy seemed to deduce he had in mind.

"I'm sure you know which that is, Paul."

He could have thought the family was imitating one of the quiz shows. If Melanie knew the title, why couldn't she say? It must be quite a few years since they'd all seen the film. No wonder the children couldn't put a name to it, and as the title came to mind at last he saw the disc where it should be, under F on the shelf. "*Fantasia*," he said for anyone who needed to know. Thumbing the disc out of its case, he slipped it into the player.

The screen grew blank, unless it had already been, as the player engaged with the monitor. In a few moments a star described an arc like the skeleton of a rainbow on the screen. While the image was familiar—the Disney logo—just now it seemed more like an omen of unnatural light. At least the disc menu lent Slater some control, and he started the film.

He remembered it well enough, and he saw that the family did. A master of ceremonies introduced the conductor and the orchestra, whose instruments began to glow as they performed a reworking of

Bach. As Slater recalled, the children had been captivated, but now
the transformation of the music into an extra sense unsettled him,
especially once the orchestra was reduced to abstract patterns that
were supposed to represent the music. They reminded him how it
was composed of electronic impulses translated by the system, and
how his perception of it consisted of electronic disturbances in his
brain; all his perceptions did—even the thought itself, not to mention the self that was having it. Although music often sent him into
a reverie, he didn't care much for this one. Since trying to make his
mind blank offered no reassurance, he did his best to confine his
awareness to the patterns on the screen and in his head.

Next came Tchaikovsky, and the children still giggled at the balletic
vegetation. Slater could have thought their amusement was a little
nervous, and the sight of flowers and mushrooms dancing as though
they had faces and brains had lost its appeal for him. It seemed to
suggest that music could bring the mindless to some kind of life—
that other forms of electronic activity might as well. The music that
followed took the shape of a mouse but also formed itself into a
broom that executed a prancing march and multiplied into countless
replicas of itself, enough to people a world. Slater might have imagined the world had collapsed from the artificiality of the situation,
because now the images turned primordial, depicting chaos before
they showed the birth and death of all life—no, just the prehistoric
kind, too distant to be remembered. Why couldn't he stop thinking?
What would happen if he did? The thought felt even more unwelcome, not least because it appeared to turn the monitor blank. The
film had reached the intermission. "Have we had enough?" he said.

The children only stared at him, but Melanie said "Why, have
you?"

Or was she asking why? Slater couldn't own up to the truth when
he didn't know what it was. "Not unless you have," he said.

He wasn't even sure if this was a plea. As he reached for the control
Melanie said "It's something we're doing together."

The orchestra returned before he would have been able to head
them off, and then the master of ceremonies coaxed the soundtrack

onstage. The sight of the unstable line creeping out of the side of the screen to cavort in time with various instruments roused all Slater's unwelcome thoughts. Eventually Beethoven drove it back into hiding, but the symphony felt like a recent memory Slater was trying to recapture, and not too accurately either. In the past he and Melanie might have exchanged winces at all the inappropriate portamento and pointed out the conductor's eccentricities to the children, but now the slithering of the violins from note to note seemed inseparable from the sinuous movements of the mythical creatures onscreen. They weren't memories, even ancient ones, but concepts that had never really existed, a thought that he found less than reassuring. A thunderstorm flung down by Zeus was sent packing by the sun, but soon the night was drawn over the land, an event rather too reminiscent of the sky outside the window, where the featureless expanse had turned black at some point Slater couldn't recall. Now what point was the film making about time? Hours didn't dance, and they certainly didn't take the form of ostriches or hippopotami. He felt as if the spectacle was undermining his grasp of the nature of time, but closing his eyes only made him nervous of what he might see when he opened them. Suppose there was nothing to see? He had to make himself hear the music in his head, and once he recalled what shapes it would be taking now—elephants and alligators—he was able to look. Another night was still to come, bringing a gigantic demon that reached down from a mountain to toy with its resurrected victims. Slater wanted to remember that it was conquered by daylight, but that didn't happen; a procession of vague figures carried feeble lights across an uncertain terrain where even the trees were indistinct, and at last the procession merged with an obscure pale radiance. "Well," Slater said and was anxious to find more to say. "I hope that lived up to our memories."

"It was a bit different," Tom said.

Since nobody else spoke, Slater couldn't avoid asking "How?"

Tom seemed to wish he'd kept quiet, and glanced at his mother and sister as though for some kind of support. It was Amy who said "I thought the sun came back at the end."

"Don't you think it does?" Melanie said, less like a question than a bid for reassurance.

"That isn't the sun," Tom objected.

"Maybe it was better," Slater tried suggesting while he wondered if they were talking just about the film. "I tell you what," he said. "If we don't see the sun tomorrow we'll go and try and find it at the weekend."

Melanie pressed her lips together as if she might have liked him to have kept the notion to himself. "Why won't we see it tomorrow?" Tom protested.

"I'm not saying we won't. There aren't any prophets here. I only meant if it carries on like this."

Tom glanced at the window, where the gap between the curtains was apparently too thin to admit even a hint of light from the street. "For ever?"

"Of course not for ever. Nothing lasts that long." Once again Slater thought he'd said too much, and now not enough. "Apart from us," he felt compelled to add.

Amy seemed not to know where to look. "Just us?"

"Now I said I'm not a prophet. They've all gone away till next time."

"Which time, dad?"

That was Tom, but Slater suspected the boy wasn't alone in wondering. "Whenever some other crowd thinks we're all due to come to an end," he said and saw this didn't appeal much to anyone. "But there are more like us who don't, aren't there? And we won."

"How did we?" Amy said.

He might have liked them simply to accept the notion, but perhaps he could hold it together. "By believing," he said and felt unexpectedly inspired. "That's all we have to do, and that answers your other question as well. Believe in whatever matters to you and it'll stay with you for ever."

He hoped that made sense or at least felt as if it should, but he didn't need any more questions. "Now I'm for an early night," he said as he shut the system down, having extracted the disc, "and I shouldn't think it would do the rest of us any harm."

Presumably they agreed, since they followed him. He could have thought they meant to queue outside the bathroom, extending the procession of family images that climbed out of the past and up the stairs. Instead they disappeared into the bedrooms as he shut the door, and he felt as if he was bursting into or at least venturing into song on their behalf, because he'd remembered a few more words to do with Barbara Allen. "All in the merry month of May, when green buds they were swelling..." It was surely a promise that life would always revive and an explanation of why the trees were keeping back their leaves until then. Otherwise he made do with the melody, interrupted by brushing his teeth, which let him retrieve another line: "Young man, I think you're dying." He was too old for it to relate to him, and Tom was certainly too young, but as soon as it was uttered he regretted having loosed it. He sang louder without bothering with lyrics, as if deedledum and doodledum could make retrospective nonsense of the line. He was playing the concerned father, not reverting to a state before he'd acquired language, and fell silent as he made for bed.

He might have inadvertently started an audition. While Melanie watched him undress and slip under the quilt they heard Amy recommence the song, though without any words that Slater could distinguish. Tom was next and just as apparently wordless, followed by his mother. As Slater listened to her contribution with his eyes shut he could have thought the family were signalling to one another, establishing where they were. He must be close to dreaming, and he fought to be aware when Melanie came to bed.

The melody she was murmuring trailed off as she returned to him. He couldn't recall turning out the light, but he must have, given the dark. As she nestled against him and captured his arm she whispered "Don't let it be like last night."

Her voice was so muted that he might have fancied he was hearing it just in his head. He didn't even know whether she had been speaking to him, but he said "Like what?"

"We'll be able to sleep now you're home," Melanie said, taking a firmer hold on his arm.

Did she mean them or the children as well, or perhaps not him at all? How could she know whether he'd slept on the plane? The flight and in particular the lurch it had suffered seemed to be his most vivid memory just now, which made him feel as though it might be repeated if he fell asleep—the lurch, at any rate. His awareness of hugging Melanie began to dissipate, consumed by the dark, and he felt threatened by sleep, but why should he feel that? Melanie was asleep—her breaths were as regular as her pulse, keeping time with it and his own—and she wasn't going anywhere so long as he kept hold of her, any more than he was. His consciousness lapsed for a moment, unless it was much longer, since as he struggled back to sentience he had to recall that he was holding Melanie. Singing under his breath might help him stay vigilant, but it was singing in his sleep that wakened him, although the man's voice didn't sound quite like his, however close it was. The words it seemed to have been finding weren't altogether accurate: not Allen but panic, and had he really heard "Young man, I think you're flying"? Perhaps the young man could be Tom after all, an idea that roused Slater to brave the vague dark, having left Melanie a hug he hoped would linger on his behalf. The boy was safe in bed; Slater was sure of it once he'd inched the quilt back from the dormant shape to reveal the dim still face. He mustn't stoop any closer—by the time he was near enough to feel Tom's breath, his own might wake the sleeper—and he contented himself with murmuring a scrap of the song like a lullaby; perhaps he'd heard it used that way somewhere. On his way back to Melanie he was dismayed to think he'd left someone out, a thought that felt like being seized by the dark, and he was in Amy's room so fast that he was afraid of waking her. When he succeeded in making out her face it was as peaceful as her brother's, and once he'd whispered the lullaby Slater retreated to his bed.

Hadn't he undertaken something else for them? Yes, he'd promised them the sun. Though he needn't alert them when it came up, he wouldn't mind seeing it do so. He regained his hold on Melanie and remembered to caress her midriff while he waited for the night to begin to grow paler. His caresses found the rhythm of the breaths he could think he was sharing with her, and perhaps his brainwaves were adopting that pulse as well, because for an instant he seemed to feel everything merge before he felt nothing at all.

The implosion of his consciousness wrenched him awake, and he clutched at the arms of the seat to save himself from plunging into whatever void awaited him. He found no arms, only a soft flatness that he couldn't even grasp. No, he was lying on his back, not flying after all. He was home in bed—alone in bed. His eyes flickered open to be met by darkness so apparently total that they winced shut at once. He was attempting to breathe when he heard Melanie say "Don't go off again, Paul. We're waiting for you."

They were at the end of the bed. Although he felt he'd only blinked, it was daylight now, the same version as yesterday's. The children were wearing their St Dunstan's outfits, and Melanie was in her business uniform. "Stay awake, dad," Amy urged.

"Then we can have breakfast," Tom said with enthusiasm.

Slater had to laugh, affectionately enough. Surely nothing could be wrong if the most vital issue was breakfast. "Give me a chance to breathe," he said.

As he heard their footsteps like a succession of heartbeats on the stairs he made for the bathroom. He did his best to sing in there, though the lyrics of the ballad kept eluding him. How was his reflection dealing with the few lines he brought to mind? In reverse or in some other kind of transformation? Obviously it was voiceless, but the sight made him feel threatened with the same lack, so that he went downstairs as soon as he could.

Three slices of toast sprang up to greet him, and Tom brought them for Amy and himself to butter while Melanie poured coffee. Slater might have protested that he could do all this, or was the routine important to the children? Perhaps it was helping them not to be nervous—about tonight's concert, of course. "Did everyone have a good night?" he said.

The pause might have implied they knew his answer would be no. After somewhat more than a moment Amy admitted "It was better."

"We heard you singing," Tom informed him.

Slater couldn't tell if this was meant to support Amy's observation. "I'm glad we're all musical," Melanie said. "Whatever can bring us together."

Surely he could take this at face value. He was working on his breakfast, though the muffled crunching in his skull sounded rather too much like some kind of collapse, when Tom said "What's that on you, dad?"

Had he seen an insect or a blemish? Slater swallowed his abruptly dry mouthful as an aid to saying "What do you have in mind?"

"The words you're putting in our heads."

Slater supposed he ought to laugh, having realised Tom was thinking of the quotation on his Texts shirt. "Maybe they were there already, Tom. They're from a famous poem."

"It's not famous to me," Tom said and gazed a challenge at his sister.

"I don't know them either. Do you, mummy?"

"Had we but world enough and time—" Melanie hesitated and then said "Had we but world enough and time..."

"You're just being an echo," Tom protested. "We can see those."

"I'm trying to think what should come next." With a reproachful look at Slater she confessed "Well, I can't."

"You know it really, though," he was anxious to remind her.

"If you say so, Derek. Now can we try and concentrate on what's important?"

Using his old name had to be a rebuke for telling her what she ought to recall, but it made him feel misperceived. Tom giggled at it, though not as if he understood, and Amy said "Who's Derek?"

"Just who I was when I was both your ages. As your mother says, it's not important. Not worth remembering at all."

"So what's the rest, dad?" Tom said. "You have to know."

"So do you. You all do." When they only gazed at him Slater said fiercely "Paul Slater."

"Not of you," Tom said with a giggle that surely had no reason to be nervous. "The rest of your poem."

"It isn't just mine. It isn't even mostly." Slater glanced down at the inverted words, only to feel as if he was plummeting into meaninglessness. *emit dna* made a certain amount of sense—it suggested leaving some kind of coded trace—but how was he to interpret *hguone drlow* or even *tub ew daH*? He could have imagined that language had begun to disintegrate or that his grasp of it had. Even when he looked up, the deranged words clung to his mind, and he couldn't think how to drive them away except by speaking. "Had we but world enough and time…"

The children giggled, but Amy said "What happens if we haven't?"

"Look, I can't think of it just now, all right? Your mother's already told you it isn't important." The outburst left him nervous, and he turned on Tom. "Why are you asking me now, anyway? You've been seeing it all month."

"Then why does it say it's the text for today?"

"Don't ask me that either. I don't do all the thinking for the shop." In an attempt to find some humour in the situation Slater added "I wouldn't blame anyone if they thought I'm not much good at doing it for myself."

"Nobody does, Paul," Melanie said, and he thought he heard an unspoken apology for having used his abandoned name. "Now let's take each day as it comes, you two. And this one's your special one, so let's keep our minds on that."

The argument had distracted him so much that he couldn't recall clearing his plate. "Your mother's right," he said, "and it's time we saw you to school."

He didn't realise that he hadn't looked out of the windows until he opened the front door to find the world too white. Of course frost had drained the parked cars of colour and turned their windows blank. All the houses had grown as pallid as ice and looked no less brittle, and the dull uncoloured sky had taken up residence in every one. How cold must the night have been to make the buds shrink back into the trees? The twigs and branches were so black that they resembled fissures in the sky. The Astra and the Viva blinked and yipped as if they were starting awake, and then the only sound was a harsh tuneless duet—Tom and Amy scraping the windscreens

with the plastic implements they'd taken from the cars. As the noises
ceased in unison Slater said "Who's going first?"

The children looked uneasy before their mother understood. "You
lead if you like," she said. "Just don't go too far."

"Dad," Amy said, "can I come with you today?"

"To the school, you mean, obviously." Since she didn't deny it he
said "Certainly you may." He climbed into the Astra as she did, and
when they slammed the doors the world went out around them.

The vibration that reverberated through the car felt unduly reminiscent of the lurch he'd experienced on the plane. It seemed to pass
through him like a wave as he managed to see what had turned the
world blank. "It's just condensation," he said before Amy could speak.

As he twisted the key in the ignition he was suddenly afraid that
the computer at the core of the vehicle would let him down. The
engine came alive, however, and he switched on the wipers and the
defrosting system. The car surrounded him and Amy with its unre-
mitting artificial breath while the wipers cleared arcs of the windscreen, revealing samples of the street, a process that put Slater in
mind of a change of scene in an old film. He turned the car out of
the drive, only to wish he'd waited for the back window to clear; the
image of the Viva in the mirror was so faint that he had to strain his
mind to perceive it at all. It gained definition as he drove along the
street at a speed that wouldn't have disgraced a funeral, so that by the
time he reached the main road he was able to see Melanie and their
son. As he accelerated gently—tenderly, he might have called it—
Amy kept her eyes on the mirror and said not much louder than the
murmur of the car "Can I tell you what happened yesterday, dad?"

"Why shouldn't you be able to?"

"Maybe we aren't supposed."

"You can always tell me anything, Amy." He felt as if he was having
to remember to add "And your mother."

The car behind them had grown no clearer by the time Amy said
"Some of the girls in my class had the thing with their tummy."

"Ah." However old-fashioned he sounded, Slater had to say "That
might be best discussed with your mother."

"I don't think she likes people talking about it." With what he could have taken for eleven years' worth of reproachfulness Amy said "You were there."

He felt forgetful and disoriented. "Where, Amy? When?"

"When I told you both about it, and Tom was there too." Having apparently needed to establish all this, she said "About how it woke me up when you were coming home."

"And now you're saying your classmates noticed it as well. Nothing too odd about that, is there? And if any of them didn't, well, some people can sleep through an earthquake."

"Who says it was one?"

"You haven't forgotten your brother."

"I wouldn't," Amy said without even a hint of the loftiness Slater might have expected, "but we're not sure it was."

"I really don't know what else it could have been."

"See, we aren't supposed to talk about it."

"I've already said you can with me." Less brusquely Slater said "What makes you think you can't?"

"My friend asked a teacher what she thought it was."

"And the teacher said…"

"She didn't." As though she resented or was made uneasy by having to expound Amy said "She took my friend to see someone and we haven't seen her again."

"To see someone how? I mean, why? To see whom?"

"The teacher wouldn't tell us. She said we better hadn't ask."

"And you really haven't seen your friend at all since?" He was sounding too much like an interrogator, but he had to say "Hasn't anyone been in touch with her?"

"We can't."

"Perhaps she was upset by being singled out like that." Slater saw that Amy thought as little of the explanation as he did. "I suppose it might be best," he said, "if you don't bring up the subject today."

"My friend, you mean."

He hadn't, and was disturbed to wonder if he should have. "Perhaps she'll be there," he tried saying. "Perhaps she's waiting to tell you all what happened." When Amy gazed harder at the mirror he said "If you like I'll see what I can find out while we're at the school." There was no response beyond the blurred murmur of the car, even when he added "Or if you'd rather I didn't I won't."

Presumably this was how she might increasingly behave at her age. They were already in sight of the school; he seemed to have forgotten there was so much open land along the route. As he drew up outside the schoolyard the Viva swelled up in the mirror, and he could have thought it was growing more solid. Amy leaned over for him to kiss her forehead, and he said almost without thinking "That'll keep your mind alive."

She gazed at him as intently as she'd watched the mirror. "Dad, will you do something for us?"

"Anything I can."

"Will you leave your phone on?"

Perhaps it was just her fervency that disconcerted him. "Why would you like me to do that?"

"Then you can see if we send you a message." She seemed not too far from pleading as she said "Just in case."

While he wasn't going to ask the question that he sensed would only make her nervous, he said "Are you meant to have your phones on at school? You don't want to get into trouble after what you were saying about your friend."

"We can put them on in the breaks. Don't you want us to call you?"

"Texts mightn't." At once he felt he was letting his family down. "You're as important," he said. "No, you're more. It'll stay on."

"Thanks, dad. You'll always be our dad." She lingered to say "And mummy's husband" before straightening up from the car to call "Dad's going to leave his phone on."

Slater hadn't noticed Tom leaving Melanie's car. At first he was unable to locate the boy's face among the dozens if not hundreds that turned towards him, and he could have imagined they'd grown as homogenous as the St Dunstan's uniform. His bad night must be catching up with him, because it wasn't until Amy went to Tom that Slater singled out his son. Didn't the two of them usually join their friends? Slater was distracted by a clank not unlike the snapping of a trap—the sound of a message. He wondered if the children were making sure he'd kept his word until he saw that the sender was Melanie. That should help, the screen said.

She flourished her mobile when he found her in the mirror. Perhaps she'd concluded as he had that the children might be seeking reassurance before the concert. He brandished his phone and then responded You as well. While this could have been clearer, she gave him a smile, and he sent her one before looking away from the mirror to see the schoolyard was deserted.

He wished he'd seen the children going into the school, especially since the reflection of the sky rendered every window blank. As he drove off Melanie followed him. He oughtn't to be so conscious of her that he failed to focus on the road, and he looked ahead to see there was traffic to be kept in mind. He was nearly at the graveyard before he realised that he didn't know when her car had vanished from the mirror.

The Astra wobbled as though it had been overwhelmed by a gale. He'd caused the turbulence; his hands jerking at the wheel had. Surely he had no reason to panic, but the car wavered again as his phone uttered its clank. He pulled into the nearest entrance to the cemetery and read Melanie's new message. Love you, it said. Still here.

He was troubled by her having needed to add the last words, and he couldn't think how to respond except by copying her message back to her, which he'd never done in his life. As he put the phone away he saw the police car lurking among the memorials. Had the police seen him use the phone while the engine was running? No, the white shape beneath the unproductive trees was a tomb, not a vehicle, and he did his best to leave the error behind along with the graveyard.

The road shrank between the huddled shops, which looked more forgotten than ever. Beyond them cars were halted on the main road, but moved off as he caught sight of them. No doubt traffic lights had released them. In the retail park the sky seemed to be on its way to leaching every vehicle of colour. Was he parking in yesterday's space? When he glanced back at the Astra he could have thought the windscreen had already grown as frosted as its neighbours, but that must be the reflection of the sky as well.

Another reflection met him at Texts, though when the pallid glass doors slipped apart he saw that to some extent it had been composed of Shelley Blake. He wondered how long she'd spent in emphasising her features, outlining her grey eyes as if to stop them growing paler, pinkening her lips. Even her silvery blonde hair looked more metallic, exhaustively touched up. Since she appeared to expect him to speak first, he felt as if he should have prepared a remark. "On time this time," he said.

"Let's hope it's every day now." Surely she didn't need to think before adding "Paul."

"Let's hope they aren't all like this one." Perhaps that sounded too unenthusiastic, and he jerked his head to indicate the sky—it felt not unlike lurching awake. "How much longer do you think we're going to carry on like this?"

"I think we'd better carry on just as we have been. That's why we're here."

She either hadn't understood or chose not to understand. The doors met behind him, shutting in an almost inaudible vaguely musical murmur. When he raised his eyes in its general direction Shelley Blake said "Is that still you?"

"Don't you know?" In case this seemed too combative he said "I mean, didn't someone start it off today?"

"It's whatever was here overnight."

"Then I expect I'm responsible." Since her expression didn't waver, not that there was much of it, Slater said "Would you like a change?"

"We don't want anything out of hand. Just be sure you play it safe."

As he wondered how much less adventurous she imagined a choice of music could be, she said "And then can you put everything in order?"

"Everything," Slater said and risked a laugh.

"All the discs." She stared at his badge as if this would remind him of his job. "All your music, Paul." As he thought of retorting that it was by no means all his she said "Make sure it's the right order."

"Which one is that?"

"The one everybody wants. There's only one." She plainly felt it was unreasonable of him to make her add "The one everybody can see."

She had to mean whichever was easiest to understand. Slater went to the racks to find the shop its music. He was disconcerted by how complicated the arrangement of the discs seemed, even to him: composers, performers, conductors, symphonies, concertos, operas, oratorios, songs... He felt incapable of making a selection until film music came into his mind, but *Fantasia* ought to strike a chord with everyone. No sooner had he thought of it than he saw the album in the rack. As the Bach prelude that conjured up innumerable macabre films began a muted thunder overhead, Slater made for the staff quarters, tugging out his badge to meet the plaque. "Paul Slater," he snarled under his breath in case the system was reluctant to acknowledge him, and felt as if he might have to say more until he heard the mechanism find in his favour.

The music followed him into the staffroom—notes that kept mounting towards a peak to fall back and recommence their climb. On the way to his locker he caught sight of the memory board, which still displayed the remnants of the message in his handwriting. How could there be more to it than he'd previously seen? He must be viewing it from an angle at which the overhead glare didn't blot out quite so many characters, faint though they were. *ERE PA LATE*—he still couldn't reconstruct the words, which left him feeling inadequate. He raised a hand to wipe out the meaningless fragments but instead hurried to his locker.

The metal door shut with a clank like the amplified sound of an incoming message. The children would be in their classes by now, and Melanie might be on the road. He wished he'd thought to ask where she was working. The music had risen into a blaze of sound suggestive of an unquenchable light, unless the film had put that into his head. It couldn't dispel the pallid blankness that surrounded him—the concrete walls—and once the time clock had contributed a random note to the music he made his way out of the room.

He didn't know how long he gazed at the racks, trying to see how the discs could be better arranged—long enough that he began to feel in danger of forgetting what the sight meant. It was music rendered solid; no, it was a kind of memory of music, fragments of the past stored in the form of impulses. He needn't dwell on that, because the idea seemed to leave him less able to read the names and words. Surely it was best to use the ones that were poking up on tags above the discs for customers to see, not that there were many of those in the shop just now. Composers had to come first, or there would be no music, or had folk music come before any composer? On second thought the alphabet must be the solution; it was the order most people knew. So a performer like Glenn Gould preceded Handel after all, and Angela Hewitt took precedence over Holst, but did she over Bach? Surely last names counted most, since some people mightn't know the others. For a moment Slater could have imagined that the racks were already in the order he'd thought up, but he had to remember that wasn't how he'd just seen them. He took hold of the handful of cases behind the letter A—composers insufficiently prolific to have name tags of their own—and moved them to the beginning, and then he set about following them.

The cases and the tags clacked like counters in a game. The sound kept driving the music out of his head, and soon he'd lost all sense of time and even of the shop around him. He mustn't grow unaware of Melanie and the children, wherever they were just now, and he was fixing as much of his mind on them as he could spare when a voice he ought to know said "Trying to put it all back together?"

He turned to be met by a blur, hardly even a sketch of a face. It regained its features as he confronted it fully—the eyes peering from beneath the overstated eyebrows, the mouth that seemed to need defining by its hairy frame, a few surplus strands accentuating the nostrils. The sight made Slater wonder when he'd last shaved: presumably this morning, since however hard he rubbed his chin he couldn't feel any stubble. "Doing my best," he said. "What can I do for you today, Mr Allen?"

"Maybe you have. You remember."

"Your order, you mean. It may be a bit soon," Slater said but made for the Information desk. "Let me see for you."

"Thank you, Mr Slayer."

Although Slater must have misheard, he hesitated at the computer. What name had he needed to type last time? The Bach hovered over him again—four notes tramping upwards, three of them outdistancing the fourth—as he remembered that the system called for his first name: no, not Derek. He keyed the four letters and brought up the customer's order. "As I say, Mr Allen…"

"Close enough."

"I'm afraid it hasn't come for you yet."

"Not a problem and maybe the opposite. Any chance you can take it off the computer?"

"I should think we'd be in time. You're saying you don't want it now."

"I think we may have remembered it wrong, the both of us." As Slater attempted to feel less incompetent the man said "It was a poem, not a song."

"It could still have been set to music."

"Maybe everything can be." Allen tilted his head towards the music that was following Bach—the Tchaikovsky suite. "Like the funguses," he said.

He must have the film in mind. Slater might have pointed out that he had the process back to front—the music had produced the mushrooms—but only said "Do you recall the poem?"

"I remember, I remember." It wasn't clear that these were the opening words until the man added "It wasn't the town where you were born, it was the house."

Rather than attempt to recall where that had been in his case Slater said "I'm afraid I don't know any music for that."

"Nobody's expecting you to. Do you know how it goes on? But now I often wish the night had borne my breath away."

Slater reminded himself that this was only a quotation. "Shall I get rid of this, then?"

"May as well. You don't want too much stuff on the system."

As Slater cancelled the order he saw his postcode vanish from the screen, and was disconcerted by how vulnerable this made him feel. He found himself taking hold of the phone in his pocket like some kind of talisman. A glance showed him it hadn't received any messages, which seemed reassuring enough to let him say "You'd have felt what my family did the other night."

"Why," Allen said with an oddly guarded look, "what did they do?"

"Nothing." The word seemed too bare, not to mention defensive. "They didn't do anything at all," Slater insisted. "I'm saying what they felt."

"Which other night?"

"Not the last one. The one before."

"The last one." Perhaps the man was simply sampling the phrase. "Nonesday, you mean," Allen said. "You're telling me I know what they felt."

"I'm assuming you must have felt it as well, knowing where you live."

"Didn't you just blank that out? What are we meant to have felt?"

"I'm told it was an earthquake."

"I don't think I'd have felt one of those."

Slater couldn't very well not ask "Why, what else was happening?"

"I don't know what you'd call it. Maybe a bit of a seizure. First one I'd had in all my life."

Though the man was visibly reluctant to talk about it, Slater felt compelled to learn "What did it do to you?"

"Put me out like a light. I don't know how long I was. Next thing I knew it was starting to be the next day."

Slater wasn't sure that he wanted to ask "Have you any idea what time it happened?"

"I'd say about midnight." Some kind of resolution made the man add "No, midnight it is."

"It sounds like what some of my family felt." Having said that, Slater was driven to add "Someone at my children's school was talking about it as well."

"What did they say to you?"

"I wasn't there. They were asking a teacher." Although he felt as if he'd already said too much, he told Allen "Apparently the teacher didn't like it much and took them to see someone."

"A doctor, would that be?"

"I don't know." In a moment Slater blurted "Nobody seems to. That's what bothers me."

"You needn't let it. They weren't one of yours by the sound of it."

"I oughtn't to be concerned just with my family."

"You want to watch what you let in your mind these days."

Before Slater could enquire what this had to do with Allen or anyone outside the family, Shelley Blake said "When you're in the shop it should be on the shop."

Slater had no idea how long she had been listening or even where she'd come from, though Allen looked unsurprised enough to suggest he'd been aware of her. "I think it is," Slater objected, "if I'm dealing with a customer."

"I'd better stop pretending to be one then, hadn't I?" Allen took his leave by adding "Thanks for looking for me."

Shelley kept her gaze on Slater, who said "I believe he's a neighbour of ours."

She might almost have been giving him a minute's silence before she said "Some thoughts are best kept to yourself."

"You don't mean that one."

It wasn't much of a joke, and even less once it was out. As if he hadn't spoken Shelley said "A lot better if you don't have them at all."

"Forgive me, what are we talking about?" When she gave him a stare as blank as the sky—it looked like a refusal to think—he said "I've never been a Finalist, if that's what you're getting at. I'm even less likely to be one now."

He wouldn't have thought it possible for her eyes to grow blanker. "I wish you hadn't brought that up," she said. "Try keeping your mind on the job."

When she moved away he turned his attention to the racks, and his awareness of her vanished like a breath, taking his rage at her admonition with it. Where had he been before he was interrupted?

Best to start again at the beginning in order not to be distracted by
the hours that were dancing in the air. Even if they were invisible,
were they rendering time more substantial? He didn't quite know
what he meant by that, especially since he'd forgotten whether they
were elephants or hippopotami. Besides confusing him, this made
him think he ought to recall something else. There was just his family, and a surreptitious glance at his mobile confirmed that they still
hadn't sent him a message, although why should he feel reassured
that there was no sign of them? Perhaps they were waiting for some
word from him.

As he brought their names into the destination window he wished
his mother had a mobile too. Was Melanie keeping in touch with her
parents? He assumed she must be, but he hadn't room for any more
people in his mind just now; he was too busy thinking of a message.
I'm all right, he typed and added so long as you are, holding
the phone as low as he could reach. Every letter emitted a muted
bleep that reminded him how electronic the communication was,
and he couldn't help feeling spied upon, even though he wasn't visible in any of the security mirrors, at least not to himself. He launched
the message and watched the icon blink to indicate that his words
were on their way. The instant the symbol subsided he put away the
mobile, and looked up to see a man and woman entering the shop.

Though he didn't recall having seen them before, he knew they
were security. They were so identically watchful that their expressions seemed to sum up the whole of them. He could easily have
fancied that their vigilance had clenched their compact faces. He
glanced about in search of a shoplifter or some other kind of crim-
inal, but couldn't even see a customer. Those of his colleagues he
could see were keeping their heads well down. He managed not to
realise who the quarry was until the newcomers paced around either
end of the music racks to close in on him.

They were in uniform, twin outfits so thoroughly grey that they
looked close to denying any colour. The woman's cropped hair was
only slightly longer than the man's, and her eyebrows were even less
defined than his, as though to compensate. Their lips and eyes were

nearly as pale as their skin, which had all the smoothness of the sky. The woman opened her mouth, but it was her partner who said "Mr Derek."

Slater did his best to feel misidentified. "That's not me."

Their attention seemed to converge on his badge. "It's on the record, Mr Slater," the woman said.

"I am, am I?" he said and felt as if his words were playing with him. "What's the trouble?"

"You won't want to discuss it here," the man said.

Slater wasn't far from panic. "Is it to do with my family?"

"It doesn't have to be."

He would have liked to hear more reassurance in the woman's voice. "You want somewhere private, do you?"

"We think you may," the man told him.

Though Slater didn't know why he should feel responsible or even if he should, he made for the staffroom. At the plaque the guards loomed on either side of him. "You know who I am," he muttered, "don't start pretending you don't," and dragged his name out from his chest to fit to the reader. The door gave, and the solid pallor of the staffroom closed around him. As he found a chair at the head of the table, which appeared to have been scrubbed completely featureless, the man sat on his left while the woman sat opposite her colleague, and Slater could have thought their faces were adding to the blankness of the room. "So," he said in an attempt to regain some sense of the situation, "what can I do for you?"

"Better do it for yourself," the woman said.

"And your family."

"A bit of a task," Slater retorted, "if I don't know what I'm doing."

They met this with a look that put him in mind of pincers gripping him. "We hear you've been having doubts," the man said.

"Hear from whom?" When their eyes grew blank as a silence rendered visible, Slater said "Has someone here been talking about me?"

"No need for that."

He wasn't sure whether the man was rebuking him, even when the woman said "We've observations of our own."

"You've been observing me, have you?" He felt as if their inex-pressiveness was swallowing his rage without a trace. "And all you've found," he said, "is I've been having doubts."

"And disturbing other people," the woman said.

"Which other people?" Slater had a disconcertingly undefined sense that he shouldn't have asked that, or indeed "Doubts about what?"

"The state of things," the man said like a warning.

"Since when haven't we been allowed to question that, whatever it is? I didn't think that was the kind of place I was living in."

"Perhaps it's time it was," the woman said.

"If it's for everyone's good."

"My god, you sound like Finalists. They couldn't see beyond their own beliefs either."

"No," the woman said, "we're the opposite."

"And they're one thing you should forget about," the man said.

Slater wasn't going to be told what he ought to remember. As incredulously as he could manage he said "Is this really all because I was asking about the earthquake?"

Nobody spoke. Their eyes might even have been trying to deny that he had and to convince him of it as well. Anger indistinguish-able from panic provoked him to blurt "Are you the same people who take children away for asking too much?"

He didn't need their eyes to tell him that they were. They could hardly arrest him for it, and he demanded "What happens to them?"

"They see the truth." Just as tonelessly the woman said "Exactly what do you think you're going to achieve?"

"You're doing nobody any good," the man said, "least of all yourself."

Slater had a grotesque sense of listening to parents. He'd found nothing to say when an electronic clank resounded through the room. "Better see what you have," the woman said.

The phone clanked again as he took hold of it, and once more as he fumbled it out of his pocket. "Take your time," the male guard said.

This infuriated Slater almost too much to let him finger the keys. We are, he saw at last, and then We are and We are. Of course that didn't mean the senders were together. Tom and Amy might be, and presumably Melanie felt able to speak for them all. "It's my family," he said.

"Are they as they ought to be?"

Before Slater could respond to her question the woman's partner said "Best concentrate on keeping them that way."

Slater was on the brink of enquiring what kind of threat this was meant to be, but only said "How do you suggest I should do that?"

"You might try responding to them," the woman said.

He barely held back from retorting that he didn't need this kind of advice. How much did she think she knew about him and his family? How closely could they have been observed? He did his best to think he was saving them as he replied Then we all are. He looked up to find the guards were gazing in the vague direction of the subdued music, Bach tramping eternally uphill. "Are you giving us that?" the woman said.

Had they even watched him choose the disc? Slater couldn't quite ask but said "It's part of my job."

"We'll let you get back to the rest," the man said.

Slater couldn't risk believing they'd finished with him until they stood up in unison. They stood aside to let him touch his badge to the inner plaque, and then they led or at any rate accompanied him to the music section, where they lingered to watch him start putting the Adams albums in sequence. "That's more like it," the man said. "Order keeps the world in shape."

"That's what you should be about, Mr Paul."

"Mr Slater," the man added or amended.

While resenting their praise Slater was disgusted to find that it came as a relief, all of which he kept to himself in the hope they would leave him alone. He concentrated on his task until he realised they'd gone away, and then he did his utmost to forget them and whatever they represented. He couldn't afford any more distractions; he had to finish before it was time to leave for the concert. The clatter of plastic reminded him of tiles in a gambling game, and he was struggling to focus on only the names when he became aware that Shelley Blake was watching him. "Don't let me take your mind off it," she said.

"I'm afraid our visitors did." Having managed to recall that she hadn't been responsible for them, Slater said "Sorry if they bothered you."

"They shouldn't bother anyone."

"They rather did me. If you're wondering—"

"I'm not, Paul. I don't want to know, and nobody else does. So long as they're happy, that's all that matters."

"I'd say at least a few more people do."

"Nobody's saying you shouldn't keep them in mind."

The conversation had begun to feel as indefinite as a discussion in a dream, and he went back to rearranging names. He hadn't time for lunch, and he could do without dealing with customers too, not that he was aware of any. The light of the sky seemed as artificially constant as the glow of the fluorescents overhead, all of which robbed him of any sense of the passing of time. When he became aware of Shelley Blake once more he could have thought she had never moved away, but his watch showed him he'd come to the end of his shift. "Well, Paul," she said.

This sounded no less neutral than the sky looked, and he strained to find some meaning in it. "I think I'm finished for the day," he said.

"Is it as it should be?"

Someone else had said the like of that recently, but he couldn't recall any more. "It is for now. I'll come back to it next time."

"Tomorrow."

"Not tomorrow." Her word felt altogether too possessive, and he had to reclaim the day. "Sunday," he said. "I'm with my family tomorrow. I should be with them now."

"I must have forgotten you weren't here." With a look that seemed to want to hold him where he stood she said "We will be."

He would have supposed so without being told, and he didn't understand her emphasis. Outside the shop the parked cars seemed

more faded than ever. No doubt the daylight was too muffled to dispel the frost, which helped to give them an abandoned look. The yip
with which the Astra greeted him sounded enfeebled, surely because
so many vehicles were in the way; he needn't panic over thinking
the electronics had run down. He started the engine and set off the
wipers to bring the world back into some kind of focus. While it
wasn't yet time for the concert, he couldn't help growing nervous
while he waited for the windows to clear.

He would have expected to find more people heading home on the
main road. Where he turned towards the school the dilapidated shops
looked grey as ash and hardly more substantial, as if they might collapse before his eyes. In the cemetery the trees were propping up the
sky, and he couldn't make out a single inscription; the stones might as
well have been blank. An open space showed him St Dunstan's ahead.
The mass of railings edged apart, letting the long blocks of the school
regain their shape, and he saw a solitary figure in the yard.

It was Melanie. He parked behind her car in the line of frozen
vehicles alongside the featureless slabs of the pavement and hurried
into the schoolyard. "Am I late?" he called.

"You just aren't," Melanie said, already heading for the main
entrance.

Beyond the doors, which were as silent as they were imposing,
a corridor that apparently had no time for colours led towards the
blurred murmur of an audience. A stretch of the left-hand wall was
occupied by overcoats unnecessarily reminiscent of abandoned
wings. As Slater hastened after Melanie the tuneless mass of voices
kept any identifiable words to itself, and he had an odd sense of over-
hearing a rehearsal. The murmur rose as though to greet him when
he opened the door to the assembly hall, where the sight of hundreds
of backs of heads seemed to render the dialogue even more secretive.
As he hurried ahead of Melanie in search of unoccupied seats he
felt no less anxious than he had in the car park. He didn't think he'd
breathed for a while by the time he located a pair of empty seats near
the middle of the third row from the bare stage. "Excuse me," he
called above the blur of voices, "are those anyone's?"

Every face between him and the spaces turned to gaze at him. Of course only their movements were identical. "They'll be yours," someone said.

All the watchers faced the stage and stood up in unison to make way for Melanie, and Slater was reminded of illustrations popping up from a book he'd owned as a child. They stayed on their feet until he passed along the row, keeping Melanie in sight, which meant the series of faces on the edge of his vision lost any individuality they had. As he sat down, the line of figures did, but he couldn't hear the folding seats for the omnipresent murmur, which had begun to seem as indistinct as the sky that was the entire content of the high windows. He found the murmur breathlessly oppressive, and was struggling to think of some conversation when it faded into silence as though a volume control had been turned down. The headmistress had taken the stage. "Welcome to St Dunstan's," she said.

He was thrown by her resemblance to Shelley Blake, though he was unable to recall how else he might have expected her to look. Her fingers were loosely intertwined like a reminiscence of a prayer, which made him feel guilty, singled out at school. He and Melanie had professed enough of a belief to have the children enrolled at St Dunstan's, but only because of its musical reputation. At least their lack of a belief was strong enough to fend off the likes of the Finalists, he told himself as the headmistress said "You know how much time we've spent getting ready for you, and I know you'll agree it has been worthwhile."

She had more to say while some of the pupils carried music stands and chairs onstage, to be followed by the orchestra with their instruments. Slater wondered why all this had been left so late, although he hadn't realised when he'd seen the stage was bare. The muted activity seemed to merge into an undifferentiated blur that distracted him from the speech, but he managed to hear the headmistress say "You've come for the music, not to hear me. Here's some I'm sure you know."

Slater did before the orchestra had played five notes. It was the *Pastoral,* and performed a good deal more to his taste than in the film or at the shop. The cartoon images seemed to be leaving him alone, and he found himself waiting for the hymn after the storm. It wasn't actually a hymn; Beethoven hadn't been naïve enough to think it would bring back the sun, and it couldn't hold off the night either. Slater was reminded of the Finalists; suppose their belief had been the strongest in the world, however briefly? They had certainly managed to convey it to everyone he could bring to mind. It might have been too powerful to have gone away, in which case what had happened to it? Of course it was irrational, but then so were its adherents, and mightn't that add to its power for them? Where had they all gone? There was no point in glancing at his neighbours—that wouldn't show him whether they were among the faithful—but the line of faces dwindling towards the walls troubled him, especially the faces at the far end, where he could have thought they were merging with the pale blurred surface. At last the symphony disintegrated into an explosion of applause, and as Slater stopped clapping the headmistress said "Now it's time for voices."

She was somewhere out of sight in the front row. The renewed murmur of the audience covered up any sounds the choir made in gathering onstage. Their faces put Slater in mind of pale flowers blooming from a mass of foliage. At first he couldn't see Amy or Tom, but then he was aware only of them. They looked at least as intent as several other people he'd encountered recently, an earnestness that didn't falter even when the children met his eyes. As they shifted their gaze to the conductor who had taken up her post in front of the choir, she raised her hands, reviving the silence. Slater saw Tom and Amy take a breath or at any rate part their lips, and found he couldn't breathe himself. He'd heard less than the first phrase when he was overtaken by the notion that he'd already known what they would sing. "In this fair town where I was born…"

Did the man who'd tried to order it have a child at the school? Slater wasn't sure the explanation could bear too much scrutiny, but surely it would let him concentrate on the performance. "All in the merry month of May…" He wasn't about to look for Allen in the audience; just the thought made the faces beside him seem far too reminiscent of an identity parade. "And death was drawing nigh him..." As he saw their mouths shaping the syllables he wondered if this was what somebody had in mind when they'd said a word was made flesh. He supposed he shouldn't think that here, and perhaps anywhere else, not least because it felt like a threat to perception. "As she was walking o'er the fields, she heard the death bell knelling..." Words were information, and he might easily conclude that all life was a form of it—a set of electronic impulses—but where did that lead him? Nowhere he thought he would choose to go, and he tried to drive the reverie out of his mind by only hearing the ballad. "Farewell..." This wasn't the last word, it was the first one of the final verse, but it seemed capable of doing away with everything that came after.

The hush that followed the final word of the choir—"Allen," which Slater could imagine was trying to remind him of someone— immediately splintered into applause that saw the children off the stage. As soon as he couldn't see Amy and Tom he was anxious to know where they were. He twisted around until he found them by the back wall, among other members of the choir. When he faced the stage again he was dogged by an impression that he'd recognised more people in the audience than he would have expected, even if he couldn't bring them to mind now. "Nothing's wrong," he muttered in case Melanie was about to ask, as well as on his own behalf.

It would disrupt the occasion too much if he were to take the family and leave. He felt as if he'd been warned not to cause disorder. Remembering that soon they would all be together helped him sit through the rest of the concert—a young pianist playing a transcription of Bach's famous prelude and fugue, a selection from Tchaikovsky's best-known ballet arranged for a chamber group whose percussion sounded oddly electronic, a soprano singing Schubert's "Ave Maria," an orchestral finale that took the listener up the mountain to meet the demon. At last the frenzy of the resurrected sank back into the graves, and the music had scarcely faded to its final note when someone burst into applause as if they couldn't bear the silence.

Slater wasn't slow to follow. Melanie joined in, and he saw pairs of hands rise up on both sides of him like a startled flock of winged creatures. As the clapping subsided and the row began to empty, Tom and Amy came to find their parents. "You really brought it alive," Melanie said. "You were stellar."

"You deserve to be up in the sky," Slater said.

Perhaps this went too far, which might explain why Amy was gazing hard at him. "Dad."

"Amy," he said and wondered why he had an impulse to add her brother's name.

"I can't see her."

More nervously than he could recall ever having heard her speak, Melanie said "Who?"

"The girl I told dad about. The one they—"

"Not now, Amy." Slater had a sense that far too many people were listening; he could even have fancied that the entire audience had halted on its way out of the hall—that if he looked he might see someone who had interrogated him. "Later," he said.

"When later?"

"Tomorrow."

It was the only answer that came into his mind, but he felt as though he'd made a promise, especially when Tom's eyes brightened. "We're going to see the sun, aren't we? You said."

"I don't know how far we may have to go."

"That doesn't matter, does it, mummy?" Amy said. "We'll all be together."

"That's all it's about," Melanie said.

Slater looked away to see that the hall was deserted, though he hadn't heard anyone leave. Being confronted by the rows of unoccupied seats made him feel like he was at a show that had come to an end, or at least to an interval. "Time we were home," he said.

The corridor wall was bare of coats. Tom and Amy had theirs—indeed, they'd put them on. The empty schoolyard felt as if the walls and the equally blank ceiling of the corridor had opened out and risen, but not enough. "Who's in my car?" Slater said as he made for the gates.

"I wish we'd just used one."

He didn't need to understand why Melanie felt that way. "We will tomorrow."

"It's my turn," Tom declared and turned to his sister. "You be with mummy."

Slater couldn't see why the boy thought he had to tell her. No doubt if Tom didn't have some strange ideas he wouldn't be a child, and the same must be true of his sister. Slater supposed he'd entertained a few odd notions when he was either of their ages, but it wasn't worth attempting to remember. He climbed into the Astra and let his son in while Melanie and Amy carried out their version of the routine. Once he'd followed the Viva away from the kerb he glanced in the mirror but couldn't see the school. All that mattered was to keep Melanie and their daughter in sight, though of course not to the exclusion of Tom. The boy seemed as intent on them as Slater was, and his voice sounded no less concerned. "Dad?"

"Tom."

"What was Amy saying happened to some girl?"

"She was spirited away for asking too much." While Slater meant this for an amiable warning, it seemed to have turned more ominous. "I don't really know and Amy doesn't either," he said. "I think it's best forgotten."

"You said you were going to talk about it tomorrow."

"I'm sure we'll have better things to do then, aren't you?" More urgently than he understood Slater said "Don't remind her and perhaps she won't remember."

Tom stared ahead so fiercely that Slater wondered what he thought he saw. There was just the other car beneath the sky that seemed to weigh on the trees, which looked close to sinking into the open spaces that bordered the road. As the Viva led the Astra into St Peter Street the trees closed in, and so did the sky as though its supports had begun to give way. Everything outside the car looked attenuated by the pallor that lingered on the windows, and even when Slater ducked out of the car in the drive the dull glare of the sky seemed to have diminished his vision. "Let's get inside," he muttered, blinking at the family to bring them into focus.

He couldn't judge how much of a difference the hall light made to the pallor that appeared to have settled into the house. "What are we having for dinner?" Melanie said.

Slater supposed she was asking for preferences, but Amy said "I'm not very hungry."

"I'm not," Tom said.

"Did you have something before the concert? Hasn't it left any room?" When they'd finished nodding and the opposite Melanie said "Then you'd better say, Paul."

"I wouldn't say no to an early night if we don't know how far I'll be driving tomorrow."

"One of us can." She might have been about to tell him not to leave them so soon, but whatever she saw in his eyes seemed to change her mind. "I shouldn't think you'll need singing to sleep," she said.

"I never have," Slater told her and was unable to recall ever having sung Tom or Amy to sleep. He didn't think he ever would. A sharp pang of loss that he didn't want to understand, never mind letting his family suspect, made him retreat to the bathroom.

As he foamed at the mouth or at any rate the teeth he wondered what was troubling him. Was there a word he ought to find significant? It wasn't retails or even relates, though it might be related to both. Of course, it was his name in the mirror. He couldn't have said why the rearrangement of the name made him feel vulnerable, but he dropped the badge face down beside the sink. The vibration of the toothbrush resounded through his head until the electronic roaming felt indistinguishable from him. Laying down his badge hadn't prevented the image in the mirror from continuing to bemuse him. What exactly did it consist of? What did he? If it was a projection of himself, what else might be? He didn't want to be alone with it or his thoughts, and he barely lingered to grab his tag.

The family came to their doors as he made for the bedroom. "We'll be early too," Melanie said.

"We won't be late," Amy told him.

Presumably this was a bid at a quip, but it sounded somehow ominous. It hung in the air until Tom pointed at the badge his father had taken off. "Now you aren't a text, dad."

Slater wasn't sure how to welcome this or even if he did. He left Melanie a hug as he slipped past her into their bedroom. As he took his place in the bed he planted his badge on the table beside it, only to feel as if he was making sure he would be identifiable in the night. Who would need to identify him? He closed his eyes and felt they were shutting out too much of the world. He thought he'd closed them for scarcely a moment, but when he opened them he saw that the window was dark.

Surely that meant he could sleep, and he would let himself once Melanie joined him. In fact she was beside him, and the room was dark as well. He slid a hand around her to be gripped hard and closed his eyes to help him concentrate on her presence, but his mind had a question for him. Had he overlooked a name? Which was the one that came first? He ought to solve the problem before he tried to sleep, so as to be ready for Sunday—not the day of the sun, which would be tomorrow. Sunday didn't mean that putting the names in order had anything to do with religion, but it seemed to be his kind of ritual, and wasn't religion an attempt to bring order to the world? Wasn't any belief? Names—his mind felt in danger of being overwhelmed by them, and there might well be a composer before Adams, perhaps someone called Abbot, though surely not Abate. And did Bach lead the Bs? Babbitt sounded possible, but Babel was something else, conceivably the mass of names in his mind. Babel had been the outcome of reaching for heaven, and he hadn't realised how many scraps of religion had lodged in his consciousness. Did he need singing to sleep after all? He mustn't disturb his family, but perhaps he could simply imagine the music. If he could just bring to mind a phrase by each composer in order, that might be better than a lullaby for him.

He didn't know how long he had been straining to think of a melody of Abbot's by the time he heard the music. At first he thought it was a man's voice—perhaps he was asleep after all, and singing—until he managed to distinguish that there was more than one, so muffled or so distant that he'd taken them for a solitary murmur. It was the ballad again; the children were breathing it, possibly in their sleep. Their voices proved they were still there in the dark, which meant he needn't go to look, let alone imagine that they were using the song to remind themselves of their own existence. Or could he be dreaming the voices? Dreams were disordered memories, after all, that adopted new shapes in the mind. He mustn't let them do that—he didn't even want to think why not—and he redoubled his hold on Melanie's waist in the hope of regaining control of his thoughts. He might have asked if she could hear the children, supposing she was awake, but she wasn't there at all.

That and his silent struggle to cry out snatched his eyes open. She was standing at the end of the bed, hand in hand with the children. "Back in the land of the living?" she said. "We're ready whenever you are."

They were indeed dressed for an outing. As he sat up, Slater peered at the window but could see nothing beyond the glass. It took him some time to grasp that the sky had stayed blank. "Still no sun," he mumbled.

"You said we'd find it," Tom reminded him.

"We'll go up if we have to, won't we?" Amy said.

"We may." Slater found he was groping about the bedside table, but he didn't need the time, never mind his name badge. "Anyway, let me get going," he said. "Someone can bring me a coffee if they like."

"There's nothing in the house, Paul."

"Nothing," Slater said and tried to sound only jovially incredulous. "Haven't we been to the shops?"

"I've had other things on my mind just like everybody else." Her desire not to worry the subject was plain as she said "We can look for something on the way if anyone's bothered."

She and the children moved towards the stairs as Slater made for the bathroom. Once the door was shut, if not sooner than that, he couldn't hear them. He was tempted to call out, but it was enough to know they were close. There was no harm in reminding them that he was, though he couldn't remember the words of the ballad. He set about humming melodies at the top, such as it was, of his voice—the various themes of the *Pastoral*. He needed to be sure they were in order, though weren't the notes themselves a form of order? What sort did they bring to the world? He was uncertain whether he could hear an echo or a voice, perhaps more than one, joining in. None of the sounds could belong to his reflection, however animated by the music it appeared to be, swaying if not dancing to the rhythms and conducting them as well. Of course this meant that he was doing so, even if it felt like mimicking an image of himself. The idea didn't appeal to him, any more than the pallor that had settled on the glass to attenuate his reflection. He left the bathroom as soon as he could, to see the family sitting on the stairs. They looked like three descending stages of a life, not unreminiscent of the photographs above them. "Was anyone singing?" he said.

"You were," Amy said, and Tom confirmed it with a giggle.

Melanie came to stand in the bedroom doorway while Slater dressed, and he couldn't decide whether she was playing a guard or a go-between. Perhaps she simply meant for some reason to encourage him to be quick. She sent the children to make a last use of the bathroom, and he had an odd sense that she'd remembered a scrap of their domestic ritual. As she opened the front door he thought at least one of the children murmured "Goodbye, house."

In the street the trees looked worn down by the pallor that seemed to have descended into them, and Slater could have fancied they were forgetting how to bud. The windows of the Viva and the Astra were blank slabs set in the pallid metal. "Who's going to drive?" Melanie said.

"I expect you two will in time." Having extracted tentative smiles from the children, he told Melanie "Let me, and you can take over if we need you to."

The Astra emitted its puppyish yip and gave them a coquettish blink, a performance that he seemed to recall amused Tom and Amy once upon a time. They climbed in the back as Melanie sat beside him, and he saw that the windows weren't too frosted after all, however uncertain the substance of the world beyond them looked. "Ready for the big adventure?" he said, and when he'd found the children in the mirror "Where do we all want to go?"

"Where the sun's gone," Tom said.

"That'll be through the tunnel," Amy told them.

"She's right, isn't she?" Slater said. "We're best going under the river if we want to catch it up."

"You're the driver," Melanie said.

As he swung the car out of the drive he lost sight of the house. By the time they reached the main road he could have thought the street had reverted to a grove; certainly that was how it appeared in the mirror, but he didn't look back. At least today's route wouldn't take him past the graveyard, where he imagined the stones and the trees deep in a secret colloquy like silence rendered solid.

There was very little traffic. He would have said all the cars they passed were parked if not abandoned, except that the occasional vehicle seemed to acknowledge his attention by moving off. Was there a fog—the frost in a less substantial form? He found it hard to make out houses, all of which appeared to be occupied by the sunless sky. Any faces he might have glimpsed at windows looked oddly nominal, more like images on screens, even if they were watching him and the family. As for any shops, it must have been too early for them to be open, and their shutters left them so blank that they mightn't have been there at all.

The road had left all the buildings behind by the time it led down to the tunnel. Beyond the slanting ramp an arch stood over each of the two deserted lanes. As soon as Slater drove beneath the left-hand arch the pale ceiling and its apparently sourceless glow closed over the car. He couldn't judge when the weight of the earth above it gave way to the burden of the invisible river, but it felt as though the blank surface that straddled the car was growing more oppressively present as the enclosed road sank lower, pressed down by the roof. The sight of the unrelieved vista that stretched more than a mile to a subterranean bend seemed to have silenced the family and, he could have thought, the car as well. Unable to think of anything he cared to say, he began to hum the reminiscences of the *Pastoral*. Before long Melanie joined in, and then the children did. Beethoven had never meant the music as a vocal quartet, but there was nobody except the family to hear. Slater didn't know how often they'd rehearsed the themes when they came to the bend, which appeared to lead up to an unrelieved pale blankness. No, there was a line of tollbooths, and he was suddenly afraid he'd come all this way to no avail. "Have we got some money?" he said not unlike a prayer.

"We couldn't forget that, could we?" Melanie said.

He wasn't sure how much of a question this might be until she displayed the coins, which reassured him for as long as he failed to notice what was odd about the tollbooths. Surely most of the barriers beyond the narrow booths used to be automatic, but now every cabin was occupied, and every face turned in unison to watch the car. He had an uneasy sense that he was close to recognising some of them—far too many, if not all—or was that a result of their expressionless official look, which was identical, not just among themselves but with everyone who'd interrogated him since he'd come home? He had to choose a booth before anyone could find his hesitation suspicious, and he drove towards the exit in the middle of the line. "Nobody say anything," he almost didn't think to mutter. "If anyone has to talk I will."

The attendant was a woman or a man with long nondescript hair—the smooth bland inexpressive face gave no indication of gender. Slater was on the way past the booth to the toll basket when the window above him slid back and the attendant leaned over the sill. "A moment, please."

The pale voice seemed sexless too. The lack of any character made the attendant seem to sum up all the officials Slater had encountered recently—an ominous summation. He saw the barrier twitch like a warning not to proceed. "What's wrong?" he blurted.

"What do you think is?"

"Nothing if you say so."

He didn't care how much this sounded like a plea so long as it let them past the barrier. The eyes gazing at him were so pale or so reflective of the sky that he couldn't distinguish the pupils. "May we ask where you're going?" the attendant said.

Retorting that it was nobody's business but the family's wouldn't make the attendant go away. Slater didn't know when all the faces in the other booths had turned to watch him. "Out for a run," he said.

"Not running away, are you?"

"What would I be running from?"

He had a nervous sense of having said too much—that the trick was not to suggest anything was amiss, even by implying that it couldn't be. The blank gaze rested on him for an indeterminate time before the attendant said "What are you taking where you plan to go?"

"Where am I, back at immigration?" Instead of demanding this Slater said "Just my family. You can see."

The attendant didn't look away from him. The blankness seemed to spread out of the eyes as the face withdrew into the booth, and Slater could have thought the features had grown altogether too indefinite. "Can we go now?" he blurted.

"Wherever you think."

He couldn't even tell which booth the muffled voice came from. Melanie handed him the coins to throw into the metal basket, and as the barrier wavered upwards he thought he heard a sound on both sides of the car, a murmur less than words—less than a sigh. A glance in the mirror as he drove onto the motorway showed him the row of narrow boxes, each peopled by a figure that looked as if it was propped up. While all of them appeared to be gazing after the car, he couldn't make out an expression or indeed a face. Then the windows of the booths turned pallidly opaque as if a single breath had settled on them, and he fixed his attention on the way ahead.

There was very little to distract him from the road. Either frost or fog must have been rendering the fields so pale. In the distance, far beyond the point at which perspective pinched the road invisible, he saw how the land rose against the sky at the horizon. It put him in mind of an act of defiance—whose, he didn't know. However remote it seemed, they had to reach it long before dark. When Tom spoke Slater stared ahead as if the boy had held his peace. "Dad," Tom insisted, "there's somewhere."

"We don't need to eat, do we? Wouldn't we rather be where you asked for?"

"We don't," Amy said. "If we stop we'll never see the sun."

In any case the Traveller's Return was shut if not abandoned, and Slater didn't spare the inn another glance. "See where we're heading?" he said. "That'll bring us closer."

Perhaps this was premature. Even if the motorway could hardly lead straight to the mountain, driving as fast as he felt able to risk didn't appear to be reducing the distance. No doubt the mountain was too far away to begin to gain stature just yet, but it looked as if the dull sunken sky was holding it down. He'd lost all awareness of gripping the wheel and treading on the pedal when Tom said "How far is it now, dad?"

"As far as you see." Surely Slater could do better than that, and he said "Don't worry, we've plenty of time."

At least he'd stopped short of claiming they had all the time in the world. For the moment the sullen sunless glow looked permanent enough, but how instantaneously had darkness fallen last night? He couldn't help reflecting that the sky was just the underside of a vast blackness. He hoped nobody would ask what time it was, not least since this would show that he wasn't alone in having forgotten a watch. When he peered at the clock on the dashboard, the digital fragments that ought to form numbers had collapsed into chaos. If he'd gone in for praying he might have begged for the computer not to let the family down any further. He found the children in the mirror and saw Amy opening her mouth. "I know what should bring it, Tom."

"What?" the boy said as though he would have liked to trust his own skepticism.

"If we sing."

Slater took her to mean it would pass the time. Her brother seemed to want to be convinced, and when she set about humming the melody he added words. "In something town where I was born..."

Slater was too intent on the road to think how to make the words more precise. Once Melanie joined in he supposed he ought to, though only with the fragments he could bring to mind. "All in the merry month of May" was the line that appealed most to him, and he sang it whenever it came around, and did his best to fend off some of the other words by humming over them. "And death was drawing nigh him…" While he didn't want to ask if anybody knew another song, especially since he couldn't think of one himself, he was long past judging how often they'd revived the ballad by the time they came in sight of a road that led off the motorway towards the mountain.

The side road meandered between fields that lay low in a mist, if frost wasn't holding them down. The route reminded Slater of any number of places he and Melanie had taken the children when they were younger, unless they'd visited the places before the children were born. Why was the mountain taking so much time to rise ahead? "Oh mother, mother, make my bed, for I shall die tomorrow…" Melanie had fallen silent, and only the children were pronouncing the words. "Here we are," she said as if she was advising not just them but the landscape.

The bulk was indeed a mountain now, blocking off the way ahead. The slopes weren't much less pale than ice and spiky as an enormous uncontrolled crystal. The road appeared to peter out beyond it, sinking into a frozen field. Alongside the road at the foot of the mountain was an extensive car park. "It's just for us," Tom said.

Slater parked the Astra and waited for the family to join him on the deserted expanse of bare earth. The car emitted a sound he could almost have found plaintive as he activated the electronic locks. Impulses like those had no emotions or sentience, he thought, and he looked hastily for something else to think. The notice beside the car park was largely illegible, and he couldn't deduce what it would have said. **ME TO MY PA**—he couldn't even judge where the clumps of letters would have fitted into the disintegrated message. The signpost indicating the path up the mountain said only **I AM TO LATE**, which he found just as incomprehensible. Perhaps it had never been in a language he recognised. "There's our way," he said.

The path took the route of a vanished stream. It bent almost at once, but he didn't bother glancing back at the car, which was already out of his mind. The smooth pale rock walls were at least twice his height, and the low sky added to the sense of climbing up a tunnel. For the moment the ascent was gentle. As Tom and Amy raced ahead Melanie called "Don't go too far."

"Can't we go to the next bend?" Amy protested.

"To see if we can see," Tom cried.

"Just stay in sight," Slater told them, finding Melanie's hand. He didn't think they would be able to see the sun from the bend ahead, where the walls were higher than ever. Was he helping Melanie climb, or was she aiding him? He couldn't recall when they had last been up a mountain, but they seemed to be equal to the task. Quite soon they caught up with the children, who were waiting impatiently at the start of the next few hundred yards of path. "It's still not there," Tom complained.

"It just means we need to go higher," Melanie said and gazed at Slater until he agreed.

Tom scrambled up the path with Amy at his heels, and their parents followed hand in hand. Were the walls growing paler as the path approached the sky? Slater mustn't imagine that the children were borrowing the pallor—at least, not unless they were climbing into a portent of the clouds, which seemed to be threatening to make them look less substantial. "Be careful," he shouted.

The walls flattened his voice, and Tom's came back even flatter. "There's nothing to be careful of."

He might have been complaining. Perhaps he was dissatisfied with the uneventfulness of the climb, if not its apparent lack of a goal. The next bend led to another quarter of a mile of track between walls not much more detailed than the sky. "We'll be there before you know it," Slater vowed, which at once struck him as careless, since it seemed to urge the children up the slope. He and Melanie were on the way to matching their speed when music caught up with him—the Beethoven that wasn't quite a hymn.

Amy swung around so fast that the dust she stirred up seemed to render her and Tom momentarily immaterial. "Who is it?" she said.

She sounded as uneasy as she and her brother looked. Of course nobody could summon the family back from their mission, but Slater wished he recognised the number on the screen. He couldn't think of a question other than Amy's. "Who is it?" he demanded.

He heard a sound that was less than a breath—just electronic restlessness—and then it seemed to form into a voice. "Who else do you think it could be, Derek?"

"It might be someone who isn't called Derek," he said and mouthed at Melanie "My mother."

"Don't upset anyone, Paul. We're here and we know who you are."

Though Melanie spoke so quietly that he almost didn't hear her, his mother apparently did. "I know you like to be Paul. I was only—" Her pause admitted static before she said "Just wanting to see how you were."

"I still am." This seemed unnecessarily clever, and he said more gently "Fine."

"Well, that was all I wanted. I should think you'd expect your mother to."

"Of course I would. How is it where you are?"

"Just the same as you remember."

"They're looking after you." In case that seemed patronising he added "They'll be there if you need them, Constance and the rest."

"I've got everything I need." This sounded final, especially when she said "And what are you doing with yourself?"

"We've gone out for a run on my day off."

"Where are you running to?"

He mustn't let this recall the interrogation at the tollbooth. "To the sun, we hope."

"I'll hope it too, then. I wouldn't mind another look at it. What about the grandchildren?"

The question seemed so vague that he felt as confused as he took her to be. "We've none."

Melanie frowned at him, and he was afraid he shouldn't have had the thought, let alone spoken it aloud. "Amy and Tom, you mean," he said hastily. "Your grandchildren. They're here with us, of course."

Or had they passed out of sight while he and Melanie were intent on the call? No, they'd halted on the path above their parents, and as he found them they stirred, waving at the phone. "They're saying hello to you," he said.

"It'll be that or goodbye, won't it? Say goodbye for me." With enough deliberation to make it her last word she added "Paul."

"Grandma sends her greetings," Slater said and brought the phone back to his face, only to glimpse a movement like an insect's on the screen. At once it vanished, and he realised he'd caught sight of its dwindling—the last of the icon that denoted network coverage. "I haven't got a signal any more," he said.

Melanie and the children took out their mobiles. "We've gone too," Amy said.

"Make that all of us," her mother said. "It doesn't matter, does it? We're all here."

"Granny isn't," Tom observed.

"She'll be where she wants to be, Tom." No doubt Melanie sensed that Slater couldn't help feeling responsible, because she added "Everyone wanted you back with us, Paul."

"Or we couldn't have done our concert," Amy said.

This was surely an exaggeration, however affectionately meant. As the children recommenced their climb he put away his mobile, and thought he saw that the screen was entirely blank. Not least in order to put that behind him he murmured "I suppose she just didn't want to feel on her own."

"Maybe she's missing Allen," Melanie said.

Slater felt as if the sky had lurched towards him, bleaching his vision nearly blank. "Who?"

"Paul." This was a rebuke and incredulous as well. "Your father," she said. "That was another reason we felt you should go and see Eileen."

Slater had a panicky sense of not knowing where his mouth was or how to use it. When he felt his lips part he had to say "I don't remember."

The children had climbed out of sight—no, they were waiting again, and when Slater focused his attention on them Tom turned to say "What don't you remember, dad?"

"About—" Slater didn't know how much he risked by admitting "About my father."

"He used to call us funny names," Amy said. "Ours but not quite."

"And he'd tell us poems," Tom said.

"And sing us songs like the one we sang for you."

As Slater gazed uphill he was no longer sure what he was perceiving. He was hardly even aware of Melanie until she said "Is that enough?"

In some way it seemed to be. He had an almost indefinable impression that he could leave the memories behind, as if they were no longer necessary to him. He felt close to weightless with shedding the burden that he hadn't even realised he was carrying. What else might have to go? He could have thought his sense of liberation had released the children, who ran with no visible effort up to the next walled-in bend. "Come and see," Tom shouted, and Amy called "We're nearly there."

In a moment they were hidden by the bend. "Wait for us," Melanie protested.

Slater did his best to keep panic out of his voice, as he thought she had with hers. "You heard your mother."

"You can hear us," Tom responded, and from further off Amy contributed "We'll sing."

"In what's its name where we were born…" Their voices were muffled by the walls if not the sky, and Slater had no time to wonder how they could have come up with the identical alteration of the lyric. He didn't try to grasp what else they sang; he was too concerned with holding on to Melanie as they followed the memory of a stream. In too little time to be worth mentioning they were at the bend, from which he saw Tom and Amy at the top of the path with their backs to him. Beyond them there appeared to be nothing at all.

Before he could take a breath to call out, the children vanished off the path. "It's all right," he blurted, clutching Melanie's hand. "I can still hear them." Surely he could, even if no words were audible as he urged or was urged by her up the path. The sky didn't recede, and he could have thought the blank surface was waiting for them. When he stepped off the end of the path onto the summit the landscape seemed to fall away on every side, and he could have fancied that it brought the sky closer. All that mattered was seeing the children ahead.

They were standing on the peak, which was flat and oddly regular, practically a rectangle, with as little colour to it as the sky. There was room on it for Slater and for Melanie as well. From this height the fields that extended in every direction looked paler still, and might have been competing with the sky for featurelessness. He couldn't recall when he'd last seen a colour. He was trying to think that only the distance was robbing the world of its details when Tom said "How did we come?"

"Dad drove," Amy said with a laugh, not as lofty as she might have wanted it to be. "Don't you remember?"

For some moments Slater was able to believe that nothing was wrong except their inability to see the road. Their ascent could have led them around the opposite side of the mountain, after all. The trouble was that he could see no roads anywhere, and searching for them had brought another issue to his notice. The horizon was unnaturally close, no more than half as remote as it should be, if even that. The flatness of the land gave it nowhere to hide, and he didn't know how far or how often he'd turned around in the hope of seeing he was somehow mistaken before Melanie said "What are you looking for?"

"I don't need anything else," he said, fixing his gaze on her and the children. "You're all here."

Although he was determined to make that the answer, he couldn't help glancing away from them. At once he wished he hadn't, because the horizon was visibly shrinking towards the mountain. His panic felt as if his insides had dropped out of him, leaving him empty of any resource. If the family weren't seeing what he saw, might that provide any reassurance? He was struggling to think how to distract them when Tom said "It's snowing, isn't it?"

While he didn't sound entirely convinced, he seemed willing to be. Slater gripped Melanie's hand—perhaps he had never let go of it—and strove to see as Tom was seeing. Surely the blankness that was advancing all around them could be an uncommon species of snowstorm, however much it looked as if the sky was consuming the world. He had to strain his vision to distinguish that the oncoming mass consisted of innumerable flakes. He was about to risk telling Tom he was right when Amy said "Suppose we'd better go back before it gets us."

At that moment Slater saw too much. Yes, the vast inexorable mass was composed of countless fragments, but they weren't snowflakes. Only their pallor had misled him. They were shards of the landscape, which was disintegrating. They put him in mind of pixels into which the world was splintering, an image reverting to its simplest components. It left them nowhere to go, but how could he tell Amy or anyone? Before he dared to speak, Tom complained "We haven't seen the sun."

Slater felt Melanie take a firmer grip on his hand. "We don't need to," she said. "We can feel it."

"I can't," Tom declared in some kind of triumph.

"I don't think I can either," Amy said.

Melanie turned towards their father and squeezed his hand. "Close your eyes and you will."

For an instant he glimpsed that she'd seen the same as he had. How could he have imagined otherwise? "Hold our hands, you two," he said with an urgency that he knew was prompted by the shrinking landscape. "We'll all close our eyes and feel the sun together."

As they faced the children hand in hand, Amy and then Tom turned to meet them. Slater found Tom's hand, which felt disconcertingly small and frail, hardly even there. Melanie took Amy's, and the girl fumbled for her brother's. The last thing Slater saw was the trust in the children's eyes. "All shut now," Melanie said, and he thought he did begin to feel the sunlight. Surely that explained why, despite the altitude, he hadn't been able to see anyone's breath. He remembered hearing that no amount of cloud could entirely block off the sun.

What else ought he to recall? Something about children—perhaps that someone was supposed to be like a little child, though weren't you also meant to put childish things away? He was glad the children were there, at any rate. Perhaps their beliefs, whatever they were, would carry the day somehow; they could well have more beliefs than he'd retained, though he couldn't speak for Melanie. Was he thinking too much in a desperate bid to cling to some sense of himself? What would happen if he failed? Suppose you couldn't feel the light if you thought about it? He had an idea that someone might be singing wordlessly, but couldn't tell whether it was him. Then the impression seemed to be overwhelmed by if not transformed into light, which was pervading every sense. He didn't know whether he was seeing it or experiencing it in some way that left words behind, but it might have been all there was to the world.

INVENTORY

CARMEN MARIA MACHADO

ONE girl. We lay down next to each other on the musty rug in her basement. Her parents were upstairs; we told them we were watching *Jurassic Park*. "I'm the dad, and you're the mom," she said. I pulled up my shirt, she pulled up hers, and we just stared at each other. My heart fluttered below my belly button, but I worried about daddy longlegs and her parents finding us. I still have never seen *Jurassic Park*. I suppose I never will.

* * *

One boy, one girl. My friends. We drank stolen wine coolers in my room, on the vast expanse of my bed. We laughed and talked and passed around the bottles. "What I like about you," she said, "is your reactions. You react so funny to everything." He nodded in agreement. She buried her face in my neck and said, "Like this," to my skin. I laughed. I was nervous, excited. I felt like a guitar and someone was twisting the tuning pegs and my strings were getting tighter. They batted their eyelashes against my skin and breathed into my ears. I moaned and writhed, and hovered on the edge of coming for whole minutes, though no one was touching me there, not even me.

* * *

Two boys, one girl. One of them my boyfriend. His parents were out of town, so we threw a party in their house. We drank lemonade mixed with vodka and he encouraged me to make out with his friend's girlfriend. We kissed tentatively, then stopped. The boys made out

287

with each other, and we watched them for a long time, bored but too drunk to stand up. We fell asleep in the guest bedroom. When I woke up, my bladder was full as a fist. I padded down into the foyer, and saw someone had knocked a vodka lemonade onto the floor. I tried to clean it up. The mixture had stripped the marble finish bare. My boyfriend's mother found my underwear behind the bed weeks later, and handed them to him, laundered, without a word. It's weird to me how much I miss that floral, chemical smell of clean clothes. End of the world, and all I can think about is fabric softener.

*   *   *

One man. Slender, tall. So skinny I could see his pelvic bone, but this was strangely sexy. Gray eyes. Wry smile. I had known him since the previous October. We drank in his apartment. He was nervous and gave me a massage. I was so nervous I let him. He rubbed my back for a long time. He said, "My hands are getting tired." I said, "Oh," and turned toward him. He kissed me, his face rough with stubble. He smelled like yeast and the topnotes of expensive cologne. He lay on top of me and we made out for a while. Everything inside of me twinged. He asked if he could touch my breast, and I clamped his hand around it. I took off my shirt, and I felt like a drop of water was sliding up my spine. I realized this was happening, really happening. We both undressed. He rolled the condom down and lumbered on top of me. It hurt worse than anything, ever. He came and I didn't. When he pulled out, the condom was covered in blood. He peeled it off and threw it away. Everything in me pounded. We slept on a too-small bed. He insisted on driving me back to the dorms the next day. In my room, I took off my clothes and wrapped myself in a towel. I still smelled like him, like the two of us together, and I wanted more. I felt good, like an adult who has sex sometimes, and a life. My roommate asked me how it was, hugged me.

*   *   *

One man. A boyfriend. Didn't like condoms, asked me if I was on birth control, pulled out anyway. A terrible mess.

One woman. On and off sort-of girlfriend. Classmate from "Organization of Computer Systems." Long brown hair down to her butt. She was softer than I expected. I wanted to go down on her, but she was too nervous. We made out and she slipped her tongue into my mouth and after she went home I got off twice in the cool stillness of my apartment. Two years later, we had sex on the gravel rooftop of my office building. Four floors below our bodies, my code was compiling in front of an empty chair. After we were done, I looked up and noticed a man in a suit watching us from the window of the adjacent skyscraper, his hand shuffling around inside his dress pants.

* * *

One woman. Round glasses, red hair. Don't remember where I met her. We got high and fucked and I accidentally fell asleep with my hand inside of her. We woke up pre-dawn and walked across town to a 24-hour diner. It drizzled and when we got there, our sandaled feet were numb from the chill. We ate pancakes. Our mugs ran dry, and when we looked for the waitress, she was watching the breaking news on the battered TV hanging from the ceiling. She chewed on her lip, and the pot of coffee tipped in her hand, dripping tiny brown dots onto the linoleum. We watched as the newscaster blinked away and was replaced with a list of symptoms of the virus blossoming in northern California. When he came back, he repeated that planes were grounded, the border of the state had been closed, and the virus appeared to be isolated. When the waitress walked over, she seemed distracted. "Do you have people there?" I asked, and she nodded, her eyes filling with tears. I felt terrible having asked her anything.

* * *

One man. I met him at the bar around the corner from my house. We made out on my bed. He smelled like sour wine, though we hadn't been drinking. We had sex, but he went soft halfway through. We kissed some more. He wanted to go down on me, but I didn't want him to. He got angry and left, slamming the screen door so hard my spice rack jumped from its nail and crashed to the floor. My dog lapped up the nutmeg, and I had to force-feed him salt to make him throw up. Revved from adrenaline, I made a list of animals I have had in my life—seven, including my two betta fish who died within a week of each other when I was nine—and a list of the spices in pho. Cloves, cinnamon, star anise, coriander, ginger, cardamom pods.

* * *

One man. Six inches shorter than me. I explained the website I worked for was losing business rapidly because no one wanted quirky photography tips during an epidemic, and I had been laid off that morning. He bought me dinner. We had sex in his car because he had roommates and I couldn't be in my house right then, and he slid his hand inside my bra and his hands were perfect, fucking perfect, and we fell into the too-tiny backseat. I came for the first time in two months. I called him the next day, and left him a voicemail, telling him I'd had a good time and I'd like to see him again, but he never called me back.

* * *

One man. Did some sort of hard labor for a living, I can't remember what exactly, and he had a tattoo of a boa constrictor on his back with a misspelled Latin phrase below it. He was strong and could pick me up and fuck me against a wall and it was the most thrilling sensation I'd ever felt. We broke more than a few picture frames that way. He used his hands and I dragged my fingernails down his back, and he asked me if I was going to come for him, and I said yes, yes, I'm going to come for you, yes, I will.

* * *

One woman. Blonde hair, brash voice, friend of a friend. We married. I'm still not sure if I was with her because I wanted to be or because I was afraid of what the world was catching all around us. Within a year, it soured. We screamed more than we had sex, or even talked. One night, we had a fight that left me in tears. Afterwards, she asked me if I wanted to fuck, and undressed before I could answer. I wanted to push her out the window. We had sex and I started crying. When it was over and she was showering, I packed a suitcase and got in my car and drove.

* * *

One man. Six months later, in my post-divorce haze. I met him at the funeral for the last surviving member of his family. I was grieving, he was grieving. We had sex in the empty house that used to belong to his brother and his brother's wife and their children, all dead. We fucked in every room, including the hallway, where I couldn't bend my pelvis right on the hardwood floors, and I jerked him off in front of the bare linen closet. In the master bedroom, I caught my reflection in the vanity mirror as I rode him, and the lights were off and our skin reflected silver from the moon and when he came in me he said, "Sorry, sorry." He died a week later, by his own hand. I moved out of the city, north.

* * *

One man. Grey eyes again. I hadn't seen him in so many years. He asked me how I was doing, and I told him some things and not others. I did not want to cry in front of the man to whom I gave my virginity. It seemed wrong somehow. He asked me how many I'd lost, and I said, "My mother, my roommate from college." I did not mention that I'd found my mother dead, nor did I talk about the three days I spent in quarantine afterwards, anxious doctors checking my eyes for the early symptoms. "When I met you," he said, "you were so fucking young." His body was familiar, but alien too. He'd gotten better, and I'd gotten better. When he pulled out of me I almost expected blood, but of course, there was none. He had gotten more beautiful in those intervening years, more thoughtful. I surprised myself by crying over the bathroom sink. I ran the tap so he couldn't hear me.

* * *

One woman. Brunette. A former CDC employee. I met her at a community meeting where they taught us how to stockpile food and manage outbreaks in our neighborhoods should the virus hop the firebreak. I had not slept with a woman since my wife, but as she lifted her shirt I realized how much I'd been craving breasts, wetness, soft mouths. She wanted cock and I obliged. Afterwards, she traced the indents in my skin from the harness, and confessed to me the CDC was not having any luck developing a vaccine. "But the fucking thing is only passing through physical contact," she said. "If people would just stay apart—" She grew silent. She curled up next to me and we drifted off. When I woke up, she was working herself over with the dildo, and I pretended I was still sleeping.

* * *

One man. He made me dinner in my kitchen. There weren't a lot of vegetables left from my garden, but he did what he could. He tried to feed me a spoonful, but I took the handle from him. The food didn't taste too bad. The power went out for the fourth time that week, and so we had to eat by candlelight. I resented the inadvertent romance. He touched my face when we fucked and said I was beautiful, and I jerked my head a little to dislodge his fingers. After the second time this happened, I put my hand around his chin and told him to shut up. He came immediately. I did not return his calls. When the notice come over the radio that the virus had somehow reached Nebraska, I realized I had to go east, and so I did. I left the garden, the plot where my dog was buried, the pine table where I'd anxiously made so many lists—trees that began with M: maple, mimosa, mahogany, mulberry, magnolia, mountain ash, mangrove, myrtle; states that I had lived in: Iowa, Indiana, Pennsylvania, Virginia, New York—leaving unreadable jumbles of letters imprinted in the soft wood. I took my savings and rented out a cottage near the ocean. After a few months, the landlord, based in Kansas, stopped depositing my checks.

* * *

Two women. Refugees from the western states who drove and drove until their car broke down a mile from my cottage. They knocked on my door and stayed with me for two weeks while we tried to figure out how to get their vehicle up and running. We had wine one night and talked about the quarantine. The generator needed cranking, and one of them offered to do it. The other one sat down next to me and slid her hand up my leg. We ended up jerking off separately and kissing each other. The generator took and the power came back on. The other woman returned, and we all slept in the same bed. I wanted them to stay, but they said they were heading up into Canada, where it was rumored to be safer. They offered to bring me with them, but I joked that I was holding down the fort for the US. "What state are we in?" one of them asked, and I said, "Maine." They kissed me on the forehead in turn and dubbed me the protector of Maine. After they left, I only used the generator intermittently, preferring to spend time in the dark, with candles. The former owner of the cottage had a closet full of them.

* * *

One man. National Guard. When he first showed up at my doorstep, I assumed he was there to evacuate me, but it turned out he'd abandoned his post. I offered him a place to stay for the night, and he thanked me. I woke up with a knife to my throat and a hand on my breast. I told him I couldn't have sex with him lying down like I was. He let me stand up, and I shoved him into the bookcase, knocking him unconscious. I dragged his body out to the beach and rolled it into the surf. He came to, sputtering sand. I pointed the knife at him and told him to walk and keep walking, and if he even looked back, I would end him. He obliged, and I watched him until he was a spot of darkness on the gray strip of shore, and then nothing. He was the last person I saw for a year.

* * *

One woman. A religious leader, with a flock of fifty trailing behind her, all dressed in white. For three days, I made them wait around the edge of the property, and after I checked their eyes, I permitted them to stay. They all camped around the cottage: on the lawn, on the beach. They had their own supplies and only needed a place to lay their heads, the leader said. She wore robes that made her look like a wizard. Night fell. She and I circled the camp in our bare feet, the light from the bonfire carving shadows into her face. We walked to the water's edge and I pointed into the darkness, at the tiny island she could not see. She slipped her hand into mine. I made her a drink in my kitchen, and we sat at the table. Outside, I could hear people laughing, playing music, children romping in the surf. The woman seemed exhausted. She was younger than she looked, I realized, but her job was aging her. She sipped her gin, made a face at the taste. "We've been walking for so long," she said. "We stopped for a while, somewhere near Pennsylvania, but the virus caught up with us when we crossed paths with another group. Took twelve before we got some distance between us and it." We kissed deeply for a long time, my heart hammering in my cunt. She tasted like smoke and honey. The group stayed for four days, until she woke up from a dream and said she'd had an omen, and they needed to keep going. She asked me to come with them. I tried to imagine myself with her, her flock following behind us like children. I declined. She left a gift on my pillow: a pewter rabbit as big as my thumb.

* * *

One man. No more than twenty, floppy brown hair. He'd been on foot for a month. He looked like you'd expect: skittish. No hope. When we had sex, he was reverent and too gentle. After we cleaned up, we drank the moonshine I'd been making in the bathtub, and I fed him canned soup. He told me about how he walked through Chicago, actually through it, and how they had stopped bothering disposing of the bodies after a while. He had to refill his glass before he talked about it further. "After that," he said, "I went around the cities." I asked him how far behind the virus was, really, and he said he did not know. "It's really quiet here," he said, by way of changing the subject. "No traffic," I explained. "No tourists." He cried and cried and I held him until he fell asleep. The next morning, I woke up and he was gone.

* * *

One woman. Much older than me. While she waited for the three days to pass, she meditated on a sand dune. When I checked her eyes, I noticed they were green as sea glass. Her hair grayed at the temples and the way she laughed tripped pleasure down the stairs of my heart. We sat in the half-light of the bay window and the build-up was so slow. She straddled me, and when she kissed me the scene beyond the glass pinched and curved. We drank, and walked the length of the beach, the damp sand making pale haloes around our feet. She told about her once-children, teenage injuries, having to put her cat to sleep the day after she moved to a new city. I told her about finding my mother, the perilous trek across Vermont and New Hampshire, how the tide was never still, my ex-wife. "What happened?" she asked. "It just didn't work," I said. I told her about the man in the empty house, the way he cried and the way his come shimmered on his stomach and how I could have scooped despair from the air by the handfuls. We remembered commercial jingles from our respective youths, including one for an Italian ice chain that I went to at the end of long summer days, where I ate gelato, drowsy in the heat. I couldn't remember the last time I'd smiled so much. She stayed. More refugees filtered through the cottage, through us, the last stop before the border, and we fed them and played games with the little ones. We got careless. The day I woke up and the air had changed, I realized it had been a long time coming. She was sitting on the couch. She got up in the night and made some tea. But the cup was tipped and the puddle was cold, and I recognized the symptoms from the television and newspapers, and then the leaflets, and then the radio broadcasts, and then the hushed voices around the bonfire. Her skin was the dark purple of infinite bruises, the whites of her eyes were shot through with red, and blood was leaking from the misty beds of her fingernails. There was no time to mourn. I checked my own face in the mirror, and my eyes were still clear. I consulted my emergency list and its supplies. I took my bag and tent and I got in the dinghy and I rowed to the island, to this island, where I have been stashing food since I got here. I drank water and set up my tent and began to make lists. Every teacher beginning with preschool.

Every job I've ever had. Every home I've ever lived in. Every person I've ever loved. Every person who has probably loved me. And now this. Next week, I will be thirty. The sand is blowing into my mouth, my hair, the center crevice of my notebook, and the sea is choppy and gray. Beyond it, I can see the cottage, a speck on the far shore. I keep thinking I can see the virus blooming on the horizon like a sunrise. I realize the world will continue to turn, even with no people on it. Maybe it will go a little faster.